****

The Gotland Deception

Book One of A World on Fire

By James Rosone
****

*Published in conjunction with Front Line Publishing, Inc.

Copyright Notice

ISBN: 978-1-967436-25-5
Library of Congress Control Number: 2025916102
Sun City Center, Florida, United States of America

Table of Contents

Author's Note:

In the coming months, we will likely release some battle maps and similar types of materials that will further enhance the reading experience and excitement of this series. You can sign up to our free, members only section on our website (www.frontlinepublishinginc.com). This is where future maps and other materials will be made available, along with our Patreon page.

I am putting together a research and reader trip to Taiwan, that will take place in the summer of 2026. If you are interested in participating in this trip, please sign up to our newsletter, so you will know when we announce the details of the trip. You can do that via our website, www.frontlinepublishinginc.com

Disclaimer: Although the story is based on events that could happen in the world, the story is entirely fictional and should be treated as such. This is a work of *fiction*. All events, characters, and organizations depicted are either products of the author's imagination or used fictitiously. While this novel incorporates real-world military platforms, defense systems, technologies, and companies, all references are based solely on publicly available information as of the time of writing.

No company, government agency, or defense contractor has sponsored, endorsed, or contributed to the development of this book. The inclusion of specific weapons systems, autonomous platforms, unmanned vehicles, software systems, or commercial entities is for fictional and narrative purposes only. The scenarios depicted represent the author's creative interpretation of how such technologies could be employed by US, allied, or adversarial forces in a future, hypothetical conflict.

Nothing in this book should be construed as reflecting actual plans, capabilities, or endorsements by any military, governmental, or corporate entity. All opinions expressed are solely those of the authors.

Chapter One:
The Dragon and the Bear

December 23, 2032
Shelby Restaurant
Blagoveshchensk, Russia

The cold bit deep, settling into Pan Min-jae's bones. He knew this was a dangerous game, but he had played it for years, slipping in and out of places men like him were never meant to be. But tonight was different. Tonight, he had witnessed men of power rarely seen together—Kuznetsov, Zhang, Sokolov.

Something big is about to happen, he realized. *But what?*

Pan moved with haste after leaving the restaurant, his hands buried in the pockets of his wool coat. He turned the phone on, waiting for the familiar buzz in his hand to let him know it had connected to its satellite cellular network. His thumb twitched, cigarette trembling as he dragged deep, nicotine steadying his nerves. With a casual tap, he synced the parabolic mic in his glasses, the fifty-meter range capturing every whisper from the Shelby's back room.

Next, he toggled to the encrypted messaging app on his phone to attach the photos and a short message to go along with the pictures of the men present at the restaurant—*Kuznetsov mentioned Dragon Bear—something big is happening. Will transmit more soon.* Then he pressed send.

There were more details to share, like the audio files the parabolic mic had captured, but these were much larger files, so he sent the photos first. He'd let the messaging app work on attaching the audio files after he'd retreated to his safe house, where he could take time to think about the meeting, the various men who were present, and what it all meant. If he was lucky, the camera built into his glasses might have recorded most of the meeting before he'd left.

Something about this meeting hadn't felt right, and the longer he stayed at the restaurant, the more his instincts were screaming at him to run. As he continued to walk his countersurveillance route, he heard the sound of footsteps behind him.

Too quick, he realized. *Too close.*

There was a shift in the air right before he heard the scrape of shoes. Pan perceived the low hum of a man flirting in Russian, and the subtle but unmistakable pull of someone moving in tandem with him.

Pan turned slightly and caught a glimpse of a couple laughing, swaying in the glow of streetlamps dotting the sidewalk. Then he thought he caught a momentary glint of light reflecting off the steel edge of a knife.

Just as Pan was reacting to the danger of a blade, pain lanced through his back, sharp and burning. His breathing locked. His legs buckled. A second thrust went deeper. Pan's phone clattered to the pavement. His vision blurred, the darkness curling in as he clawed for the device, fingers trembling.

With all the strength he had left, he tried to reach for the phone—tried to transmit his intel. But a boot slid forward, pressing heavily against the device. The audible crunch of glass and plastic shattered his last hope of sending the message.

Just then, he heard a deep voice murmur above him. "He won't be completing his spy mission tonight."

The woman he'd spotted as part of the flirtatious couple knelt beside him and began to rifle through his pockets. The last thing Pan saw was the smirk on her face before the void swallowed him whole.
****

Shelby Restaurant

Kirill Andreyevich Kuznetsov swirled his vodka, watching the way the liquid caught the dim golden light. Around him, five men sat in quiet anticipation, their faces carved from stone, waiting for the final act of the evening.

The room smelled of cedar, old smoke, and history soaked into the very foundation of the building. Deals had been made here, wars whispered into existence over a toast and the flick of a wrist. It was such an unassuming place to hold such meetings that it had gone unnoticed until now.

The heavy oak door creaked open again, a momentary gust of frigid air sweeping into the room before it was promptly closed. The man entering was Dmitry Mirov, his deputy and head of Special Operations for National Security Affairs. The man better known as The Undertaker walked confidently toward them, his movements unhurried, his expression unreadable. He stepped around the table to Kuznetsov's side and took his seat, then reached for his Beluga Epicure, downing the vodka before leaning in to whisper, his breath barely stirring the air.

"It's taken care of. We have his phone."

Kuznetsov's lip twitched, the closest he ever came to a smile. He lifted his glass. "Good."

Seated across from Kuznetsov was Zhang Weihao, the director of the Central National Security Commission. He slowly sipped tea, his expression carefully neutral.

Zhang studied Kuznetsov as if searching for the invisible strings he was pulling. The air in the room thickened, the weight of decisions made pressing upon them all.

"Let's talk about Taiwan—you're certain this strategy of yours will not interfere with our plans?" Kuznetsov asked Zhang, hoping for a straight answer. "Goryunov has spent years preparing for this. It can't be derailed at the last minute."

"You can be assured, Kuznetsov, that our wayward province will not derail the grand strategy," Zhang said dismissively. "Besides, the naval units involved are not drawn from our North Sea Fleet. They have no impact or interaction with the Arctic operation."

"Still, it is an unnecessary risk right before things begin," Kuznetsov countered, unconvinced this sideshow wouldn't bleed over into their carefully laid plans. Too much was at risk for this to fail at the last moment.

Zhang stared at him for a moment, not saying anything. "The time to settle the Taiwan issue is now," he finally explained. "With our joint plan underway, Europe and America will be powerless to intervene—a hostage to circumstances beyond their control. Besides, the plan has been in motion for years. It is too far along for us to turn back."

Kuznetsov raised an eyebrow in surprise. When he spoke, his voice was like tempered steel. "Hmm, then we best hope your plan works. This year, this moment—we won't have a better time to act than now. In eighteen weeks, the world as we know it will be gone. And a new world will be reborn in its place—one led not by the West but by the East." Zhang set his cup down with deliberate precision. "The Americans will be overextended. They will scramble when it begins, but they will not know where to defend."

Mirov poured himself another drink, his smirk barely concealed. "They still believe in their markets. By the time they understand, their economy will already be in flames."

Lieutenant General Sergei Orlov sat back in his chair as he rolled an unlit cigarette between his fingers. "The simulations are complete," he added. "NATO's response time is predictable. They will hesitate." His gaze flicked toward Zhang. "We will not."

This was why Orlov was called The Chess Master. His mind worked several steps ahead of his opponents'. It was a skill Kuznetsov had put to good use when he'd appointed him Director of National Security Operations. The man worked in the shadows. Few knew of him; those who did feared him. He was the man who effectively ran the nation's private military contractors.

Cuī Zemin smiled coldly as he stared at Orlov, then shifted his gaze to Kuznetsov. "When the time is right—they won't know what hit them."

Kuznetsov nodded to Cuī, the man known as The Ghost. Cuī was the director of the Ministry of State Security 6th Bureau—Special Affairs Division. It was Orlov and Cuī who were responsible for lighting the flames that would set the world on fire.

Raising his glass, Kuznetsov gave a final toast, the weight of history settling upon them. "Then, gentlemen… let the firestorm begin."

The vodka burned as it went down, smooth and inevitable. The servers returned, sensing the moment was right to serve the plates of honey-drenched medovik, an indulgence before the storm was unleashed. They ate in silence, savoring the final moments before the world burned.

****

December 28, 2032
Visby, Gotland
Sweden

For Klara Hedevig, it was just a usual Tuesday. Christmas had come and gone and now it was time to get back to work. She was up before the sun, keeping the curtains drawn as she prepared a thermos of blackcurrant herbal tea and toasted rye crispbread with foraged jam—routine, austere, and very Swedish.

From her third-floor apartment in Innerstad, the old walled city portion of Visby, Klara tracked foot and vehicle traffic along a minor route that NATO contractors had been using to reach the Gotlands Regemente (P18) depot. Using a thermal monocular and spotting scope mounted behind a discreet wool curtain, she logged plate numbers, convoy time stamps, and fuel resupply intervals, then coded her notes into her Coastal Weather Drift database. All entries appeared as wind vectors and temperature records from a weather buoy, shared weekly to a cloud repository hosted in Tallinn.

Just before dawn, Klara donned snow boots and winter gear for a short "migratory overwintering survey" of marshland just south of Visby Harbor. She carried with her thermal binoculars with birding overlays, a standard Leica scope, and a backpack-mounted omni-antenna disguised as a folded bird blind frame—used to passively scan for encrypted VHF comms from new SHORAD nodes.

Along her way, Klara encountered local joggers, retired birders, and a curious border collie or two. She greeted everyone warmly. They were all used to her habits by now. In a waterproof Rite in the Rain notebook, she jotted "bird notes."

Having completed her cold-weather recon of equipment staging, she headed back home, defrosted her boots, and walked the few blocks over to her day job at the Baltic Resilience & Renewables Initiative. She sat down on the yoga ball seat at her upcycled desk, stretched her back, and cracked her knuckles.

She knew she had two actual grant proposals to write that day, but before she did that, Klara followed her usual ritual. She opened her laptop, logged in to a VPN, used a TOR browser to further obscure her IP address, opened the DuckDuckGo search engine, and logged in to her usual birding messaging boards. She typed up some of her real observations from her morning walk. "I spotted a small group of Bohemian waxwings near the cemetery this morning. I estimate approximately thirty females and twenty males." Her message also held code words for her handler to interpret. She clicked through some of the other posts until she discovered one that interested her.

I finally have another message from Viktor, she realized as she noticed the specific phrasing in a post about European robins along the shaded stone walls.

Klara logged into her Tuta email account, which was fully end-to-end encrypted, including subject lines and metadata. There, in the drafts folder, was a new email waiting for her to read.

Viktor Mikhailov, her GRU/SVR handler, also knew the password to her account and had typed up a note for her. Because the email was never sent to anyone, it was basically impossible for any intelligence agencies to intercept. This was one of the main ways they had communicated for the last ten years or so.

"It is time to move ahead with the advertising campaigns for the Baltic Wings Festival," he wrote. "Anders Ulfsson, the director of Gotland's Visit Gotland office, has made assurances that the Baltic Wings Festival will be listed on the high-traffic Nature Events calendar. Should he give you any trouble or insist on any unreasonable vetting procedures, remind him of how much he loves skiing and ask him how he enjoyed his all-expenses paid trip to Courchevel 1850 in France.

"Further, I have approved your request for funds to rent that cluster of cabins on Fårö Island," Viktor continued. "Once that site is set up, we will begin to send some of our preliminary RVs with equipment your way. They will camp at Lauters Hamn and make individual drop runs to our cabins with supplies."

It's finally becoming real, Klara thought. She had already been planning the Baltic Wings Festival for a little over a year—getting participation from other legitimate NGOs who were interested in her vision of an event that combined bird-watching with environmental talks and activities. She had arranged various illustrious speakers from all over Europe, figured out catering, security, and volunteers to run the program, and reserved various campsites, cabins and Airbnbs all over Gotland in preparation for an influx of around a thousand visitors, which was unusual for early May.

Klara gleefully turned on the advertising blitz she had arranged for the festival and opened up the registration. Soon, the money would begin pouring in, and the groundwork would finally be laid for one hundred GRU/SVR agents to flood the island all at once, traveling with various legitimate NGOs under passports from Germany, Estonia, Lithuania, Ukraine, and Poland.

Of course, there would be real attendees at her event. Klara had done a lot of groundwork, and her day job gave her the bona fides to run this event. Plus, her side project, as head of the Baltic Wings NGO, cemented her as a staunch environmentalist and a lover of birds, so she'd easily snagged Dr. Anu Ristmägi of the Estonian Ornithological Institute and Dr. Elias Thorne, professor of environmental systems at the University of Kiel, Germany, among others.

She went over the program for the Baltic Wings Festival once more, making sure she had all her t's crossed. Not only did each site hold very real interest for bird and nature lovers, each had some proximity that would provide strategic tactical advantage. For example, the activities she had advertised for Fårö Island highlighted the migration routes of the ruff, which was known for its showy breeding plumage and lek behavior, flaunting extravagant head tufts and collar feathers in open marshes. At the same time, agents on the island would enjoy a strategic position where there were very few law enforcement personnel to make any sort of resistance.

When she was finished with those initial tasks, Klara decided it was time for a break and walked to St. Hans Café, situated next to the St. Hans church ruin that she frequently visited, especially during the warmer months, when the café had outdoor seating set up in the ruins itself. It made for a great ambience when meeting with academic liaisons or hosting "sustainability fellows."

"By yourself today, Klara?" asked the manager, a woman named Annika Bragefeldt.

"Yes," Klara responded with a smile. "I just finished some major tasks for BRRI, and I thought I should celebrate."

"Ah, well, we are happy to have you on this dreary January morning," Annika replied. "Do you want the usual?"

"Yes, please," answered Klara.

"One St. Hans Blend with Gotländsk Saffranspannkaka, coming up," said Annika.

Soon, Klara had her hands around a mug of warm tea and a beloved Gotland specialty—a saffron pancake served warm, made from rice pudding, cream, saffron, and egg, topped with local dewberry jam. It was very traditional—a cultural heritage dish that balanced austerity with indulgence, like the island itself.

Annika was a retired teacher turned café manager, and a bit of a busybody. Always suspicious of outsiders, she kept meticulous records and had her eye on everything. Klara had managed to get on her good side by being extremely predictable and showing her true love of all things Gotland. Later, she would talk Annika into sharing all the new local gossip with her.

Klara smiled. *It's all paying off,* she realized. All these years of habits, of tiny rituals, had allowed her to hide in plain sight…and now she was ready to spring her trap.

****

Twelve Years Earlier
October 2020
Eurasian Climate Youth Summit
Riga, Latvia

The breakout room smelled faintly of wet coats, cheap coffee, and ambition. Klara Hedevig sat cross-legged on the carpeted floor, the required six feet away from a UN volunteer from Estonia and a "rewilding specialist" from Kyrgyzstan who kept quoting Žižek between sips of birch sap tonic. His mask hung from one ear whenever he drank, and he promptly put it back on after each sip. Around her, twenty young, masked climate delegates debated decarbonization equity frameworks in the Baltic–Black Sea corridor.

But Klara wasn't listening anymore. Her gaze was fixed on the man near the bookshelf, in the gray wool blazer with the pale pink tie: Dr. Sergei Anatolyev, introduced earlier as a visiting lecturer from the Saint Petersburg Institute of Eco-Geopolitics.

He had asked only one question during the last session—but it sliced through the fluff like a hawk through mist.

"If EU green transition funds are being used to build LNG terminals in Klaipėda and Świnoujście, are we really discussing energy resilience—or just NATO logistics in disguise?" he'd probed.

That was when Klara had first looked up.

Now, as the group dispersed for lunch, he crossed the room toward her.

"You're the student from Lund, yes? The LUMES program?" he asked, voice low, warm. He spoke precise English, but with a slight Russian accent.

"Yes," Klara replied, cautious but curious. "Klara Hedevig."

He nodded. "You spoke earlier about Gotland's offshore wind potential. Your passion was clear."

"Not that it matters," she said, a little sharper than she meant to. "Sweden just approved a military expansion zone over the best wind corridor. NATO takes priority."

Dr. Anatolyev chuckled quietly. "Spoken like someone who still believes the system should live up to its promises."

She wasn't sure if he was mocking her—but she didn't recoil.

"I read your name in the delegate list," he continued, producing a slim pamphlet from his satchel. It was a Russian-language academic quarterly titled *Geopolitika i Ekosfera*. He opened it to a page he had dog-eared.

"This piece," he said, tapping a paragraph. "It made me think of your thesis abstract. Disrupted migration routes, pipeline conflict zones, the NATO-fossil linkage. You might find it... clarifying."

Klara flipped the page. The article was titled "Green Empires and Gray Militaries: Western Ecology as Strategic Hegemony."

Her eyes scanned the first few lines—references to Lithuanian radar emissions, Polish shale gas corridors, avian behavioral shifts across NATO air bases...

She looked up at him. "You've read my abstract?"

"I make it a point to study promising minds," he said simply. "Especially those that haven't yet been dulled by institutional compromise."

He smiled again, almost fatherly.

"There's a reception tonight," he added. "Nothing official. Just a few of us—independent researchers. Eurasian, Central European, postcolonial climate voices. You might enjoy it more than the recycled net-zero slogans in the plenary hall."

Klara hesitated.

"Where?" she finally asked.

He passed her a folded slip of paper. Just an address and a time.

"No pressure," he said. "But I suspect you'll find the conversation... more honest."

And with that, he left her standing in the corner of a Baltic conference room, holding a Russian ecology journal in one hand and a handwritten invitation in the other—her first breadcrumb down a path she didn't yet know she'd follow.

But she would.

****

That Evening

The building wasn't marked. All she found was a lacquered green door beside a closed flower shop on Ģertrūdes Street, a few blocks from the city center. There was no banner, no NGO flag—just a small sticker on the door that read "Common Ground Baltic."

Inside, she found warm lighting, quiet jazz, and the low hum of conversation in at least four languages.

Klara paused just inside the doorway, suddenly aware of how Scandinavian she looked—tall, windblown, carrying a canvas bag filled with summit notes and a copy of *Doughnut Economics*.

Then someone approached—a woman in her late thirties, dark hair tied back, black mask, no visible makeup around her eyes, Baltic-knit sweater and felted wool skirt.

"You must be Klara," she said.

Her accent was hard to place. *Is she Latvian?* Klara wondered. *Russian?* But neither quite fit.

"I'm Irina," said the woman. "Sergei mentioned you might come."

Klara smiled cautiously beneath her mask. "I wasn't sure if I'd be welcome."

Irina's eyes sparkled. "You are exactly the kind of person we welcome."

She gestured toward the gathering. There were maybe thirty people scattered between couches and standing tables, sipping tea or Georgian wine. No one wore a lanyard. A small projector flickered slides on the back wall—photographs of steppe fires, flooded grain fields, and black oil lines slicing through bird migration maps.

One slide read, "Kazakhstan: Migratory Disruption in the Trans-Caspian Axis."

Klara blinked.

"That's my thesis topic," she said aloud.

Irina tilted her head. "Then perhaps you're already one of us."

They sat together on a small settee beneath a bookshelf lined with Russian-language climate theory and old Worldwatch Institute reports. Klara noticed a sticker on one of the mugs that read, "There is no neutrality in ecological collapse."

"Tell me," Irina said, pouring herbal tea into mismatched ceramic cups, "do you believe your government is serious about saving the climate?"

Klara hesitated. She'd said things—angry things—in dorm rooms and in student forums. But this was different.

"I believe they're serious about pretending," she said. "Sweden talks like Greta. Spends like Exxon. We green-wash our missiles now."

Irina gave a slow nod. "You see clearly, then. Most don't, not at your age."

Klara looked down at her tea. "Sometimes I feel like I'm being told to organize deck chairs on the *Titanic*," she said quietly. "And if I say that out loud, I get uninvited from grant panels."

"And what if," Irina said, "there were ways to do more than just 'organize chairs'?"

Klara glanced up. Irina's voice was gentle—*never forceful*.

"Ways to right the ship?" Klara asked.

"To fix the berg hole in it," Irina corrected. "To save the passengers."

Irina leaned in slightly.

"We don't need saboteurs, Klara. We need *witnesses with access*. Architects who've read the blueprints. You don't need to shout. You need to see, and pass it along."

Klara felt something stir in her—recognition…respect.

"I'm not a spy," she said reflexively.

"No," Irina replied. "You're a scientist. An idealist. That's much more useful."

A young man nearby asked Irina a question in Russian, and she excused herself to answer. Klara sat in silence, watching the projector switch to a grainy photo of a US airfield carved into wetlands outside Constanța, Romania. Below it was a graphic of displaced stork migratory routes.

While she was watching the slideshow, someone placed a small handwritten card on the table beside Klara. "Field Ecology Exchange: Central Asia. Spring semester. Eurasian Avian Corridors Grant. Full stipend."

It was an opportunity, an open door. Klara traced the paper's edge with her fingertip.

She wouldn't decide tonight. But she already knew which way the wind was blowing.

****

May 2022
Avian Migration Research Post
Foothills of the Zailiyskiy Alatau Mountains
Outside Almaty, Kazakhstan

The birds always came just after sunrise—no matter how many times Klara Hedevig checked the tracking data the night before, it was never the GPS tags or the drones that gave them away first. It was always the horizon—the widening shimmer of wings catching heat against snowcapped ridgelines.

She raised her binoculars, following the ragged line of demoiselle cranes as they coasted low over the scrub, angling east along the same corridor as the pipelines below. Feathers and fossil fuels traced the same paths—her thesis was practically writing itself now.

Suddenly, there was a female voice behind her: calm, precise, low frequency. "You left your GPS enabled yesterday. That's three times this month."

Klara didn't turn. "It was intentional. I needed to draw the motorbike off."

Irina's boots crunched closer. Klara glanced back. Irina wasn't wearing a jacket today—just her long gray sweater-coat and sun-scorched trousers. She held no visible weapon, but Klara assumed she still carried the ceramic folder knife in her boot.

"And the rider?" Irina asked.

"Lost him in the open market. Took the service road, looped through the back of the tech bazaar. Dropped the burner in a clearance crate of Nokia chargers."

Irina stepped beside her. "And if it wasn't a drill?"

Klara didn't answer immediately. The cranes were fading now, gliding out of visible range toward the eastern steppes.

"I wouldn't have stopped at the market," she said quietly. "I would have used the gravel spill near the depot to lay down the spare phone, cracked it open, stripped the battery, and left the SIM in the nearest drainage slit, then walked through the fuel corridor checkpoint wearing the survey jacket, not the field vest."

Irina said nothing at first, then gave a small, approving nod. "Better."

They stood in silence for a few moments more.

Then Irina offered a sealed envelope.

"Your assignment."

Klara took it and slit it open with her thumbnail. Inside were a profile photo, two names, and a loosely redacted itinerary for a Czech-funded NGO biodiversity director visiting the Korgalzhyn Biosphere Reserve.

"Why him?" Klara asked.

"Because his satellite surveys don't match his published resolutions," Irina replied. "Because his last trip to Georgia involved a forty-eight-hour stop in Ankara with no listed conference. And because if he's using species tagging as a cover for field ISR, we need to know which side he's selling to."

Klara tucked the envelope into her weathered field manual.

"I'll add him to the marsh team rotation," she said. "Ask about his tracking drone specs. Play the data ethics angle."

"And his driver?" Irina asked.

"I'll let him follow me," Klara responded. "See if he gets greedy."

Irina smiled faintly. "You're learning," she said.

"No," Klara replied. "I already learned. I'm just refining."

They turned to leave the overlook. Below them, the dry plain stretched toward a half-decommissioned KazTransOil relay station—a dot on her thesis map, a keyhole for SVR signals intelligence.

Klara knew she'd spend the afternoon cataloging crane banding data, updating her academic dashboard, and submitting her nightly upload to Lund University via a clean VPN pipe routed through Novosibirsk. She also knew she'd be testing a new encrypted messaging protocol passed to her two days ago by a contact posing as a bird-tagging intern from Tatarstan.

This was her new normal now: feathered migrants by day, electronic ghosts by night.

And she loved it.

Chapter Two:
Presidential Finding 32-33

December 30, 2032 – 1647 Hours
National Security Advisor's Office
White House
Washington, D.C.

The radiator clanked its familiar rhythm as National Security Advisor Jim Batista hunched over the DNI's year-end assessment. Outside, snow fell steadily past his window, already accumulating three inches on the South Lawn. Twenty degrees and dropping—a proper D.C. winter.

He'd read the report twice already, but the numbers still seemed impossible. Russia's GDP had grown forty-seven percent in three years. Unemployment was down from twenty-two percent to three. Infrastructure projects that would have taken decades were now completed in months. All thanks to those damned robots.

"The GR-3R 'Drevnik' units have revolutionized Russian industrial capacity," the report stated in the bloodless prose of intelligence analysis. "Current estimates suggest 400,000 units operational across mining, construction, and manufacturing sectors. While these humanoid platforms demonstrate remarkable capability in civilian applications, assessment indicates they remain unsuitable for military deployment. Susceptibility to jamming, vulnerability to high-powered microwave systems, and limited autonomous decision-making restrict combat applications."

Batista set the report aside, massaging his temples. At least that was something. Bad enough that Russia and China had formed the largest military alliance since the Warsaw Pact. If they'd managed to create an army of combat robots too…

A sharp knock interrupted his thoughts.

"Come in."

Secretary of Defense Thomas "T. J." Varnell entered, bringing a gust of cold air from the hallway. Snow still dusted his shoulders, a sign he'd likely come in via the West Wing basement instead of the covered entry his motorcade would typically use. If Batista had to guess, whatever Varnell's reason for stopping over, he didn't want it to show up in the official logs.

"Mr. Secretary." Batista stood. Despite their long friendship, protocol mattered. Varnell outranked him in the chain of command, even if they both reported directly to the President.

"Jim." Varnell didn't take the offered chair. Instead, he moved to the window, watching snowflakes swirl like ash outside the West Wing office. His voice was low, edged with something Batista rarely heard from him—unease. "Did you read the President's Daily Brief this morning?"

Batista nodded slowly, already dreading where this was going. "I take it you're referring to the cable from the Beijing Station?"

"That's the one." Varnell turned, arms crossed. "The Station Chief at the embassy flagged the preliminary agenda for this year's National People's Congress. Buried deep in the proposed resolutions were two items—subtle, but loaded."

Batista raised an eyebrow. "Let me guess, Taiwan?"

"Bingo. But it's worse than usual." Varnell walked over and dropped a red-striped folder on Batista's desk. "The details are inside. They're reaffirming the 'One China' line, but they've taken it a step further and rewritten the language entirely. Now they're referring to the President of Taiwan as the 'Provincial Governor of Chinese Taiwan.' The entire ROC government's been downgraded to provincial officials under Beijing's authority. It's legal fiction—but designed for maximum humiliation."

Batista exhaled through his nose, cold fury flashing across his face. "Damn, talk about throwing gas on a fire."

"Yeah, and that's not the worst of it," Varnell continued. "The agenda includes a sweeping counter-narcotics initiative. You know that synthetic drug called *Vortex*—the one that's already killed three hundred thousand Chinese youths the past six years?"

Batista nodded. "Yeah, it's their version of our fentanyl crisis. Let me guess; they're still blaming *us* for it."

"And more. They're now accusing us of engineering a new Opium War."

Batista frowned. "I've seen the MSS statements… I figured it was just propaganda fodder for domestic consumption."

"It is and it isn't. The draft enforcement plan for countering it now includes maritime inspections—targeting inbound cargo vessels from 'non-compliant jurisdictions,'" Varnell said, quoting directly. "You want to guess which island got named."

Batista's gaze sharpened. "Taiwan, of course."

Varnell nodded. "The civilian coast guard gets the lead. But the fine print authorizes the PLA Navy to support inspection operations. Refuse inspection, and the vessel is presumed complicit in narcotics smuggling. That's the legal trick—they're not calling it a blockade. It's a civilian-led anti-drug enforcement effort. But we both know it'll be used as a pretext for more."

"Great, just what we need on top of everything else," Batista muttered, grabbing the folder, reading it quickly. "This reads like a war plan dressed in a narcotics policy."

"That's what the Beijing Station Chief thinks," Varnell replied grimly. "He believes it might be tied it to a cryptic tip we got from Seoul before their man went dark. Remember that South Korean operative— Pan Min-jae? He caught wind of a backroom meeting in Blagoveshchensk. The operative mentioned something called *Dragon Bear*—Russian and Chinese officials talking about coordinated something and overextending the West."

Batista's spine stiffened as the pieces began to fall into place. "You're saying this might be more than some anti-drug operation?"

"I'm saying it's a slow-rolling operation masked by lawfare and op-ed outrage. And if we're not ready for whatever it is, come April fifteenth, the PLA Navy will be inspecting commercial vessels in the Taiwan Strait under color of law—and daring us to stop them."

Batista looked out the frosted window, his breath fogging the glass. "Four months, huh?"

"Four and a half," Varnell corrected quietly. "That's all the time we've got to decide. Do we call their bluff, or do we let them redraw the map without firing a shot?"

Batista muttered a curse under his breath. "It's BS, Mr. Secretary. A blockade in all but name."

"It's also a test." Varnell finally sat, his movements sharp with tension. "We've suspected this might happen eventually. If I had to guess, Beijing wants to see if we'll blink. If we'll submit and accept this as a new normal," Varnell said angrily. "Four and a half months, Jim.

That's all the time we've got before they start strangling Taiwan's sea lanes and we have to make a tough choice."

Batista muttered a curse under his breath. "It's BS, Mr. Secretary. A blockade in all but name."

"It's also a test." Varnell finally sat, his movements sharp with tension. "We've suspected this might happen eventually. If I had to guess, Beijing wants to see if we'll blink. If we'll submit and accept this as a new normal," Varnell said angrily. "Four and a half months, Jim. That's all the time we've got before they start strangling Taiwan's sea lanes and we have to make a tough choice."

Batista reached into his desk safe, withdrawing a folder marked with classification stamps and a single code word: AZURE SENTINEL. He slid it across to Varnell.

"Presidential Finding 32-33. Signed this morning at 0900."

Varnell broke the seal, his eyes tracking rapidly across the authorization. His eyebrows rose. "Jesus. Five billion in black funding? Expedited weapons transfers bypassing ITAR?"

"The Taiwan Working Group gets whatever they need," Batista confirmed. "No bureaucracy, no delays. Marcus Harrington's people can have Roadrunners, Barracudas, Seekers—the entire autonomous arsenal fully delivered and operational before April fifteenth."

"If the Chinese don't sink the ships carrying them," muttered Varnell.

"They won't. Not yet." Batista pulled up a map on his secure tablet. "Beijing's not ready for that level of escalation. But come April fifteenth…"

"Yeah, I get it. Meanwhile, two weeks later, we've got the start of this EDEP exercise before the May Day celebration." Varnell set the finding aside. "If these DIA reports are correct, we're looking at two PLA Group Armies deploying to Western Russia. I've got EUCOM screaming for more assets. Poland wants another armored brigade on rotation during the exercise. Then the Baltics are raising hell, convinced Russia's going to pull another 2022 and steamroll across the border."

"What's your gut tell you?" asked Batista, eyeing him closely.

Varnell was quiet for a moment. Outside, the snow intensified, obscuring the Washington Monument. "My gut says we're looking at a coordinated move. China takes Taiwan while Russia annexes the Baltics, creating their long-sought-after land bridge connecting them to

Kaliningrad. It's a classic two-front dilemma, with NATO pinned down in Europe, and America stuck with a choice of going all in to help Europe or coming to the aid of our Asian partners. It's a lose-lose situation any way you cut it."

"Which is why TSG matters." Batista tapped the folder. "Six hundred operators embedded with Taiwanese forces. Each one can manage twenty autonomous platforms. That's like having twelve thousand soldiers. It's a force multiplier that's going to make a difference."

"Hmm, the jury in my mind is still out on that one. Contractors, Jim... I'm not so sure about this." Varnell's tone carried his ongoing disapproval of the idea. "I don't like it one bit."

"Respectfully, you don't have to like it, sir. You just have to make it work," Batista replied, keeping his voice respectful but firm. "We both know we can't put active-duty troops on Taiwan right now. Not without triggering the very war we're trying to prevent. But PMCs? That gives us deniability. It places the decision in the hands of Taiwan."

"Sure, until they start dying. These are Americans, nearly all of them are military veterans. If that happens, and we begin to see dead Americans in the streets of Taipei. Congress will want answers," Varnell countered.

"Probably. But by then, it'll be too late for hearings. The bullets and missiles will be flying." Batista stood, moving to his wall display. Satellite imagery showed the Taiwan Strait, with PLA Navy vessels marked in red. "Look at the buildup in the ports opposite Taiwan and within five hundred kilometers of it. They've moved three of their four carrier groups to this area. Forty-plus amphibious vessels. This isn't for an exercise. They're pre-positioning assets, testing logistics, and planning an invasion."

Varnell sighed audibly as he stood and joined him at the display. "What about our autonomous naval program? Reeves keeps promising those unmanned surface combatants will even the odds."

"They will, but they're still in testing. The *Intrepid* task group won't be fully operational until April." Batista highlighted friendly assets in blue. Pathetically few compared to the red swarm. "It's our Hail Mary against their shipbuilding capacity, we've always known that."

"Time, it always comes down to time we don't have." Varnell checked his watch. "Look, I'm supposed to brief the President in twenty minutes about this Taiwan development. What should I be telling him?"

"The truth. Tell him TSG is moving, but we're obviously going to have to accelerate its timeline. Assure him we'll have Taiwan hardened before the shipping inspections start," explained Batista. "And tell him it might be helpful to pray Beijing doesn't accelerate their timeline."

The radiator clanked again, a counterpoint to the gravity of their discussion. Varnell picked up the presidential finding, studying it once more.

"You trust Harrington?"

"I served with him in Iraq. He's solid."

"He'd better be." Varnell moved toward the door, then paused. "Jim, I've got the SECNAV and the Joint Chiefs breathing down my neck about force allocation. If this goes sideways, if Congress gets wind of what we're authorizing…"

"It won't go sideways." Batista returned to his desk. "Marcus knows what's at stake. TSG isn't just defending Taiwan. They're defending the first Island chain and our entire Pacific architecture."

Varnell grunted, nodding slowly. "When do you brief Harrington?"

"Tonight. Crystal City, 2000 hours." Batista glanced at the snow, now falling in thick sheets. "Weather permitting of course."

"In this town, my friend, the weather's the least of our problems." Varnell buttoned his coat as he prepared to leave. "Keep me updated. And, Jim? No surprises. With another term, I've got a chance to fully modernize the entire Defense Department. Last thing I need is a scandal derailing everything we've worked toward."

"I know. Understood, Mr. Secretary."

After Varnell left, Batista sat alone in his office, the weight of the decision settling on his shoulders. Outside, Washington disappeared behind a curtain of white. But his mind was eight thousand miles away, on an island democracy that didn't know it had months to prepare for war.

He pulled up the secure comms channel to TSG. Time to set the wheels in motion. Time to see if six hundred contractors and an arsenal of autonomous weapons could deter an empire.

The radiator clanked one more time, like a countdown clock marking time until April.

Chapter Three:
Taiwan Working Group

December 30, 2032
1770 Crystal Drive
Crystal City, Virginia

The six-story office building in Crystal City was a masterpiece of hiding in plain sight. Building 1770 was no different from the other nearby buildings that housed various government offices and the myriad of contracting companies supporting one government agency or another. But that was a facade for the public. Within the building, hidden behind faux storefronts and secret entrances, was a hidden world of classified workspaces and intelligence workings. It was the quintessential example of how Washington's overt and covert worlds blended seamlessly together.

When Marcus Harrington reached the elevator leading to his workspace, two security guards greeted him—one seated behind a desk, the other standing vigilant near the elevator doors. Marcus nodded, recognizing the tailored suit jackets designed to conceal weapons. Standard procedure in this line of work.

"Evening. Here to access the mainframe?" the seated guard asked, delivering the authentication phrase with practiced neutrality.

"Yes, terminal four, yellow protocol," Harrington responded, completing the countersign that granted him elevator access.

The guard gave a curt nod. "You have a visitor. Room 412."

Harrington stepped onto the elevator and pressed the button for the fourth floor, a slight smile crossing his weathered face.

Three years ago, he'd been savoring retirement on Thailand's Phi Phi Islands, sipping fruity drinks and living the carefree life of a beach bum. After two decades in special forces and ten tense years in the world of private military contracting, he desperately needed to decompress. The PMC work had paid well, but the constant strain of wondering if each day might be his last had worn him to the bone.

Thailand had felt like the natural choice. Having worked closely with the Thai military throughout his career, he appreciated that a few grand a month allowed him a comfortable, stress-free lifestyle. He might still be there if Jim Batista, a former SOF operator and longtime colleague, hadn't called out of the blue with an offer he couldn't refuse.

When Batista had become National Security Advisor, he'd offered Marcus a chance to lead what had eventually become the Taiwan Study Group. TSG was a concept they'd discussed for years back on their ODA team: an unconventional approach aligning with the US's public stance on Taiwan while quietly ensuring the island's continued independence.

Operating openly as a private military company with the Taiwanese government's consent, TSG provided scalable support beyond what the Pentagon could easily deliver. Congressional oversight and diplomatic sensitivities made official channels slow and cautious. As a PMC, TSG could act decisively, maintaining enough separation from Washington to give Batista precisely the strategic flexibility he needed Harrington to exploit.

When he arrived at Room 412, with its mahogany conference table, ergonomic chairs, and neutral artwork, it looked like any other executive meeting space—but that was the point. To the trained eye, the door's thickness and the faint hum of active RF jammers hid its SCIF rating in plain sight. The room was designed to be a bubble of absolute security in a city where walls routinely had ears and spies were everywhere.

When Harrington arrived, Batista was seated at the table, patiently waiting for him. They had known each other a long time, several decades, in fact. They had fought together, bled together, suffered and shared triumphs. It was a friendship built over time through collective sacrifice. While they didn't always see eye to eye on everything, they were one when it came to protecting this country and ensuring that no matter what happened in the future, it would be America and her allies that came out on top.

"Marcus, good to see you," Batista said, getting straight to the point. "Sorry for calling you in like this, especially right before the New Year."

Harrington took a seat opposite him at the table. "It's fine, Jim. Sorry I couldn't meet earlier—family commitment. I'm guessing this meeting has something to do with that big EDEP exercise scheduled for spring?"

He paused briefly, eyes narrowing thoughtfully. "Call me paranoid, Jim, but having exercises in the South China Sea, North Pacific, Middle East, and Eastern Europe—all at once? You guys at the White House must be chewing glass by now." Harrington's gallows humor surfaced predictably, drawing a weary smile from Batista.

"Something like that," Batista laughed. "With the election over, I was hoping this spring exercise was the only thing we'd have to worry about. Have you seen the size of this thing? We're talking about the entire Eurasian Defense and Economic Pact flexing at once—Russia and China leading the charge with their junior partners all playing along. Damn, if you thought the REFORGER exercises in the eighties were big—I'm just glad the Europeans finally got serious about rearming a while back. They're asking if we'd consider running a beefed-up EuroDefender exercise this year. I think it's doable and the President will likely go for it too."

"Makes sense, given what EDEP has become," Harrington nodded. "Four years since Moscow and Beijing signed that pact, and look at them now—free movement of people and capital across member states, integrated supply chains, and a mutual defense clause that makes NATO's Article 5 look conservative. From what I've heard, the Japanese are thinking this exercise might be a decoy for an attempt to seize the Miyako Islands. A few contacts I have in Saudi told me that the crown prince, MBS, thinks the Iranians are going to make a play to further consolidate their control of Iraq or maybe try to reconstitute that Achaemenid Empire the new regime's been touting since coming to power."

Harrington leaned forward. "No one in the Middle East is comfortable with the Iranians, Afghanis, and Pakistanis being part of EDEP. Having them backed by Russian military tech and Chinese economic muscle? That's a nightmare scenario. And don't get me started on North Korea having free access to Chinese ports and Russian energy. If BRICS and the old Warsaw Pact had a child raised on steroids, it'd be EDEP."

Batista laughed at the analogy, but his expression quickly sobered. "Yeah, except this version spans from Vladivostok to Tehran, Pyongyang to Islamabad. Hell, with Myanmar, Laos, Cambodia and Sri Lanka signed on, they've got the Bay of Bengal practically surrounded. As they say, amateurs talk tactics, professionals talk logistics. For all of our sakes, I'm hoping this exercise is just them testing their new integrated command structure and supply chains, not a lead-up to something more."

He paused, then added, "But there's another wrinkle. NSA picked up something interesting—backed up by our friends in Tokyo and Seoul. Looks like Beijing's planning to propose some kind of new customs inspection regime at the People's Congress in March."

"Customs inspection?" Harrington's eyebrows rose. "What kind of scope are we talking about?"

"That's the thing—we don't have all the details yet. From what we can piece together, they're framing it as a drug enforcement initiative. But, Jim, you and I both know if they implement something like that, Taiwan's going to be caught in the net."

"A drug enforcement action that just happens to give them legal cover to board and inspect any vessel they want," Harrington said slowly. "Including ships bound for Taiwan."

"Exactly. Until the proposal actually drops or they release more details, we're operating on fragments. But between this and the EDEP exercises..." Batista shook his head. "That brings me to the reason I called you here. That document we discussed a while back, the one that says 'break glass in case of emergency'...well, the President considers this an emergency." Batista slid a folder across the table to him.

Harrington opened it, raising an eyebrow when he saw the letterhead. His eyes quickly read it, noting the language, the monies allocated, and the waivers for ITARS and export-controlled items.

"Unfortunately, recent events have compressed our timeline," Batista continued. "Between Beijing's rhetoric, this recent customs announcement, and the ongoing demonstrations on Kinmen and Matsu, it's increasingly looking like they're gearing up to do something stupid. We need to be ready for whatever it is."

Batista pointed to the document. "Marcus, this supersedes your previous authorization. President Ashford has removed any and all procurement restrictions. You now have direct acquisition authority for the full suite of autonomous systems."

Harrington nodded, continuing to scan the document with practiced efficiency, mentally cataloging the expanded authorities. "The Anduril package is substantial. Fury combat drones, Lattice C2 architecture, autonomous interceptors—"

"Everything," Batista interjected. "Plus the newest generation of Epirus Leonidas counterdrone systems and Saronic's coastal defense platforms. Full-spectrum electronic warfare capabilities. The whole arsenal. We can't go light on this—we have to go all in if we're going to make it work."

"Good, and the funding mechanism?"

Batista pulled another folder from the classified bag he'd brought and slid it across the table. "This is your funding document and authorities. You have four-point-eight billion dollars to spend. It's being channeled through three separate funding vehicles. Defense Production Act authorities have been invoked with the primary contractors on anything we need that we don't already have on hand or in the production pipeline."

Marcus whistled softly. "Damn, you know this is a significant escalation from our current footprint of slowly and steadily boiling the frog, right?"

Batista shrugged. "We're adapting to overcome. The timeline has changed, but not the President's strategy. He still believes our best weapon is to use economic pressure as our primary leverage against China. But he's purchasing this insurance policy via TSG in case it fails." Batista tapped the finding. "Your teams need to expedite the defense in depth strategy that makes Taiwan too costly to invade."

"Yeah, I can see that. We've been doing a lot of that with the ROC Marines and a couple of Army units. We are doing the best we can with the people we have, but right now I'm running everything with just two hundred and thirty-six people. I've got a hundred and ninety of them deployed in-country between Penghu and Tamsui as mobile training teams. If you are wanting us to go operational, actually assist the ROC in repelling an attack, two hundred and thirty-six people isn't going to cut it."

"Agreed, and we are addressing that." Batista extracted a USB drive. "The authorization includes recruitment of four hundred additional contractors. Names have been pre-vetted, and the ones still on active duty can be transferred to support TSG via JSOC and the Agency. Everything you need, their backgrounds and documentation are on here." He passed the drive across the table and Harrington pocketed it.

"And should things go kinetic, are there limits on our involvement or do we have a free hand to operate as we see fit?"

Batista leaned forward, looking Harrington in the eyes. "Marcus, if things go kinetic with the PRC, we're in trouble. Not just us, but everyone else on our side of the ledger. Publicly, the Taiwan Study Group is a registered private military contractor that's been hired to provide training and assistance to the armed forces of the Republic of China as they modernize their military. Privately, there are only five people in their government who know TSG has been contracted to fight on behalf of, and alongside, ROC government forces. Let's hope it doesn't come to that, but should it, TSG is legally protected."

"Good, I'm glad we've got that covered. Let's talk about training—it's going to be an issue. For the past year we've been working to build an organic train-the-trainer program within the services. This will eventually allow them to become self-sufficient rather than dependent on us. If our timeline is to have everything in place and ready to go by April—and even that date is pushing it—not only do we need to increase our trainers by a factor of four, but we also need ten times the current number of operators capable of using these various AI and drone platforms. We're talking about hundreds of autonomous platforms that require specialized operator knowledge, which we have to impart in a very short period of time."

Batista grimaced, acknowledging the problem. "And this is why you get paid the big bucks, Marcus. To figure things out and solve the problems others can't. That said, I'm not going to leave you high and dry with no outside help either. For the next ninety days, your training guru, Elena Bell, and her staff will have priority access to the Naval Special Warfare facilities on Guam. This should give you additional help but, more importantly, a secluded place to train specific tactics without the prying eyes of CCP collaborators. I won't tell you how to run your training, but I'd focus on counterdrone and coastal defense capabilities first. That's where we'll get the maximum deterrent effect the fastest and get the best bang for our buck. If the PLA gets a foothold on Taiwan…well, just try and make sure that doesn't happen."

For a couple of minutes no one spoke as Harrington finished the documents. It was a lot to take in. The whole purpose of the Taiwan Study Group was to aid the ROC government in utilizing advancements in AI and autonomous weapon platforms to offset the PLA's obvious across-the-board numerical advantage. This change to their mission was a lot to take in. He effectively had four and a half months to have all the gear, equipment, and personnel ready inside Taiwan to turn TSG into a private military force that could directly fight against the People's Liberation Army alongside the soldiers and sailors they'd been training.

"This is a big ask, Jim. Do we really have to be operationally ready by April fifteenth or is there a little room on the timeline?" Marcus asked, rising from his chair.

Batista collected the folders, placing them in the classified bag he'd brought before answering. "I'd like to say you have more time, and maybe you will. But in terms of supplies arriving via boat, I think you have to plan on having everything you need in place before April fifteenth. You also need to keep in mind, the last time Russia announced a training exercise of this scale was nearly eleven years ago, when it invaded Ukraine. We fundamentally failed to deter Putin from crossing that Rubicon and unleashing years of devastation. We cannot make that same mistake and fail to disabuse the PLA generals and President Ouyang of this belief that they can militarily seize Taiwan."

As they exited the conference room, Batista lowered his voice. "Marcus, the President wanted me to tell you something. He wants you to know this isn't just about Taiwan. This is about replacing the democracies of the West with the digital autocracies of the East. It's about replacing the old unipolar world order with a multipolar one divided into spheres of influence across Asia, the Middle East, and Europe. This is about who will control the resources to build the technologies of the future. It's why we see moves being made across Africa. It's why EDEP includes the Stans, Mongolia, Iran and Afghanistan. If they succeed in subduing Europe and defeating America, there's nothing left to stop them from securing complete domination over everything. We have to stop them."

Marcus nodded once. He knew the stakes.

"I'll contact you through the established channel when the first shipments are underway and send updates as things progress," he said.

"I know you will, and the President knows it too. Good luck, Marcus, and Godspeed."

Chapter Four:
Task Force Nightfury

January 7, 2033 – 0900 Hours
Centurion Facility, Sublevel 1
Rosslyn, Virginia

The C4ISR suite hummed with electronic life. Wall-mounted displays cycled through threat matrices, satellite feeds, and network traffic patterns. Coffee steam rose from a dozen cups scattered across the mahogany conference table. Outside, big fluffy cotton balls of January love continued to fall around the Arlington glass towers of Rosslyn City, but down here in the digital cocoon, the weather might as well not exist.

Jim Batista stood at the head of the table, studying faces. His team looked rested, a minor miracle after the holidays given how crazy the lead-up to them had been. It had been a rough year, and he knew this year wasn't going to be any better. He needed them rested—he needed them focused. He just hoped the ten days of rest he'd given them hadn't dulled them.

"Morning, people. And happy New Year!" Batista's Utah drawl cut through the ambient hum. "I hope everyone enjoyed their break, 'cause the enemy didn't take one and it's time we get back to earning our keep." He turned to his FBI liaison seated to his right. "Darnell, you're up. What's our domestic picture looking like?"

Special Agent Darnell Cross straightened in his chair. The former Philly beat cop turned cyber specialist was a technical wizard when it came to hunting digital adversaries. He tapped his tablet, sending his screen to the main display.

"Happy New Year to you too, boss. I wish I had better news to start the year, sir." Cross's Philadelphia accent thickened under stress. "We've been tracking increased PLA cyber activity against critical infrastructure since Boxing Day, December twenty-sixth."

The screen filled with network diagrams. Red intrusion attempts spider-webbed across port facility schematics.

"Primary targets are industrial control systems at our major automated ports." Cross highlighted nodes. "LA, Newark, Miami, Houston. They're probing the AI management systems that run container operations."

Batista leaned forward. "Probing or penetrating?"

"So far...just probing. But it's sophisticated stuff." Cross pulled up attack vectors. "They're targeting the junction points where human operators interface with autonomous systems. The handoff protocols."

"Smart," muttered Colonel Rooke from across the table. The CYBERCOM liaison studied the patterns with professional interest. "Hit the seams, not the armor."

Cross nodded. "Exactly. They know our port automation runs on predictive algorithms. Crane movements, truck routing, container stacking, it's all AI-optimized. Corrupt those decision trees..."

"And you turn efficiency into chaos," Batista finished. "Got it. Casualties? Any companies fall victim?"

"None yet. Our defensive measures held." Cross's jaw tightened. "But here's what keeps me up at night."

New graphics cascaded across the displays. Port throughput statistics. Dependency charts. Supply chain vulnerabilities mapped in painful detail.

"Houston handles forty percent of our military petroleum imports. LA processes sixty percent of transpacific container traffic. Miami's our primary pharmaceutical gateway." Cross let the numbers sink in. "We're talking strategic choke points. And the PLA knows it. That's why these ports were targeted and not others."

"Huh, that's interesting. How close did they get?" This from Alicia Morane, the CIA's Deputy Director for Foreign Operations. Her voice carried the weight of someone who'd seen networks burned, and burned a few herself.

"Too close, if you ask me." Cross pulled up forensic data. "They penetrated the demilitarized zones at three facilities. Got within two network hops of the operational technology layer before our AI-enabled intrusion detection caught them."

"Attribution confidence?" Batista asked, curious if it was the same known actors or someone new.

"We're high confidence on this one. The digital fingerprints are pretty well known by the NSA at this point. We traced the attacks back to PLA Unit 61456, their critical infrastructure warfare group. It stumped us at first, but looking back on similar attacks, we found the codes matched against what we saw in the Colonial Pipeline sequel from last year and the year before. Sloppy if you ask me, but we'll take it."

Mara Whitford, the State Department liaison, removed her reading glasses. "That's good work, Darnell. It sucks that Beijing will deny involvement. They always do."

Cross shrugged. "Eh, so what? Let 'em deny it. We know it was them and we stopped them." Cross's street edge began to show in his tone. "So, if you can believe this, we actually got lucky on this one. We've got packet captures, malware signatures, even sloppy OPSEC on their command infrastructure. It would appear one of their operators forgot to sanitize his time zone data. Using that and some other tools, we back-traced the attack to, I kid you not, the Shangri-La Hotel."

Batista nearly spat his coffee out. "Whoa, wait a second. You guys managed to trace this hacker back to a hotel in Guangzhou?"

Cross nodded. "We did. But without a visual verification to know if it's legit, we can't say for certain that it truly originated there and wasn't a proxy."

Batista sat back in his chair, absorbing the information. Around the table, his team processed the implications. The PLA hackers had been targeting American port automation processes for years. The automation of America's transportation and logistics networks had been a game-changing revolution in productivity. Fewer workers, faster throughput, predictive maintenance. Unfortunately, that efficiency now looked like a new vulnerability.

"OK, recommendations. I mean, is it possible we could get eyes on that hotel, maybe see if there's something to it?" Batista asked, keeping his tone neutral.

Cross straightened as he answered. "We're coordinating with DHS and with port authorities on immediate patches that should take care of the issue. But, sir, we need a more thorough security review of our automation architecture."

"OK, meaning?"

"Meaning we built these systems for efficiency, not necessarily resilience." Cross pulled up architectural diagrams. "Every automated crane, every autonomous truck, every AI scheduler, they're all potential attack vectors. We need air gaps, manual overrides, offline contingencies in case next time we don't get so lucky and prevent them from having some fun inside our systems."

"Huh, yeah, fat chance of that. That'll cost billions," Rooke observed.

"I don't know about that, but it's cheaper than losing a port for six months," countered Cross, meeting his gaze. "I mean, ask Baltimore what happened when their terminals went down in twenty-eight. That resulted in seven billion in economic losses."

Batista turned to Dr. Helena Yuryevna, their disinformation specialist. The former Russian academic studied the attack patterns with unsettling intensity. "Helena? You look like you've got something."

"*Da*, I am thinking..." Her accent thickened when she concentrated. "These probes, they are not random. Look at the timing."

She commandeered the display, overlaying attack time stamps with other data streams.

"December twenty-sixth, they probe LA. December twenty-eighth, Houston. January second, Newark. January fourth, Miami." She paused. "Now look at ship arrivals."

New data flowed across the screen. Container vessel schedules. Chinese-flagged ships highlighted in amber.

"Every attack coincides with COSCO vessel arrivals. The hackers are using their own ships as collection platforms." Yuryevna smiled coldly. "Very clever. Park a signals intelligence suite in a container, intercept local wireless traffic during port operations."

"Good Lord, really?" Cross began scribbling out a message to send after he returned to his computer. "Damn, I need to alert the field offices about this once our meeting's over."

"No worries, but do it quiet," Batista cautioned. "No need to tip our hand yet. Let's see if maybe we can try and catch 'em in the act."

As Cross wrote urgently in his notepad, Batista studied the broader picture. The PLA wasn't just probing defenses, they were mapping vulnerabilities. Building target packages. Preparing.

"All right, people. Good catch on this." Batista's tone sharpened. "Darnell, I want you coordinating with Evan at NSC. We need a classified annex on port vulnerabilities added to the next Presidential Daily Brief."

"Copy that."

"Rooke, work with CYBERCOM on active defense measures. If the PLA wants to play in our networks, let's make sure they find some surprises."

The cyber commander grinned. "I've got some ideas. Honeypots that look like ICS vulnerabilities but actually map their attack infrastructure."

"Do it. Helena, work up some counternarratives. When Beijing denies involvement, I want us ready to expose their operations."

"With pleasure." The Russian's smile could have frozen vodka.

Batista checked his watch. Twenty minutes into the meeting, and already his year looked complicated. "Mara, State's going to need talking points for our allies. Especially Singapore and Rotterdam. If the PLA's hitting our ports, theirs are probably next. Oh, and see if we have anyone in Guangzhou who might be able to pay a visit to this hotel to do some recon work for us."

"Sure, I can look into that for us. I'll draft something today," Mara confirmed.

"Good." Batista surveyed his team once more. "Questions on the port situation?"

Silence. They were professionals. They knew the stakes.

"All right, then." Batista pulled up the next agenda item.

The displays shifted to some recent high-resolution satellite imagery. The first image it showed was the Trans-Siberian Railway's main hub located at the Russian-Chinese cities of Zabaikalsk–Manzhouli. This was the predominant route for both passenger and rail freight moving between the two countries. The caption next to the image indicated that sixty percent of all freight moving into Russia from China traversed this line.

The second and third images showed two air bases in Belarus, Balbasava and Baranovichi. Both had undergone extensive modernization and expansion over the past five years. They now had additional parking aprons flanked on either side with overhead protection and drone nets to help protect the autonomous one-way attack drones and loitering munitions. The high-resolution images showed increased air cargo activity, and neatly parked rows of wheeled military vehicles ranging from four- and six-passenger vehicles to larger five-ton transports and fuel trucks.

"OK, people. Let's talk about the elephants in the room." Batista's voice cut through the tension as he began. "First, let's start with this announcement from Foreign Minister Qiao. Apparently, the PRC plans to refer to President Ching-te as Governor of Taiwan Province."

He paused, letting that sink in. "I've directed the Taiwan Study Group to accelerate the timeline for the delivery and operational status of their mission to be ready by the first of April. What I need to know from the rest of you is this: Does the PRC plan to enforce these customs inspections with military force via a civil police action? A Hong Kong 2.0. Is this more saber-rattling, or the start of the next round of trade talks with the Grain Consortium?"

Mara Whitford leaned forward. "Jim, I need to share something first."

Evan Rallus raised a hand as Alicia started to speak. "Hold up, Alicia. We'll circle back to you. Go ahead, Mara."

"Thanks." Mara's fingers drummed once on the table. "I reached out to a friend, Alex Donnelly, at our Beijing embassy. We've worked on different projects together for going on fifteen years, so I know him pretty well. He's now the Economic Unit Chief, Political Section."

She glanced briefly at her notes. "For a little more than three years, Alex has regularly met with Zhao Lifen—he's the Deputy Director, Trade Policy Coordination Office. They meet weekly for breakfast and lunch, sometimes both if it's important. Alex said Zhao's a pragmatist, walks the line at Commerce. Officially handles trade messaging before his office and our embassy. Unofficially, however"— her eyes swept the room—"he's become State's back channel for de-escalation."

"So I asked Alex, is this more chest-thumping from Ouyang? Same rhetoric we've seen since twenty-eight?" Mara's expression tightened. "Yesterday, Alex left me a voicemail. His voice was... off. Spooked, even—"

"Really? What did he say?" Alicia couldn't wait this time, concern etching her features.

Mara nodded slowly. "Zhao told Alex to ensure President Ashford understood something: Ouyang was going to be firm on Taiwan." She let the words hang. "Does that mean he'll escalate to a direct conflict? Alex wasn't certain. But in the three years he and Zhao have been meeting, he's never been this blunt."

The room was absorbed by quiet, with no one speaking for a moment.

Batista finally broke the silence. "OK, then, I think we have our answer. We'll circle back in a few days and discuss how we should respond to this once we've had some time to think on it. Now that we've solved world peace and ended homelessness," Batista joked, trying to break the tension of the moment before shifting to the next meeting update, "Rooke, you mentioned your people at CYBERCOM had an update on some unique offensive capabilities. Floor's yours."

Colonel Everett Rooke sat a little straighter in his chair, the former NSA operative's fingers unconsciously tapping binary patterns on the table. His North Carolinian drawl emerged, clipped and precise.

"Yes, sir. My team's been developing a new tool kit targeting Russian rail infrastructure." He pushed his brief to the main display for everyone to follow along. "Specifically, we've gained persistent access to their automated rail-line-switching systems."

The screen filled with some technical schematics. Rail networks spider-webbed across Russia, Belarus, Iran, China, and the Stan countries, pulsing in an amber color.

Batista smiled as he leaned back in his chair. "Very nice. Walk me through it. How'd you get in and what are you able to do with it?"

"Patience and luck." Rooke allowed himself a thin smile. "Thankfully, the Russian rail network management system uses a version of Huawei routers that we're familiar with and have exploited in the past. Chinese hardware, Russian implementation. Neither side fully trusts the other, so it's created some vulnerabilities that we've been quick to identify, and that's allowed us to create a series of back doors we can access later on at a time of our choosing."

"Ha-ha, good one, Rooke. The seams once again for the win," Morane laughed.

"Exactly. If it ain't broke, don't fix it," Rooke said, sharing a humorous moment with Morane before turning serious again. "As we moved through their system, we identified the weak link we could exploit to sow some chaos and cause serious damage when the time comes. What we found was a component part, a timing controller chip that still accepts firmware updates." Rooke smirked as he highlighted code snippets. "Huawei pushes out a series of patches quarterly. We've been injecting our own code into those patches for going on eighteen months now."

"Christ almighty!" Cross's hand tightened on his coffee cup. "You've been inside their rail network for a year and a half?"

"Yes, observing only. At least until now." Rooke's expression hardened. "Given current tensions, we've gone ahead and developed some active measures."

New graphics flowed across the displays. The Trans-Siberian Railway stretched across eight time zones. A handful of choke points glowed red.

"The Russians have eight rail lines connecting their Far East oblast to European Russia. But geography's a beast." Rooke zoomed in. "They're funneled through six major tunnels and eight critical bridges. Right now, Chinese engineering teams working with a few thousand of those GR-3R 'Drevnik' humanoid robotic workers are helping expand the rail bridge and tunnel capacity. But until those projects are finished, they're limited to using just three operational tunnels."

"Ah, those make for some nice bottlenecks," Batista observed.

"Yeah, massive ones. Seventy percent of their military logistics flow through these choke points." Rooke pulled up a traffic analysis report. "In peacetime, this is manageable. In a war…"

He let them fill in the blank.

"Yeah, I get it. So what's the play?" Batista's tone stayed neutral.

Rooke's fingers resumed their binary drumming. "Simple physics. Their automated switching system prevents collisions by routing opposing traffic to holding tracks when necessary. As we continue to observe their rail schedules, we've mapped when the gates get turned on to divert the trains to the holding tracks."

The display showed train movements in real-time simulation. Green arrows flowing east and west, diverted smoothly at junction points.

"When authorized, and only when authorized, we flip those gates." His voice dropped. "An eastbound military transport carrying tanks. A westbound fuel train. Both doing eighty kilometers per hour and neither is diverted."

The simulation continued to play out, the two arrows converging on each other until they merged into one—impact.

"On one track, we engineer a head-on collision inside a tunnel." Rooke's drawl vanished, his tone sharp. "On another track, we time a collision to occur on a bridge span. Either way, you're looking at weeks of cleanup, and a hell of a mess. If we're lucky, it could take months to repair and restore traffic. Our bottlenecks become corks."

Silence fell. Around the table, operators who'd seen death up close processed the implications. Hundreds dead, maybe even thousands. Infrastructure crippled. Supply lines severed.

Cross's Philly accent cut through. "That's... Jesus. The crews..."

"Not crews. Military logistics personnel." Rooke met his gaze. "They're valid targets under the laws of armed conflict."

"Still." The FBI agent's jaw worked, but he said nothing more.

Dr. Yuryevna leaned forward, her academic detachment intact. "If such an event occurred, controlling the information space would be critical, especially in the immediate moments and hours after it happens."

All eyes turned to the Russian exile.

"Railroad disasters resonate deeply in Russian psychology. There is a history of this happening, and it is almost always a result of incompetence and corruption. Lives wasted over greed." Yuryevna's fingers traced patterns on the table. "We would not claim credit, *da*? Instead, we flood Telegram channels with speculation. Maintenance failures covered up. Embezzled safety funds. Officials more concerned with Beijing bribes than Russian lives. We sow doubt between allies where none previously existed."

"I like it. Turn their people against their own government," Mara observed.

"Is already happening. We simply amplify." Yuryevna's smile could have etched glass. "Perhaps leaked documents showing rail officials' Swiss bank accounts, videos of Chinese advisors living in luxury while Russian workers die. The narrative writes itself."

Before she even spoke, Batista saw the gleam in Yuryevna's eyes as a plan took shape. "Jim...you could let me tinker with CHIMERA. I could generate some deepfakes we could test and make ready to use when the time's right?"

The room stirred when she mentioned CHIMERA. Cognitive Hyper-Intelligent Media Engine for Realistic Alteration was TF Nightfury's most potent digital tool. In the wrong hands, it could make anyone say or do anything on video, complete with perfect audio matching—a dangerous capability they wielded carefully, and under the strictest of rules.

Batista sat back as he absorbed the discussion happening within his team. Cyber weapons were clean in theory, code instead of bombs and bullets. But when the time came to launch this attack, it would leave a trail of death and destruction in its wake.

"Colonel, if it comes to it and we need to authorize this attack, what's your confidence level on a clean execution without a digital trail leading right back to us?"

"If ordered—high. We've run simulated attacks over a thousand times without a single trail of evidence that could be traced back to us." The cyber commander's certainty was absolute. "Give the word, hoss, and pick the trains. Within a few hours, physics takes over."

"You're absolutely certain about the attribution?"

"Yes. We're ghosts inside their systems," Colonel Rooke confirmed as he pulled up a forensic analysis. "The attack uses their own switching logic against them. There's no malware signatures to look for. No external connections to back-trace. To the investigators, it'll look like the catastrophic failure it was."

"And if we nudge them a bit with CHIMERA, they'll believe whatever narrative we feed them," Yuryevna added.

Batista smiled slowly. Another tool of war. Another crossed line in defense of his country.

"All right, Colonel, Yuryevna. Keep the capability warm but weapons tight. This is a wartime-only option unless directed otherwise." Batista checked his watch. Nearly noon. "And on that cheerful note, let's break for lunch. Reconvene at 1400."

Chairs scraped back. Conversations sprouted in small groups. Special Agent Cross caught up to Colonel Rooke near the door. "Hey, Colonel, out of curiosity, does it bother you that some of these actions you talk about will invariably lead to the death of civilians who are certain to be caught in the crossfire??" The FBI agent's voice carried an edge. "It seems cold how we choose who lives or dies when these people are just doing their job."

Colonel Rooke paused, studying the younger man. "I do. I think about it every day." His drawl returned, softer. "The same way I think about our port workers if the PLA succeeds in their attempts to harm our people. It's war, and war has casualties."

Rooke's hand found Cross's shoulder. "We're supposed to be better?"

He leaned in. "You think we're the good guys. They think they're the good guys. Know the difference?" His eyes hardened. "I want *my* kids to have a future. Not theirs. If they win, *my* family loses."

Cross stared, uncertainty shifting to understanding. The weight of their decisions was suddenly real.

Chapter Five:
Baltic Disaster

January 27, 2033 – 0434 Hours
HSwMS *Lulea* (*Lulea*-Class Corvette)
Baltic Sea, Southeast of Gotland

The Baltic Sea lay shrouded in predawn darkness, its surface disturbed only by the gentle wake of merchant vessels following the invisible highways of international shipping lanes. Twenty-three nautical miles southeast of Gotland, Sweden's strategic island fortress, the HSwMS *Lulea* maintained her patrol station.

The *Lulea* was a cutting-edge warship, barely three years out of the shipyard. At 2,400 tons and 110 meters in length, this corvette represented Sweden's leap into next-generation naval warfare. Her sleek hull incorporated the latest in signature management technology, while her combined diesel-electric and gas turbine propulsion system balanced efficiency with a sprint capability exceeding thirty-two knots. Armed with RBS-15 Mk4 antiship missiles, a 57mm Bofors gun, and the latest Saab 9LV combat management system, she was built specifically for the confined waters and complex threats of the Baltic.

Tonight, she ghosted along at eight knots on electric power alone, her passive sensors cataloging the electronic heartbeat of every vessel within sixty kilometers.

Lieutenant Commander Mats Algotsson hunched over the communications console in the state-of-the-art combat information center, his face illuminated by the blue-white glow of LED displays. The flash priority header from NATO Maritime Command made his stomach tighten. He read the message twice, then grabbed the internal phone.

"Bridge, CIC. Wake the captain. Immediately."
****

Captain Henrik Dahl arrived on the bridge at 0441 hours, his uniform crisp despite the hour. Twenty years in the Swedish Navy had trained him to transition from deep sleep to full alertness in seconds. The concerned expressions on his officers' faces gave him an additional boost of adrenaline—something was up.

"Talk to me, XO."

Algotsson handed him a tablet displaying the encrypted message. "MARCOM alert came in twenty minutes ago. High priority. A US Air Force RC-135 Rivet Joint detected anomalous electronic emissions from a Chinese-flagged vessel approximately forty kilometers from our position."

Dahl scrolled through the report, his expression hardening. The American surveillance aircraft, bristling with signals intelligence equipment, had picked up military-grade radar emissions from what should have been a civilian freighter. They were short bursts, precisely timed—the kind of pattern used to test targeting systems.

"Which vessel?" asked Dahl.

"MV *Hai Qing 678*, sir," Algotsson replied. "Bulk freighter, sixty thousand tons. Departed Saint Petersburg thirty-six hours ago, declared destination Shanghai via the Suez Canal. Currently making ten knots on bearing two-three-five, following standard shipping lanes through the Baltic."

Lieutenant Stefan Lindström added from the navigation plot, his fingers tracing routes on the holographic display, "Sir, at her current course and speed, she'll pass directly over the GosNet-1 cable junction in approximately three hours."

Dahl felt his jaw tighten. The fiber-optic lifeline connected Gotland to Sweden and mainland Europe, carrying everything from civilian internet traffic to military communications. Damaging it could cripple the island's digital infrastructure for weeks.

"Pull up her history," Dahl directed.

Lindström's fingers flew across the haptic interface. "Chinese registry, home port Shanghai. This is her fourth Baltic transit in eighteen months. She always travels along the same route—picks up cargo in Saint Petersburg, usually grain or timber, then returns to China." He paused, highlighting a section of data. "Sir, she was in the vicinity during the Estonia-Finland cable incident last October. One of three vessels that could have been responsible."

"Never proven," Algotsson added quietly.

"No," Dahl agreed. "But suspicious enough." He moved to the large tactical display dominating the bridge's forward section. The Baltic stretched before them in three-dimensional representation—shipping lanes marked in blue, territorial waters in various shades, critical infrastructure pulsing red. The *Hai Qing* appeared as a yellow icon, plodding steadily toward their cable.

"Range?" asked Dahl.

"Thirty-eight kilometers, sir. She's approaching Fårö Island to our north."

Dahl studied the geometry of the intercept. The *Lulea*-class's powerful MTU diesels could close the distance in under an hour—but doing so would light them up on every sensor in the Baltic. Stealth took priority. That meant the Chinese freighter would have time to finish whatever it was doing and cover its tracks.

"Helm, come to course two-seven-zero. Increase to fifteen knots on electric drive only. Let's position ourselves for a closer look without lighting up our heat signature."

"Two-seven-zero, fifteen knots electric, aye, sir."

The corvette's advanced electric motors increased power smoothly, her hull cutting through the calm seas with minimal noise. Through the bridge's panoramic windows, Dahl could see the first hints of dawn painting the eastern horizon deep purple. The morning twilight would help—that gray zone between night and day when visual identification became difficult.

"Sir," the electronic warfare officer called out from her station. "I'm picking up intermittent signals from the *Hai Qing*'s bearing. Same characteristics as the MARCOM report. Seven-second bursts at irregular intervals."

"Can you classify them?"

"Running them through our database now, sir. Preliminary analysis suggests fire control radar. Specifically matching Chinese Type 366-2 characteristics—that's their latest maritime targeting system."

Fire control radar on a cargo vessel returning from a routine grain pickup. Dahl felt the pieces falling into place. This wasn't just intelligence gathering—someone was testing targeting solutions on every naval vessel, platform, and critical infrastructure node they passed.

"XO, what's our rules of engagement regarding suspected threats to critical infrastructure?"

Algotsson had already pulled up the relevant orders on his tablet. "Under NATO Baltic protocols and Swedish maritime law, we're authorized to investigate any vessel demonstrating hostile intent toward undersea cables. Visual inspection, query, and if necessary, boarding for inspection."

"But only if we can establish probable cause," Dahl added. He knew the game—international waters meant international law. One wrong move and Sweden would face a diplomatic nightmare with China.

"Captain," Lindström interrupted. "Recommend we maneuver to position ourselves along her port side as she approaches the cable. Best angle for visual inspection of her hull and any deployed equipment."

Dahl nodded. "Make it so. But maintain EMCON—no active sensors until I give the word. I want to see what she's doing before she knows we're watching."

"Understood, sir. Computing intercept course for visual range at first light."

The bridge settled into focused efficiency, each officer bent to their task. The *Lulea*-class's advanced automation meant a smaller crew could fight the ship, but it also meant each person carried greater responsibility. Outside, the Baltic began to lighten, revealing scattered fog banks that would provide perfect cover for their approach.

"One more thing," Dahl said quietly to Algotsson. "Have the boarding team prep their gear. Full tactical loadout. If this goes sideways, I want options."

The XO nodded and reached for the intercom. Below decks, six of Sweden's best maritime interdiction specialists would soon be checking weapons and rehearsing procedures they'd practiced a thousand times.

Dahl returned to the tactical display, watching the gap between hunter and prey slowly shrink. The Chinese freighter continued her steady advance toward home, her crew likely thinking of families waiting in Shanghai, unaware that Swedish eyes now tracked their every move.

In ninety minutes, they'd have visual confirmation of whatever the *Hai Qing* was really doing out here.

He just hoped they'd be in time to stop it.
****

0602 Hours

Seventy minutes later, after a slow and stealthy intercept, the corvette finally closed in on her target.

"Visual range in thirty seconds," Lieutenant Lindström announced.

Captain Dahl raised his binoculars as the first rays of sunlight painted the Chinese freighter's hull rust-orange against the pewter sea. The MV *Hai Qing 678* moved steadily through the calm waters at a sluggish five knots, her deck stacked with containers bearing the logos of various shipping companies. Black smoke drifted from her single funnel. She was an older vessel, and probably burning cheap bunker fuel.

"Anything unusual?" Algotsson asked, scanning with his own optics.

Dahl systematically examined the freighter from bow to stern. Nothing seemed out of place. Standard navigation lights, proper flag display, crew moving about their morning duties...

"Wait." He fine-tuned the focus. "Port side, amidships. What's that?"

A thin line ran down the ship's hull, barely visible against the rust-streaked metal. As the *Hai Qing* rolled gently in the slight swell, the line alternately tightened and slackened, creating a subtle disturbance in the water.

"I see it," Algotsson confirmed. "Looks like... cable?"

Lindström enhanced the corvette's optical sensors, throwing the magnified image onto the bridge display. The line appeared to originate somewhere near the anchor housing, running down the hull at an angle before disappearing into the water. The wake it created was barely noticeable—unless you were looking for it.

"Sir," Petty Officer Erik Nilsson spoke up from the sensor station. "I read an article a few weeks back about a similar incident. A Chinese vessel cut a fiber-optic cable between the Philippines and Taiwan. Filipino Coast Guard spotted a cable hanging from the anchor housing, creating a wake just like that. Only noticed it because they were running fast enough to make it visible."

Dahl felt his blood run cold. "Distance to GosNet-1?"

"Eighteen kilometers on her current course. At present speed, she'll cross it in... fifty-three minutes."

"Not on my watch." Dahl turned to his communications officer. "Get me a channel to that ship. International bridge-to-bridge."

"Channel sixteen open, sir."

Dahl grabbed the handset. "MV *Hai Qing*, MV *Hai Qing*, this is Swedish warship *Lulea*. You are ordered to stop immediately and prepare for inspection. Acknowledge."

Silence.

"MV *Hai Qing*, this is Swedish warship *Lulea*. Stop your vessel immediately. This is not a request. Acknowledge."

The radio crackled. A heavily accented voice responded in English. "Swedish warship, this is *Hai Qing*. We are in international waters conducting lawful passage. We have done nothing wrong. We will continue our voyage."

Dahl's jaw tightened. "*Hai Qing*, you are suspected of preparing to damage critical underwater infrastructure. You will stop immediately, or we will take necessary action to stop you."

"Negative, Swedish warship. We are peaceful merchant vessel. Any interference is act of piracy. We continue to China."

The transmission ended with a decisive click.

"They're calling our bluff," Algotsson said quietly.

"Then let's show them we're not bluffing." Dahl turned to his weapons officer. "Light them up. Full targeting radar. Let them know we mean business."

"Fire control radar active, sir. Locked on target."

On the bridge speaker, they could hear renewed chatter from the Chinese vessel—urgent voices in Mandarin. But the freighter maintained course and speed.

"Sir," Lindström called out. "At current rate, we have forty-eight minutes before they reach the cable."

Dahl made his decision. "XO, launch the boarding team under standard inspection authority. If we get ROE escalation from MARCOM, we'll shift to full combat protocols.."

Algotsson was already moving. "Aye, sir!" He grabbed the intercom. "Flight Deck, Bridge. Spin up the helicopter. Combat launch, hostile boarding. Six-man team, full tactical loadout."

The response was immediate. "Flight Deck, aye. Spinning up now."

Through the bridge windows, Dahl could see the hangar doors sliding open. The NH90 helicopter emerged on its handling system, rotor blades beginning to unfold. The boarding team sprinted across the deck in full combat gear—helmets, body armor, MP5 submachine guns, and tactical radios.

"Helm, increase to twenty knots," Dahl ordered. "Put us in optimal position to support the boarding."

"Twenty knots, aye."

The *Lulea*-class corvette surged forward, her gas turbine joining the diesel engines. The distance to the Chinese freighter shrank rapidly.

"*Hai Qing* is accelerating," the radar operator reported. "Now making eight knots... ten knots."

They were running. That confirmed Dahl's suspicions—innocent vessels didn't flee from lawful inspection.

"Time to cable?"

"Forty-two minutes at their current speed."

On the flight deck, the NH90's rotors reached full speed, the downwash creating a localized storm of spray. The boarding team leader gave a thumbs-up to the deck officer.

"Sir," the communications officer interrupted. "Flash traffic from MARCOM. Rules of engagement confirmed. We are authorized to use all necessary means to prevent damage to critical infrastructure."

"About time," Dahl muttered. He keyed the intercom. "Flight Deck, Bridge. You are cleared for launch. Execute hostile boarding. Stop that vessel."

"Flight Deck, aye. Launching."

At 0608 hours, the NH90 lifted off in a thunder of rotors, banking sharply toward the fleeing freighter. Through his binoculars, Dahl spotted the six-man team checking their fast-rope equipment. Lieutenant Jonas Eriksson, the boarding team leader, was one of Sweden's best. If anyone could stop the *Hai Qing*, it would be him.

"Sir," Algotsson said quietly. "If they resist?"

Dahl didn't lower his binoculars. "Then we do whatever it takes to protect that cable. The diplomatic fallout will be someone else's problem."

The helicopter raced across the gap, closing on the Chinese vessel like a predator swooping on prey. In the morning light, Dahl could see crew members on the *Hai Qing*'s deck pointing and gesturing at the approaching aircraft.

Forty minutes to the cable.

The race was on.

****

0612 Hours
MV *Hai Qing 678*

Within four minutes of lift off, the NH90 was hovering twenty meters above the freighter's deck, rotor wash sending loose debris skittering across the containers. Lieutenant Jonas Eriksson gave the signal—two fingers pointed down—and his team began their descent.

Petty Officer Lars Andersson slid down the rope fast, boots hitting the deck hard. He immediately moved left, his B&T carbine up, covering the approach from the bridge.

Corporal Nina Holm dropped beside him, sweeping right toward the container stacks. The Karlsson twins, Erik and Magnus—landed simultaneously, spreading the perimeter. Petty Officer Mikael Lindqvist rolled behind a ventilation housing, scanning for threats.

Eriksson grabbed the rope, ready to follow his team down. Through the helicopter's open door, he could see Sergeant Johan Svensson preparing to descend after him.

The first muzzle flash came from the bridge wing.

Three rounds punched through the NH90's thin aluminum skin. Eriksson heard them impact—sharp metallic cracks that made his blood freeze. Then came the sound every soldier dreaded: turbine failure.

The engine coughed, then sputtered. Black smoke billowed from the exhaust port.

"Taking fire!" the pilot shouted over the intercom. "Engine hit! Losing power!"

There were more muzzle flashes. The shooter had an AK-pattern rifle, firing short bursts with trained precision. Bullets sparked off the helicopter's fuselage, spider-webbing the cockpit glass.

Eriksson dropped. There was no time for the rope—he hit the deck hard, rolling to dissipate the impact. Pain shot through his left ankle, but he forced himself up, weapon ready.

Above him, the NH90 lurched sideways, the pilot fighting dying controls. Black smoke poured from the engine compartment in thick, oily clouds. The helicopter spun, its tail rotor struggling to maintain authority.

"Get clear!" Andersson screamed.

The boarding team scattered as the NH90 descended in a barely controlled crash. The pilot managed to level out momentarily, trying for the open deck space between container stacks. For a heartbeat, it looked like he might make it.

Then the main rotor clipped a container edge.

The blade shattered with a sound like breaking thunder. Composite fragments exploded outward in a lethal cloud. The helicopter pitched violently, rolling onto its side as it slammed into the deck.

Metal screamed. Glass shattered. The fuel tank ruptured.

The explosion came a half second later—a ball of orange flame that climbed thirty meters into the morning sky. The shockwave knocked Eriksson flat, heat washing over him like a physical blow.

"Contact left!" Holm's voice cut through the chaos.

Two figures emerged from behind a container stack, rifles raised. Chinese military—not crew. They moved with tactical precision, using the smoke and flames as cover.

Eriksson's team reacted instantly. Trained reflexes took over. B&Ts barked in controlled bursts, the disciplined fire of professionals. The first Chinese soldier spun and fell. The second dove behind a cable spool, returning fire.

"Bridge shooter still active!" Lindqvist called out, then grunted as a round caught his shoulder plate. The armor held, but the impact drove him to one knee.

More automatic fire erupted from the superstructure. How many hostiles? The intelligence had said civilian crew, maybe a small security detail. This was a military operation.

"Andersson, Magnus—flank right!" Eriksson ordered, ignoring the spreading flames from the crashed helicopter. "Everyone else, suppress that bridge position!"

As the smoke swirled around, he spotted movement through the windows near the forward deckhouse. Two figures dressed in civilian clothes looked like they were bashing some sort of equipment with hammers. Then he spotted a flash mixed with sparks. He realized whoever was inside the deckhouse was there for sabotage. Then he spotted a second flash, then a third.

"Lieutenant! It looks like they're trying to destroy equipment!" Holm shouted, tracking the new targets.

Eriksson knew if those were thermite grenades, the ship was in for much worse trouble than the fire currently burning on its deck. A thermite grenade generated a chemical fire that burned at over 2500 degrees Celsius, hot enough to melt through steel, certainly hot enough to reduce computers and hard drives to slag. The real problem, Eriksson realized, was how they would put it out once they had secured the ship.

Another burst of rifle fire from the bridge forced Eriksson down behind a bollard. Rounds sparked off the metal inches from his head. The Chinese had turned their merchant vessel into a kill box, and his team was caught in the middle.

Behind him, ammunition in the crashed helicopter cooked off—small explosions that sent tracers arcing across the deck in random directions. The fire was spreading, feeding on spilled aviation fuel that ran in burning rivers between the containers.

Screams came from inside the wreckage. Someone was still alive in there. Eriksson's heart clenched—the pilots, maybe Svensson if he'd been caught in the crash. But there was no way to reach them through that inferno.

The ship's deck had become a vision of hell—flames, smoke, the sharp crack of gunfire, and the acrid stench of burning metal and flesh. And somewhere beneath it all, that cable still dragged through the water, counting down the minutes until it reached GosNet-1.

Time was running out.

****

0621 Hours

Eriksson's earpiece crackled through the gunfire. "Jonas, this is Lulea Actual. Priority message."

He pressed deeper into cover as another burst from the bridge showered him with paint chips. "Go ahead, Actual!"

"You need to reach the pilothouse immediately. Turn that ship—she's twelve minutes from the cable. Whatever it takes, Jonas."

"Copy that." Eriksson quick-peeked around the bollard. They were twenty meters away from the superstructure. The bridge was two levels up and there was at least one shooter still active up there.

"Moving to bridge!" he shouted to his team. "Holm, Lindqvist—base of fire on that shooter. Andersson, twins—we're going up the starboard ladder. Move!"

The team reacted instantly. Holm and Lindqvist opened up with their ACP556 PDWs, the Swiss-made weapons chattering in precise bursts. The compact 5.56mm carbines were perfect for shipboard operations—short enough to maneuver in tight spaces but packing enough punch to penetrate cover.

"Go, go, go!"

Eriksson sprinted across the open deck, his team tight behind him. Rounds cracked past, but Holm's suppressing fire was doing its job. They reached the external ladder and started climbing, taking the steps two at a time.

A figure appeared at the top—a Chinese sailor with a rifle. Magnus Karlsson's ACP556 barked twice. The man tumbled backward.

They burst onto the bridge wing. Through the windows, Eriksson could see two men at the helm, one wrestling with the wheel while another worked frantically at a laptop. The bridge shooter spun toward them, bringing his rifle around.

Eriksson fired through the glass. The window exploded inward, his rounds catching the gunman center mass. The man crashed into the chart table and went down.

"Bridge secured!" Andersson called out, sweeping the space with his weapon.

But Eriksson was already moving to the helm. The Chinese helmsman backed away, hands raised. The officer with the laptop made a final keystroke, then threw the computer over the side through the shattered window.

"Off! Everyone off!" Eriksson commanded in English, gesturing with his carbine.

Through the forward windows, he could see their salvation—a rocky outcropping marked on the chart as Rute Misslauper Sälområde. It was maybe three kilometers away.

If we could beach the ship there…

Eriksson spun the wheel hard to starboard. The freighter responded sluggishly, its sixty thousand tons of steel reluctant to change course.

Come on, come on!

"Engine telegraph to stop," he ordered Karlsson. "Kill the engines."

The twin fumbled with the controls for a moment due to the Chinese labels—then found the right lever. The vibration beneath their feet changed, then ceased. Momentum would have to carry them now.

Fire had spread across the main deck. The crashed helicopter was an inferno, and the thermite-ignited blazes in the deckhouse were merging into a single conflagration. Black smoke poured from ventilators and hatches.

"Sir!" Holm barked through his earpiece. "The fire's spreading below decks. We've got maybe five minutes before this whole ship goes up!"

Eriksson checked their heading. The rocky shore of Rute Misslauper Sälområde was dead ahead, growing larger. They were two kilometers away. He calculated how long it would take to get there at their current speed.

He made the hardest decision of his career. "All call signs, abandon ship!" he ordered. "I say again, abandon ship. Rally at the stern, starboard side. Move!"

He gave the wheel one last adjustment, lashing it in place with a length of rope from the flag locker. The ship would hold this course now, driving itself onto the rocks.

The team gathered at the stern rail, the heat from the advancing fire growing intense. Below them, the Baltic stretched cold and dark. Eriksson could see the *Lulea* racing toward them, maybe eight hundred meters out.

"Inflation on my mark," he commanded, hand on his life vest's CO_2 cartridge. The team lined up along the rail. Through the smoke, he glimpsed Chinese crew members doing the same on the port side—the fight forgotten in the face of the growing inferno.

"Mark!"

They jumped.

The Baltic in January hit like a sledgehammer. Even through his dry suit, the cold was paralyzing. Eriksson pulled his inflation toggle. The vest expanded with a sharp hiss, yanking him back to the surface.

"Sound off!"

"Andersson!"

"Holm!"

"Erik here!"

"Magnus—good!"

"Lindqvist—wow, that's cold!"

Five, thought Eriksson with sadness. They'd lost Svensson in the helicopter crash, along with both pilots. Three good men were dead. But five had survived.

It was 0633 in the morning when Eriksson finally turned in the water to see the ship they'd just abandoned. The *Hai Qing 678*, trailing flame and smoke like a dying comet, drove itself onto the rocks of Rute Misslauper Sälområde with a grinding screech of tortured metal. The bow lifted, crumpling, and the vessel shuddered to a halt, hard aground, flames reaching into the morning sky.

Had they not diverted the Hai Qing when they did, it would've reached GosNet-1 and severed a critical communication link connecting Gotland and the Nordic States to the Continent. Now, the cable was safe, but it had cost the lives of three Swedish sailors—sailors with families who were about to be notified in the coming hours their loved one had paid the ultimate price in the protection of their freedom. It was a price those families would now feel, and Eriksson and his survivors would carry with them for the rest of their lives.

As Eriksson floated in the water, waiting to be picked up. He hoped for all of their sakes their leaders in Stockholm would understand the sacrifice they'd just paid and send a message to Russia and their Chinese cronies this type of behavior would not stand.

Turning to the sound of motors approaching, Eriksson saw the *Lulea*'s RHIB was bouncing across the waves toward them. Squinting against the morning light, Eriksson could see Captain Dahl on the corvette's bridge wing, watching through binoculars as the ship moved closer.

Soon, hands were pulling him from the freezing water. Eriksson allowed himself one moment of satisfaction. The cable was safe. The mission, despite everything, was complete.

But three empty spaces in the boat were a reminder of the cost of freedom.

****

Office of the Prime Minister
Rosenbad Building

Stockholm, Sweden

"The Swedish government expresses profound regret for the loss of life during the incident involving the Chinese-flagged vessel MV *Hai Qing 678* in the Baltic Sea on Tuesday. However, we firmly assert that our naval forces acted decisively and lawfully to protect critical national and European infrastructure. The vessel was intercepted based on credible intelligence indicating an attempt to damage the GosNet-1 undersea fiber-optic cable, a vital artery for Sweden's communications network. When the vessel refused to comply with lawful orders and subsequently fired upon our NH90 helicopter, resulting in the tragic loss of three Swedish servicemen, our forces took necessary measures to neutralize the threat, prevent further damage, and redirect the vessel away from sensitive infrastructure. We commend the bravery of our personnel, who, despite significant risk, ensured the safety of our nation's strategic assets.

"Sweden is committed to transparency and will conduct a thorough investigation into the incident, including the role of suspected People's Liberation Army Navy personnel operating covertly aboard the MV *Hai Qing 678*. We call on the Chinese government to cooperate fully in establishing the facts, particularly regarding the vessel's activities and the use of military-grade equipment, such as thermite grenades, which escalated the situation. The protection of undersea infrastructure is a shared European priority, and Sweden's actions were consistent with international law and our obligations to safeguard regional security. We urge all parties to exercise restraint and engage in dialogue to prevent further escalation, while reaffirming our resolve to defend our sovereignty and critical infrastructure against any threats."
****

Global News Agencies
Deutsche Welle (*DW*)

Swedish Forces Storm Chinese Vessel After Fatal Helicopter Crash in Baltic Sea
On Tuesday, a deadly confrontation unfolded off Sweden's Gotland Island, when Swedish naval forces intercepted the Chinese-flagged cargo vessel MV Hai Qing 678,

suspected of attempting to sabotage the GosNet-1 undersea fiber-optic cable. After the vessel ignored orders to stop, a Swedish NH90 helicopter attempting a boarding operation was shot down by an unidentified shooter, crashing onto the ship's deck, killing three Swedish military personnel, and sparking a fire exacerbated by thermite grenades. Swedish special forces redirected the burning ship to prevent damage to critical infrastructure, but the incident claimed eleven lives, including eight Chinese crew members—some of them alleged to be covert PLA Navy personnel—and one Swedish soldier. Seven Chinese crew were rescued, and while Sweden defends its actions to protect vital infrastructure, China condemned the operation as piracy, escalating tensions in the Baltic region.

****

BBC News

Baltic Confrontation: Chinese Vessel Fire Kills 11 After Swedish Boarding Attempt

A diplomatic crisis looms after Swedish naval forces intercepted a Chinese cargo ship suspected of threatening undersea cables near Gotland, leading to a helicopter crash and deadly fire that claimed eleven lives, including three Swedish military personnel and eight Chinese nationals, with questions remaining about the presence of military equipment aboard the ostensibly civilian vessel.

****

Russia Today (RT)

NATO Aggression: Swedish Military Attacks Chinese Merchant Ship, 11 Dead

Western militarization of the Baltic Sea claimed eleven lives as Swedish forces launched an unprovoked assault on a civilian Chinese cargo vessel, using the pretext of "cable protection" to justify their deadly raid that witnesses describe as "reminiscent of colonial-era piracy."

****

Washington Post

11 Dead After Swedish Military Confronts Chinese Ship Near Critical Data Cables

Swedish naval forces' attempt to inspect a Chinese cargo vessel suspected of endangering Baltic Sea internet cables turned deadly Tuesday when the operation sparked a fire that killed eleven people, raising urgent questions about maritime security, the protection of critical infrastructure, and the rules governing military intervention in international waters as tensions between NATO and China continue to escalate.

****

Global Times (环球时报)

Swedish Military Pirates Murder Eight Chinese Sailors in Unprovoked Attack

A peaceful Chinese merchant vessel was brutally assaulted by a Swedish warship in international waters, with eight innocent Chinese citizens murdered after Swedish commandos illegally boarded the MV Hai Qing 678 *and set it ablaze, demonstrating the West's return to gunboat diplomacy and its determination to strangle China's legitimate maritime trade through naked military aggression.*

Chapter Six:
Patriotic Movement

January 28, 2033
Xiamen, Fujian Province
Lao Niu's Claypot Kitchen, Back Room

A greasy ceiling fan spun above the table, its cracked blades stirring the heavy air just enough to keep the cigarette smoke from settling. The walls were yellowed with age, the door sealed tight. In the adjacent kitchen, cleavers pounded pork cartilage in rhythm with a local radio station piping out soft revolutionary ballads from the '60s.

Cuī Zemin waited in silence. The man known in intelligence circles as The Ghost sat with his arms folded, his porcelain teacup untouched. He wasn't here for comfort.

The door creaked open.

Two men stepped in, wiping the rain off their sleeves. Hao Lei went straight for the seat across from Cuī, his coat still damp. Gao Rong took the corner seat, spine straight, eyes sharp.

Neither of them spoke first.

Cuī broke the silence.

"You've cultivated your orchard well," he said quietly, voice like sand over smooth stone. "Now it's time to harvest."

Gao gave a curt nod. "We've been pruning carefully."

Cuī slid a thin red envelope across the table. It wasn't fat. It didn't need to be.

"The operation is simple," he continued. "February twelfth, coordinated gatherings across Kinmen and Matsu. I want government buildings, city halls—places with camera angles and emotional resonance."

Hao's left eyebrow rose. "No ferry insertions? No 'volunteers' from Fujian?"

Cuī allowed himself the faintest smile. "Unnecessary. You already have the population. You helped build it."

And they had.

Over the last decade, as infrastructure had expanded—housing towers, vocational campuses, and ferry terminals—thousands of new residents had settled across the islands. Subsidized mortgages, priority hiring programs, cultural "reconnection" grants—each application had been quietly vetted by the MSS or their provincial affiliates. Slowly, Kinmen and Matsu became less Taiwanese frontier and more mainland forward extension.

Instead of an invasion, they had slowly taken over through demographic shaping.

"Half the apartment blocks south of Chenggong Road are full of pro-reunification families," Hao muttered. "We used to count rooftops. Now it's doorways."

"And they vote," Gao added. "They sit on local councils. Run clinics. Teach."

Cuī leaned forward. "You've normalized loyalty. That's harder to reverse than fear."

The Ghost pulled a flash drive from his coat pocket and placed it on the table. "This contains the media starter pack: sample slogans, optimized hashtags, and visual assets. Tie them to 'youth-led' imagery. Highlight the abandonment narrative. You know the arc."

Gao nodded. "We've been pushing it already. 'Taipei left us to rot.' 'Kinmen has no voice.' It's sticky."

"And the students?"

"More fervent than we expected," Hao said. "A few took red envelopes. Most came through the forums. Line groups, Signal chains, subreddits. They found each other."

"Who seeded those networks?" Cuī asked calmly.

Gao answered without hesitation. "We did. Three years ago."

Cuī nodded once. The timing was sound.

"The youth will march first," he said. "Let them scream betrayal. Let them drape themselves in nostalgia for something they never lived through. Our job is not to control them—it's to guide the flood once it breaks."

Hao took the envelope, sliding it inside his coat. "So, what happens if Taipei overreacts?"

"Then they lose the frame. A truncheon on a protester's face is worth more than ten manifestos."

"And if they don't respond?"

Cuī looked him dead in the eye. "They will."

The Ghost stood then, adjusting his coat. "One last thing," he said, his voice low. "Phase two—should it come—is already in place.

No need for ferries or fatigues. The house is built. The keys are simply waiting to be turned."

And with that, he vanished into the winter rain, leaving the room as quiet as it had been before he entered.

Hao stared at the flash drive.

Gao reached for the tea and finally took a sip.

"Time to set the match," he said.

****

February 12, 2033 – 1447 Hours
Jincheng Township Government Plaza
Kinmen Island

The plaza had become a furnace.

What had begun as coordinated chants and student-led speeches was dissolving—now chants overlapped, flags tore in the wind, and young men were shoving the police line. Thin-lipped conscripts, barely older than the protesters themselves, gripped plastic shields with whitening knuckles.

Above the crowd, on the second-floor balcony of a tea shop, Gao Rong watched it unravel in real time.

"Too soon," he muttered.

Hao Lei stood beside him, sweat darkening his collar. "I know that kid—front row, black hoodie. He was in the dorm chat six weeks ago asking about ferry discounts. Now he's screaming for blood."

Down below, a protester launched a paint balloon. It splattered across a police visor, triggering a surge. Three students rushed forward, slamming into the shield line. A baton swung. Once, twice, and a girl went down, screaming.

Gao's burner phone buzzed.

"PLA cell's breaking cover. Civilian gear discarded. Beach axis open. Kinmen command element en route."

The second message read, "Engage ROE breach. Justify military intervention."

Gao looked up. "They're coming. It's now."

Across the plaza, an unmarked white box truck screeched to a halt just off Zhongzheng Road. Four men spilled out, dressed like aid workers. Their posture gave them away. Each had squared shoulders, close-cut hair, and the unmistakable gait of a man trained to kill quickly. Each wore a red armband that read "People's Relief Front."

One carried a duffel. Another unzipped it, revealing wrapped metal pipes and riot shields stenciled with Chinese characters. They moved fast—blending into the crowd, passing out gear. Within minutes, ten protesters were suddenly armored. And armed.

A makeshift formation advanced on the outer police flank, swinging pipes at plastic riot shields. One ROC conscript went down hard, helmet cracking on the curb. Another tripped under a tangle of limbs. His sidearm was visible—exposed.

A protester lunged for it.

Gunshots cracked.

The crowd screamed, splintering like shattered glass. Two people hit the pavement—one protester, one police officer.

That was the ignition.

Behind the crowd, PLA special operations cells posing as humanitarian volunteers dropped their disguises and moved—tactically, surgically—into alleyways and rooftops. Some fired blank rounds. Others used rubber bullets. The point wasn't to kill.

It was to make it all look out of control—to give Beijing a reason to "restore order."

Hao swore, ducking as a whizzing canister exploded against a nearby pillar, releasing gray smoke. He yanked Gao by the sleeve. "We've got to go. Right now."

Gao nodded, stuffing the monocular into his bag. "We'll slip past the old market road. Meet extraction at the harbor."

They advanced quickly—keeping low, avoiding cameras. But the tea shop owner burst out the side door and pointed at them, screaming, "You! I *saw* you—filming the crowd! You're agitators!"

From across the alley, a local militia officer—recently recruited from a PRC-friendly security agency—whistled and shouted, "Hey! Stop!"

Gao broke into a sprint. Hao hesitated.

"Go!" Gao barked. "I'll shake him!"

But Hao turned the wrong corner—straight into two PLA-affiliated militia in plainclothes. They grabbed him hard, forcing him against the wall.

"Name!" one barked. "Who sent you?"

He stayed silent.

A fist slammed into his gut. He went down hard.

Gao didn't look back. He heard the scuffle, the shouts, but he couldn't afford to stop. The plaza was collapsing into a war zone, and phase two was well underway.

By the time Gao reached the harbor and slipped into the tide of evacuees posing as ferry-bound tourists, he'd ditched his phone and jacket. His face was soaked with sweat, his eyes cold.

Above the city, smoke was rising. Sirens wailed

Hao would be among the dozens detained that afternoon, likely listed as "an unknown instigator," unnamed in official press releases. He would be a ghost, just like the ones who trained him.

Gao would report the arrest up the chain, along with his final message to Cuī Zemin: "Storm achieved. Narrative fracture complete. MSS element compromised. Phase two continues."

And then he boarded the ferry for Xiamen, leaving Kinmen behind in flames.

Chapter Seven:
Future of Naval Warfare

January 30, 2033
Naval Support Activity
Panama City, Florida

National Security Advisor Jim Batista sat rigid in his chair, reading the detailed outline of the unmanned combat vessels that comprised Task Group 79.2, "Jericho One." His fingers traced the specifications as he recalled the first time he'd seen these vessels when they were just PowerPoint fantasies presented by his former employer, Palantir.

Batista had sat in on one of the meetings in the early 2020s, when the idea of UCVs had first been pitched. Admirals who had spent careers commanding billion-dollar manned warships had dismissed the concept of having unmanned frigate-class warships augmenting manned ships.

Whose side are they on? Batista had wondered. *The US or China?*

Still, the SECNAV had greenlit the program in the mid-2020s, and it had taken just six years to go from concept to operational deployment. That was a verifiable miracle, considering the Navy had started work on the DDG(X) program to replace the *Ticonderoga*-class guided-missile cruisers in 2022 and still hadn't settled on the final requirements so a prototype could be built as of 2033.

The Navy wasn't exactly known for efficiency as a general practice. Over the last couple of decades, it had taken over five years just to finish the *designs* for the *Constellation*-class frigates, let alone build any of them. It had nearly driven Batista to drink.

But change was coming, like a freight train. It had been ramping up for a while, actually. Batista thought back to the tour of Saronic's facility in Austin he and his fellow Palantir employees had taken in 2025. He'd expected another dog-and-pony show—some Silicon Valley startup promising to revolutionize warfare with "vaporware" and venture capital arrogance. Instead, he'd found a converted catamaran production facility churning out *Corsair*-class vessels using automotive assembly techniques. Young engineers worked alongside grizzled Navy contractors, welding commercial radar arrays onto hulls built from the same aluminum used in F-150s.

He recalled Saronic's CEO explaining, "We're not building yachts." They walked past workstations, where students fresh from MIT were installing targeting software originally developed for virtual reality video games. "Think of these things like iPhones that float and kill. When one breaks, you don't fix it—you build five more."

That philosophy had shattered forty years of Navy doctrine. Where a *Burke*-class destroyer was costing the Navy two and a half billion a ship and taking five to six years to build, a *Corsair* cost five to six hundred thousand dollars per ship and just seven to twenty-one days to build. Of course, the old guard of the five big Defense Prime companies that had controlled the US defense industry since 1993's "Last Supper" threw a big stink. But Batista knew they were only howling because the *Corsair*s threatened their bottom lines.

Admiral Blackwood, the then-Chief of Naval Operations, had practically vomited his coffee during a Joint Chiefs briefing when Saronic pitched the idea to start building newer classes of large, unmanned autonomous vessels. Batista still remembered a captain on the admiral's staff joking, "You can't be serious—disposable warships? What's next, cardboard carriers? Tupperware cruisers?"

Batista had wanted to choke the man. Instead, they listened as the Tech CEO explained the design for their 140-meter-long *Doomhammer*-class arsenal UAV. It would augment manned ships like the Burkes or a carrier strike group with a capable, long-range hypersonic strike and defense platform, capable of carrying 96 VLS cells and two 150kW directed energy weapons.

"With a large, modular, mission-capable UAV platform like the Doomhammer, the Navy will have a new way of projecting power into the Pacific...or *wherever* these UAVs are directed," the CEO of Saronic had concluded.

Regardless of what the admiral and the Defense Primes thought, the math of the problem facing them was unescapable. The Jiangnan and Dalian shipyards in China had launched sixteen Type 055 destroyers between 2014 and 2032, while American shipyards had completed eighteen Arleigh Burkes in the same amount of time. The problem was that the PLA was also producing other highly capable destroyers, frigates, and submarines at a rate US shipbuilders had no means of keeping up with. In thirty years, the PLA Navy had achieved something unthinkable—numerical and tonnage superiority over the US Navy by the year 2032. No matter how *anyone* had rationalized it, the traditional shipbuilding the Navy had relied on for decades could no longer compete with the manufacturing powerhouse China had become. America had needed a new playbook—one written in code rather than steel if it had any hope of winning the wars of the future.

The DARPA Replicator program had provided the blueprint—not massive shipyards requiring thousands of skilled welders, but distributed production using civilian manufacturing. Anduril was mass-producing missiles and their Fury drones at production rates not seen since the end of World War II. Shield AI was now assembling underwater systems in plants that previously manufactured jet skis. Even traditional defense giants, while slow to adapt, had finally caught on. Huntington Ingalls was now operating "ghost yards" at the Toledo Shipyard in Ohio, at the General Dynamics NASSCO facility in San Diego, California, and at the Fincantieri shipyards of northern Wisconsin. They were dispersed far from vulnerable coastal yards the Navy had relied on the past couple of decades. With the introduction of modular construction techniques borrowed from prefab housing, the rate of construction of these unmanned combat vessels was beginning to outpace the rate of Chinese manned ship production.

The key to success with the ACVs was the constant reminder to the Navy brass that they weren't meant to replace their treasured carriers or submarines. They were meant to augment them and overwhelm America's enemies. Using swarm tactics backed by AI-battle managers, decisions could be made in nanoseconds. Lose ten unmanned surface vessels in a battle? Build twenty more before the end of the month. It was a change in how the Navy viewed its warships. No longer was it a race to match manned ship for manned ship with China. It was now a race to field more missile and drone platforms than China could hope to defend against. At least, that was the theory.

Now DARPA was several years into the Pentagon's Replicator program as it scrambled to find ways to counter the Chinese Navy's shipbuilding juggernaut. While Batista was generally optimistic about the changing trajectory, his jaw tightened as he reviewed current readiness levels. Theory required execution, and execution required hulls in the water. Every delay meant the equation shifted further in Beijing's favor.

"Captain, that was an impressive video of each of these ACVs, but let's dispense with the fancy projections of what these autonomous weapons are supposed to do and talk about why I'm looking at a task group that's supposed to be fully operational but is currently at sixty-six percent strength," grilled Batista, his voice cutting through the noise of the AC running in the background.

Hammond acknowledged the question as he tapped something on his tablet. The monitor displayed another slide, one highlighting operational vessels in blue. "Sir, two-thirds of our autonomous combat vessels are deployed with the USS *Intrepid*, currently homeported at Pearl. In a couple of days they will be conducting a simulated naval engagement and live-fire exercises near Adak, and the Bering Sea."

Batista raised an eyebrow, leaning forward to ask. "Live fire, eh? OK, that doesn't answer my question about the other third. Where are they?"

Hammond shifted uncomfortably. "Production delays—"

Batista's hand slammed the table in frustration. "Unacceptable, Captain. I'm looking at a roster that shows your Pacific Task Group Jericho-1 at sixty-six percent. Atlantic Fleet's Hazar-1 is at fifty percent. Your second Pacific group, Jericho-2?" He scrolled through his own read-ahead on his tablet. "Forty percent. These were supposed to be at full strength three weeks ago."

Admiral Vos intervened. "Jim, I understand the frustration. No one is more irritated by these production delays than I am. We've been encountering some serious supply chain issues that we're still trying to—"

"Sorry to cut you off, Admiral, but I've got to call BS on part of this. Six months behind schedule. That's what this read-ahead says." Batista's voice dropped to a dangerous quiet as he briefly held his tablet up, then placed it back on the table. "I know the Navy's already submitted requirements for triple the current production. How exactly do these companies plan to meet that when they can't fulfill this first order?"

A woman in a tailored suit whose badge said Huntington Ingalls cleared her throat before interjecting. "Mr. Batista, we have been very open about the challenges our Newport News production facility has faced. From a critical shortage of skilled labor to materials needed for the construction of the Doomhammer arsenal. We're back on track—"

"On track for what? The current order? Or the tripling the Navy needs? And who the hell is coming up with the names for these ACVs— Doomhammer? What is this, a play off of Warhammer 40K or something?" Batista retorted hotly.

A representative from Anduril Industries corrected him. "It's World of Warcraft, not Warhammer."

All eyes turned to the young-looking representative from Anduril, waiting to see how Batista would respond. "Huh, World of Warcraft... Aiden, is it?" Batista shook his head. "I think it's been fifteen years since I played WoW with my kids. Let me guess, this is your CEO's idea?"

The Anduril rep, Aiden, smiled and nodded. "It was. I suppose it could be changed if that's really necessary. These platforms are basically software built to kill. He wanted to let the dev guys name the ACVs."

Batista grunted but didn't press the issue. He didn't care about the names. What he cared about was that they performed as intended and that the shipbuilders could deliver in the time and numbers requested.

Fixing Aiden with a hard stare, Batista pressed on. "You and the Navy can call these things whatever you want, so long as you deliver. Now, speaking of production and specifically your company, is Arsenal-1 going to be able to keep up? You're not just feeding the Navy. The Army wants more Roadrunners, and the Air Force is screaming for more Barracuda-500s."

Aiden smiled confidently. "Sir, that won't be an issue. Arsenal-2 in Texas went fully operational last month. Arsenal-3 in Kansas comes online next week and Arsenal-4 in Stuttgart is already producing."

"Stuttgart?" Batista's eyebrow rose in surprise.

"Yes, sir. We're filling pre-position stocks as we speak. Dutch Harbor, Pearl, Guam, Sasebo, Robertson Barracks." The rep pulled up production figures. "Even forward positions in Poland, Germany, and the UK. It's actually one of the bright spots in the Replicator program," Aiden replied.

Batista studied the numbers, his expression softening marginally. "Finally, some good news." He turned back to Hammond and Vos. "So missiles we can build. Ships, still a struggle apparently. When will these task groups reach full strength?"

Vos nodded for Hammond to take the question.

"By end of summer, sir. We've been addressing the bottlenecks for more than a year. They're clearing. Boeing's Long Beach facility just doubled their Seeker-class production line. Shield AI opened two new autonomous underwater vehicle plants—"

"Whoa, hold up there," Batista interrupted again. "You said end of summer?"

"That's correct," Hammond confirmed.

Batista looked around the room, then pulled up a production comparison he'd been briefed on by the DIA a few days earlier. "A couple of days ago the Defense Intelligence Agency was able to verify what I'm about to tell you. The Jiangnan Shipyard in Shanghai launched eight Type 058 autonomous corvettes in December. Eight of them in one month. That's on top of their already insane building of conventional warships."

The Saronic rep countered, "Mr. Batista, those are incredible numbers. I would like to point out our Defiant-class arsenal stealth ship uses our modular construction technique. This means once the new facilities in Toledo and northern Wisconsin are operational—"

"There's that word again—operational. OK, when is it scheduled to be operational?"

"Six weeks for Toledo. Eight for northern Wisconsin. We should be cranking out ACVs a rate of four per month. That's a fully autonomous stealth ship the size of a corvette with forty-eight VLS extended-range naval strike missiles."

"We're stuck with summer, aren't we?" Batista sighed, frustrated by the delays and little he could do about it. "Listen, the Eurasian Defense and Economic Pact is going to be running the largest military drills since the height of the Cold War in the 1980s starting in early May. I'm a big believer in deterrence. So is the President. And in order for deterrence to work, you have to have a military force capable of deterring aggression. I'm not confident we're there, and I don't think the people in this room are either."

Batista stood, gathering his materials. "Here's what's going to happen. Admiral Vos, the SecDef and I have to provide a weekly update to the President on this issue. That means I need a weekly update on the

ACV Task Group's readiness. Not a monthly progress report—a *weekly* report that's being given to the President. Every vessel that comes off the line, I need to know about it. We are on the clock, Admiral; we need them fielded and ready immediately."

"Understood, sir. We'll make it happen," the admiral confirmed, nodding to Hammond to make sure it did.

Batista turned to the industry reps. "For years, we've talked about reindustrializing the defense sector to build the weapons of war necessary to win the wars of the future. You've got distributed production beginning to come online, and that's good. I want you to start drafting up contingency plans for those facilities. Ask yourself what happens if we lose those facilities on the coasts? Can the West Coast and the Great Lakes facilities pick up the slack? What about expanding production along the Mississippi? These are contingencies we should be thinking about and developing plans for just in case. It's always better to have a plan and not need it than to need a plan and not have one."

The reps nodded grimly, taking notes.

"Arsenal production of missiles and autonomous combat aircraft stays the priority next to shipbuilding," Batista continued, looking at Aiden, the Anduril rep. "I don't care if you have to run your factories on twenty-four-hour shifts. The one thing we've done right thus far is missiles. Keep it that way."

"Understood, sir," Aiden confirmed.

Batista turned to leave, then paused at the door. "One more thing. These live-fire exercises *Intrepid*'s running—I want real-world testing data. Figure out how well these systems will perform when Chinese EW tries to jam them. Do what you can to simulate what happens when a Seeker autonomous submarine goes up against Chinese Navy Type 039C AIP subs."

Captain Hammond nodded. "I'll coordinate with Captain Trammell personally."

"Good, do that." Batista's expression softened slightly. "Look, I know I'm pushing hard. But if this exercise turns into something more... we could be in serious trouble."

The room remained silent, the weight of his words settling over them.

"If this goes hot," Batista continued, "these ACVs become our force multipliers. One destroyer captain controlling a distributed fleet of unmanned systems—that's the kind of edge we need. But only if we have them built, deployed, and the bugs worked out." Batista fixed each person with a final stare. "No more delays, people. We're running out of time."

Outside, Batista strode down the corridor, his footsteps echoing off polished floors as he headed toward the exit and the waiting vehicle. As he climbed into the SUV, his phone buzzed—a message from the President. *How did the briefing go?*

He paused, looking back at the building as his driver headed toward the flight line. He typed: *Better than expected. But we're cutting it close. That situation in the Baltic, that's our immediate concern.*

The President's response came quickly: *How concerned should I be?*

Batista thought about what had happened, the discovery of the PLA Navy secretly obtaining targeting data of NATO member ports ahead of EDEP's May exercise. He typed: *Very. We need to meet soon, before I fly to NATO.*

The President replied: *OK, tomorrow. 10 a.m. See you then.*

Batista breathed a sigh of relief. He sent a text to the others he'd wanted for the briefing as the driver pulled up to the aircraft. *Tomorrow—we'll figure things out tomorrow*, he thought as he climbed the stairs to the government plane and returned to Washington.

Chapter Eight:
Stormy Waters

February 1, 2033
USS *Intrepid* DDG-145 Task Group 79.2 – "Jericho-1"
IVO Kodiak Station
Aleutian Islands, Alaska

Captain Asa Trammell gripped the armrests of his command chair as the bow of *Intrepid* crashed through another mountain of gray-green water. The impact sent a shudder through ten thousand tons of steel, rattling coffee cups and testing the magnetic locks on loose gear. The deck tilted twenty degrees to starboard before another wave crashed over the bow, the sea reminding Trammell who was boss.

"Steady as she goes, helm," came the voice of Lieutenant Commander Robert Walsh, calm and steady even as he grabbed a stanchion to keep his feet. "Maintain three-two-zero."

"Aye, sir. Course three-two-zero," the helmsman responded, his knuckles white on the controls but his voice steady.

Trammell watched like a beaming father as his bridge crew danced with the storm. Chief Kowalski moved between stations like a boxer in the ring, never losing his footing despite the ship's wild gyrations and the punch of the waves. Petty Officer Martinez called out radar contacts even as his scope flickered with sea return. The newest ensign, Baker, fresh from Annapolis, managed the AEGIS updates with hands that trembled only slightly.

Through the bridge speakers came the metallic soundtrack of modern warfare—the click of keyboards, the hum of cooling fans, the measured cadence of sailors doing their jobs while nature tried to kill them.

"Track four-eight-two-one bears two-seven-five, fifteen miles," came from CIC. "Probable merchant, southbound."

"Roger, correlating with AIS," confirmed Petty Officer Martinez.

Competence under pressure—the foundation of naval power since men had first gone to sea in warships. Those were the words Trammell's first skipper had told him many years ago—something he'd instilled in his officers. Technology was changing things, and you either kept up or you got left behind. In the business of warfighting, being left behind wasn't an option.

Through the rain-lashed windows, Captain Asa Trammell caught glimpses of the future riding alongside them. A Stormwatcher-class unmanned combat surface vessel, one of the specially designed air-defense variants, crested a wave two hundred yards off the port bow, its angular hull shedding water like a breaching whale. It carved effortlessly through the slate-gray chop with quiet efficiency, half-swallowed by mist and foam, like a ghost refusing to be seen for too long. It was one of the many semi-autonomous combat vessels his task group would put through their final paces today.

The weather was hell. That was the point.

He remembered his conversation with Vice Admiral Reeves shortly after accepting command of the USS *Intrepid* and the autonomous strike group it would shepherd. Reeves wasn't just a strategist—he was a true believer. A surface warfare officer who'd clawed his way up during the lean years, watching the Navy bleed capability with every early retirement and every bloated contract that delivered too little, too late.

"Congress will scream," Reeves had said, eyes fixed on the glossy, sensor-rich interface of the new CIC consoles. "But they screamed about the carrier too, once upon a time."

Trammell had nodded then. He understood the politics, but more than that, he understood the stakes. For years, the Navy's procurement pipeline had been choked by legacy thinking. Gold-plated hulls. Manpower-intensive platforms. Endless spiral upgrades.

In contrast, companies like Saronic, Shield AI, and Anduril moved like predators in blue water. They weren't just building hulls— they were designing fleets of thinking weapons, nodes in a kill web that could fight, fail, learn, and adapt faster than any crewed ship ever could. Their approach was ruthless, elegant. Hardware as disposable. Software as sovereign.

Reeves had leaned closer that day. "Asa, we both know the next fight isn't going to give us six months to spool up. It's going to be fast, brutal, and decided by whoever commands the battle space—digitally and physically. Whoever dominates autonomy… wins."

Now, with the *Intrepid* pacing behind the ACVs like a watchful shepherd, Trammell felt the weight of that truth. Ahead, the autonomous vessels moved through the broken weather like wolves stalking between trees, their comms quiet, their coordination nearly flawless.

This wasn't a test of weapons. It was a test of trust.

"Captain." His executive officer appeared at his elbow. Robert Walsh had the solid build of a former linebacker and the steady demeanor of a man who'd seen enough sea duty to respect the ocean without fearing it. "METOC shows this mess clearing by 0900. We'll have decent conditions for the demonstration."

Trammell nodded, eyes still on the Sentinel Stormwatcher as it disappeared into another valley of water. Despite its 279-foot length, the stealthy unmanned vessel cut through the waves like a giant surface board. Hidden within its angular features were a series of removable weapon pods that gave the vessel a capability Trammell still marveled at.

In its present form, it carried twenty-four of the versatile multirole SM-6 missiles. Two quad-pack SeaRAM launchers flanked the superstructure, providing close-in defense against missiles and drones, while a pair of quad-pack ESSM interceptors for short-range aerial threats. Mounted fore and aft were twin 150kW Cobalt beam lasers, capable of silently scorching incoming targets mid-flight. Amidships, beneath a retractable panel, sat the dish-like emitter of the Epirus high-powered microwave system—designed to fry the guidance systems of entire drone swarms in a single burst. All of it was slaved to GIDEON's combat AI, allowing the Stormwatcher to engage threats across multiple domains without a human aboard.

"How are our metal friends handling it?" Trammel asked.

"The Seeker AUVs are in their element. The acoustic interference is actually helping them practice noise discrimination. The surface units…" Walsh paused. "Stormwatcher-3 is reporting some visual degradation from salt accumulation on its camera lens."

"Damn, it's still operational, right?" Trammell asked.

"Affirmative. All green, sir. The GIDEON-AI is keeping them tighter than a drum section," Walsh confirmed.

GIDEON-AI. The Guided Intelligence for Decisive Enemy Obliteration Networked-AI. Some contractor's idea of a biblical reference, as Gideon went up against a much larger and better equipped force and still won. Trammell appreciated the symbolism, even if the acronym was a bit forced. Then again, all the ACVs seemed to have been named after different MMO games. He guessed that was what happened when you put a bunch of gamers and engineers in charge of creating autonomous warships.

"TAO to Bridge," came Meilof's voice over the net, clear and direct. "Combat systems are green across the board. All autonomous platforms show link integrity and are holding final tasking."

Trammell allowed himself a small smile. His tactical action officer, Lieutenant Commander Alice Meilof, had a way of cutting through military stuffiness that either charmed or infuriated her superiors. Lucky for her, Trammell fell into the former camp.

"Acknowledged," Trammell replied. "I'll be in CIC in five."

"Aye, sir. I'll hold the conn," Lieutenant Walsh said.

Trammell stood, timing his movement with the ship's roll. Years at sea had tuned his body to the subtle shifts underfoot—momentum, steel, and balance forming an instinctive rhythm. He paused at the bridge wing door for one last look at the formation: manned command at the center, unmanned teeth fanned out like wolves on the hunt.

He stepped through the watertight hatch and into the stairwell, the sound of the storm dulling behind armored bulkheads. The ship vibrated faintly beneath his boots, not from stress or strain but from the quiet hum of hundreds of processors working in concert—the digital nervous system of a new kind of warship.

Two decks down, the hatch to CIC hissed open, and he walked into a radically redesigned combat information center. The *Intrepid* was one of four of the new Flight III variations of the *Arleigh Burke* destroyers, designed to manage and operate more than a hundred autonomous combat vessels (ACVs) at a time. A portion of the forward section of the original CIC had been converted into a flagship operation suite with billeting for an additional twelve personnel should an admiral make the *Intrepid* their flagship. The biggest change was the halving of its flight operations, repurposing half the hangar deck into a battle management control room (BMC-R). The BMC-R would manage the task group's ACVs while the CIC would manage the overall battle, much like the *Ticonderoga*-class guided-missile cruisers had prior to being retired.

Trammell entered without ceremony, the operators focused solely on their tasks. He wasn't one for enforcing outdated protocols, requiring people to rise when he walked into a room. They were too busy and too focused on their jobs for him to insist on breaking their concentration just to acknowledge him entering or leaving. That kind of protocol was for shore duty and vessels without the pace and demands of the *Intrepid*.

Gone were the rows of outdated cathode displays, gray-painted consoles, and banks of operator chairs arranged like a Cold War command post. *Intrepid*'s CIC had been rebuilt from the keel up—sleek, light-paneled, and immersive. The ceiling was lower, more insulated, fitted with embedded LED light strips that changed to match the ship's alert status. The space was quieter too, and divided into sections that managed subsurface, surface, and airspace, making it easier for each group to remain focused on their assigned areas.

A panoramic augmented-reality wall spanned the forward bulkhead, giving real-time overlays of the maritime battle space, with autonomous vessels marked in pale blue, enemy positions in red, and the *Intrepid*'s systems woven into the tactical mesh in gold. Dynamic mission zones hovered in soft rings around each ACV, updating live from GIDEON's predictive matrix.

To port, a transparent projection surface hung in the air, displaying the weather cell in vivid 3D. To starboard, a smaller holo-table rendered the nearby island terrain, helping the ACVs plan terrain-masking and sonar screening paths through choke points. A digital heat map of sensor occlusion bloomed and contracted as weather and wave action shifted.

To the rear of the CIC was the battle management control room. This was the brainstem controlling and coordinating the ACVs. Unlike the CIC, this space was designed with rows of reclining operator pods that ringed a central command pit, a quarterback calling the shots, integrating the various types of ACVs. Depending on the function of the ACV the pod was manned by one or two sailors, typically overseeing a cluster of autonomous vessels. While the operators didn't drive them, they coached them, ensuring it was a human who gave a kill order, not an AI. Like quarterbacks scanning for a receiver, the operators made the final call in engaging targets.

Above them, a circular command halo suspended from the overhead projected the active warfighting data. It was here that GIDEON's intentions—often unfathomable in raw code—were translated into human-readable battle logic. Not just what the machines were doing, but why.

What he liked most about the design of the new modular console stations was how each workstation was configurable to the operator. Each crew member could arrange the station to best fit the way their mind worked, determining what went where and whether the monitor was vertical or horizontal. No one was buried in paperwork or shouting over radios like in the past. AI agents handled coordinating messages and radio traffic, allowing humans to manage the exceptions or items the AI flagged for review.

Captain Trammell descended into the CIC's command station, joining Lieutenant Commander Alice Meilof, who was seated at the central console, hands dancing through holographic interfaces like a conductor channeling Beethoven. Her short-cropped hair was still damp from her trip topside to clear the water droplets left by a wave that shouldn't have fouled the camera. He liked that about Alice, never afraid to get her hands dirty when needed. Right now, he thought, she wore the focused expression of someone juggling chainsaws, aware of the risks but determined to put on a show.

"Captain in CIC," Senior Chief Jake Thompson announced, his eyes never leaving his station.

Trammell slid into his command seat. "Status, TAO. How's our robotic ghost fleet holding up?"

Meilof smiled at the reference to their unmanned ships, her fingers continuously typing as she replied. "Nominal across the board, sir. Though Stormwatcher Three's optical sensors are degraded by thirty percent from salt accumulation. It's still within operational parameters, but we should have Anduril find a way to better protect it from being splashed during storms. It's not like we can pull over and clean the camera lens."

"The Seekers?"

"Having the time of their lives. They're learning to filter out natural noise faster than projected."

Trammell studied the displays. Icons representing the opposing forces (OPFOR) units were already positioned around the exercise area—Dutch Harbor's contribution to their final evaluation. Each icon bore Chinese or Russian naval designations, their movement patterns programmed to mimic known PLA Navy and Pacific Fleet doctrine.

"Sir?" A stocky man in khakis with the Anduril logo on his polo approached. "We met briefly the other day—I'm Eric Schreck, Anduril systems integration. I wanted to let you know we've completed final diagnostics on GIDEON's engagement protocols. All safeguards are verified active."

Seated behind Schreck were two more contractors hunched over portable workstations. Trammell had met them and Schreck a couple of days ago when they'd come aboard during their pit stop at Kodiak Coast Guard Station. One of them was from Saronic Technologies, the other from Shield AI. Both were programmers for the Seeker-class AUVs and the Judicator-class stealth arsenal ACVs, the drone vessels carrying forty-eight land-attack cruise missiles or extended-range naval strike missiles.

"Yes, I remember. Are there any concerns I need to be made aware of, Mr. Schreck?" Trammell kept his voice neutral, his eyes locked on the man standing before him.

"No, sir. Just the usual first-run jitters, Captain. This exercise is the first time GIDEON's coordinated a force-on-force engagement of such complexity. We've got manual override protocols ready if anything looks like it's deviating from the standard operating procedures or established rules of engagement."

"Excellent, Mr. Schreck. It's important we have the ability to take manual control back of any of our surface or subsurface platforms, should the need arise. You mentioned we could initiate this if we spotted one of the units deviating from the SOP or ROEs, but how are you defining a deviation?"

Schreck shifted uncomfortably, weighing his response carefully. "Hmm, I guess a deviation would be targeting friendly units or ignoring weapons-tight commands. Basically, anything that would make tomorrow's headlines read 'Navy AI Goes Rogue,' or something along the lines of 'Robotic Warships—Terror of the Seas.'"

Trammell laughed at the fictional headlines but appreciated the point he was making. "Very well, Mr. Schreck. If you see anything unusual or get a sense the AI is taking actions beyond its programming, you take immediate action and find me, understood?"

"Understood, sir," Schreck assured him and returned to his station.

"CIC, Bridge." Walsh's voice crackled overhead. "Crossing into exercise area. T-minus ten minutes to commencement."

Meilof's hands flew across her controls. "All right, people. Time to see if eighteen months of development was worth the taxpayers' money." She pulled up a three-dimensional display. "I've got our units configured for demonstration pattern Alpha—defensive screen transitioning to offensive sweep once OPFOR shows hostile intent."

"Very well. And our OPFOR composition—what are we looking at?" asked Trammell as he leaned forward to get a better look.

"Oh, Dutch Harbor's throwing us a real party, sir. They're simulating a reinforced PLA Navy surface action group. Two Type 055 destroyers, three Type 054A frigates, and six Type 056A corvettes. Subsurface picture shows two Type 039C AIP boats," Meilof confirmed.

Thompson whistled low. "That's a lot of metal."

"That's the point, Senior Chief," Meilof replied. "If we can't handle this with three Stormwatchers and two Seekers, the whole concept's dead in the water."

Trammell rose from his seat, moving to stand beside Meilof at the command console. Through the holographic display, he could see his task group's electronic nervous system—data streams flowing between platforms at light speed, decision trees branching and pruning in nanoseconds.

"How's Dutch Harbor managing their side?" he asked, curious how they were going to handle their set of ACVs.

"They've got a mirror setup to ours. Lieutenant Rodriguez and his team, plus contractors from the same companies are going to push the boundaries of our system." Meilof highlighted the OPFOR control node on her display. "They're using the HYDRA-AI. It's basically GIDEON's evil twin. Same base architecture, different tactical libraries and approach to learning."

The countdown timer steadily moved toward zero, now sixty seconds out.

Trammell keyed the 1MC. "All stations, this is the captain. Exercise Kodiak-33 will commence in one minute. This is it, everyone. We are about to prove that autonomous warfare isn't science fiction. It's science fact, and it's here."

He turned to Meilof. "Lieutenant Commander, you have my authorization to activate GIDEON. Weapons free under exercise parameters."

Meilof's expression hardened with concentration. "Aye, sir." Her fingers moved across the haptic interface with practiced precision. "GIDEON, this is Intrepid. Authentication Zulu-Nine-Whiskey. Execute demonstration package Alpha. Autonomous operations authorized."

The transformation was immediate but subtle. Every display in the CIC seemed to sharpen, as if coming into focus. Data streams reorganized themselves, inefficiencies vanishing as GIDEON optimized every connection. The AI's presence was felt rather than seen—a vast intelligence spreading across the quantum-encrypted links between platforms.

"GIDEON online," Meilof reported. "Establishing tactical mesh... confirmed. All platforms report ready for autonomous operations."

On the main display, Trammell watched his Stormwatchers adjust their formation. The movements were small—a few degrees of heading change, minor speed adjustments—but the effect was dramatic. What had been a standard escort formation became something organic, breathing with the rhythm of the storm. Twenty minutes into the exercise, the first signs of the enemy appeared.

"Contact," Thompson called. "Confirmed, OPFOR units going active. Detecting search radars consistent with PLA Navy Type 364 and Type 382 systems."

"GIDEON's responding," Meilof reported. "Stormwatchers are... interesting."

The three Stormwatchers had begun what looked like random course changes. But Trammell recognized the pattern from his study of the system. They were creating electromagnetic ghosts, using the storm's interference to multiply their apparent numbers. To the OPFOR's sensors, three vessels would look like nine.

"Vampire, vampire," Thompson announced with clinical calm. "The lead Stormwatcher just detected an OPFOR missile barrage."

"Don't tease me, Senior Chief, give me numbers and types of inbounds," quizzed Meilof as Trammell watched her take control of the situation.

Senior Chief Thompson swiftly answered. "Aye, ma'am, it's coming in now. First wave consists of twenty-four YJ-18s. Time to impact four minutes. Second wave is larger, thirty-six YJ-18s, impact in seven minutes. Oh wow, damn, Stormwatcher just detected a third wave. The OPFOR is launching twelve YJ-21s, time to impact five minutes."

Captain Trammell's pulse quickened as the threat profile came through—an onslaught of inbound Chinese missiles, each a flying stick of death. At the top of the list was the YJ-21, a hypersonic antiship ballistic missile developed to punch through even the most advanced AEGIS defenses. Capable of reaching terminal speeds above Mach 10, it was designed to kill or cripple capital ships with a combination of kinetic impact and deep-penetration warhead detonation. Alongside it were salvos of YJ-18s, China's primary sea-skimming cruise missile, notorious for its subsonic approach and terminal sprint at Mach 3. It was the classic saturation tactic naval warfighters had feared for years—a multivector, multispeed assault aimed at overwhelming layered defenses through sheer volume and complexity. The OPFOR wasn't just probing; they were trying to break the shield.

"Whoa, that's a hell of a barrage. How is GIDEON responding?" Trammell asked Meilof.

"GIDEON's initiated full battle group defense," Meilof replied, eyes locked on her console. "All three Stormwatchers have fanned into intercept arcs—SM-6s are already in flight, prioritizing YJ-21s by predicted impact vector. Secondaries are tracking the cruise wave; SeaRAMs and lasers are holding fire for leakers in the sprint phase. Sidewinder turrets are on standby, slaved to shared targeting data. GIDEON's adjusting posture every second—this is a live fire net, not a picket line."

Trammell watched in fascination as the Stormwatchers transformed their scattered formation into something he'd only seen once in a simulation. Instead of each ship creating its own defensive bubble, they merged their sensor pictures and weapons employment zones into a single integrated defense. The lead Stormwatcher's radar painted targets while the trailing units remained silent, their missiles guided by their sister ship's data while their ship kept its radars off, preventing them from being quickly identified.

The holographic battle space flared with dozens of red arcs, all converging on the task group in staggered waves. Twenty-four YJ-18s came in low, sea-skimming just above the wave tops. Behind them, thirty-six more broke over the horizon in a second volley. Higher still, twelve YJ-21s screamed in from the stratosphere, their trajectories sharp and fast—maneuvering ballistic arcs with hypersonic velocity profiles.

"Splash twenty-two," Senior Chief Thompson exclaimed excitedly. "Two leakers from the first wave—heading straight for Stormwatcher-2 and Stormwatcher-3!"

The Stormwatcher-class unmanned surface vessels (USVs) shifted formation instantly. The GIDEON-AI had already predicted the surviving missile paths, retasking additional interceptors before Thompson had finished speaking.

Trammell watched on the display as the SeaRAMs roared virtually to life, digital missile tracks reaching out for the incoming sea-skimmers still bearing down on them. Intermixed with the missiles were precision laser bursts from the vessel's cobalt beam turrets, which zapped targets as they crisscrossed the simulated sky. The last two YJ-18s blinked out seconds later, the defenses holding.

"Heads up, here comes the second wave. They're entering Stormwatcher-2 and Stormwatcher-3 laser envelope now," announced Meilof as calmly as one could with dozens of incoming missiles. She continued, "Thirty-six YJ-18s inbound. Hang on, it looks like GIDEON is overclocking its targeting cycles. It's moving to rotate Sidewinder packs for full quadrant saturation."

Trammell could barely keep up with what was happening but saw that the holographic board continued to grow denser with activity. Blue and gold icons on the ocean's surface representing friendly assets were swarming into defensive alignments. The trio of Stormwatchers layered their beams and missiles like a living wall. The ACVs fired missiles in pairs, some tripled, others stacked at different altitudes to hedge against evasive programming.

"Eh, there are too many," Meilof muttered from the BMC-R pit. "They're coming in too fast to react to them all."

"Hang on, intercepts are happening...nine down...fourteen...twenty-two," Senior Chief Thompson announced excitedly. "Splash thirty-one—ah crap," he reported grimly before adding, "We've got five leakers from the second volley zeroing in on Doomhammer-1, Zealot-2."

Trammell watched three simulated impact icons blossom in red against the 524-foot-long Doomhammer-class unmanned surface vessel arsenal ship. The Huntington Ingalls Industries ship wasn't out of action yet, but a third of her ninety-six VLS cells were down. The two other hits against Zealot-2 blotted her from the board, a simulated kill against one of Trammell's patrol-boat-sized counterdrone vessels.

"Ballistic missiles inbound!" Thompson exclaimed as the digital representations of the YJ-21s came diving in.

"Hypersonics incoming at Mach 8! GIDEON's engaging," Meilof announced, the tension evident in her voice. "Hot damn! We scored six mid-course kills with the SM-6s. Whoa, a pair of missiles look like their guidance systems got fried by a microwave hit from Stormwatcher-1's Leonidas-III. Their tracks are way off course, headed for empty water. That leaves four missiles remaining, all headed for the *Intrepid*."

Trammell was amazed by the results, something he knew they wouldn't have been able to achieve without the aid of AI. Still, as he watched the remaining missiles still bearing down on them, he held hope the ACVs would come through in the end, if not, the *Intrepid* would engage the leakers.

"Stormwatcher-2 and 3 are engaging," Thompson updated as the vessels changed course and speed. "They're attempting to herd the last four missiles into a convergence path for the cobalt beams."

The Stormwatchers mounted a pair of 150kW cobalt beam lasers for hard kills in the terminal phase of a missile or drone attack. The laser turrets were mounted in a port and starboard fore and aft configuration to provide full 360-degree rotational fields of fire for layered engagement. With an effective range of two to five kilometers depending on the weather, it was a last-ditch weapon capable of firing eight to twelve bursts per minute, per turret, with no limits on its sustainability at that rate. Mounted port and starboard or in a staggered dorsal-fore/aft configuration

On the display, the simulated kill box lit up as the trap was sprung. The three Stormwatchers saturated the final vectors of the incoming missiles. The SeaRAMs engaged on staggered timing while the Leonidas-III pulsed microwave bursts across the last known glide paths of the incoming missiles. Three of the four YJ-21s vanished, swatted from the sky at the last second. The fourth changed its path, angling in for a different ship, causing the interceptors and microwave pulses to miss it entirely as it slammed into the Stormwatcher-3.

"Hit on Stormwatcher-3," announced Meilof, her eyes narrowing as she rapidly read the incoming diagnostic reports. "Node severed. Autonomous control lost. Stormwatcher-3 is offline, destroyed. The Warden logistics USV is initiating recovery protocols."

The room was silent for half a beat. Then Trammell exhaled. "OK, we just got bloodied. This fight's not over and we're not out of it yet!"

"Aye, sir," Meilof said. "We've got this."

The next ninety minutes of the exercise became a doctoral thesis in autonomous warfare as Trammell's crew continued to push their unmanned vessels to their limits. The Dutch Harbor's OPFOR threw increasingly complex scenarios at them, from coordinated submarine attacks to electronic warfare cyberattacks and even a repeat of an even larger simulated hypersonic strike. Each time, the GIDEON-AI adapted, learning not just from its successes but from the patterns in OPFOR's tactics and how its human operators reacted to each iteration and action.

"They're getting frustrated," Meilof observed during a brief lull in the exercise. "HYDRA's started using nondoctrinal approaches. That last attack pattern was pure improvisation."

"Good," Trammell said approvingly. "Real enemies won't stick to the playbook either. It's important for GIDEON to understand that."

The contractor from Saronic, a thin man who'd introduced himself as David Liu, looked up from his workstation. "Excuse me, Captain, we're seeing some interesting emergent behaviors in the mesh network. The platforms are starting to anticipate each other's actions. It's like they're developing their own tactical language of sorts."

"Huh, is that a problem or something we need to be worried about?" Trammell quizzed.

"No, not yet. I only bring it up because it's something we didn't model for. In fact, GIDEON's efficiency has increased by twelve percent since the exercise started."

"Wow, that's pretty amazing. Make sure to continue to document everything. I'm sure your people will want to study this further after everything is over," Trammell replied. This was what exercises were for. To test ideas, systems, and tactics before they were tested in war.

The exercise slowed as they finished going through the final elements that needed to be tested. Once they had completed the digital force-on-force test, they switched to live firing actual missiles and zapping target drones to test the lasers. This gave everyone a chance to do more than just test the ACVs' computer-simulated battles—it allowed them to run through the process of firing missile salvos and then having to conduct missile reloads while underway. By the end of the day, the crew was exhausted, and so was Trammel. When the call to ENDEX was heard, it couldn't have come at a better time.

"Good job, everyone. Secure from exercise stations," Captain Trammell ordered. "I want GIDEON placed in standby mode and all ACVs returned to escort formation."

The displays showed his small robotic fleet re-forming around *Intrepid*, as if the intensity of the day had never occurred. But the data told a different story.

"Sir, we're receiving the preliminary battle damage assessment from Dutch Harbor OPFOR," Meilof announced, a note of satisfaction in her voice. "OPFOR losses: two destroyers, three frigates, six missile boats, two submarines. Total kill probability: ninety-four percent. Our losses…" She paused for effect. "One, and one damaged ACV."

The CIC remained silent for a moment. They had proven something today. They'd proven that a handful of unmanned combat vessels, properly coordinated, could defeat a force many times their size.

"Well, Mr. Schreck," Trammell said quietly, "what are your thoughts on how GIDEON performed today?"

The contractor rubbed his chin before responding, weighing his answer carefully. "Honestly, Captain? It performed better than we modeled, better than I thought it might. The emergent behaviors, the adaptive tactics, GIDEON's not just executing preprogrammed responses anymore. It's actually learning, adapting. From a programmer's perspective, that's either very good or very scary, depending on how you want to look at it."

"Interesting. From my perspective, this concept of autonomous naval warfare works," Trammell offered, then turned to his senior chief. "Thompson, what's your take?"

The veteran sailor looked thoughtful. "Sir, I've been running combat systems for sixteen years. What I just saw… it's like watching the first radar-guided missile hit its target. You know everything just changed, even if you don't know how yet."

Trammell nodded slowly. "Alice, download all exercise data. I want a full analysis ready for Admiral Reeves by 0800. Include the emergent behavior patterns—he'll want to know about those."

"Aye, sir." Meilof's fingers were already flying across her console. Then she paused, looking up at him. "Captain? We just changed naval warfare. You realize that, right?"

Trammell looked at the displays one more time. Outside, the storm picked up again, dark clouds and stormy waters threatening a rough night. But inside *Intrepid*'s electronic heart, the future hummed with quiet efficiency. They'd proven the concept. Now they had to scale it up, train with it, and prepare for the day when the missiles would be real and the stakes absolute.

"I realize it, Lieutenant Commander. Question is whether we changed it fast enough."

He thought of the intelligence reports, the satellite imagery of Chinese shipyards, the growing Eurasian Alliance. Time was not on their side. It never had been. But today, in the gray violence of the Bering Sea, they'd proven that numbers weren't everything. One ship, a handful of robots, and an AI that learned—properly wielded, it might just be enough.

The real test was yet to come.

Chapter Nine:
Loose Lips

February 2, 2033
Innerstad, Visby
Gotland, Sweden

The scent of grilled lamb and vegetables lingered in the kitchen, competing with the pine tang of the wood-burning stove. Klara leaned back on the worn linen sofa, wineglass in hand, legs folded beneath her. She looked perfectly at ease, her features soft in the amber glow of the lamp by the bookshelf. Across from her, Lars moved with a practiced ease, stacking plates in the kitchen sink, sleeves rolled to his elbows, revealing forearms speckled with sawdust from the morning's shift at the GEAB substation, where he had reworked some safety mechanisms for the electrical line from mainland Sweden.

"You know," she said, swirling her glass just enough to keep his eyes on her, "for a man who works twelve-hour days and drills on the weekend, you make a mean dinner."

Lars chuckled, tossing a dish towel onto the counter. "I make a point of feeding people I like. Occupational hazard of growing up with two older sisters."

Klara tilted her head. "Mmm, lucky me."

She rose and crossed to the counter, lightly brushing against him as she set her glass down. Her fingers traced the edge of a laminated training schedule pinned to the fridge, subtly scanning it—dates, unit numbers, logistics.

"Your next Home Guard drill... that's the joint readiness thing, right?" she asked casually, as if recalling something he'd mentioned weeks ago.

"Yeah, big one." Lars nodded, drying his hands. "We're supporting P18 with inland security sweeps. Moving supply caches, establishing fallback zones outside Slite and Klintehamn. Kind of a distributed logistics test."

She gave a soft whistle, feigning mild surprise. "That's serious. Do they expect... something?"

Lars shrugged, eyes narrowing just slightly—half cautious, half flattered by her interest. "There's chatter. Nothing formal. But the regional command wants every unit's readiness above seventy percent in case we get mobilized. Even our little battalion's getting new kits and ammo inspections. It's kind of crazy, there's been a lot of movement lately, far more than normal. Heck, they're rotating four units from the mainland to Gotland for familiarization training on the island."

Klara leaned in, her body language playful, intimate, giving him attention without pressing.

"Wow, that sounds… big, but what do I know? I'm a simple girl with simple needs." She winked playfully at him. "Will you be at the airfield again? It's close, we might be able to meet up for lunch," she suggested, tone warm, an eyebrow raised with practiced curiosity.

He smiled. "Mmm… not this time. That's B Company's turf. We're doing grid security along the coastal relay lines—GEAB's worried someone might tamper with the fiber link or the backup diesel feeds."

She kissed his cheek, letting it linger. "My handsome protector of all things fragile."

He turned, hand resting lightly on her waist. "You know, it'd be easier to protect you if you lived here."

She laughed genuinely, then sobered just a hair. "Lars…"

"No pressure," he added quickly, reading the shift in her posture. "I just… we already spend most nights together."

She traced a finger along the edge of his shirt collar, gently grounding the moment.

"I love being with you. You know that," she said softly. "But I also love waking up alone sometimes, making my tea in silence, walking through my own door. It's not about you—it's just how I stay balanced, how I separate my work from my personal life."

Lars looked away, nodding slowly.

She stepped closer. "And with the Baltic Wings Festival only a few months out, I'm drowning in logistics. Environmental permits, press kits, volunteer assignments. Once that's behind me… I'd really like to revisit this conversation."

He gave a half smile. "So, you're saying there's hope."

"Hmm, I'd say there is a little more than hope," she whispered, brushing her lips against his. "But not just yet."

As she kissed him again, longer, deeper—her mind quietly filed the intel away: southern fallback sites, GEAB grid focus, B Company at

the airfield. The map of the security situation on Gotland was beginning to take shape.
****

Following Day
St. Hans Café
Visby, Gotland

Snow flurries swirled along the cobbled lane outside as Klara ducked into her favorite café, the warmth of cinnamon and cardamom greeting her like an old friend. The bell over the door chimed once—soft, familiar.

Annika Bragefeldt looked up from behind the counter, eyes twinkling behind her oversized readers. "Ah, Klara, my favorite bird whisperer returns."

"Only for tea," Klara replied with a smile, brushing snow from her sleeves. "And maybe a bit of gossip, if you've got any steeping."

Annika chuckled, setting down a tray of saffron buns. "I always have something brewing. The usual?"

"Please."

Moments later, Klara settled into her favorite corner seat, a warm St. Hans Blend between her hands and a Saffranspannkaka already halfway to her mouth. Annika leaned across the counter like a cat preparing to pounce.

"So?" Annika began, voice lowered. "Did you hear the PM's comments about that Chinese ship the Navy intercepted?"

Klara raised her eyebrows. "Bits and pieces. They said it was a freighter, right? I heard something about it burning for days just off the shore near Smöjen, at least that's what Lars said."

"Oh, it was a bit more than that, Klara," Annika said with a wave of her hand. "I have a cousin whose son is in the Home Guard near Slite. He says there were gunshots…even a helicopter crash."

Klara widened her eyes, letting the shock register just enough. "Seriously? Lars didn't tell me anything about that. I thought we were still in the realm of peacetime."

Annika leaned in further. "Apparently, the ship was too close to the undersea cables. The ones that keep us connected. Some think it was trying to… cut them, like what's been happening between Estonia and Finland."

Klara let the silence stretch for a breath, then said carefully, "Wow. That would explain the uptick in patrols lately. Lars did say something about how his Home Guard unit's been repositioning gear—mentioned something about fiber links and relay nodes being critical. He didn't go into details, but… he's been a bit tense lately."

"Mm-hmm." Annika nodded sagely. "And have you noticed all the new antenna rigs on the ridge south of town? Not cell towers. Something else."

Klara made a mental note—someone else was observing the buildup. It was time to tighten her recon routes. But she simply said, "It's almost like we're preparing for something we're not allowed to say out loud."

"Exactly," Annika replied, pleased. "It's almost like saying Voldemort." She laughed at her own joke before continuing. "And here's the worst part, Klara: no one's saying anything officially. Just rumors, whispers from busybodies like me. But if those cables go down—poof—no banking, no internet, not even landlines. We'd be blind and deaf overnight, cut off from the outside world."

Klara sipped her tea, warm and sharp on her tongue. "I had no idea. It sounds like we would be very vulnerable if that happened," she murmured, then added, "Ugh, I can't even imagine the confusion something like that would cause, especially with all the extra visitors coming this spring for the Baltic Wings Festival I've been organizing. Makes me wonder if the government is doing enough to keep the peace. We're a small country, we just want to be left alone."

Annika gave her a look—part question, part concern. "Well, I don't know about the government. I'm just a simple shopkeeper. But did I hear that right, you're still going through with that birding festival?"

"Of course," Klara said lightly. "If we cancel every time someone sneezes in Moscow or Beijing, we'll never get anything done. Besides, it might be good for morale. People need something to focus on… something that feels *normal*."

Annika nodded. "True, you're not wrong. Just… keep your eyes open, dear."

Klara smiled. "Always."

As Annika moved off to help another customer, Klara leaned back, letting the tea and tension settle. The cable attack had nearly succeeded—barely stopped in time. But the narrative was already morphing into local myth: rumors, half-truths, and strategic uncertainty.

Exactly as planned, she thought.

Now, all she had to do was find ways to keep stoking the right fires at the right times. As she sipped her tea, her mind began to plot ideas, scenarios working themselves over in her head.

Chapter Ten:
Don't Cause a Panic

February 8, 2033
US European Command Headquarters
Building 2314, Patch Barracks
Stuttgart, Germany

The secure conference room on the second floor of the headquarters building was steeped in history, having served the American Army since 1945 and the German Army dating back to 1936. Sitting at the polished mahogany table brought back memories of Jim Batista's time in uniform, before his retirement, back when he had been a warrant officer. He set his ceramic mug down on the table. The bitter liquid had done little to cut through the jet lag gnawing at his bones. Outside the windowless room, a light snow dusted the Swabian hills surrounding Vaihingen, a suburb of Stuttgart where US European Command was headquartered. Inside the room, it was anything but cold as the temperature rose with the pressure of events.

"Gentlemen, let's dispense with the pleasantries," Batista said, his Utah accent sharpening each word. "We have a Chinese spy ship burned to the waterline off Gotland, eleven dead, and NATO ports cataloged like a targeting package. All this while Moscow and Beijing prep for the largest military exercise since the 1984 REFORGER. I'm a student of history, so tell me how we're not looking at 2022 all over again."

General Nathaniel Calder, dual-hatted as both EUCOM Commander and SACEUR, leaned forward in his chair. The Spartan coin he habitually carried clicked against the table as he set it down. At fifty-eight, Calder still looked like he could run a 5K before breakfast—and often did, much to his staff's exhaustion.

"Jim, the parallels aren't lost on any of us," Calder said, his Colorado drawl carrying the weight of command. "But there's a difference between preparation and provocation. We start flooding the Baltics with armor, we might just give Goryunov the excuse he's looking for."

Secretary of Defense T. J. Varnell shifted in his seat, his fingers drumming a pattern on his tablet. The former tech magnate turned

Pentagon chief might have traded the casual look of Silicon Valley for tailored suits, but his mind still worked in algorithms and decision trees.

"With respect, General, when has restraint ever deterred Russian aggression?" Varnell's California-neutral accent carried an edge. "Georgia, Crimea, Donbas—each time we showed restraint, they took it as weakness."

Lieutenant General Mark "Bear" Sheridan, Deputy EUCOM Commander, rubbed the bear claw pendant in his hand like a fidget—a nervous tic his staff knew meant he was deep in thought. The Alaskan's massive frame dwarfed his chair, making him appear even larger than he was.

"The Swedes are spooked," Sheridan said, his voice rumbling like distant thunder. "Can't say I blame them. That Chinese ship was mapping their infrastructure like they were planning an invasion. Hell, they had thermite grenades. That's not intelligence gathering, that's sabotage prep in case they got caught."

Batista nodded. "Yeah, which brings us to the elephant in the room. Prime Minister Lindqvist reached out through back channels. She wants to know when we can have NATO forces on Gotland to help shore up their defenses ahead of this May exercise."

The room fell silent for a moment as they thought about the request. The Swedish military maintained a small contingent of forces on the island but had never offered to host NATO forces behind the occasional exercise. The island was effectively an unsinkable aircraft carrier in the middle of the Baltic Sea, a prize Russia would love to capture should hostilities break out between NATO and the Eurasian Defense and Economic Pact.

Major General William "Duke" Morrison, the SOCEUR Commander, stopped spinning his wedding ring—a sure sign the special operations chief was now fully engaged. The former Delta operator's scarred hands told stories his classified record couldn't. "It should go without saying, Gotland's the key to the Baltic," Morrison said, his Arkansas drawl slow and measured. "It was a prime target during the Cold War and it's a prime target now. If the Swedes are willing to allow us to station assets there, we should take them up on the offer. With a proper A2/D2 setup, we could bottle up the Baltic and provide an aerial umbrella of protection that would extend over Kaliningrad, Lithuania, Latvia, Estonia, Sweden, and Norway. It also gives us a safe position to fire extended-range rocket artillery over those countries and the likely avenues of attack into NATO territory should the ChiComs and Russians decide to get froggy."

Calder picked up his Spartan coin, rolling it between his fingers. "You're the strategist, Jim. What are you thinking? What's the President's temperature on this?"

Batista leaned back, studying the faces around the table. These were warriors, not politicians. They understood the knife's edge they walked. "President Ashford has preauthorized the forward deployment of the 1st Armor and 3rd Infantry Divisions if needed," Batista announced, watching their reactions. "He's taking this seriously, as am I. The question is, what do we put on Gotland that provides deterrence without escalation?"

"I think Duke already suggested it," replied the SecDef. His fingers tapped on his tablet, pulling up force deployment options. "I've been war-gaming this since the Baltic incident and I think I might have something that could work. We could deploy the First Battalion, 59th Air Defense Artillery. They could provide an umbrella over the entire region. Patriot batteries for the high-altitude threats, HIMARS for precision fires. Leonidas-IIIs for counterdrone. It gives us a mobile, lethal, defensive, and offensive option should we need it."

"Smart," Calder said, setting his coin down with a decisive click. "But they'll need security. Can't have another Khobar Towers on our hands."

"Second Battalion, 503rd Infantry from my 173rd," Morrison suggested. "Paratroopers. Light, fast, and used to working with European partners. One company on Gotland, the rest of the battalion stages from Riga."

Sheridan pulled up a map on the wall display, his thick fingers surprisingly delicate on the touchscreen. "Creates a triangle—Gotland, Riga, Helsinki. Any Russian move gets caught in a crossfire."

"And if this exercise turns hot?" Batista pressed. "Like Ukraine in 2022?" The room fell silent again. They all remembered how quickly "exercises" had become invasions.

Calder stood, moving to the map. Despite his lean frame, he dominated the room. "Then we implement Joint Task Force Sentinel. Full anti-access, area-denial umbrella from the Danish Straits to the Gulf of Finland."

He traced the coverage area with his finger. "Patriot batteries here, here, and here. HIMARS positioned to cover the Suwałki Gap and the Estonian border. Navy assets surge forward from the North Sea."

"I can have 1-59 ADA moving within seventy-two hours," Varnell said, already composing deployment orders in his head. "The 173rd can follow within a week."

"What about the Europeans?" Morrison asked. "Can't do this unilaterally."

Batista nodded. "That's my next stop. Mons, then Stockholm. I'll get Stubb on board."

Alexander Stubb, NATO's Secretary-General, was a pragmatist who understood the delicate balance between alliance cohesion and decisive action. The Finnish politician had learned hard lessons about Russian intentions.

"The Germans will balk," Sheridan warned. "They always do when it comes to antagonizing Moscow."

"Let me worry about Berlin," Batista said. "Right now, I need to know we can execute if given the green light."

Calder moved back to his seat, picking up his coin again. "Jim, I can have TF Sentinel operational within three weeks. But I want more than just the 173rd. If this goes sideways, I need heavy metal close at hand and additional airpower to counter the increase in PLA Air Force units arriving in the region."

"First Armor's at Fort Bliss, ready to roll," Varnell confirmed. "Third Infantry at Stewart. We could have a full armored corps in Europe within a month. I can schedule two F-22 squadrons from the 325th Operations Group out of Tyndall, a pair of F-15EXs from the 4th Operations Group from Seymour Johnson, and the 4th Fighter Squadron's F-35As from Hill. That beefs your airpower up by five squadrons of stealth fighters and frontline aircraft."

"Do it, quietly," Batista said. "We'll call it a readiness exercise. How about EuroShield-33, or whatever you think is best? But I want options."

Morrison leaned forward. "My teams have been tracking Russian Spetsnaz activity in the Baltics. Unusual patterns. Tourist visas that don't match tourist behavior. We might already have infiltrators in place."

"All the more reason to move fast," Calder said. He looked around the table, meeting each man's eyes. "Gentlemen, we're walking a tightrope. Too little response, and we're inviting aggression. Too much, and we might trigger exactly what we're trying to prevent."

Batista stood, signaling the meeting's end. "Then we'd better have perfect balance. General Calder, I want TF Sentinel's deployment plan on my desk by tomorrow. Duke, get your snake eaters ready—I have a feeling we're going to need them. T. J., start working the logistics. If we're doing this, we're doing it right."

As the others filed out, Calder lingered. The two men stood by the window, watching the snow fall on the headquarters of America's European shield.

"Jim, you know what this looks like, right?" Calder said quietly. "Forward-deploying air-defense and precision fires? That's not just deterrence. That's preparation for a fight."

Batista nodded slowly. "I know, Nate. Question is, do they?"

"The Russians? They wrote the playbook we're reading from." Calder pocketed his coin. "*Maskirovka*. Deception. Exercises that aren't exercises. We're just playing by their rules now."

"Then let's make sure we play to win," Batista said.

****

Three Hours Later
Secure Video Teleconference Room

Batista sat alone in the darkened SVTC room, the glow from multiple screens casting harsh shadows across his weathered face. The secure link to Washington had just connected, and President Lawson Ashford's imposing six-foot-four frame filled the primary display. Even through the encrypted connection, Batista could see the strain in the President's tired eyes. All of Ashford's years in the military, working in agricultural logistics, and his time as the governor of Kansas hadn't aged him nearly as much as his time in the presidency. His once chestnut-brown hair had grayed considerably. Batista wondered if he'd lost more weight with a bit of concern, since Ashford was already quite lean.

"Jim, I've read your initial assessment," Ashford said, his Kansas drawl more pronounced than usual, a tell that he was deeply concerned. "Bottom-line it for me. Are we looking at another Ukraine?"

Batista had served in uniform under four presidents, but Ashford was different. The former governor and visionary who'd led the creation of the Grain Consortium understood logistics and supply chains better than most generals. He grasped that modern warfare was as much about industrial capacity as battlefield prowess. It was why he had supercharged the Pentagon's Replicator program and accelerated the implementation of autonomous weapon platforms across the services. They were doing more with less, with greater capability than ever before.

"I'm not sure I'm ready to say that yet, but the parallels are concerning, Mr. President," Batista said, choosing his words carefully. "The way I see it, Mr. President, is we have two problems we're facing and no good solutions for how to deal with them. The first problem is the US and NATO and our continued challenge with Russia. The second problem is China. Their involvement changes the calculus entirely."

"Oh, how so?"

"Eh, people may differ on what led to the 2022 Russo-Ukraine War, but ultimately, that war was about territorial expansion. The Russians were trying to create a buffer zone along the Dnipro River, Sea of Azov, and the Black Sea. It's a shame that poor leadership on the part of Europe and the US led to the war beginning in the first place and its eventual outcome. What we have to do now, Mr. President, is make abundantly clear to Russia and the Chinese our spheres of influence are better served through trade and economic activity than through force of arms," Batista explained.

"The thing is, Mr. President, this somehow feels bigger. Like this is part of a greater, more strategic plan in play. This incident around Gotland, in my mind, is a bigger deal than our Swedish and European allies may be willing to accept. It feels coordinated, the Russian and Chinese Navies working in tandem toward a common goal." Batista paused, looking off camera for a moment, searching for the right words. "I know the emphasis of your next term, Mr. President, is meant to be on how we can find a way to bridge these geopolitical, economic, and social divides between the Western-led democracies and what's transformed into this Eurasian Defense Economic Pact, EDEP. But we might have to face the reality that, despite our desire to achieve some sort of normal coexistence between our sides—as worthy a goal and as noble a gesture as yours and Europe's is—we don't have a willing partner opposite us that sees it the same way."

Ashford nodded slowly, leaning back in his chair and looking up toward the ceiling, collecting his thoughts and weighing what to say in response. The 2020s had been a rough decade for the West, from COVID lockdowns to unheard-of levels of digital censorship to the brutal, barbaric war in Ukraine and the Middle East. People were looking for calm, for stability and for economic security at home.

The country was just starting to recover from the economic impact of running a $40 trillion deficit. Ashford's push during his first term to create the Grain Consortium or GC, a cartel of like-minded nations that rewarded farmers for producing ever-growing quantities of food for the government to buy and then sell at guaranteed prices and quantities, had reduced global famine and food shortages by half in just the first couple of years. It had also brought in enormous tax revenues for the government as it sought to begin the process of paying down the deficit. But it was his radical approach to restructuring how entitlement programs were funded that had really ended deficit spending and shored up the programs for future generations, even increasing benefit payments at the same time.

"Jim, as always, I appreciate your pragmatism and ability to see the world as it is, not how us politicians wish it was," Ashford began, weighing his words carefully. "When the voters saw fit to give me a second term, they did so because they wanted their elected leaders in Washington to address the problems here at home. Not nation building abroad or attempting to be the global cop, the country always sticking its nose into the affairs of others. That said, if Goryunov and Ouyang believe me to be weak, or think that we will sit idly by while they redraw the borders of nations in a way that suits them, they have another thing coming.

"Next month, the GC is meeting in New Delhi to discuss ways to further increase rice production. Separately, they are hosting a trade delegation with representatives from EDEP. They're looking to establish a long-term deal for the bloc, as opposed to their individual members negotiating deals on their own. How do you think Moscow or Beijing might react if we looked to use these negotiations as leverage to de-escalate things before this May exercise begins?" Ashford asked.

Batista hated the principle of the idea, as it would punish the citizens rather than the leaders it was meant to influence. "I'm hesitant to use something like food over a country, especially one we're not at war with. If that's the route you'd like to go, Mr. President, then perhaps we should dangle a better deal for them than they otherwise might get, but we make the deal contingent upon them scaling back the size and scope of this exercise. And we make it abundantly clear—should they decide to turn this exercise into something more, all deals are off. If Russia or China start a war, it'll negatively impact all the members of EDEP, not just belligerents. I think we could use this to help shape the kind of peaceful outcome we want to see," Batista replied.

"Jim, are we too late? Should we have pushed this leverage a year ago when the GC officially came into being?" quizzed Ashford, a hesitant look on his face, like he had made a mistake and was only just now realizing it.

Batista shrugged. "That's hard to say, Mr. President. All I know is since we got that report from South Korean intelligence, DragonBear—I'm just not sure. All signs point to this exercise being cover for something bigger. It seems to me the Russians are preparing to secure the Baltic States and create that long-sought-after land bridge to Kaliningrad, like they did in Ukraine with Crimea."

Ashford nodded, then sat forward as he asked, "And this Gotland force, Joint Task Force Sentinel—you think this will deter them, along with those other deployments T. J.'s recommending?"

"I think so. It's a credible deterrent," Batista replied. "Air-defense umbrella, precision fires, just enough ground forces to secure our assets. It's small enough not to provoke, large enough to complicate their planning if they wanted to try and seize the island."

"Walk me through the timeline."

Batista pulled up a deployment schedule on his tablet. "1-59 ADA begins movement in three weeks. Equipment follows by sea and air. Initial operational capability on Gotland by March fifteenth. Full TF Sentinel operational by April first."

"That's fast."

"Has to be. The EDEP exercise kicks off May first. If they're planning something, that's their window."

The President was quiet for a moment, his weathered hands folding and unfolding on his desk. "Jim, I grew up watching wheat futures. You learn to read patterns, spot the signs before the storm hits. What's your gut telling you?"

Batista considered the question. In thirty years of service, his instincts had saved more lives than any intelligence report. "My gut says this is different, sir. Bigger. The resource allocation, the timing, the coordination between Russia and China—it's unprecedented. They're not just testing their readiness capabilities like they claim. They're preparing for something."

"Then we'd better be prepared too," Ashford said. "You have my authorization for TF Sentinel. But, Jim—"

"Sir?"

"Keep it quiet. Last thing we need is the *New York Times* running 'US Prepares for World War Three' headlines. That helps nobody."

"Understood, Mr. President."

"And, Jim? That armor you mentioned, the 1st Armor and 3rd Infantry Division? Start the movements. Call it a training rotation. But I want them ready to roll into battle if this goes south."

"Agreed. I'll get it in motion, sir."

The President nodded, then leaned forward. "One more thing. What's your take on Gotland? Can the Swedes hold it if push comes to shove?"

Batista thought of the map, the narrow straits, the strategic position. "With our help? Yeah, not a problem. Without it? Not a chance in hell if the Chinese are involved."

"Fair enough. Then make sure that doesn't happen. Whatever it takes," the President directed, then cut the feed.

Batista was left alone with his thoughts and the weight of what was coming. Outside, the snow continued to fall on Vaihingen, each flake adding to the blanket of white covering the base. Soon, he thought, they'd know if this was just another exercise or the prelude to something worse.

He stood, gathering his materials. Mons awaited, then Stockholm. Allies to reassure, defenses to coordinate, and always, always, the ticking clock counting down to May.

As he left the conference room, Batista couldn't shake the feeling that they were already playing catch-up in a game whose rules they didn't fully understand. The question wasn't whether the storm was coming—it was whether they'd be ready when it hit.

Chapter Eleven:
The Rehearsal

February 13, 2033 – 0630
Type 055 Destroyer *Zunyi*
Yulin Naval Base
Hainan, China

Rain hissed gently against the windows of the bridge, each droplet shimmering under the amber glow of Yulin Naval Base's floodlights. Captain Shen Tao studied the tactical display intensely, the tight scar above his eyebrow twitching—a permanent reminder of the violent typhoon that struck Woody Island during a disastrous exercise last October.

The Navy had been conducting its largest amphibious landing exercise, transporting twelve of their jack-up barge systems from Yulin Naval Base to Woody Island. When a typhoon swept into the area before they could secure the landing barges, seven of the twelve had been lost. Three more had been severely damaged. In a single day, Mother Nature had dealt a crippling blow to the PLAN's amphibious landing capabilities, leaving the Navy scrambling to replace the lost barges and the crews that had manned them.

The new Shuiqiao barges, or "battle barges" as some called them, sat highlighted on Shen's display. "One hundred ten meters, one hundred thirty-five, one hundred eighty-five," Shen murmured, visualizing each barge variant's position and function. They would deploy sequentially—shallow to deep water—to form a temporary eight-hundred-meter pier for rapid offloading.

"Sequential deployment," he said quietly. "In theory, that's how it's supposed to work."

His secure phone buzzed. Admiral Deng Litian's caller ID flashed, a comforting yet stern reminder of the immense pressures at hand.

"Iron Wolf." Deng's voice resonated warmly despite the tension. "Reviewing the exercise parameters again, are we?"

"Yes, Admiral." Shen gazed out the window, watching civilian ferries, converted roll-on/roll-off ships, materializing from the rain like phantom vessels. "Considering the disaster from last October, we are attempting a highly ambitious recovery. We're compressing six months of training into three weeks."

Deng sighed. "Correction, Captain. The Central Military Commission has compressed six months of training into three weeks. They provide the timeline and mission. We execute it."

Lightning briefly illuminated the horizon, followed by rolling thunder. Shen watched deck crews hurriedly securing cargo on the ferries. While officially, the vehicles concealed beneath the tarps were "agricultural equipment," in reality, they were unmistakably armored vehicles.

"I reviewed the reports you sent. Intelligence suggests the Taiwanese have been substantially upgrading their defenses," Shen said carefully. "It seems the Americans are supplying autonomous underwater drones and surface vessels. I'm concerned this so-called Ghost Fleet concept could render our tactics and preparations obsolete."

A silence stretched uncomfortably between them. Shen wondered if he'd overstepped.

"Tao," Deng said finally, deliberately, "do you remember why we named you the Iron Wolf?"

Shen almost smiled at the memory from long ago. "I do. My first captain said I was too stubborn to quit, yet too smart to charge blindly into a fight."

"Exactly. Tomorrow's exercise at Yalong Bay isn't just about proving the new jack-up barges can deploy efficiently," Deng explained firmly. "It's about demonstrating that despite setbacks and adversaries' new toys, our human ingenuity and perseverance remain unmatched. Machines can malfunction and fail, Tao. Our resolve does not."

Commander Gong Jun approached, a weather report clutched tightly in his hands. Shen quickly concluded the call and turned toward his executive officer. "Give me the forecast, Commander."

"Sea State Three predicted during the exercise window, Captain," Gong replied, voice steady but eyes uncertain.

"Hmm, manageable," Shen acknowledged, exchanging a brief, uneasy glance with his XO. "But let's not forget what happened last October, Gong. Command thought that storm was manageable too."

Lieutenant Commander Zhu Mingzhe, Zunyi's operations officer, joined them. "Captain, the four Shuiqiao barge teams are reporting ready. All three variants operational. The maritime militia crews are ready, and the training officers are aboard and ready to assist."

Shen nodded solemnly. Six days to practice and implement the skills they'd been taught with their instructors on hand should be more than enough time. "Great, and our escort disposition—are they ready for their part in all of this?"

"Yes, sir," Zhu answered. "The *Zunyi* will lead and act as the command-and-control vessel for the landing force with *Nanjing*, *Wuxi*, and *Changsha* providing aerial cover for the task force. The four Shuiqiao barge teams will advance toward the beach, supported by twelve Type 054A frigates and two Type 901 supply ships. A squadron of J-11s and J-15 will provide air cover, while Z-8 and Z-20 helicopters land the initial assault force and Z-10s from Hainan provide close-air support. Everything is ready."

On paper, the exercise was impressive. But Shen felt a gnawing apprehension as he imagined unseen autonomous vessels lurking beneath the waves like silent predators. He sighed, recalling Admiral Deng's insistence. "The Southern Fleet Commander, Admiral Chen Weiming, has made our priorities clear. We are to get our Shuiqiao barge teams certified and ready to join the fleet and whatever operations we could be tasked with."

Zhu's tablet chimed with perfect timing. "Captain, speak of the devil. We just received the fleet command orders. Ferries begin loading at 0800. We begin escort operations to Yalong Bay by 1000 hours."

Through the rain-streaked windows, Shen watched more ferries arrive, hulls heavy with their disguised cargo. Each ferry could carry a mechanized battalion. The task force could rapidly deploy a significant amount of combat power to a hostile shore, assuming the Shuiqiao barges performed flawlessly.

"XO, gather department heads in the wardroom immediately," Shen instructed decisively. "I want to prepare the crews thoroughly on the kinds of autonomous threats we may encounter. Oh, and, Zhu—instruct every sonar operator to review the acoustic signatures of our Dragon Pearl unmanned underwater vehicles. I don't want our sonar operators getting them confused with the recently identified acoustic signatures of those American UUVs. If Americans are going to seed the waters around Taiwan with their drones, I want our people practiced at identifying them immediately."

"Yes, sir, Captain," Zhu promised, leaving to make it happen.

Once alone, Shen revisited the deployment plans and how these jack-up barges were supposed to work. The first of the three barges was the *Shuiqiao-110*, which had four deployable jack-up legs that would anchor the barge into the shallows near the coast, lifting the barge platform out of the water. Positioned at the front of the barge was a drawbridge-like structure that lowered a ramp several hundred meters long, onto a beach or the scrub just past it.

The second barge was the *Shuiqiao-135*, a slightly longer barge with six jack-up legs that lifted the barge to either float on the surface of the water or rise just above it. The third and final barge was the *Shuiqiao-185*. This was the largest of the barges, with eight jack-up legs that extended into deeper water, forming the pier's end for ferries and roll-on, roll-off ships to dock with and offload their vehicles. There were also several angled docking entrances for additional ferries to use. Once connected, the entire system of barges could extend between four hundred and four hundred and fifty meters in length, providing a mobile, improvised pier in contested waters.

Tomorrow, Shen's squadron would escort the vessels to the training grounds where they would deploy the Shuiqiao barges under simulated combat conditions. Their primary training objective was to count the number of vehicles they could unload per hour.

Smooth is fast; fast is life, Shen reflected. The more armored vehicles they could put ashore per hour, the higher the chances they could secure a beachhead before the enemy could push them into the sea.

Chapter Twelve:
The Weight of Duty

February 15, 2033
4-70th Armor Regiment
Fort Bliss
El Paso, Texas

The Silverado's Duramax diesel engine growled as SFC Ramon Torres pulled into his driveway. He sat for a moment, engine ticking as it cooled, staring at the basketball hoop mounted above the garage. The net hung limp in the windless El Paso evening.

How do I tell them? he wondered.

Through the living room window, he could see his wife, Maria, helping their daughter, Sophia, with homework at the dining table. The warm glow of home life before him was bittersweet as he became aware that he was about to shatter it.

He grabbed his patrol cap from the passenger seat and headed inside.

"Daddy!" Four-year-old Carlos launched himself from the couch, Spider-Man pajamas already on despite it being only six thirty.

Torres scooped him up, inhaling the scent of Johnson's baby shampoo. "Hey, *mi hijo*. You already ready for bed?"

"Mommy said if I put on PJs early, I could stay up for the Spurs game."

"Smart move." He set Carlos down, ruffling his hair. The boy scampered back to his Lego fortress on the carpet.

Maria looked up from Sophia's math worksheet, her smile faltering. Sixteen years of marriage had taught her to read his face like a tactical map. She must have seen the weight he carried as soon as he walked through the door.

"Sweetie, finish that problem. I need to talk to your dad." Her voice stayed steady, but Torres caught the tremor beneath.

"But, Mom, I don't get fractions," Sophia protested. Ramon couldn't help but smile to himself—his daughter was twelve, going on twenty-one.

"I'll help in a minute, *mi hija*." Maria stood, smoothing her nurse scrubs. She hadn't had a chance to change yet after her shift at Del Sol Medical Center.

They met in the kitchen. Maria pulled a pair of Dos Equis from the fridge, which was another tell. She only drank beer when she needed to brace herself.

"When?" she asked.

Simple. Direct, he thought. *That's Maria.*

"We got the warning order today. We deploy by month's end."

Her hand tightened on the bottle. "Europe?" she pressed.

"Poland," Ramon confirmed.

"It's the exercise—the one on the news, isn't it? With the Russians and Chinese?"

He nodded. Through the doorway, he watched Isabella, their eight-year-old, building a Lego creation with Carlos. Miguel, twelve and obsessed with Call of Duty, hadn't even looked up from his Xbox.

"It's just an exercise, right?" asked Maria. Her eyes betrayed that she knew better, even as the words left her lips. She'd been an Army wife too long.

"That's what they're calling it," Ramon replied. He took a long pull from his beer. "We're bringing the new robotic tanks, the Ripsaws. It will be their first operational deployment."

"Robots." She laughed, but it came out bitter. "They can send robots but still need to take you."

"Someone's gotta tell the robots what to shoot."

Silence stretched between them. From the living room came the crash of Lego blocks and Carlos's delighted shriek.

"How long?" she asked.

"Unknown. Could be ninety days. Could be…" He didn't finish.

Maria set her beer down and moved over to be close to him. Her head found that spot on his chest where it had always fit perfectly, even back in Riverside High School when he was just a linebacker with dreams bigger than Jacksonville, Florida.

"I watch the news, Ramon," she said. "This feels different."

"It is different," he answered as he put his arms around her. There was no point in lying. She'd see through it anyway.

"The kids—Miguel's tournament is next month," Maria said, holding back tears.

"I know." The weight of missing moments pressed down. "I know, baby."

She pulled back, hands framing his face. She looked at him with those same brown eyes that had watched him ship out to the Middle East and Europe. But they'd been younger then. Back then, they hadn't had a mortgage, or four kids with soccer practice and orthodontist appointments.

"You come back to us," said Maria. It wasn't a request. It was an unspoken order.

He smiled. "I always do."

Maria held his gaze for a second. "I'm serious, Ramon. You come back to us."

He kissed her forehead, breathing in deeply. Maria smelled like vanilla perfume mixed with hospital antiseptic. It was a familiar aroma that brought him comfort.

She sighed, then motioned with her head toward the family room. "Come on. Let's tell them together," she offered, leading him into the chaos of domestic bliss.

After a moment, Maria had gathered everyone in the living room. Ramon had done this before, but it never got easier. Miguel paused his game, which was a minor miracle. Sophia closed her math book. Isabella and Carlos continued building a tower between them on the carpet.

"Kids, Dad's got something to tell you." Maria's hand found his.

Ramon cleared his throat. "You know how sometimes Dad has to go away for Army stuff?"

"Are you deploying?" Sophia asked, too perceptive for twelve. "Is this like that time when you went to the Philippines a few years ago? Or when you went to Romania?"

"Yeah, *mi hija*. Except this time, they're sending me to Poland. Back to Europe."

"I know where Poland is," Miguel piped up. "It's next to Russia and Ukraine. Are you fighting Russians?" he asked.

"No fighting—no one is fighting anyone right now," Ramon tried to reassure them. "We're just going over to do some training, and making sure everyone stays friendly."

Carlos looked up from his blocks. "How long?" he pressed. The hardest questions always seemed to come from the smallest voices.

"A few months, buddy. I'll be back before you know it."

"But you'll miss my tournament." Miguel's voice cracked. He was caught in that stage between being a boy and a teenager.

"I know. I'll try to watch online if I can."

Isabella crawled into his lap. "Can you take Whiskers?" she asked, referring to her stuffed cat that she carried with her everywhere. It was worn threadbare from love. "So you won't be lonely?"

His throat tightened. "That's a great idea, princess."

"This is because of what's on the news, isn't it?" Sophia asked. Once again, she was too smart for anyone's good. "I heard on the news that the Chinese and Russians are doing something big in Europe, the Middle East, and Asia."

Maria intervened, saving him from answering. "Dad's job is to keep us safe, Sophia. Sometimes that means going places to make sure nothing bad happens."

"Like a superhero," Carlos announced. "Except with tanks—a tank superhero."

"Something like that, *mi hijo*."

They talked until bedtime. Sophia wanted to make sure that he packed his winter gear because it would be cold there. Carlos was confused about the time zones and was amazed that when it was bedtime at their house, Ramon would be eating breakfast. And Miguel wanted assurances of staying connected.

"We'll video chat every chance we get," Ramon promised.

Finally, Maria herded the younger ones upstairs. Sophia lingered, curled next to him on the couch.

"You're scared," Sophia said. It wasn't really a question, more of a statement.

Ramon considered lying but decided against it. "A little, I suppose. It seems tensions have been building for a while now. I don't know what it all means, but it's generally not a good thing when lots of military units from opposing sides are in such close proximity to each other."

"Yeah, Lisa's dad mentioned something like that the other day when he said her uncle was going to England for a few months. He's a fighter pilot in the Air Force," his daughter explained. "I think Mom's scared too. She only drinks beer when she's worried."

Ramon laughed softly. "Wow, you think your mom is that easy to read?" he teased.

His daughter shrugged. "I don't know about that. It's just about the only time I see her drink one of your beers."

"Huh, you're pretty good at noticing things, aren't you?" he asked.

"Well, someone has to when you're gone," she answered nonchalantly.

He smiled at her. "My little soldier. I like it. Hey…can you promise me something?"

She looked up at him, nodding slowly.

"Go easy on your mom, and your brother. I need you to step up, help take care of your mom and the littles till I get back, OK?"

She smiled. "I always do." She hugged him tight, kissed him on the cheek and headed upstairs, leaving him alone with the weight of leaving.

****

Later, in their bedroom, Maria lay against his chest. The house was quiet except for the hum of the air conditioner.

"Remember when you first deployed?" she whispered. "It was 2018. I was so scared, I threw up every morning for a week."

"You were pregnant with Miguel."

"That too." She traced circles on his chest. "But mostly scared. Now I'm just…" She searched for the word. "Tired, I guess. Tired of goodbyes. Tired of explaining to the kids why Daddy missed another Christmas, another birthday."

He winced at the comment. It stung, but he knew it was true. It was an unfortunate part of being a soldier. "I know. Maybe I should have gotten out six years ago when I hit the midway point, but now with sixteen years in…" He sighed. "Hell, the sergeant major says I should make master sergeant once they post the cutoffs. That bump in pay will be nice."

She sighed too. "Money doesn't do us any good if you're not here." She propped up on an elbow. "Ramon, we're not eighteen anymore. I see what's happening over there. This isn't like Afghanistan or Syria. This is—"

"Different. I know," he finished for her.

"Do you? Russia, China, this isn't like Afghanistan, Syria, or Iraq." But her anger deflated as quickly as it had come. "I'm sorry. I just—" Tears came then.

He held her while she cried for a moment, releasing the anxiety and fear she felt.

"Hey." He tilted her chin up. "Remember what you told me before my first deployment?"

"That if you died, I'd kill you?" she replied through a watery laugh.

"Ha-ha. No, not that. You said you'd be here. No matter what happened. That this"—he gestured to the space between them—"doesn't break."

"Sixteen years, four kids, five deployments." She wiped her eyes. "I'm still here."

"Me too," he answered, leaning in to kiss her.

They made love then, desperate and tender, knowing he would be gone soon. Afterward, she fell asleep curled into him, one hand fisted in his shirt like she could anchor him home.

Ramon lay awake, thinking of her, the sound of her breathing, the faint scent of her shampoo, and how lucky he was to have found his soulmate. Down the hall, he heard one of the kids cough. In the kitchen, the ice maker in the freezer churned out another batch of ice cubes into the tray. These were the ordinary sounds of home. The sounds and smells he'd carry with him to Poland, and whatever the future held.

On the nightstand, his phone buzzed. He reached for it and found an email from the battalion S3.

Equipment inspections at 0600. It was midnight, and his mind was racing.

Ramon thought about the Ripsaw systems arriving tomorrow. They were autonomous killing machines, but they still needed men to guide them. The irony wasn't lost on him. They could build robots to fight, but they couldn't build robots to say goodbye.

Maria stirred, murmuring something in her sleep. He pulled her closer.

Three more days. Three more breakfasts. Three more bedtime stories. Three more chances to bank memories against whatever comes next.

Outside, a siren wailed somewhere in El Paso. The world spun on, oblivious to one family's countdown to goodbye. Ramon closed his eyes and tried to sleep. Tomorrow would come soon enough. It always did.

Chapter Thirteen:
Blackjacks

February 19, 2033
Bravo Company "Blackjacks"
2nd Battalion, 503rd Infantry Regiment (Airborne)
Carpegna Training Area
Marche, Italy

A white-hot flash lit the tree canopy for a fraction of a second—like a camera strobe on full burn. A beat later, thunder rolled across the hills, low and steady. The first fat drops of rain fell, pattering against pine needles and striking Mercer's gear with soft, hollow taps.

The forest stank of churned loam, ozone, and cordite from the blank rounds fired in earlier drills. Wet bark. Sweat. Pine oil. The layered scent of training.

Captain Alex Mercer lay prone beneath a tangle of low-hanging branches, rain bleeding off the brim of his boonie hat. A thin flicker danced across the bottom of his visor as his AR-HUD recalibrated for low light. His view lit up in a pale green overlay—terrain lines, unit icons, and simulated hazard markers.

He didn't blink.

Ahead, the gravel road twisted through a natural cut in the ridge. First Platoon's kill zone. Everything about the approach screamed textbook, which made him more interested in what they couldn't see.

"They'll be in position any second now," murmured Sergeant First Class Victor "Vic" Santana beside him. The Bronx native spoke low, the mic on his chin strap picking up just enough to route to their fireteam net.

Vic flicked water off the laminated terrain sheet mounted to his forearm. His gloved hand hovered near a tablet—connected wirelessly to the TES-X training network, the Army's next-gen combat simulator that synced their weapons, sensors, and helmets into one real-time kill grid.

"Shame about the rain," he muttered.

Mercer's eyes didn't move. "If it ain't raining, we ain't training."

Vic grunted. "Yeah, well. I'd kill for one op where my ass stays dry."

The radio on the wet ground between them chirped.

"Valkyrie-7, Valkyrie-13. Movement on the road. I count six. Over."

Staff Sergeant Cole Travis. Calm as ever. His voice fed straight through Mercer's earpiece via the secure comms channel. The visor's heads-up display marked his transmission with a soft amber ping.

Vic keyed his response. "Valkyrie One-Three, Valkyrie One-Seven. Solid copy. Call when the tail clears the zone. Out."

Then he slid through the mud and pine needles toward First Lieutenant Reid Matthis, who crouched five meters back. Mercer didn't need to hear the whispered exchange.

This wasn't about control—it was about watching the plan collapse.

Mercer had briefed none of them on the full scenario. They thought this was a lane ambush. Simple. Predictable. But while First Platoon watched the road, Third and Fourth Platoons were already maneuvering, creeping up the high ground on their right and sloping low around their rear.

TES-X emitters mounted to rifles, haptic recoil modules, and infrared target sensors on their vests would all feed real-time telemetry back to his command tablet. This wasn't about who got lucky shots—it was about squad cohesion, comms discipline, and how fast they could adapt when things went sideways.

AR overlays would soon simulate the impact zones of artillery and drone strikes, force players to react to suppressive fire and partial casualties. The system would lock out weapons and "wound" soldiers with temporary loss of motion in affected limbs. Total immersion.

He didn't smile.

The test was already underway. They just didn't know it yet.

Mercer adjusted his visor, zooming in on the heat bloom of six bodies moving through the trees.

Let's see if Matthis figures it out in time.

****

The rain hadn't let up, and now it hissed off the tree canopy like oil on a skillet. Visibility dropped. Sound carried weird through the wet.

First Lieutenant Reid Matthis lay behind a moss-covered stump, visor pulled low as his HUD tracked First Squad from Second Platoon moving into the kill zone.

They were good. Disciplined. Their TES-X signals painted them in clean blue icons, spacing tight, heads on a swivel. Their rifles—sim-modified M7s—registered hot, ready to "fire" laser pulses synced with their recoil modules and blank adapters.

Everything was proceeding perfectly.

Which was what worried him.

He narrowed his eyes. "Where the hell are the other squads?"

Only six signals. First Squad, clearly. The rest of Second Platoon—Second, Third, and Weapons Squads—should be stacked along the southern ridge, blocking escape. But no movement. No pings. No sound.

"Vic," Matthis said, voice low. "Where's the rest of Spectre?"

Vic frowned. Glanced at his forearm tablet. Nothing.

Matthis's stomach twisted.

Something was off.

Vic tapped his mic. "All Spectre elements, report status."

Silence.

Then—

"Contact front!"

Gunfire erupted.

Crack-crack-crack—not real rounds, but the TES-X blank rifles thundering like they meant it. Lasers streaked through the air, visible only through the HUD as faint red trails. Half of First Squad lit up—vests chirping, visors flashing damage overlays.

"Oh crap—they see us!" someone shouted.

"Back up, back—!"

Matthis twisted to Vic. "It's a feint—Spectre's bait. We've been made!"

He keyed to Travis. "Reorient west! Collapse fire onto—"

Too late.

Third Platoon surged from the underbrush—Reapers, full force, rifles glowing with laser strobes as they stormed up the flank.

Matthis's squads scattered.

Simulated fire lit the ridge. Digital overlays mapped out where suppression fire was hitting. One AR indicator showed a virtual grenade go off in their rear element—two blue icons blinked red, disabled by system rules.

"Smoke! Now!" Matthis barked.

Vic yanked the pin on a 2033 smoke canister—thermal and IR-dampening, designed for both cover and AR masking—and lobbed it toward the right slope.

Pop-hissss.

A thick fog bloomed, churning like ghost vapor as rain pushed it sideways.

"Reaper elements closing from the south!" someone shouted.

Matthis spun. "Fourth Platoon—damn, they're pinching us!"

Red icons flooded the HUD. Gravediggers. They were coming hard, simulating mortar splash with visual overlays that forced his men into scatter movement. Their AI was working perfectly—smart fire arcs forced breaks in Matthis's cohesion.

He didn't hesitate.

"Fall back! Move! Use the smoke—bound back to Delta!"

They moved—some tagged "wounded," limping as motion feedback slowed their lower limbs, others "dead," visors blacked out, watching helplessly from the ground.

Matthis stayed behind, herding the rest, rifle at the ready.

His test wasn't whether he could win.

It was whether he could lead in the chaos.

And Mercer was watching.

****

Bravo Company Tactical Operations Center
Carpegna Training Area
Marche, Italy

The scent of wet canvas, hot plastic from field servers, and burned cordite clung to the TOC like smoke in a barbershop. The rain hadn't let up. It beat against the roof in steady rhythms—background noise for the after-action debrief.

Lieutenant Colonel Patrick Brenner stood with arms crossed, an unreadable expression on his face. Combat fatigues soaked around the cuffs, boots caked in Italian mud. His eyes tracked Mercer first, then shifted to First Lieutenant Matthis, who stood at parade rest, helmet under his arm, uniform streaked with grime and sweat.

"You trained him well, Captain," Brenner said without preamble. "Held it together when the op flipped. Got his people out. That's what I like to see."

Matthis opened his mouth to speak, then hesitated. He cleared his throat. "Respectfully, sir, it was Vic—Sergeant Santana—and the squad leaders are the ones who ran the platoon out of that meat grinder. I just held the leash."

Mercer gave a faint smirk behind him, arms folded. Brenner chuckled, eyes never leaving Matthis.

"Good answer. You taught him well," he said, glancing over at Mercer. "He already knows it's the NCOs who run the platoon, not the officers."

Mercer met the battalion commander's gaze. Held it for a beat. "He'll make us proud, sir."

Brenner nodded once. That was all it took.

The room fell into silence for a moment. Then Brenner's jaw flexed. He dropped his hands to his hips, a shift in weight punctuating what was coming next.

"I just got a warning order." His voice dropped a register. "Division's flagging our battalion for forward posture in the Baltics. Could be tied to a big exercise spinning up around the first of May."

Mercer's eyes narrowed. Matthis shifted his grip on his helmet but didn't speak.

"Nothing's official yet," Brenner continued. "But if this goes the way it smells, we're wheels-up with a reinforced task force. Could be Poland. Could be Gotland."

Silence returned, heavier this time.

"I'll put you in for that Ranger School slot," Brenner added, looking at Matthis. "But if this deployment drops, I can't guarantee it sticks. You might lose the date."

Matthis gave a single nod. "Understood, sir."

"I'll fight to hold it or get you a new slot down the line if it gets scrubbed. Your packet's strong. You've earned it."

"Thank you, sir."

Brenner nodded again. No salutes, no more words. He stepped back out into the rain, alone.

Mercer looked at Matthis, then turned back to his field monitors. Outside, the storm deepened.

The next war wasn't coming. It was already moving. He could feel it in his bones.

****

February 21, 2033
173rd Airborne Brigade Combat Team
Caserma Del Din Vicenza, Italy

The room was cold, the lights dimmed to half, and the soft hum of the HVAC filled the silence between spoken words. Rows of officers in MultiCam uniforms filled the seats—company commanders, battalion staff, and brigade planners. Most had flown back from field training less than thirty-six hours ago. Tired and exhausted.

Brigadier General Carter Ashford stood at the front, flanked by a pair of intel officers from the S2 and a large operations display screen dividing the world into three theaters—Eastern Europe, the Russian Far East, and the North Pacific.

"This isn't routine," Ashford began, voice clipped, his West Point cadence sharpened with combat-seasoned restraint. "What you're about to see is classified, SECRET-NOFORN. No one is to discuss this with anyone outside of this room."

The screen shifted—zooming in to reveal the Leningrad Military District, a broad swath of northwestern Russia encompassing Saint Petersburg, Murmansk, and the surrounding Leningrad and Arkhangelsk Oblasts, stretching from the Barents Sea in the north to the Gulf of Finland in the west. Its reach hugged the Finnish border for over a thousand kilometers, ran along Lake Ladoga, and extended south along the borders of Estonia, Latvia, and Lithuania. Major transport corridors from Vologda and Moscow funneled directly into the district's staging areas—now glowing red on the screen.

To the southwest, a smaller but highly sensitive zone lit up: Kaliningrad Oblast—a Russian exclave wedged between Lithuania and Poland, completely landlocked from Russia proper. "There's no overland access to Kaliningrad," Ashford noted. "Only way in is by sea or air. I'm going to hand things over to the S2 to bring us up to speed on the bigger picture of what's going on and what this 'exercise'"—he added air quotes—"actually looks like."

He stepped back.

Major Grace Elliott, the brigade S2, stepped forward. Her voice was calm, clipped. "Bottom line up front: this isn't just a training event. The scale and logistics footprint suggest it's meant to prove they can surge fast—and sustain it."

She tapped a control. The display zoomed on Kaliningrad's coastal ports.

"Over the last ten days, we've seen a sharp increase in sealift traffic inbound to Kaliningrad, especially into Baltiysk and Kaliningrad Port. Cargo manifests are either sealed or falsified, but imagery shows military containers, vehicle crates, and radar assemblies being offloaded under security."

A new frame snapped up—satellite stills of freshly cleared terrain, dirt berms, and defensive batteries under camo netting.

"They're also building out new air-defense positions—likely short- and medium-range systems. Possibly Pantsir-S1 and S-400 being repositioned around key airfields. There's movement at every known site."

Elliott shifted the slide again—this time to a broader theater map showing European Russia.

"Same pattern north of Kaliningrad, across the Leningrad Military District. We've picked up increased activity at major airfields from Pushkin to Olenya—more sorties, more ground crew, more aircraft moving. On the surface, it's a readiness drill. But it's a big one."

She paused. A final overlay filled the screen—a simplified representation of Russian and Chinese rail lines stretching from the Far East across the continent.

"We're also watching a significant spike in Chinese rail and road traffic coming out of Xinjiang and Inner Mongolia, feeding west into central Russia. Large convoys—armor, fuelers, containerized equipment—headed toward staging areas in Moscow and Leningrad Districts. This has been building for about two months."

She looked out across the room.

"No way to know how long it took to prep that much equipment—but it didn't happen overnight."

She nodded once, then stepped back.

Ashford returned to the front, his tone flattened. "None of this changes our immediate orders—but you need to understand the environment we're stepping into. This isn't just Baltic theater noise anymore. It's a full-spectrum, multifront show of force. NATO wants presence. Visibility. We're part of that line. We're not here to provoke. But we will be seen."

Ashford turned to his S3, Lieutenant Colonel Tony "T. Z." Zitrion, motioning for him to speak on the deployment orders the brigade just received. As he walked forward, the map behind them zoomed in again—Poland, Lithuania, Latvia, Estonia. Icons bloomed blue and amber as NATO units repositioned eastward. Sweden and Finland glowed green along the upper edge of the display.

"This is where we come into the picture," T. Z. explained, his tone sharp, his piercing. "Washington, Tokyo, Seoul, and Brussels are spooked with the scale and scope of this exercise. SHAPE, and our Asian allies, are right to be suspicious after what happened in Ukraine in '22. No one wants to be caught unprepared, so as a precaution, EUCOM, in coordination with our NATO allies, is going to temporarily reinforce the border regions where they plan to conduct their exercises.

"In short, NATO wants to establish an anti-access, area-denial capability over the Baltic Sea that can extend to include Kaliningrad and the northeastern NATO border. The land component of this JTF will consist of the US 173rd and the US forces that'll comprise the A2/D2 element that'll deploy to Gotland and Sweden proper—more on those units later. The rest of the JTF will consist of Swedish and Finnish local ground, air, and naval forces. Additional NATO naval assets will come in the form of German and Danish corvettes to augment the local Swedish and Finnish naval forces. Outside of local air assets, NATO will provide an air element from a Dutch F-35 squadron, and US AWACS support from England," T. Z. explained as he stepped back to let Ashford close the briefing out.

"Look, I don't have a crystal ball to tell you if this is just a training exercise and show of force by this new Pan-Eurasian Alliance or the prelude to some massive war that's about to start." Ashford paused to look his battalion commanders in the eye. "What I can tell you is this. Regardless of what happens, this is a great opportunity for us to do some hard-core training, and that's how I intend to look at this until it materializes into something more. For now, prepare yourselves and get your commands ready to deploy. The first units are rotating north on the first of April. We're to be in position and ready by the fifteenth. A lot has to happen between now and the end of March. Let's show Big Army and everyone else why we're the best. Dismissed."

Chapter Fourteen:
Steel Across the Atlantic

March 2, 2033 – 0630 Hours Local Time
Port of Gdańsk, Poland

Salt wind cut through SFC Ramon Torres's OCP combat blouse, the fabric stiff with sea salt and cold as he stood on the dock, watching the morning sun paint the Baltic a gunmetal gray. The USNS *Watkins* loomed above him, her cargo cranes swinging M1E3 Abrams tanks from her hold like toys.

"Sixteen years in, and it still makes me nervous watching them dangle my tank over water," SFC Ramon Torres said to himself. He didn't take his eyes off Alpha-22 as it swayed above the dock.

First Lieutenant Adam Novak appeared beside him, his collar pulled high on his combat shell jacket, shoulders hunched against the wind. "Three years in, and I'm just trying not to throw up watching it."

Torres grunted agreement, eyes locked on Alpha-22 as it swayed thirty feet above the concrete. That was his tank, his crew, his responsibility.

"Least they made it." The LT's breath hung in the frigid air like smoke. "When I heard they were routing through Hamburg first, I figured we'd be here till April."

"Hamburg's backed up with commercial traffic. Gdańsk gave us priority." Torres thumbed on his tablet, scrolling through the manifest on its cracked screen. "All four tanks are accounted for. Ripsaws are coming off the *Fisher* in about an hour."

The port bustled with controlled chaos. Polish longshoremen worked alongside US Navy cargo specialists, their shouts a mix of English, Polish, and the universal language of arm-waving. A platoon of Polish land forces patrolled the perimeter, MSBS Grot rifles cradled casually but ready.

"You sleep on the flight?" Novak asked.

"Some." It had been twelve hours from Fort Bliss to Ramstein, another fourteen by bus to Gdańsk. His body still thought it was midnight in Texas.

"How'd Maria take it?"

Torres watched Alpha-22 touch down, chains rattling as dockers rushed to secure it. "Like she always does. Strong in front of the kids, fell apart after."

"Sixteen years, four deployments—"

"Five," Torres corrected. "Syria counted, even if it was just six months."

"Right." Novak shifted, uncomfortable with the personal talk. Torres thought Novak was a good kid, but even as a West Point graduate, he was still learning that leading meant knowing your NCOs as people, not just soldiers.

A Polish major approached, his English crisp despite the accent. "Sergeant Torres? Major Kowalski, 11th Armored Cavalry Division. I'm your liaison for the transit to Drawsko."

Torres saluted. "Sir. This is Lieutenant Novak, our platoon leader."

Kowalski returned the salute, then extended his hand. "Welcome to Poland, gentlemen. Your reputation precedes you—1st Armor's finest, yes?"

"We try, sir." Novak shook hands, finding his command voice.

"Your route is secured. We'll move in convoy—Polish lead and trail elements, your vehicles in the center. The roads are clear, but…" Kowalski paused. "There have been incidents. Russian sympathizers, mostly graffiti and protests. Nothing serious."

Yet, Torres thought but didn't say.

"Distance to Drawsko?" Novak pulled out his own tablet, probably triple-checking the route Torres had already memorized.

"Three hundred twenty kilometers. Five hours with rest stops. Your soldiers are already boarding buses, correct?"

"Yes, sir. They left Ramstein an hour ago."

Torres's phone buzzed. It was a text from Sergeant Burke: "Alpha-22 secured. Starting inspection."

"Excuse me, sirs. I need to check on my crew."

Torres jogged across the dock, dodging forklifts and cargo nets. The Abrams sat massive and patient, condensation already forming on its composite armor. Burke stood on the front slope, running through his checks.

"How's she look, Nate?"

"Intact. Some surface rust on the track pins, but nothing major." Nathan Burke, a Nebraska farm boy turned tanker, knew machinery like some men knew women. "Munoz is checking the bustle rack. Boone's underneath, inspecting the running gear."

"Good." Torres circled the tank, eyes cataloging every bolt and weld. He'd learned to spot trouble before it spotted him. A loose track pin in Romania had nearly cost him his first tank.

"Sergeant Torres!" PFC Munoz appeared from behind the turret. "Permission to ask a question?"

"Ask away."

Munoz hesitated. "My girl, she says the protests in Warsaw got pretty heated last week. Anti-NATO stuff. Do you think we're gonna have any problems while we are here?"

Torres considered his answer. Munoz was twenty, from Jacksonville just like him and Maria. He had steady hands on the loader's controls, but this was his first real deployment.

"Poland invited us, Munoz. Most folks here remember what Russian occupation looks like. A few protesters don't speak for the whole country."

Munoz nodded. "Roger, Sergeant. That's good to know."

As Munoz returned to work, Torres knew he hadn't been completely honest with him. He'd listened to the intelligence briefs the S2 had given prior to them leaving Bliss. Pro-Russian and -Chinese information operations were running at full speed across Poland and most of Europe—especially after that incident off the coast of Gotland. The discovery of Chinese naval officers conducting espionage activities from a commercial vessel had really shaken things up in Europe. In addition to regular sabotage against undersea cables in the Baltic Sea, Asia, and the Caribbean, small acts of sabotage were starting to appear at rail junctions and port facilities across major logistic nodes in Europe and even back home. It felt like the world was slowly shifting beneath their feet and they didn't even know it.

"Hey, Sarge." Boone emerged from beneath the hull, coveralls already filthy. "Trans is good, but we're down about two quarts of hydraulic fluid. Looks like normal seepage, but still, there has to be a way to keep it from leaking like that."

Torres shrugged. He knew how to do regular maintenance on his tank, but he was far from a grease monkey who might know how to solve a problem like that. "Ugh," he commented. "OK, Boone. Get it topped off before we roll. Burke, you and Munoz check the ammo storage. I want every round secured."

Torres headed back to where Novak now stood with Major Kowalski and a Polish captain by the name of Piotr Sikoa studying a tablet map.

"—avoid the A1 through Toruń," Captain Sikora was saying. "There's construction delays, plus it takes us too close to Kaliningrad."

"How close?" Novak asked.

"Hundred fifty kilometers at the nearest point." Kowalski's expression darkened. "Close enough for those Russian Helios ISR drones or even those new Chinese Winged Dragon high-altitude surveillance drones. We've been spotting more of these drones edging Polish airspace as they monitor our ports and the rail and road networks entering from Germany. For an exercise, they sure are conducting a lot of surveillance across much of our country."

For a moment, no one spoke as the words hung in the salty air. The Russians had always maintained a presence in their Kaliningrad enclave, but the recent arrival of some Chinese units was beginning to cause alarm in Poland and even Germany that this so-called exercise might become something more. The Kaliningrad pocket was strange—a piece of Russia wedged between Poland and Lithuania. The so-called Suwałki Gap was the only thing separating Russia from its proxy Belarus.

"Geez, are these drones armed?" asked Novak.

Kowalski shrugged, his smile not reaching his eyes. "Who knows these days. When they first announced this new military and trade pact, I genuinely thought we might begin to see a period of normalcy with Russia. You know, neighboring countries trading with each other and perhaps moving beyond our past. Now? Who knows what Moscow and Beijing think anymore."

A horn blast drew their attention. The USNS *Fisher* was maneuvering into the adjacent berth, her deck stacked with shipping containers. Inside those boxes were four M5 Ripsaw autonomous combat vehicles, the platoon's new silicon-brained partners.

"Ah!" Kowalski brightened. "Your robots arrive. We are very curious about these systems."

"You and me both, sir." Torres had done the training at Fort Bliss, but three weeks wasn't enough to trust his life to a machine.

Novak's phone buzzed. He frowned at the screen.

"Problem, LT?" Torres asked.

"Text from Captain Morrison. Third Platoon had an issue clearing German customs. Some paperwork glitch with their Ripsaw's AI classification."

"They get it sorted?" Torres pressed.

"Yeah, but they're twelve hours behind now." Novak pocketed the phone. "We might be running our validation exercises shorthanded."

Torres shrugged. In sixteen years, he'd learned that plans were just suggestions. "We'll adapt."

The next two hours blurred. Tanks were offloaded, inspected, and fueled. The Ripsaws emerged from their containers like lethal insects—low, angular, bristling with sensors and weapons. Each one cost more than most Americans made in a lifetime.

Torres watched the civilian technicians fuss over Ripsaw Two-One, his platoon's assigned unit. The thing looked wrong somehow. Tanks had personalities, quirks you learned like a spouse's moods. The Ripsaw just sat there, cameras swiveling with mechanical precision.

"Creepy, right?" Staff Sergeant Granger appeared beside him, coffee steaming in the cold. "It's like it's thinking."

"It *is* thinking," Torres insisted. "That's the point."

"Yeah, but thinking *what*?" asked Granger. He was eight years in and steady as bedrock; he didn't rattle easy. But the Ripsaw had them all on edge.

"Right now? It's probably calculating firing solutions on those seagulls," Torres teased.

Granger laughed, breaking the tension. "As long as it doesn't mistake *us* for seagulls."

By 0900, the Polish HET crews had arrived. Torres watched the first M1300 Heavy Equipment Transporter back up to Alpha-21, its hydraulic ramps lowering with a mechanical whine.

"Easy with my baby!" Torres called out as Polish operators guided his tank onto the flatbed.

Torres's counterpart was right to be nervous. Loading seventy tons of tank onto a transporter required millimeter precision. One wrong move and you'd throw a track or worse.

"Your men seem competent," Novak observed, watching the Polish crew work.

Major Kowalski nodded with pride. "They move our Leopards and K2 Black Panthers regularly. American tanks are heavier, but the principle is the same."

Alpha-22's turn came next. Torres climbed up beside the Polish loadmaster, a grizzled sergeant who looked like he'd been doing this since the Cold War.

"Beautiful machine," the Pole said in accented English, patting the Abrams's armor. "Much heavier than our tanks."

"She'll ride steady?"

"Of course. We secure with twelve-point tie-downs. Could drive upside-down and she wouldn't budge." He grinned, gold tooth catching the morning sun.

Torres watched Burke guide Boone up the ramps, tracks clanking on steel. The tank settled onto the flatbed with a satisfied groan of hydraulics.

"Perfect," the loadmaster declared. "Now we chain her down."

The process was repeated for each tank. By 1030, all four Abrams sat secured on their transporters. The Ripsaws, lighter and more compact, loaded faster onto smaller flatbeds.

"Convoy brief in five," Kowalski announced.

They gathered near the lead Polish escort vehicle, a Rosomak APC bristling with antennas. Captain Sikora spread a laminated map on the hood of a vehicle.

"Gentlemen, our route." Sikora traced the highways with a laser pointer. "A1 to Grudzi, then S6 north to Słupsk, finally S11 to Drawsko. Total distance three hundred twenty kilometers."

"Anticipated threats?" Novak asked.

"Minimal. Some anti-NATO graffiti reported near Tczew. Possible protesters at the Słupsk interchange. Local police will clear them before we arrive."

"How about speed? What are we allowed to travel?" asked Novak nervously.

Captain Sikora calmly replied. "Sixty kilometers per hour maximum. EU road regulations. The transporters are heavy—we don't want to damage civilian infrastructure."

Torres calculated. Five hours minimum, plus stops. They'd reach Drawsko well after dark.

"Rest stops every ninety minutes," Sikora continued. "Designated truck stops only. Your soldiers remain with vehicles at all times."

"What about security during transport and at the rest stops?" Torres asked before Novak could.

Sikora seemed unfazed by their questions as he continued to calmly respond to them. "Two Rosomaks front, two rear. Police coordination at major intersections. Polish Police have a SWAT team on standby, though we expect no issues."

Famous last words, Torres thought.

"Questions? No? Then mount up. We depart in twenty minutes." Sikora wrapped up the briefing as he gathered up his map and notebook.

Torres found Burke prepping their escort JLTV. They'd ride separately from the tanks, standard procedure for road moves.

"You good to drive first shift?" Torres asked.

"Roger. Munoz wants to ride turret."

"Negative," Torres replied. "Too visible. We're guests here, not occupiers. Windows up, weapons concealed."

Burke nodded. "Munoz won't like it."

"Munoz will survive. Make sure everyone has water and snacks. Long ride ahead."

Torres's phone vibrated. It was a text message from Maria: "Kids off to school. Sophia made honor roll!"

He smiled, then typed back: "Tell her I'm proud. Miss you all."

"Miss you too. Stay safe over there."

He pocketed the phone without responding. Safe was relative when you were moving seventy-ton tanks across a continent balanced on a knife's edge.

"Sergeant Torres!" Kowalski waved from his command vehicle. "Ride with me for the first leg? I'd like to discuss integration procedures."

Torres looked at Novak, who nodded. "Go ahead, Sergeant. I'll keep an eye on things here."

The Polish major's vehicle was surprisingly comfortable—cushioned seats, climate control, even cup holders. It was the lap of luxury compared to American trucks.

"Coffee?" asked Kowalski, offering a thermos as they pulled onto the highway.

"Thanks." Torres accepted gratefully. It was proper coffee, not the motor oil Americans usually brewed.

Behind them, the convoy stretched half a kilometer. There were four tank transporters, four Ripsaw carriers, escort vehicles, and support trucks. They were a steel serpent winding through Poland.

"Your first time moving through Poland?" Kowalski asked.

"Did a rotation here in 2018," Torres replied. "Just training then."

"Ah, simpler times." The major navigated through Gdańsk's industrial district. "Now we have Russian troops in Belarus, Chinese advisors in Kaliningrad, and everyone pretending this is normal."

"You think it kicks off?" Torres pressed.

Kowalski considered. "My grandfather fought the Nazis. My father prepared to fight the Soviets. I hoped my son would know peace." He shrugged. "History has other plans."

They passed graffiti on a warehouse wall. "NATO GO HOME" was lettered in red spray paint. It was fresh, by the look of it.

"Ignore that," Kowalski said quickly. "Russian propaganda. Most Poles remember what occupation means."

But Torres noticed the major's knuckles whiten on the steering wheel.

The highway opened up, with the Baltic coastline visible to their right. The convoy maintained perfect spacing, with Polish efficiency on display. Torres found himself relaxing slightly.

His phone buzzed. It was a text from Burke: "All good back here. Munoz sulking about the turret."

"Tell him I'll buy him a pierogi in Drawsko," Torres replied.

They made their first stop at a truck stop near Tczew. Torres supervised the tie-down checks while Polish military police kept curious civilians at a distance. A few truckers took photos, but there were no incidents.

"Smooth so far," Novak commented, stretching his legs.

"Long way to go yet, LT," Torres replied.

Back on the road, Kowalski grew more talkative. He talked about his son, who had served in the Polish Army's 16th Mechanized Division. His wife apparently taught school in Warsaw. Normal life continued, despite the gathering storm.

"You have children?" the major asked.

"Four. Oldest is fourteen, youngest is six," Torres answered.

"Difficult, being away," said Kowalski.

"Part of the job," said Torres, even though his heart felt a familiar ache. Miguel's tournament was in three days. Sophia was working on her quinceañera planning. Life moved on without him.

They passed through Słupsk without incident, the promised protesters nowhere in sight. Either Polish intelligence was wrong, or local police had been very efficient.

"Two hours to Drawsko," Kowalski announced as they turned onto S11.

The landscape changed, and coastal plains gave way to forests and lakes. The sun dropped toward the horizon, painting everything gold.

Beautiful country, Torres admitted to himself. *Worth defending.*

His phone rang. It was Captain Morrison.

"Torres, you tracking our position?"

"Yes, sir. ETA 1900 hours."

"Good. Ripsaw briefing pushed to 2100. Division commander wants to address everyone first. Mandatory formation at 2000."

"Roger, sir. Any word on Third Platoon?" asked Torres.

"Delayed again," Morrison explained. "German rail workers threatened a strike. They're trying to route through Czech Republic."

More complications. Torres wondered if the delays were coincidence or something deliberate.

"Oh, and, Sergeant?" Morrison's tone shifted. "Good work in Gdańsk. Major Kowalski sent positive feedback about your professionalism."

"Just doing my job, sir."

"Keep it up. Morrison out."

Kowalski smiled. "I may have mentioned your excellence to my liaison."

"Appreciated, Major."

"Professional courtesy. Your country sends its best to help defend ours. The least we can do is acknowledge it."

They crested a hill, and Drawsko Pomorskie sprawled before them. The training area's lights twinkled in the gathering dusk.

Almost there.

"Final stop," Kowalski announced over the convoy net. "Fuel and tie-down check before we enter the training area."

The truck stop was military-controlled, and Polish MPs were already in position. The convoy pulled in with practiced precision.

Torres dismounted, his legs stiff from sitting. He walked the line of transporters, checking each tank. Alpha-22 sat patient and massive, waiting to be unleashed.

"How're we looking, Burke?" asked Torres.

"Solid, Sergeant. No issues. The boys are ready to get these beasts off the trucks."

"Soon enough," Torres replied with a smile. "We'll offload at first light. Tonight's about getting settled."

He checked his watch: 1830. Thirty minutes to Drawsko, then it would be a scramble to prepare for the division commander's brief.

"Mount up!" Kowalski called. "Final push!"

The convoy rolled through Drawsko's main gate as darkness fell. Security was tight—Polish and American MPs checked credentials, swept mirrors beneath vehicles, and utilized dogs to sniff for explosives.

"Welcome to Fort Trump," someone muttered over the radio, using the unofficial nickname for the expanded American presence.

They followed guides to the armor assembly area. Even in darkness, Torres could see the buildup. Rows of vehicles and stacks of equipment were the infrastructure of deterrence.

"Tomorrow, we offload," Kowalski said as they parked. "Tonight, we rest. Your barracks are in Area 7, Building 42."

Torres shook the major's hand. "Thanks for the smooth ride."

"My pleasure. We'll work well together, I think."

Torres gathered his platoon as they dismounted. He saw tired faces, but they were still alert.

Good soldiers, he thought with pride.

"Outstanding movement, men. Grab your gear, find your bunks. Formation at 1950 in the company area. Look sharp—division commander's watching."

They dispersed into the night. Torres lingered, looking at the tanks on their transporters. Tomorrow they'd roll off, ready to train...and ready to fight, if necessary.

His phone buzzed. It was Maria again. "Kids in bed. Carlos asked if tanks have beds too. I told him tanks sleep standing up."

Tores smiled and typed, "Smart kid. Tanks do sleep standing up. Give them all a kiss from me."

"Already did. Love you."

"Love you too."

He pocketed the phone and headed for the barracks. Whatever the division commander had to say, whatever was building in the east, would wait until tomorrow.

Tonight, he had soldiers to take care of. The rest was above his pay grade.

But as he walked through the Polish night, past tanks and robots and the machinery of modern war, Torres couldn't shake the feeling that pay grades wouldn't matter much longer.

Something was coming. They all felt it.

The question was when.

Chapter Fifteen:
Enemy Within

March 3, 2033 – 20:41 Hours
Lotus Pond, Parking Deck Level 4
Kaohsiung, Taiwan

The rooftop lot was empty, except for a single Toyota sedan with a black duffel in the trunk and a view of the city lights below. Cuī Zemin stood with his back to the rail, face half lit by the orange glow from a flickering lamp overhead. As always, he was still…watchful. The wind tugged at his long coat.

"You're looking well," he said, eyes scanning Hao Lei's face.

Hao nodded stiffly. "They kept me seventy-two hours. No formal charges. Just questions."

"No bruises," Cuī observed.

"Not on the outside."

Gao Rong stepped forward, shifting his weight. "We heard your diplomatic channels worked fast."

Cuī didn't confirm or deny it. "The arrests were unfortunate. But instructive. Taipei blinked. International media turned your footage into a feature. Hong Kong diaspora pages picked it up. BBC called it a 'soft uprising.'"

He pulled a folder from inside his coat and laid it on the car's hood. "Time to scale the model," he said.

Gao flipped it open. Inside were maps—National Taiwan University, Kaohsiung Medical University, Tamkang, Shih Hsin. Target-rich environments, annotated with red markings for entry points, dormitory zones, and student union buildings.

"The youth are already restless," Cuī stated. "Your job is to give them a purpose."

Hao raised an eyebrow. "Taipei and Kaohsiung are different beasts. You don't flip a capital city with slogans and live streams."

Cuī looked at him. "We're not flipping cities. We're lighting brushfires. Unrest doesn't have to win. It just has to exhaust."

He tapped the folder. "You'll focus on the universities. Use the Kinmen footage. Push it through underground forums and diasporic networks. Emphasize betrayal, division. Frame it as 'Kinmen was just the start.'"

"There's already chatter," Gao interjected, voice low. "After Kinmen, a few campus chapters of that old Reunification Society tried organizing. The turnouts were small. They got no traction."

"Then seed new leaders," Cuī said simply. "You've done it before. Use local faces, sympathetic faculty, dorm reps with activist streaks...anyone who wants to be seen as the next voice of the movement."

He opened his palm and revealed a small slip of paper—six digits, two letters. "These are Telegram wallet codes. Consider these 'emergency funds.' Track expenditures. Remember, bribes are crude—credibility is better."

Then Cuī's tone shifted. "You'll also expand your media front. Push content from the West. Show how American campuses are 'awakening' to the injustice."

Gao frowned. "You mean the Berkeley protests?"

Cuī nodded. "UC Berkeley and San Diego. Small groups. Mostly international students—some ours, some not. But the optics are valuable. Showing American youth echoing Chinese grievances adds legitimacy."

Hao scoffed. "They're waving signs about colonial overreach and Asian identity. None of them could find Kinmen on a map."

Cuī didn't smile. "They don't need to," he countered. "They just need to be loud."

The Ghost stepped closer to the car, lowering his voice further. "America has its own house fire. Your job is to connect the embers. When someone in Taipei sees a protest in Kaohsiung, then a crowd at UCSD, then a live stream from Berkeley—they start to believe there's a movement. They see Taiwan as out of sync. They think something bigger is coming."

Gao folded the folder shut. "And when do we pull back?" he asked.

"You don't," Cuī replied flatly. "While you're at it, I want you to make sure you're incorporating anger at this new synthetic drug, 'Vortex.' Make sure to gin up as much outrage as possible about its import from the West. 'Taiwan isn't protecting us' should be a common theme."

"We can do that," Gao agreed.

He dropped a new burner phone beside the envelope. "Next check-in is March fourteenth. Use the same Signal channel. If you're compromised, burn everything. Do not engage Taipei's National Security Bureau. They're watching the foreigners now."

Hao looked up, eyes narrowing. "We're not foreigners."

Cuī held his gaze. "No. But some of your neighbors are."

He turned without another word and disappeared down the stairwell. He offered no farewell.

All that was left was the hum of Kaohsiung's lights, and a quiet sense that the matchbox had been opened once again.

Chapter Sixteen:
The Matrix of Survival

March 12, 2033
Presidential Retreat
Yangmingshan National Park
Taipei City, Taiwan

President Ma Ching-te stood at the window, watching the mountain mist cling to ancient pines like ghosts refusing to let go. There was something calming about how the foggy mist drifted across the volcanic peaks, obscuring the four armored SUVs as they wound up the narrow access road to his private weekend retreat. It was that time of year when the spring rains were a daily affair, leaving everything gleaming.

Waiting behind President Ma Ching-te in silence were four of Taiwan's most powerful defenders, summoned personally to attend this secretive meeting—a meeting that would decide the fate of their nation. Chief among them was Defense Minister Theresa Kao, a former flight pilot. As usual, she sat ramrod straight, waiting for their guests to arrive and the meeting to begin. Sitting next to her was his NSB Director Chao Ming-hsien, the head of his intelligence agency, scrolling through encrypted feeds on a hardened tablet, occasionally muttering darkly about mainland SIGINT reports. The PRC's Ministry of State Security had been causing all sorts of problems for them on the islands of Kinmen and Matsu; the noose of the mainland constantly tightened around them. Standing hunched over, Admiral Han Ji-cheng, his naval chief, was studying nautical charts spread across the lacquered table while they waited, making pencil marks with surgical precision. Last but by no means least was Lieutenant General Wu Jian-tai, Commandant of the ROC Marine Corps. He stood near the wall-mounted display, his arms crossed, studying coastal defense overlays with the intensity of a man who'd spent his life preparing to repel the PRC's version of D-Day, the eventual invasion of Taiwan.

"They're almost here. They're through the final checkpoint," Chao announced without looking up. "ETA two minutes."

President Ma turned from the window. The weight of twenty-one million lives pressed against his shoulders, a familiar burden that had aged him a decade in five years. "So, what are your opinions on the men we're about to meet?"

"Solid. They've delivered on their promises so far," Kao said evenly. "One hundred and twenty contractors embedded with our forces for the past eighteen months. The training quality offered has far exceeded our expectations."

"True, but training isn't fighting," Admiral Han countered, not unkindly. "When missiles fly, mercenaries sometimes remember their bank accounts."

Lieutenant General Wu's jaw tightened. "These aren't Wagner types, Admiral. These are vetted, highly trained operators. Many of them have decades of experience in the Middle East, Europe, and Africa. They also have personal stakes in seeing the mainland defeated."

"Perhaps, but personal stakes don't stop waves of hypersonic missiles and drones, do they?" Han replied coldly.

A knock interrupted their discussion. Ma's security chief entered and nodded once. The Americans had arrived.

Marcus Harrington entered first—he was tall, six feet four inches. His weathered face moved with the controlled economy of a man who'd spent decades in hostile territory. Behind him came someone new. Ma noted his compact build. He was maybe five-ten, with the kind of dense muscle that came from swimming rather than weightlifting. The second man had a salt-and-pepper beard, trimmed tight. His eyes tracked every corner, every shadow, he looked like he knew how to wage violence if directed.

"Mr. President," Harrington said, offering a crisp handshake. "Good to see you again. Thank you for making time for us. May I introduce Commander Ryan Mitchell, USN retired. He's TSG's new country manager for our growing Taiwan operations."

Mitchell stepped forward, grip firm but not trying to prove anything. "Sir. Honor to meet you. Honor to be part of this mission."

Ma smiled, noting the Bostonian accent—a reminder of his own Harvard days. "Commander Mitchell, the honor is mine. Your reputation precedes you."

"All bad, I hope," Mitchell deadpanned, then seemed to catch himself. "Sorry, sir. Nervous habit."

The ghost of a smile crossed Ma's face. *Americans and their compulsive humor.* "Please, sit. We have much to discuss."

They arranged themselves around the table—Taiwan's leadership on one side, the Americans on the other. It was just like negotiating a business deal, Ma thought, except the commodity was survival, and they came offering the means to ensure it.

Harrington slid a sealed portfolio across the polished wood. "Mr. President, I was instructed by National Security Advisor Jim Batista to share this with you and your team. It's Presidential Finding 32-33, signed seventy-two days ago. It explains the surge in deliverables and activity of the past few weeks. Jim felt it was important you see this, and to leave no doubt in your mind about President Ashford's commitment to Taiwan's defense."

Ma broke the seal and scanned the document. His English was flawless. Years of study at Georgetown had seen to that, but Harvard had taught him to read slowly, absorbing the details people often missed. "Am I reading this correctly? You are increasing your numbers from one hundred and twenty to six hundred contractors by the end of April. And you'll have full autonomous weapons release authority. Expedited technology transfer." He looked up in shock. "Jim was right, your president is serious."

"Deadly serious," Mitchell interjected. "Nobody wants this going kinetic. But like Morpheus once said—'Unfortunately, no one can be told what the Matrix is.' We're about to show you."

The reference hung in the air. Harrington shot Mitchell a look that said *maybe dial back the movie quotes*.

Ma passed the document to Kao, who began reading with professional intensity. "Wow. The funding is substantial. Four-point-eight billion. I mean, don't get me wrong, that's great. But money doesn't sink landing craft or shoot down helicopters."

"No, ma'am, it doesn't," Mitchell agreed. "But these will." He produced a ruggedized tablet, fingers dancing across the screen. "May I?" He gestured toward the main monitor in the room.

Ma nodded. A moment later, the room's main display flickered to life, showing technical schematics that made Admiral Han lean forward involuntarily.

"As I alluded to earlier, we have a substantial gravy train of supplies arriving in the coming weeks. Let me walk you through what all is coming," Mitchell began, his Boston accent thickening with enthusiasm. "First up, some nasty little devils the techies came up with—

smart mines. And not just any mines. We're delivering a thousand of these Sea Guardian units. Let's just say these aren't your grandfather's tethered sea mines either. These are equipped with passive sensors and networked AI. They decide when to detonate based on a programmable target value we determine."

The display shifted to show deployment patterns and a second sea mine. "We call these Wraiths. We have six hundred of them arriving. What makes these unique is how they work; they can hunt and attack in swarms. But more than that, the onboard targeting AI is able to reference a library of PLA Navy schematics of the vessel it's preparing to attack, to find its weak spot before plowing into it. For instance, it will aim for the vessel's magazine or engineering section, areas of the vessel where its impact would likely lead to a secondary explosion. There's a higher chance of a ship kill this way."

Admiral Han's pencil stopped moving as he realized how many in total were coming. "Are those numbers right? A thousand mines with AI networking?"

"Sure is, but that's just the appetizer," Mitchell continued. "We got the main meal still coming. Two hundred forty Hammer Sharks. They're one-way attack UUVs with thousand-pound warheads. They sprint at sixty knots once they're within five kilometers of their targets."

Lieutenant General Wu leaned forward. "Oh, my Marines could deploy these from shore positions. We could wreak havoc on a landing force approaching the coast."

"Exactly, General. But here's the kicker, we have forty-eight Seeker XLUUVs that arrived last night. These are the big boys of autonomous underwater vehicles, and they can pack a hell of a punch. They can each carry twelve light torpedoes. These autonomous mini-subs can be programmed to loiter in a particular area, or they can be directed to hunt for enemy subs in a geofenced area. These bad boys are designed to deny the enemy sea control of wherever you direct them to for weeks."

The display cycled through surface vessels next. "For chaos on top of the waves, we have these bad boys. Four hundred Zealot fast-attack boats. Each carries four naval Hellfires and a MANPAD quad pack, plus a two-hundred-and-fifty-pound suicide charge for when things need to get personal."

"Wow, like a swarm of angry wasps," Wu murmured appreciatively.

Mitchell grinned. "Oh, it gets better, Admiral. We got six hundred Feiying drone boats for ISR and strike missions. These are smaller autonomous boats, designed to scout ahead, launch loitering munitions, then kamikaze with a two-hundred-and-fifty-pound bomb once they've spent their munitions, or they can be redirected back to be reloaded and sent back on another mission."

President Ma studied the numbers, his mind racing through the tactical permutations. "This is...substantial. More than I thought possible. Am I to also understand that most of this equipment has already arrived or is arriving before the end of the month?"

Harrington answered for Mitchell. "Yes, Mr. President. A lot of the equipment that could be sent via commercial air cargo has been steadily arriving via DHL, FedEx, and UPS. Some of the items have come via cargo vessels inside of shipping containers. When absolutely necessary, the US Air Force has made a handful of deliveries to Hengchun Airport. From there, a lot of it is moved to Camp Renshou, and then further dispersed to the locations where we've been told to hide them. Our goal, Mr. President, is to have as much of this equipment ready for your forces ahead of the mainland's April fifteenth deadline."

President Ma nodded. "Your people have done a lot to aid our country. We are forever in your debt for the help you have given. I do not mean to appear ungrateful or suggest that what you have provided isn't enough or won't make a difference. I believe it will. We are facing more than just the world's largest navy. Should it come to war, our country will likely be swarmed with one-way kamikaze drones, ballistic and cruise missiles, and this is before the PLA Air Force and Army helicopters swarm the skies over our country. How do you plan to help us deal with this threat—or do we just have to absorb it?"

Harrington motioned for Mitchell to continue his brief. "Mr. President, that's something we have considered as well and it's something we have a solution for," Mitchell said eagerly as he resumed his brief. "To answer your question about air defense, we have you covered. As of right now, your Air Force has ten Patriot PAC-3 batteries with eight launchers per battery fitted with a mix of CRI, MSE, and GEM-T interceptors. This gives your forces a total of eighty launchers with four missiles apiece or three hundred twenty missiles. We're providing an additional five batteries with eight launchers apiece, bringing an additional hundred and sixty missiles."

Defense Minister Kao's eyes widened. "Whoa, wait a second. You're saying you somehow managed to find and then cut through mountains of red tape to deliver five additional Patriot batteries? That gives us a starting missile capacity of four hundred and eighty interceptors! How in the hell did you manage to do that?" She stumbled over her words, dumbfounded by the news.

Harrington interjected, responding to her question directly. "Minister Kao, on behalf of my country, I must apologize for the unprecedented years' worth of delays your country has endured. I wish there were a way for me to undo the unquestionable mistakes of the past in delivering these kinds of weapon systems you purchased earlier, but I can't. I can, however, assure you we worked miracles with National Security Advisor Batista and President Ashford to expedite the delivery of these systems to your country now."

Minister Kao bowed her head slightly, seeming to accept his apology. She then motioned for him to continue.

"In addition to strengthening your air and missile defense capability, we've also finished delivering, as of this morning, three thousand Anduril Industries Roadrunner Block III interceptors," Harrington went on with a mischievous grin. "This is the newest generation of Anduril's flagship reusable interceptor and has been upgraded to use a multiband radar plus IR and even LIDAR targeting system. Its range has been increased from ten kilometers to twenty, and it boasts a top speed of Mach 2.6. When we integrate this with the Patriot batteries. The airspace over your country is going to be difficult at best for the PLA to defeat—effectively creating the porcupine effect we believe will deter the PLA from even attempting to seize it."

Mitchell pulled up another screen as Harrington finished. "Turning Taiwan into a porcupine is only part of the solution. We also need to make sure the PLA knows if they try to seize your country militarily, you can throw a few punches of your own. It's a lesson we learned from the Russo-Ukraine War. It's not enough to defeat the drones and missiles being fired at you. You have to fire a few back at 'em and hit 'em where it hurts. This is where the offensive package we're providing will come into play. One of the keys of deterrence is being able to hit back. To accomplish this, we've once again turned to Anduril

Industries' Barracuda autonomous cruise missiles. We procured a varying number of all three variants. The 100 series is for close work, sixty miles if ground-launched and eighty-five miles if launched from an aircraft. It packs a forty-pound kinetic or modular warhead. The Barracuda-250s are for medium range, one hundred and fifty miles if ground-launched and two hundred if fired from an aircraft. Its warhead size is the same as the 100 series. The 500 series is your deep-strikes option. It has a range of five hundred and fifty miles if ground-launched and one thousand miles if air-launched. It also packs a larger punch, with a one-hundred-pound warhead."

Mitchell paused a second as he read something on his tablet. "Our final delivery should arrive on March thirtieth. Oh, ha-ha, I told you what they are, but I forgot to tell you how many. My bad." The others just stared at him, waiting for him to get to the point. "Um, yeah, so, a total of eighteen of 'em are on the way. Five hundred of the Barracuda-500s, seven hundred of the 250s, and the remaining six hundred of the shorter-range Barracuda-100s."

The room suddenly fell silent as the implications of this weapons package finally began to sink in. TSG wasn't just providing them with enough weapons and missiles to have Taiwan lose slowly, as had happened in Ukraine. They were providing them with the quantity and types of weapons to hold their own and, if necessary, defeat the mainlanders should they attempt to seize control of their island.

Harrington leaned forward as he spoke. "I know this sounds like a lot, and technically it is, Mr. President. But one of the key lessons we learned from the Russo-Ukraine War was the necessity to pre-position as many weapons as possible before the war starts. Unlike Ukraine, which shares a land border with multiple NATO countries, Taiwan is surrounded by the sea. And it's a sea that is going to be brimming with PLA surface and subsurface warships. Should hostilities begin, we won't have the luxury of bringing in outside supplies when we run low. We'll have what we have on hand, and that's likely all we're going to have."

NSB Director Chao nodded in acknowledgment. He adjusted his glasses, then said, "The coordination requirements for all of these systems is going to be challenging—"

"Yes, it is," Mitchell answered before Chao could finish. "And one of the biggest challenges we'll have to overcome at the outset is the initial saturation barrage of one-way kamikaze drones, ballistic and cruise missiles and aircraft. This isn't something that can easily be handled by human operators. It's why we've spent a lot of time and effort creating OrchidNet, an AI battle manager that will sync the distributed defensive nodes between your Air Force's air and missile defense and the new systems we're providing.

"I know it can feel scary to trust an AI-controlled battle manager. But the fact is no human operator or team of operators is going to be able to identify, track, and then prosecute the kind of saturation barrage the mainland is going to fire at Taiwan. The difference between surviving and defeating the enemy in the first hours and days of this attack will be determined by the side that employs and utilizes the best AI system. If that's us, via OrchidNet, then I firmly believe we will deter the mainland from launching a ground invasion. If we fail, if the enemy succeeds in overwhelming us, then we'll fight them block by block once they're ashore."

Admiral Han set down his pencil. "I have to admit, I'm impressed. This isn't just material support to hurt the mainland. This is a complete defensive ecosystem."

"It is. And as you have shared with us in prior meetings. The enemy will try to overwhelm us with their drone swarms. That's why we've included one hundred twenty Leonidas-III high-power microwave systems to the package," Harrington added. "These can be vehicle- or static-mounted and hard-kill a drone's electronics from a kilometer away, degrading its sensors and controls at three. But here's the thing— all this hardware needs trained operators. That's where the four hundred and eighty additional contractors we've brought over come into play."

President Ma stood, pacing to the window. Outside, mist swirled through ancient pines. "Show me a deployment concept."

The display transformed into Taiwan's geography and Mitchell overlaid defensive zones with the various weapon systems.

"Sea Guardians and Water Prisons here"—blue fields appeared in the strait—"covering primary approach routes. The Hammer Sharks and Seeker units patrol these sectors."

He gestured, and icons scattered across the coastline. "Zealot boats based at fishing ports. They'll blend with commercial traffic until activation. Feiying scouts will provide early warning."

"The Penghu archipelago?" Wu asked.

"We turn it into a fortress. Patriot batteries here and here. Roadrunners in pop-up positions. Leonidas systems covering the beaches."

"Kinmen and Matsu?" Ma asked without turning.

"Minimal deployment if that," Chao interjected firmly. "Those islands are intelligence traps. Any system we place there—"

"Becomes a gift to the PLA," Mitchell finished. "Correct. Tony Soprano had it right—'Those who want respect, give respect.' We respect their ability to probe those positions."

Ma turned back. "Your contractors. Six hundred men. How do they integrate into all of this?"

Mitchell's expression sobered. "We embed with your units. Ten-man teams with each Patriot battery. Twenty operators per Seeker squadron. Fifty maintaining the Pulsar suites."

"Combat roles?" Wu pressed.

"When it goes loud?" Mitchell's jaw tightened. "We're wherever the metal meets the meat. But our primary mission is keeping these systems operational under fire."

"Think of us as force multipliers," Harrington emphasized. "In special forces, we have a saying: 'by, with, and through our allies.' Just one TSG operator can manage twenty autonomous platforms. That's the equivalent of twelve thousand additional combatants."

The math hung in the air—six hundred men becoming an army through technology.

"Huh...and the timeline to make this all happen?" Kao asked.

"Most of this equipment is already loaded on ships and on the way. The first deliveries hit Kaohsiung in two weeks," Mitchell said. "We expect full deployment by May first. We'll run your crews through certification of the systems as they arrive."

President Ma returned to the table. "This is a big delivery. The mainland is bound to see these preparations. They'll know what's happening."

"Good. Let them," Mitchell replied. "That's the whole point. Deterrence through demonstrated capability. They need to see what they are facing and decide it's not worth it. We nut this place up, turn it into a porcupine they won't want to bite, and if they do, we sting 'em hard."

President Ma nodded. "And if deterrence fails?"

Mitchell leaned back. "Then we give them what Colonel Kurtz promised in *Apocalypse Now*: 'Horror has a face, and you must make a friend of horror.'"

This time, no one smiled at the movie quote.

Ma looked at his defenders. "Admiral Han—naval integration?" he asked.

"The autonomous submarines change everything," Han said slowly. "Forty-eight platforms with nearly six hundred torpedoes…good night. All of that combined with smart mines…" He shook his head. "We're going to turn the straits into a killing field."

"General Wu, thoughts?" President Ma Ching-te asked.

"Oh, my Marines can work with this." Wu's eyes gleamed. "Feiying scouts feeding targeting to shore-based Barracudas, Zealot boats screening our flanks—we could hold Penghu indefinitely, and keep them from establishing a beachhead with those bridging barges they've been training on."

"And how about you, Director Chao? What say you?" Ma stared at his chief spy.

The intelligence chief removed his glasses, cleaning them thoughtfully. "The electronic warfare suites interest me. Twenty Pulsars could create dead zones where their command networks fail."

"I agree, Director," Ma replied, then turned to his defense minister. "Thoughts, Minister Kao?"

She closed the funding document, then looked him in the eyes. "With ten Patriot batteries plus three thousand interceptors, we could maintain air defense even under saturation attacks."

Ma absorbed their assessments. Each saw possibilities through their professional lens. But he saw the larger picture—a small island becoming a fortress, protected by silicon and steel rather than flesh alone.

"One concern," Ma said finally. "These systems—they're American. If Washington's political winds shift…"

"Ah, well, that's why we're training your people," Harrington said firmly. "It'll be a full technology transfer. Your engineers will learn maintenance, and your operators will learn tactics. In twelve months, you'll be self-sufficient."

"Twelve months," Ma repeated. "Beijing may not give us that long."

"True," Mitchell replied. "Then we accelerate. Train the trainer, give crash courses. Your people are smart and motivated. We can cut training time if needed and focus more on training trainers who can carry on without us, if it comes to that."

The room fell silent. Through the window, the afternoon sun broke through clouds, casting golden light across the valley below. Taiwan's beauty had always been its blessing and curse—too precious to abandon, too small to defend conventionally.

"OK. I'd like your professional assessment," Ma said to Mitchell. "If the PLA comes next month—before full deployment—what happens?"

Mitchell met his gaze directly. "We make it cost them. Every ship that enters the strait faces smart mines. Every landing craft meets a Hellfire. Every transport aircraft flies through Roadrunner swarms."

"Casualties?" asked Ma.

"Theirs? Catastrophic. Ours?" Mitchell paused. "We'll bleed. But we'll make them bleed more."

"And your six hundred men?"

"We hold the line where it matters most: command nodes, radar sites, and ammunition dumps." Mitchell's voice hardened. "We've all written letters home already. We know the deal."

President Ma Ching-te studied the American's face—it was weathered, scarred, but steady. These weren't corporate mercenaries. They were true believers, buying time with their lives.

"Show me," Ma said finally. "If Beijing comes tomorrow—not May, not next year, tomorrow—how do your six hundred men help us survive?"

****

Marcus Harrington watched Mitchell's fingers dance across the tactical display, pulling up deployment scenarios with practiced efficiency. The younger man had the technical details down cold, which was a good sign. But selling hope to a president facing annihilation required more than spreadsheets.

"Sir," Harrington interjected smoothly, "before Commander Mitchell walks through the tactical response, let me address the strategic picture."

President Ma turned from the display, eyebrow raised. Behind him, Taiwan's military leadership shifted their attention like wolves catching the scent of new prey.

Harrington stood, his six-four frame commanding the room without trying. "You asked how six hundred contractors help Taiwan survive. The answer's simple—we don't let it come to that."

"Hmm. Deterrence is fine in theory," Admiral Han said dryly, "but theories don't stop landing craft."

"No, sir, they don't. But eighteen hundred cruise missiles do." Harrington moved to the window, gazing out at mist-shrouded peaks slowly fading as the afternoon sun burned them away. "President Ashford didn't authorize five billion dollars because he's fond of scenery. The PRC is as big a threat to our country as it is to yours. Helping to defeat the PLA here helps ensure they won't defeat us elsewhere."

He turned back. "If Taiwan falls, the entire first island chain collapses. It leaves Japan exposed. Australia becomes isolated and ripe for the taking. Every shipping lane from Singapore to Seoul falls under the control of the PLA Navy."

Defense Minister Kao leaned forward. "I mean no offense when I say this, but Washington has a history of abandoned allies."

"Taiwan's not Afghanistan, or Vietnam." Harrington's voice carried the weight of absolute conviction. "That presidential finding isn't just a piece of paper. It's a message to Beijing. If they cross the line, if they choose to wage war, we're going to bleed them dry."

"Your contract," NSB Director Chao said carefully, "it covers combat operations?"

"Every contingency." Harrington pulled a document from his jacket. "Article Seven, Section Three. 'In the event of military aggression against the Republic of China, TSG personnel are authorized to engage in direct combat operations in defense of allied forces and critical infrastructure.'"

Lieutenant General Wu studied the contract language. "Mercenaries don't typically sign up for last stands."

"We're not typical mercenaries." Harrington's jaw tightened. "Every TSG operator volunteered knowing the stakes. This isn't about paychecks. They're compensated well, but this is about more than money. My people see Taiwan as America's front line. You fall, we fall. It's simple math. We fight them here, so we don't have to back home."

President Ma moved back to the table. "Assuming your conviction matches your contracts, logistics remain problematic."

"Which brings me to my next point." Harrington leaned forward. "Mr. President, your strategic reserves need work."

That statement was met with silence. Taiwan's leadership exchanged nervous glances with each other.

"We're aware of our limitations," Ma said carefully.

"Three months of food and fuel might be decent for a typhoon. But they are insufficient for a siege, and a siege is what you have to prepare for." Harrington kept his tone respectful but firm. "Technically, Beijing doesn't need to invade. They can blockade your ports and wait for hungry citizens to demand surrender."

"And what are you suggesting?" Admiral Han's voice carried an edge.

"Six months minimum. Preferably nine if you can." Harrington spread his hands. "I know it's expensive. I know storage is limited. But hunger breaks nations faster than bombs; it always has."

"The cost—" Kao began.

"Is nothing compared to capitulation." Harrington met each leader's gaze. "Double your grain reserves. Triple pharmaceutical stockpiles. Diesel, aviation fuel, ammunition—everything."

"Storage facilities would be primary targets," Wu commented.

"Of course they will. That's why you distribute caches. Spread it out in mountain bunkers and civilian warehouses." Mitchell pulled up a map showing potential sites. "We've taken the liberty of mapping over two hundred locations you could use. Spread the risk around and minimize the loss."

"There's another element," Harrington added. "Food production. Every apartment balcony should have planters. Every park becomes a victory garden. Schools teach hydroponics."

President Ma's expression shifted—something between surprise and satisfaction. "Actually, in that department, we've made significant progress there."

The military leaders straightened. This was news to some of them.

"Oh, do tell, if you can," Harrington prompted.

Ma gestured to Chao, who pulled up classified imagery on his tablet, casting it to the main display. Tunnel entrances appeared, carved into mountainsides.

"We call it Project Morning Glory," Ma explained. "We're three years into development. Hydroponic facilities are housed inside hardened tunnels. They're temperature-controlled, with LED growth lights powered by geothermal."

The images shifted, showing vast underground chambers filled with vertically growing towers. Lettuce, tomatoes, beans, and rice sprouted in precise rows.

"Current capacity?" Harrington asked, genuinely impressed.

"As of now, twelve facilities are operational. Each produces enough fresh vegetables for fifty thousand people daily." Pride crept into Ma's voice. "Not enough for twenty-one million, but combined with reserves—"

"You double your timeline," Harrington finished. "Outstanding. Why wasn't this in our briefings?"

"Classification concerns," Chao said. "These facilities are strategic assets. Their locations—"

"Stay secret. Understood." Harrington nodded approval. "What about protein?"

"We have fish farms in three locations and chicken coops on government building rooftops." Ma almost smiled. "We learned from Singapore. Urban farming at scale."

Mitchell whistled low. "That's next-level prep. Like the Oracle said, 'You're not here to make the choice. You've already made it.'"

"The choice to survive," Ma agreed. "But calories don't stop missiles."

"No, sir. But they buy time." Harrington stood again, moving to the display. "Commander Mitchell, show the President our deployment timeline."

Mitchell pulled up a Gantt chart. "Week one—first Sea Guardians arrive. Our people work with your Navy to establish command protocols. Week two—Patriot batteries start landing. We integrate with your air-defense network."

The timeline scrolled forward. "By week six, half the autonomous systems are operational. Week ten, full deployment. Week twelve, your operators achieve basic certification."

"And if Beijing moves before week six?" Han asked.

"Then we fight with what we have." Harrington's voice hardened. "Every TSG operator knows the mission: protect the equipment, keep it operational, and make the PLA bleed for every meter."

"Bluntly," Mitchell added, "we're speed bumps with guns, buying time for these systems to do their work."

President Ma absorbed this. "Your casualties would be severe."

"If we are at war with China, chances are, our casualties would be severe no matter where we fight." Harrington spoke stoically, without a hint of emotion. "We've all made that calculation, Mr. President. If we didn't die here, it'd be somewhere else." The room fell silent.

"There's something else you should consider," Defense Minister Kao said slowly. "Public opinion. If American contractors die while defending Taiwan—"

"Then I'm sure the media will run with it." Harrington nodded. "It's no different than when American blood was spilled when volunteers chose to fight defending democracy in Ukraine, or any other fight."

"You aren't afraid your deaths might be used as propaganda?" Wu questioned.

"With social media and everyone having a phone dialed into the internet, I'm sure there will be a few viral moments." Harrington met his gaze. "However, if six hundred Americans die while defending Taiwan's freedom, that tells Beijing America isn't abandoning its allies."

President Ma stood, motioning for the others to stay seated while he walked to the window. The setting of the sun painted Taipei in beautiful golden hues. This was his country, his city, and it was his responsibility to defend it.

"You genuinely believe we can deter them?" Ma finally asked.

Harrington stood and joined him at the window. "Sir, I've fought in Iraq, Afghanistan, Syria, and a few other places in this world. I've seen determined people with inferior weapons hold off superpowers. You have superior weapons and determined people; that is not something to underestimate or dismiss lightly."

Harrington gestured at the city below. "Twenty-one million free citizens," he said. "A first-world economy, and democratic values. That's worth protecting, Mr. President."

Lieutenant General Wu stood slowly. "I've heard many briefings in my time, many assurances from friends and allies. This feels different."

"It should," Mitchell replied. "We're not Pentagon staff officers who rose through the ranks making promises they can't deliver. We're the tip of the spear, the trigger-pullers they send when force is the only answer. We're Uncle Sam's hellions, his killers when there's no other choice but violence of action."

President Ma returned to his seat. "You mentioned blockade scenarios. Walk me through TSG's response."

Harrington nodded to Mitchell, who pulled up new overlays.

"A blockade requires surface vessels maintaining station." Mitchell highlighted patrol zones. "Zealot boats operate in wolf packs. Ten boats, forty Hellfires. How many destroyers can they spare?"

"Submarines would be the real threat," Han observed.

"Seeker XLUUVs hunt subs," Mitchell acknowledged. "Forty-eight platforms with nearly six hundred torpedoes. We turn their advantage against them."

"Air cover?"

"Patriots and Roadrunners create defensive bubbles. If there's three thousand interceptors rotating through launch sites, their drones, helicopters, and aircraft face constant attrition." The display showed radius circles expanding from Taiwan. "Push the defensive perimeter out two hundred miles, and you make their blockade stations untenable."

"They could stand off further," Wu suggested.

"Sure, but then shipping routes reopen." Harrington spread his hands. "Blockades require proximity. Distance equals gaps. Plus, you have to keep in mind, the US Navy is going to wreak havoc on the PLA Navy. The Air Force is going to want a piece of the action too. This isn't going to be a one-sided affair, by any means."

President Ma studied the display, then sighed deeply. "Your assessment…honestly, can we really hold?"

Harrington met his gaze directly. "With full deployment? Preparation? Your people's courage? Hell yeah, we can hold."

The President stood, extending his hand. "Mr. Harrington, Commander Mitchell. On behalf of the people of Taiwan, I want to thank you for your steadfast dedication and your willingness to fight and die if necessary, defending our people."

Harrington shook firmly. "The honor is ours, Mr. President, but let's save the thanks for after we win. We've got work to do between now and then."

As they prepared to leave, Ma asked one final question. "Humor me. Just tell me why. Why do you and your men choose this?"

Harrington paused at the door. "We're warriors, Mr. President—sheep dogs who have chosen a life of service to protect the flock. We fight for those who can't, to defend the cause of freedom," Harrington explained. "I know it sounds silly. But some things matter more than living. Freedom, democracy—those ideas have to be fought for, and have to be defended. If we just give up, if we choose to look the other way, what kind of future does that leave those who come after us?"

Leaving the residence as they walked toward the waiting vehicles, Harrington felt good about the meeting. He really hoped it wouldn't come to war with China.

But if it does, he thought, *God help them. Because my men and I will unleash holy hell on them.*

Chapter Seventeen:

Sky Soldiers

March 13, 2033 – 14:23 Hours Local Time
Bravo Company, 2nd Battalion, 503rd Infantry Regiment (Airborne)
Visby Airport, Gotland

The C-130J Hercules banked hard left, and Captain Alex Mercer felt his stomach lurch. Through the porthole, Sweden's unsinkable aircraft carrier materialized from Baltic haze—ninety miles of limestone and forest, ringed by cliffs that looked ready to repel invaders.

"Two minutes!" The loadmaster's voice crackled through the cabin.

Mercer keyed his throat mic. "Blackjacks, final checks."

Around him, thirty-four paratroopers from his advance party stirred. Body armor adjustments. Weapon slings. The familiar pre-insertion ritual that meant business was about to begin. First Sergeant Elijah "Big E" Tanner moved down the aisle like a prowling bear, checking gear with practiced eyes.

Senior NCO Daniel Holloway leaned close. "It's too bad we can't arrive via a combat jump, sir."

"Yeah, that's *one* way to make a first impression on the locals," Mercer mused at the idea of him and his men parachuting into the Visby airport like an invading army. "But we're here to assure the locals, not scare them."

The Herc touched down with a controlled thump, engines screaming in reverse thrust as the pilots slowed them down and began to taxi to the military side of the airfield. Peering through the window, Mercer spotted their welcoming committee. A contingent from the Gotland Regiment, CV90 infantry fighting vehicles and Patria armored personnel carriers arranged in precise formation, a company of soldiers in their distinctive M90 woodland camo waiting for them at parade rest. They looked impressive, professional, and cautious. Exactly what Mercer expected from a nation in the crosshairs of whatever game it was the Chinese and Russians were playing.

As the aircraft came to a halt, the ramp began to lower, revealing the beauty of the Swedish island of Gotland, home to some 63,000 people, 25,700 of whom lived in Visby, the provincial capital. No sooner had the ramp touched down than a strong, Baltic wind hit Mercer like a cold slap across the face. He could taste the salt and smell the sea mixed with scents of jet fuel and fresh pine. Mercer led his advance team onto the tarmac as he made his way toward an officer waiting to greet them.

"Good afternoon! You must be Captain Mercer," the Swedish officer announced as he walked toward him.

Mercer smiled. The colonel who approached had the weathered look of someone who'd spent more time in the field than behind a desk— Lindqvist, his name tape read. As the officer came to a stop, Mercer snapped a salute. "Colonel Lindqvist. Bravo Company, Second of the 503rd Airborne. Honor to be here, sir."

Colonel Lindqvist returned his salute crisply. "Welcome to Gotland, Captain. It is an honor to welcome you to our island. Your reputation precedes you." His flawless English and tone gave the impression of a learned man. "Your commander said you had previously served in the Ranger Regiment once upon a time, yes?"

Mercer smirked at the mention of his time in the Regiment. The last time he'd been to Gotland was during his time with the Rangers. He wasn't sure if anyone from back then would still remember him.

"I did, but that was a long time ago, sir."

"Ah, I thought I recognized your name. I was a newly promoted major when your Ranger unit parachuted onto the Tofta Range. That was a fun exercise if I recall." Lindqvist's eyes crinkled slightly at the memory. It was one of the few times Mercer could remember when his Ranger company had found themselves mauled in an exercise.

With a motion for Mercer to follow him, he led them past the soldiers standing in formation waiting to receive them. "You Rangers gave us a hell of a run for our money that day, Captain. Come, let us put the past behind us and discuss the present. We have much to plan for."
****

The convoy rolled through Visby's medieval walls forty minutes later, GAZ Tigers and Mercedes G-Wagons navigating streets built for horses, not vehicles. Mercer rode with Lindqvist in the lead vehicle as the colonel drove dangerously close to the edges of buildings and the occasional parked car. The airport was just north of Visby. The P18 or Gotland Regiment was located six miles southwest of Visby, near the Tofta firing range. This area hugged the western shore of the island and was where the majority of the military barracks and activity on Gotland took place. As they exited the city into the countryside, the colonel broke the silence.

"Captain, when does your main force arrive?" Lindqvist asked, his eyes on the road.

"Week from Thursday. Hundred and twenty personnel, plus equipment," Mercer replied, keeping his tone neutral. "Our heavy gear follows by ship in the coming weeks."

"Hmm, OK. And the Patriot batteries?"

"Ah, well, I can't speak to Task Force Sentinel's timeline. We're just the security element."

Lindqvist grunted. "One company to protect Patriot batteries that can engage targets three hundred kilometers away. That's an interesting allocation."

Mercer had had the same thoughts when he'd been given the orders. It seemed he wasn't the only one who thought they were a little light in providing security for what was obviously a strategic asset and thereby a target.

"We make the most of what we have. Besides, paratroopers work best in small teams," Mercer offered in response. "My understanding is our battalion headquarters along with Alpha and Charlie Companies are located at Berga Naval Base, with Delta Company situated at Muskö Naval Base. If we need a QRF force, Alpha Company is it. I think we'll be fine with your people and won't need them."

"Hmm, we'll see," Lindqvist responded as he turned onto a forest road. "Do you know where the rest of the 173rd is going?"

"Latvia, near the Adazi military base just northeast of Riga," Mercer replied. He then asked, "Just between us, Colonel, what do you think of this EDEP exercise in a few weeks? You think the Russians and Chinese are preparing for war or just trying to scare us?"

The colonel was quiet for a moment. "That's hard to say, Captain. The Russian and Chinese economies are starting to benefit from this economic pact they have formed. It's hard to believe they would want to risk all of it for a war I don't think they are yet ready to fight, let alone win."

"Yeah, that's my thinking too. It's hard to tell sometimes with all the saber-rattling. You would think after their thumping in Ukraine, they would take some time to maybe learn from their mistake and not try something as foolish as invading their neighbor again," Mercer replied as their vehicle turned onto another road leading into a forested area.

A few minutes later, the Gotland Regiment's headquarters building came into sight, seeming to materialize from the pine trees surrounding them. Mercer smiled as he took the sight in, observing how the buildings had been designed to blend in with the terrain around them. As they drove closer, he soon spotted strategically placed berms, suggesting hardened positions and defensive works beneath them. It was clear the Swedes were preparing their positions for whatever might come of this exercise, leaving nothing to chance.

Pulling up to the front of the building marked "Headquarters, P18 Gotland Regiment," Mercer followed Colonel Lindqvist inside. Maps covered nearly every wall of the first room he'd walked into, some of them rendered in topographical detail, with defensive sectors marked in neat Swedish script and English next to it. The half dozen officers near a conference room table turned to greet him. Mercer recognized the looks. Professionals assessing the Americans who'd just arrived in their backyard.

Colonel Lindqvist motioned for Mercer and his people to take a seat as he walked toward the front of the room. "Gentlemen, I would like to introduce you to Captain Mercer," he announced loudly in English. "Captain Mercer is the commanding officer of Bravo Company, 2nd Battalion, 503rd Airborne Infantry. They are the security element for the Patriot and HIMAR batteries that should start to arrive in the coming weeks. Let's go ahead and do some introductions. Captain Lindholm, why don't you lead off for us."

A younger captain stepped forward. "Afternoon, Captain. I'm Captain Joran Lindholm. I command a tank platoon. We're the heavy armor for the regiment. Do your soldiers have experience working with or coordinating operations with armor?"

"We do. We've worked with Bradleys and Abrams at Grafenwoehr and participated in the last NATO exercise in Romania last summer," Mercer replied confidently. "I'm aware your unit operates the

Leopards. We're used to working with them as well. They aren't too much different."

"Yeah, perhaps. But our terrain is difficult." Lindholm gestured to the map. "Gotland, as you can see, is forests and farmland. We have some open areas for maneuver, but not many. One thing we do have plenty of is places for infiltrators to hide."

Mercer sensed someone walking up behind him. He turned to hear First Sergeant Tanner comment, "Infiltrators, you say? Sounds like what we used to deal with in Afghanistan. Except you all have better roads."

That drew a few laughs, breaking the ice and the tension.

A major with an intelligence insignia on his collar leaned forward. "I'm Major Stenqvist, the regiment's S2. What would you say is your biggest threat you need to be ready to handle?"

Mercer knew he'd be asked a question like this and had prepared for it. "That's a good question, Major Stenqvist. I'd say we have a couple of viable threats we need to watch for—the first being Spetsnaz infiltration. They could come in the form of tourists, or if an attack is underway, they could come via airborne or even a seaborne assault. Second, and more likely, drone swarms. Say this Russian-Chinese EDEP exercise turns kinetic. They'll likely try to saturate our defenses with drones before sending cruise missiles," Mercer explained, then softened his tone. "Major, this is your home. My men and I are not to occupy Gotland or garrison it for months or years. We're here to help defend it until whatever this exercise is passes and we can all go home."

Stenqvist smiled, nodding in agreement. "Let's hope you are right, Captain. And if this defense needs to become an offense, what then?"

"Well, we do what paratroopers do best. We adapt, and we punch the ChiComs and Ruskies in the face and stomp on them until they say uncle," Mercer replied, which elicited a few more laughs and some brash boasting about who would kick the enemy the hardest.
****

Following Day

The site reconnaissance began at dawn the next day. Three Swedish liaison officers joined Mercer's team—Captain Elin Boström from Air Defense, Lieutenant Nils Sandberg from Logistics, and a grizzled Home Guard officer who introduced himself simply as Bertil. His rank and name tape read Captain Sonevang. Mercer recognized him as the 32nd Battalion commander of the Gotland Home Guard. His unit functioned similar to how a National Guard unit would back in the States.

"Shouldn't we address you as captain, sir?" Sergeant First Class Dan Holloway asked the older man.

"No, it's OK. On Gotland, most of us Home Guard don't really bother much with professional ranks. We have them because we are told we must, but we are generally on a first-name basis. Around here, everyone knows me as Bertil, but you can call me captain if you must," the older man replied, his rugged and weathered face turning into a grin. "You see, I have been teaching history on this island for thirty-two years. I have students, now adults who send their children to my classes," he laughed, explaining how he was as much a fixture of the island as the trees around them. "That is why everyone knows me as Bertil, not captain."

Their convoy wound north from Visby, past limestone farmsteads and wind-twisted pines. Every few kilometers, Bertil pointed out local details, which roads flooded in spring, where cell coverage died, which farmers were "reliable" versus "talkative" when it came to developing credible sources and informants.

Mercer was studying his tablet's tactical overlay when he said, "The airport is obvious for us to locate the Patriot radar at. But where else should we consider setting our other radars up, and the launchers?"

Bertil held a hand out for Mercer's tablet. Taking the device in hand, he looked it over, then pointed to something. "You are right to point out the obviousness of the airport. This point here, the Grönt Centrum near Romakloster, would be a good location for you to set up the radar, command trailer and power unit for the Patriot battery and that Leonidas device you were telling us about. It is not a good idea to concentrate too many of your critical units around the airport. It is best to disperse them away from the population centers. The Centrum is centrally located on the island, and it has good lines of sight across many of the inland approaches toward Visby from the Baltic coast."

While they were speaking, Boström pulled over near a forested ridge. "Here, Captain Mercer. This is Gråtmon Hill. It has good elevation and natural concealment."

Mercer got out of the vehicle, his boots crunching on the frost-brittle grass that the sun hadn't yet warmed. The position overlooked some routes from the east heading toward Visby. The area from which they'd pulled off the road provided them with some dense overhead forest cover, something that would come in handy if the enemy was using FPV drones to scout the area. Near the road they'd just exited was a logging road that ran further into the forest, offering more overhead concealment if they wanted to try and place one of the Patriot launchers or a HIMAR vehicle.

"Yeah, you're right, Bertil. This is a good spot. What's the distance to Visby?" asked SFC Holloway as he gave an approving nod to Mercer.

"Twelve kilometers," Lieutenant Sandberg supplied. "Far enough to avoid civilian interference. Close enough for quick resupply when needed."

Tanner was already pacing the perimeter, measuring fields of fire. "We could fit a Patriot launcher or a HIMAR truck here and easily keep it concealed or relocate quickly if we needed."

"You have to be careful with the trees. They will interfere with the launcher coverage," Boström warned.

"True, but better to have to move to find an opening in the tree coverage to fire than eat a Kalibr missile because we're too exposed to their spotter drones," Tanner countered. "Concealment over convenience is sometimes worth it if it can keep you alive."

They spent three hours walking the site. Holloway marked positions on his GPS, command post here, ammunition storage there, generators tucked behind natural berms. Standard dispersal pattern, adapted for Gotland's terrain.

"What about personnel?" Mercer asked Lindqvist, who'd remained silent during the survey. "Where would you like to have my troops billeted?"

"Not in Visby." The colonel's tone was firm. "The population is… concerned about militarization. They do not want to make Visby a military target, especially after the incident with that Chinese spy ship. We have a former military camp in Roma, the Grönt Centrum, that we would like to offer to your people. It dates back to our conscription days and has since been converted into a boarding school of sorts. It now teaches sustainable green farming and things like that. It's vacant this semester for some renovations, so it's ideal for our needs right now," Colonel Lindqvist explained. "The grounds have dormitories we can use as sleeping quarters and living spaces for your people. It's a good facility, Captain. We can turn some of the school rooms into offices for your headquarters as well, and the surrounding grounds offer protected berms and forested areas where you can position some of the Patriot vehicles and plenty of space for you to park your vehicles and establish a good perimeter."

"Excellent, can we head over there now and take a look?"

"Yes, of course. It's not a hotel or anything, but it'll do." Lindqvist almost smiled. "It's Swedish military luxury."

****

Grönt Centrum
Gotland

Roma Military Camp sprawled across a shallow valley twenty-five kilometers southeast of Visby. Built during the Cold War, expanded in fits and starts, and then turned into a vocational school a decade after the Cold War ended, the place was only recently undergoing refurbishment into an alternate reserve military encampment for wartime use or contingency operations like now.

From the moment Mercer saw the place, he had to admit, this was better than he had hoped for. It had running water, bathrooms, showers, a cantina, and warehouses where they could store gear and supplies. While it was clear the facility was still actively being used for civilian purposes, the buildings themselves still retained that utilitarian charm for which military architecture was known.

"Well, boys, looks like this is going to be home sweet home," Sergeant First Class Holloway loudly announced as the soldiers walked into the building.

The buildings, returned once again to barracks, were indeed basic. They were long buildings with open bays, metal bunks with folded-over mattresses, and communal showers that promised tepid water. But the bones of the building were sound—thick walls, good sight lines, and multiple exit routes. It even had a restaurant that looked to have been a mess hall at one point.

"We can work with this," First Sergeant Tanner declared, already mentally organizing platoon areas. "Weapons cleaning station there. TOC in that end room. Comms can set up—"

An explosion of Swedish erupted nearby. Two Home Guard soldiers were unloading equipment from a truck, apparently disagreeing about proper procedure. The argument grew heated.

"Problem?" Mercer asked Bertil.

The old teacher sighed. "Göran thinks ammunition should be stored in the old bunker. Erik says it's too damp. They've had this argument for three years."

"And?" Mercer asked.

"They're both right." Bertil shrugged. "The bunker is secure, but moisture is bad for long-term storage. Welcome to Swedish consensus-building, Captain. Everyone discusses until everyone agrees."

Mercer laughed. "How long does that usually take?"

"Sometimes minutes. Sometimes years." Bertil's eyes twinkled. "But once decided, we commit fully. No half measures."

A cultural note filed away. Mercer had worked with dozens of allied forces over the years. Each had their quirks. The Swedes seemed methodical, careful, and prone to debate. But their preparations showed attention to detail that spoke of competence.

"Sergeant Holloway will coordinate billeting details," Mercer told Colonel Lindqvist. "What about local support? Fuel, food, medical?"

"Already arranged. Our quartermaster will brief your logistics NCO. Medical support from Visby Hospital for serious casualties. Field treatment here." Lindqvist paused. "One suggestion, Captain."

"Sir?"

"Your men. When they have liberty, remind them they are guests. Gotland does not see many foreign soldiers. Most will welcome you. Others…" He spread his hands.

"Understood. We'll maintain a low profile," Mercer assured him.

"Good. Because if this exercise across the water becomes something more, we'll need the population's support. Fear makes poor allies," replied Lindqvist.

****

Later That Evening

Alex finally found a quiet spot to call his wife. He'd been gone two days now, and he'd promised he would do his best to stay in touch while he was gone. He knew tomorrow was a big day for her and he wanted to make sure she knew he hadn't forgotten. Pressing the phone to his ear, he smiled as Maddie's familiar voice came through, warm yet tinged with a hint of nerves.

"Hey, babe," she began softly, a gentle sigh following. "How are things going on your end? You guys getting settled?"

"Yeah, we're getting things sorted," he began. "You know this place is beautiful, Madz. You were right, Gotland is beautiful."

She laughed. "Hey, can I get you to say that again while I record it?"

He scrunched his eyebrows. "Huh? What?"

"You know, that part where you said I was right?" she replied while stifling a laugh.

"Ha-ha, you got me there, Madz. OK, I'll say it again, slow for you...you were right. Did you get that?" he joked good-naturedly with her as she laughed. He missed that—hearing her laugh.

"So, you know tomorrow's launch day," she began. It was the release date of the third book in her series, which she had been working on feverishly for months. "I really wish you were here for it. It just won't be the same celebrating it without you at da Mario."

He smiled softly, picturing their favorite spot vividly—the cozy Italian bistro in Creazzo they'd made their tradition on every release day. "I wish I was there too. I know it's going to be amazing, Madz."

She sighed again, worry creeping into her tone. "I really hope so. We've put so much into this ad campaign. If it doesn't take off... I'm just worried about the finances, the nanny, all of it."

"Hey, trust the process," Alex reassured her gently. "You've done everything right. Just focus on the kids, enjoy the day, and let the launch happen. We'll deal with whatever comes afterward."

"Thank you," she murmured, gratitude softening her voice. "Speaking of the kids, they're doing great. The twins adore Caroline—honestly, hiring her was the best decision we've made in a long time."

"And Alex Junior?"

"Your mini-me?" Madz laughed lightly. "He's a handful, but Caroline manages him like a pro. Seriously, that woman deserves a medal."

"I'm glad it's working out," Alex said, warmth and relief easing his worry. "I know it's been tough without your mom around."

"Yeah," Madz agreed quietly, her voice momentarily thick with emotion. "But having Caroline here these past six months has been a lifesaver. I don't know how I would've managed the new book without her."

"You're doing great, Madz," Alex reassured her again. "Tomorrow's going to prove it. You're an amazing writer, and the world is finally going to see that."

"I hope you're right," she whispered, courage returning to her voice. "Stay safe, Alex. Come home soon."

"Always. Love you."

"Love you more, Blackjack Six."

Chapter Eighteen:
Setting the Trap

March 15, 2033
Yulin Naval Base
Hainan, China

It was 0900 hours, and already the Fleet Auditorium's air conditioning had lost its battle against Hainan's relentless humidity and the body heat of the nine hundred officers packed within.

Captain Shen Tao had arrived early, securing a seat among familiar comrades halfway up the tiered rows. He noted how those in the auditorium subtly divided themselves—veteran commanders clustered together, exchanging knowing glances heavy with unspoken implications, while younger officers and fresh-faced academy graduates sat toward the front, animated and oblivious to the weight of history poised to fall upon them.

"Attention on deck!" a voice boomed from the auditorium's rear. Instantly, nine hundred naval officers snapped upright, rigid and respectful, as Admiral Chen Weiming, Commander of the Southern Fleet, entered with his entourage.

From his vantage point, Shen glimpsed his mentor, Vice Admiral Deng Litian, face grim and resolute. Alongside him walked Vice Admiral Wu Guangxi, the fleet's political commissar, whose usually composed expression was now tense with unusual seriousness.

"Take seats!" echoed from the stage as Admiral Chen reached the podium.

Chen's gaze swept over the gathered officers, the intensity of his stare reinforcing the gravity of the moment. "Gentlemen, ladies, today marks a significant turning point in the naval history of our great nation. Each of you and your ships will be central to the future of the People's Republic of China. The responsibility on your shoulders cannot be overstated. What we discuss today remains strictly within these walls. Security teams have verified our privacy, and your phones are secured. Any unauthorized discussion will be considered treason, punishable by the full force of the state."

The auditorium's atmosphere shifted palpably, excitement tempered by the solemnity of Chen's words.

"Yesterday, the National People's Congress voted unanimously to enact the Drug Enforcement Act of China 2033—DEAC-33—a law designed explicitly to safeguard our youth from the lethal narcotic known as 'Vortex.' As you know, this deadly drug has already taken over three hundred thousand young Chinese lives, threatening the health and productivity of our nation's workforce."

He paused, allowing the weight of the statistic to settle over the assembly.

"The People's Congress has authorized, under national and international law, the establishment of the Maritime Sovereignty Protection Zone. This measure will ensure rigorous customs inspections of all vessels entering Chinese ports, explicitly including those bound for the Taiwan province, whose authorities have failed to control the flow of illicit substances endangering Chinese citizens."

The main screen illuminated with a detailed map of the Taiwan Strait, the new inspection zones marked clearly in red. Shen's pulse quickened. The choke points were unmistakably deliberate—Penghu approaches, the Pratas corridor, and the northern strait narrows.

"The maritime authorities have formally requested naval support to enforce this new legislation," Chen continued, his voice firm and authoritative. "The Central Military Commission has fully endorsed our participation."

Captain Wang Jian leaned in close, whispering, "Maritime authorities. He means the militia fleet."

Shen nodded grimly. Everyone knew these fishing vessels carried more electronics than fish, and crews more proficient with weapons than nets.

"Rules of engagement." The screen transitioned, outlining explicit operational guidelines. "Vessels failing to comply with inspection demands or exhibiting resistance will be boarded. Resistance is defined broadly—failure to stop, encrypted communications, crew resistance, or deviation from established routes." Chen's voice hardened. "Your discretion is paramount."

Shen understood immediately. The rules weren't designed to avoid confrontation—they practically guaranteed it.

"Force composition per enforcement zone includes one destroyer squadron, two frigate flotillas, militia support, aerial coverage, and standby submarine assets." Younger officers straightened with pride; veterans recognized an ominous escalation.

Assignments appeared on-screen. "Northern Zone—Destroyer Squadron 9. Central Zone—Squadron 12. Penghu Approach Zone—Squadron 15, Captain Shen Tao commanding."

Shen's jaw tightened imperceptibly. Penghu was a critical flashpoint, its waters crowded and its defenses formidable. His squadron would be at the heart of the operation, visible to global scrutiny within minutes of any incident.

"Packets before you contain detailed operational boundaries, protocols, and militia coordination guidelines," Chen announced as sealed folders circulated.

Shen opened his folder, his heart sinking at the text: "Militia vessels will initiate close-approach maneuvers to facilitate inspection opportunities. Naval units maintain overwatch and escalate upon noncompliance or hostile intent."

Translation: the militia will provoke, and naval forces will respond decisively, thought Shen.

A younger officer raised his hand. "What about Coast Guard coordination, Admiral?"

"There will be no Coast Guard involvement," Chen responded sharply. "This is exclusively a naval operation supporting civilian customs authority. Our actions have clear and firm legislative backing."

"Intelligence indicates significant Taiwanese military concentrations, including autonomous defense systems advised by American personnel," Chen continued, his tone unyielding. "Your primary mission is the enforcement of national sovereignty. Noncompliant vessels attempting to evade inspection or displaying hostile actions will be decisively stopped."

Captain Nie Yuhang stood, cautious. "Sir, what if American vessels intervene?"

"Any interference will constitute a direct threat to Chinese sovereignty," Chen stated coldly. "Intelligence assessments indicate the Americans are unlikely to risk direct confrontation. Autonomous systems may probe our operations. Observe, record, but engage only if hostile intent is clear."

He concluded gravely, "You have thirty days. Prioritize boarding drills, small-boat maneuvers, and strict fire discipline.

Remember, we enforce the law, but stand prepared to defend our national integrity. Unless provoked, we do not initiate conflict—but we will not tolerate challenges to our sovereignty."

As officers filed out, murmurs reflected mixed apprehension and determination. Shen's mentor, Vice Admiral Deng, subtly approached him. "Penghu will define this entire campaign. Trust your instincts, follow your orders. The nation's future depends on this."

Shen nodded solemnly. He understood clearly now—the Navy's role was provocatively structured under the undeniable legitimacy provided by DEAC-33, a legal framework masking an inevitable escalation.

As Shen stepped outside, heat washed over him, matching his inner turmoil. His phone buzzed. Messages from home were innocently unaware of the storm approaching. He responded briefly, unable to promise safety, only duty.

Thirty days.

He glanced toward Yulin Base, steel hulls gleaming ominously under the tropical sun.

The countdown to confrontation had begun, cloaked in legality but poised for history-altering consequences.

****

Later That Evening

Rain hammered Admiral Deng Litian's residence with tropical fury, each drop exploding against terra cotta tiles like liquid shrapnel. Captain Shen Tao paused in the covered entrance, watching water cascade off traditional eaves onto manicured gardens now churning with mud.

"Tao!" Deng Litian appeared in the doorway, trading his uniform for a simple cotton shirt that made him appear more grandfather than fleet admiral. "Come in, before you drown."

Inside, the house radiated quiet wealth and historic discretion— Ming dynasty vases shared space with silk scrolls of a bygone era. Deng led Shen to an antique cabinet, where he withdrew an expensive bottle of fine alcohol and a pair of ornately decorated glasses.

"Maotai," Deng said reverently as he showed him the bottle. "Fifty-year reserve. From simpler times."

"When were times ever simple?" Shen replied.

Deng chuckled softly. "Truth." He poured two glasses for them in his study. "But at least our enemies used to be human."

They drank, the fiery baijiu burning away pretense. The study in his base housing home resembled a command center, masquerading as a scholarly retreat. He had maps layered upon maps, a secure terminal glowing softly on his desk, and a wall-mounted display showing real-time naval positions across the Pacific and into the Arctic.

"Hungry?" Deng gestured to a simple meal—rice, steamed fish, vegetables. "My wife insists admirals eat like peasants. Keeps us humble."

They ate quietly, thunder punctuating the clink of chopsticks. Shen noticed Deng's eyes repeatedly drifting to the map display, especially focused on deployments in Russia and Iran.

Finally, Deng set down his bowl. "Tao, what do you know about this spring's exercise taking place in Western Russia, the Great Plains of Iran, and the Bering Sea?" he asked.

"Just that this exercise is supposed to test the logistical capabilities of the Eurasian Defense and Economic Pact's ability to transport large numbers of men and materials across great distances, assemble them into formations, and then conduct joint military exercises between our alliance partners. It's fairly similar to the annual NATO exercises held in Europe each summer and fall."

"That's what you are supposed to know." Deng moved to the wall display, enlarging deployment patterns. "What would you say if I told you this giant exercise was cover for something bigger? Something no one will see coming?"

Shen's chopsticks froze midair. "Are you serious? This exercise has been in the planning for more than a year. Heck, the Army has deployed two entire Group Armies to participate in it. What could it possibly be cover for, if not this exercise?"

"Tao, look more closely at the map," Deng encouraged, highlighting positions for him. "The Russians are massing a VDV division near the Finnish and Norwegian borders. They have deployed the 1st Tank Army opposite the Baltic States of Estonia, Latvia, and Lithuania. We have deployed the 82nd Group Army to Belarus, opposite Suwalki, Poland. The 1st PLA Naval Infantry Brigade is training with the Russian Marines in Kaliningrad, opposite the Swedish island of

Gotland. In the Middle East, the 79th Group Army is deploying with the Iranian Republican Guard Corps and the Pakistani 9th Mechanized Brigade along the Khuzestan province of southwestern Iran, opposite the city of Basrah along the Shatt al Arab river, adjacent to a series of strategic rail and highway routes connecting the energy fields of southern Iraq and northwest Kuwait. Do you see it now, Tao?"

Suddenly, it crystallized in Shen's mind. He hadn't noticed it earlier, but now it was glaringly obvious. He looked to Deng with newfound awe at his strategic brilliance. "Whoa, I think I see it. This entire time—this whole exercise, the hype, all of it—it's been nothing but a giant ruse. It's a pre-positioned threat to Europe and America, designed to keep them paralyzed. If they interfere with our actions against Taiwan, this so-called 'exercise' could pivot into a full-scale invasion—one they're not ready to repel. The whole thing is a feint. Brilliant."

"And the Padawan becomes the Master. While the world watches the EDEP exercise continue to unfold, we will be making our move to rein in the renegade province of Taiwan, using the passage of DEAC-33 as the legal pretext for our actions. The inspections at sea, justified by protecting our people from the deadly narcotic Vortex, are the tip of the spear," Deng explained. "When your squadron initiates inspections near Penghu, the world's media and Western navies will be completely absorbed by the ongoing exercises taking place along the Baltic Sea and the shores of Kaliningrad—not Taiwan. Not until it's too late."

Deng touched the display again, shifting to the Arctic and Northern Pacific. "When the world's attention suddenly shifts to Taiwan, that is when the EDEP exercise transforms into a full invasion of critical islands, harbors, and airstrips here—the Bering Strait. Meanwhile, Russia and our North Sea Fleet will rapidly secure the Arctic passages and gateways into the Bering Sea: Attu Station, Dutch Harbor, and St. Lawrence Island. With control of these areas, Tao, China and Russia will not merely dominate the global trade routes stretching from the South China Sea to the Bering Sea—we will control the future of Arctic commerce as it continues to be unlocked by the melting of polar ice.

"This means China and Russia will be positioned to dominate European and American trade corridors for the remainder of the twenty-first century. The brilliance of our plan, Tao, is that by paralyzing the

West with the threat of simultaneous invasion across Eastern Europe and the Baltics, we force them into inaction just long enough for us and our EDEP allies to seize control of our objectives and entrench ourselves beyond their capacity to dislodge us."

The sound of thunder crashed outside as Deng finished speaking. The lights of the room flickered ever so briefly before returning like nothing happened.

Shen sat there for a moment, thinking over what Deng had just shared. It was incredible, but also scary. "This explains so much—why you have been pushing us so hard these past few months, the rigid timelines, the invasion barges…all of it," Shen realized. "It all has to integrate with the announcement of the DEAC-33 legislation and customs inspections just as it has to integrate with the EDEP exercise. It's brilliant, Admiral."

"Yes, it is. And it took years to plan and make ready. Two empires reclaiming their spheres of influence, while America spreads itself impossibly thin and tears itself apart from within. We leverage the West's own fear of escalation. The same fear that made them hesitate in Ukraine will render them powerless now," Deng explained confidently.

Shen considered the implications before responding. "Sir, about the intelligence reports you shared with me about those autonomous naval vessels Taiwan's been receiving—supposedly from some American private military contractor. What happens if Taiwan fights harder than originally anticipated? What if those autonomous weapons inflict serious losses on my squadron in the Penghu area? If I understand the reports correctly, they're trying to turn the waters around Penghu into an autonomous killing field."

Deng's voice was grim but resolute as he responded. "If that happens, Tao, then it escalates. Obviously, it would mean your squadron would take losses. That may unfortunately be one of the prices we'll have to pay to achieve victory. If that is the case, we suffer whatever losses are necessary to achieve our strategic objective—the Penghu archipelago. You and I both know the capture of Penghu means Taiwan will be on borrowed time. If we have to, we simply embargo the island and starve them into submission."

Deng paused what he was about to say, staring at the digital map before speaking. "In the end, Tao, it's not like America is going to willingly trade the city of Los Angeles for Taipei. And it's not like

Europe would dare risk nuclear war over territories thousands of kilometers away. Just look at how paralyzed they were during the Russo-Ukraine War. The mere mention of nuclear weapons caused them to falter, exactly when they had Russia on the ropes. Instead, they allowed Putin to save face and turn certain defeat into strategic survival. Trust me, Tao—Europe and America will do the same in Asia. They'll blink."

Shen felt a shiver run down his spine at how casually his mentor spoke of nuclear war, of loss beyond anything he imagined. As he thought of his family in Beijing, he asked, "Admiral, you may be right about Europe, maybe even America. But are we prepared to risk losing Shanghai for Penghu if that's what it comes to?"

"That is a question for the CMC and the Politburo. Your mission, Tao, is to make sure it never comes to that. Give Taiwan a bloody nose, not a mortal wound. If things go according to the plan, then America will be too busy to respond with enough force to stop us."

Shen felt the urge to laugh, catching himself just in time.

"What's so funny, Tao?" asked Deng, his perceptive eye missing nothing.

"I was remembering a phrase an American boxer named Mike Tyson used to say," Shen began. "He said everyone has a plan until they get punched in the face."

Deng laughed, a deep, loud belly laugh. "Oh, Tao, I needed that. He is right, of course. No plan survives first contact. That is why I push you commanders so hard: to make you resilient, to force you to adapt and bounce back from each setback. I only hope I have prepared you commanders for the battles we are about to face," confided Deng.

Outside, the rain intensified. The wind howled through the palm trees as the eye of the storm approached.

Deng's tone softened as the rain grew louder. "There's something else I want to tell you; it's personal."

Shen waited quietly, letting him speak when he was ready.

"You know my son, Minghao, he recently took command of the *Long March 21*, one of our Type 094 nuclear-powered ballistic missile submarines. He's currently on deployment in the Arctic... our insurance policy if things spiral out of control..." Deng murmured softly, his mask slipping to reveal the same paternal anxiety a parent feels when their child is serving in the Armed Forces.

"I remember. Minghao was beyond excited when he learned he was selected for command of a *Jin*-class. But, sir, we do have some control in the escalation," replied Shen, reminding him they weren't completely powerless in what happened next.

"Do we?" Deng answered as he moved to the window, staring into the storm. "Or are we simply pretending to control the forces beyond human grasp?"

A flash of lightning illuminated the garden outside the window as Deng's voice grew softer. "Once first blood spills, Tao, control becomes an illusion. Follow your orders. Ensure your squadron does its job and brings us a swift victory before this plan has a chance to spiral out of control into something we'll regret."

Shen nodded soberly. "The rules of engagement practically guarantee—"

"Do not open this unless the situation demands it," Deng interrupted, handing Shen a sealed envelope from his desk safe. "It carries my personal authority. I trust you, Tao. Use your judgment over Beijing's. If you receive orders that endanger your survival, your crew's, perhaps the world's—don't hesitate to use this letter. I'm giving you the freedom to act wisely in a time of chaos."

Shen accepted the envelope; the weight of it felt beyond its paper and wax. "Of course. If I may, what does this letter say?"

"It says whatever you need it to say to cover and authorize whatever action you deemed necessary to take to ensure the survival of yourself, your crew, and our world, if necessary." Deng's eyes met Shen's with profound trust.

The sound of thunder crashed once more, close and violent as the windows shook.

"We're manipulating forces we barely understand," Deng continued softly. "Beijing sees opportunity. Moscow sees necessity. Washington sees threat. But no one sees the full picture."

He displayed a final map—global trade routes, populations, and critical infrastructure. "A conflict over Taiwan doesn't remain local. NATO responds, India and Pakistan destabilize, Korea moves opportunistically. The system unravels."

"Huh. Yeah, no pressure or anything," Shen remarked quietly.

Deng smiled faintly. "Command is always pressure. Either we direct it, or it directs us."

As Shen prepared to leave. Deng escorted him to the door, handing him an umbrella—an empty gesture amid the storm's fury.

"Tao, in the coming days, expect the unpredictable," Deng warned.

Shen nodded, then stepped into the chaos of the storm, rain pelting sideways, nature asserting its dominance. He hesitated at the threshold. "Admiral, if escalation spirals—"

"Then we'll answer the defining question of our time," Deng responded solemnly. "Does humanity control its tools, or do they control us?"

Lightning split the heavens, illuminating a landscape of fury. Shen saw with stark clarity the perilous brink they stood upon.

He hurried to his car, rain drenching him instantly. Inside, he clutched Deng's envelope tightly, a lifeline against potential catastrophe. The sound of thunder rolled ominously across Yulin Naval Base. In thirty days, their meticulously planned trap would be sprung. God help them all when it was.

Chapter Nineteen:
Yanks Are Coming

March 17, 2033
Swedish Armed Forces Headquarters
Lidingövägen 24, Stockholm

When the secure video from NATO headquarters in Mons, Belgium, disconnected, General Michael Claesson, Chief of Defense, turned to face the heads of the Army, Major General Johan Hallberg; Air Force, Major General Bengt Wilkson; and Navy, Rear Admiral Patrik Nilsson. His aide brought up an interactive map of the island of Gotland for them to discuss. Highlighted on the map was the main city of Visby along with the port and airfield. To the south lay Tofta Barracks and the accompanying Tofta Range, home of the Gotland Regiment P18 and the 32nd Home Guard Battalion, the Gotland Grönt Centrum in Roma, and key road networks that connected the island.

General Claesson cleared his throat. "Generals, I hope this talk with Secretary-General Stubb and SACEUR General Calder helps to assure you that Sweden, along with Finland and our Baltic cousins, will not be left alone in the face of this enormous exercise occurring in Belarus and throughout the Leningrad Oblast—especially in light of recent developments."

Claesson paused, his voice growing more measured. "As we were on the call, the Chinese Foreign Minister, Qiao Wenli, formally announced from Kaliningrad the commissioning of a new military facility. They're calling it the 'Northern Hawk Airfield'—it's that old Soviet base, Chernyakhovsk. This new facility is now jointly operated by the PLA Air Force and the Russian Federation. Hours later, Minister Qiao traveled to Baltiysk to officially commission what they're calling the 'Kaliningrad Special Logistics Zone.'"

Rear Admiral Nilsson leaned forward. "A logistics zone? That's their cover story?"

Claesson nodded grimly. "Precisely. But it's what's behind that facade that concerns us. The PLA Navy announced the establishment of Task Group Changfeng-21, officially designated as the PLA Baltic Fleet Detachment. Their stated purpose is to ensure safe passage for Chinese and EDEP vessels through the Baltic Sea. This fleet is formidable,

Admiral. We are talking about guided-missile destroyers, frigates, corvettes, submarines, and even an amphibious assault capability. More alarming, they've openly stated this move is designed to prevent what they call 'future disasters like the Gotland incident,' a clear reference to the confrontation we had off our own coast."

Hallberg shifted uneasily. "What about ground forces?"

"Minister Qiao also confirmed that ground units participating in their EDEP-Defender exercise will remain permanently stationed in Kaliningrad. We're talking heavy armor, mechanized infantry, attack helicopters, and significant air-defense capabilities."

Major General Wilkson exhaled, shaking his head. "This changes the security equation in the Baltic region completely. With their most advanced fighter and ISR aircraft based less than three hundred kilometers from our shores…"

"Exactly," Claesson affirmed sharply. "We must calibrate our responses carefully, bolstering Gotland's defenses without handing Moscow or Beijing a pretext for escalation. NATO has committed the American 2-503rd Infantry Regiment and enhanced anti-aircraft and missile defense assets to Gotland precisely for this reason. I expect each of you to ensure your branches are prepared, vigilant, but disciplined. We will maintain readiness without provoking unnecessary tensions."

He surveyed each officer deliberately. "The strategic balance is shifting beneath our feet. Our job now is to make certain Sweden remains firmly anchored. Coordinate closely, plan carefully, and keep me apprised."

General Claesson then turned directly toward Colonel Anders Lindqvist, commander of the Gotland Regiment.

"Colonel Lindqvist, the Americans are already on the island with their advance party, but as you know, they've deployed only Bravo Company of the 2-503rd Infantry Regiment to Gotland. Alpha and Charlie Companies are currently slated for basing at the naval facility near Stockholm, with Delta Company near the submarine base at Muskö. Given Minister Qiao's latest announcement and the sheer scale of the Chinese deployment in Kaliningrad, what's your assessment?"

Lindqvist straightened, his expression serious. "General, frankly speaking, one American company—regardless of its capabilities—will barely be enough to protect the Patriot and HIMARS batteries. With the Chinese now openly basing a significant force just across the sea, I strongly recommend you press NATO to deploy the entire battalion here, or at the very least, one or two additional companies. If we're to credibly cover island-wide security, countersabotage patrols, and rapid responses to potential infiltration, I'll need more soldiers and more equipment than we currently have."

Claesson nodded thoughtfully. "You're right, Colonel. Given today's announcements, it's clear Gotland is no longer merely symbolic—it's a potential front line. I'll raise this immediately with the Americans and General Calder at NATO. In the meantime, we must prepare as if Bravo Company is all we'll have. Beyond the American presence, what else will you need to hold the island effectively? Would a targeted call-up of local reservists suffice, or do we need immediate mainland reinforcements?"

Lindqvist replied without hesitation. "General, given the scale of what's happening in Kaliningrad, targeted reservist call-ups would help. It would minimize strain elsewhere in the country, allowing us to strengthen island security without weakening the mainland. But even then, we can't rely solely on reservists and Home Guard units to defend the critical infrastructure at Visby, the countryside, and the air base without creating dangerous gaps."

Captain Joran Lindholm, commander of the island's Leopard 2 tank platoon, leaned forward, interjecting calmly, "Sir, we've already begun positioning armor just north of the airport—hidden from public view but close enough to rapidly respond. I've consulted with our American counterparts; we're all in agreement about dispersing Patriot and HIMARS batteries into hardened, camouflaged sites. No co-location. No proximity to civilian population centers."

Next to him, Major Mikael Stenqvist affirmed, "Fallback positions for both US and Swedish missile systems are already under preparation. If missiles start flying, we'll need more dedicated transport assets to ensure rapid repositioning."

Across the table, Captain Elin Boström, liaison from the Eastern Air Defense Command, adjusted the overlay on her tablet, her voice professional yet tense.

"Our fighters will maintain continuous air patrol coverage over Gotland and the surrounding Baltic Sea, fully coordinated with NATO's air policing operations. NATO's asked us specifically for increased coastal patrol craft presence and additional SHORAD coverage around the Patriot and HIMARS reload points, as well as ISR units operating near Tofta."

She looked directly at Claesson. "With your approval, we can redeploy an additional RBS 70 team to the southern ridge and a mobile IRIS-T launcher near Slite. That would fill the blind zones effectively without overtly militarizing the entire island."

Captain Bertil Sonevang, representing the Gotland Home Guard, folded his arms firmly. His tone was calm yet resolute. "General, our troops are already actively patrolling the woods, cliffs, and coastlines quietly but effectively. If saboteurs arrive, we'll find them quickly. However, clear operational boundaries must be established with NATO personnel. We'll coordinate with them, but under no circumstance will the Home Guard be subordinated directly to foreign command structures. Islanders will not tolerate Gotland becoming a permanent NATO forward operating base."

Claesson raised his hand reassuringly. "I fully understand your concerns, Lieutenant. That's exactly the careful line we must navigate. NATO's presence here is necessary, but optics and islander sentiment matter greatly. Colonel Lindqvist, I trust you'll handle coordination personally with the incoming American commander at Tofta. Captain Boström, maintain tight airspace coordination with NATO's Joint Force Air Component. And, Captain Sonevang, I authorize immediate mobilization of two reservist platoons at your discretion."

The general then gestured back toward the interactive map, emphasizing the northern and western regions of Visby. "Make sure launcher sites are positioned north and west of the city, carefully concealed, far from residential areas. No convoys through the city center. NATO uniforms should only appear in town at our invitation or in clearly approved circumstances."

He paused, letting the weight of his words sink in. "Task Force Sentinel isn't simply here to reinforce us; it's a strategic trip wire. With the situation in Kaliningrad unfolding rapidly, Gotland is directly in the crosshairs. Gentlemen, let's ensure we remain ready without becoming reckless."

Each officer exchanged solemn, determined nods, fully grasping the gravity of the task before them.

****

Following Day—Late Morning
Northern Gotland Ferry Crossing
Fårö Island

The wind coming off the Baltic was crisp but tolerable, a reminder that spring hadn't quite made up its mind. The small ferry pitched gently as it glided across the narrow sound separating Gotland from Fårö, its deck empty but for a few cars and a solitary van. A gull screeched overhead.

Mikko Rautio stood at the railing, hands stuffed into the pockets of his waxed canvas coat, eyes scanning the northern coastline as it emerged—windswept, sparse, and quiet.

"Perfect light," he murmured in Finnish, lifting his phone to snap a few reference shots of the approaching shoreline. "Soft shadows. The raukar will look incredible once the fog lifts."

Sanna, seated behind the car's windshield with her tablet balanced on her knees, looked up from the outline she'd been refining.

"Chapter five," she called out. "The jarl's longship makes landfall here. Midsummer storm. The cliffs feel like teeth as they approach."

Mikko smiled faintly. "That's good. We should hike out to Langhammars at dusk—catch the rocks under the low sun."

From anyone listening, it was ordinary enough. Writers in their element. A couple escaping to the silence of the islands for historical inspiration. That was the point.

But Mikko had already logged the position of the new relay antenna near Fårösund on the way up from Visby. And the coastal defense radar near Bungenäs, barely visible through the pines, had been rotating on a tighter interval than usual. Noted. Time-stamped. Logged.

As the ferry ramp clanked down onto the short stretch of dock, Sanna slid her sunglasses on and adjusted her scarf.

"I messaged Eva—the Airbnb host. She left the keys in the box by the porch, like last time. The house sits just beyond Ryssnas," she said casually. "She mentioned something about the historical society hosting a local exhibit in Visby next month. Might be worth supporting. Good visibility for the channel."

"Perfect," Mikko replied. "We'll offer to contribute. Maybe a special episode on the Brotherhood of Raukar."

"Or a short AI-animated sequence," she added, tapping her stylus. "Something eerie. The land gods never left."

The roads of Fårö were as they remembered—narrow, edged with early spring frost, and lined with scrub pine and open rock. The farther north they drove, the fewer cars they saw. When they passed a Home Guard checkpoint near a coastal trailhead, Mikko offered a friendly wave. The soldier didn't stop them—just logged the license plate like always.

By the time they pulled into the gravel driveway of their Airbnb—a weathered timber cottage tucked into the woods just west of Norsta Auren—the sun had pushed through the cloud layer.

The porch creaked beneath their boots. Mikko opened the lockbox and retrieved the key with a practiced hand. Inside, the cottage smelled faintly of smoke and cedar. A welcome basket sat on the kitchen table—locally made crackers, a jar of juniper honey, and a handwritten note:

Welcome back, Sanna & Mikko! Hope your writing goes well. Let me know if you need anything. Weather should hold through the weekend. Eva.

Sanna smiled. "She thinks we're writing the sequel to *Daughters of the Iron Wind*. We may need to actually write it now."

Mikko dropped their bag by the door and peered out the window toward the trail leading north.

"We'll give them something worth filming," he said quietly. Then, louder, "Let's take the drone out tomorrow. Sunrise over the cliffs?"

Sanna nodded. "And this afternoon, we visit the old fishing harbor. I want to walk the ridgeline."

From this cozy little hideaway, nestled between folklore and granite, the map of Gotland's defenses would soon take shape—piece by careful piece.

Chapter Twenty:
Everyone Knows Bertil

March 18, 2033
Bravo Company Headquarters
2nd Battalion, 503rd Infantry Regiment (Airborne)
Gotland Grönt Centrum

By the fourth day, patterns emerged. The Swedes worked in careful layers—planning, discussing, implementing with quiet efficiency. They knew every trail, every cove, every farmer who might report unusual activity. Home Guard members like Bertil seemed to materialize from the forest itself, bearing local intelligence and strong coffee.

Mercer's advance team adapted. Sites were selected for the incoming Patriot batteries—dispersed positions that balanced concealment with coverage. Ammunition would be cached in small lots, never concentrated. Fuel dumps were positioned near civilian stations, hidden in plain sight.

"It's like building a ghost defense," Holloway observed over dinner in Roma's mess hall. "Everything scattered, nothing obvious."

"That's the point." Mercer pushed reconstituted beef around his plate. The Swedes had apologized for the limited menu—supply chains were still adjusting to the sudden influx. "If Ivan comes calling, he won't find neat targets."

"Think he will?" Staff Sergeant Landon McRae asked. The designated marksman had spent the day scouting sniper positions with his Swedish counterpart.

"Above our pay grade," Tanner interjected. "We prepare for yes and hope for no."

Through the mess hall windows, dusk painted Gotland's forests purplish black. Somewhere out there, Russian satellites were photographing every new antenna, every vehicle movement. The chess pieces were sliding into position.

"Sir?" A Swedish corporal appeared at Mercer's elbow. "Colonel Lindqvist requests your presence. Priority message from your headquarters."

Mercer exchanged glances with Tanner. Priority messages rarely brought good news.

The Swedish command post was a study in organized efficiency, filled with banks of radios, digital displays showing real-time air traffic, and a coffeepot that never seemed to empty. Lindqvist handed Mercer an encrypted printout as he walked in.

"The deployment schedule for the remainder of your unit has been accelerated," the colonel said simply. "They now arrive in four days."

Mercer scanned the message. He suspected someone in Brussels or D.C. was getting nervous with all the saber-rattling going on. When the military accelerated the timeline of deployment, it was usually because something was heating up.

Mercer turned to Lindqvist. "Can Visby handle the sudden influx of the airlift?"

"Eh, we'll make it work." Lindqvist's tone suggested Swedish determination kicking in. "You have a lot of heavy equipment coming?"

"Some. Mostly JLTVs, our unarmored infantry support vehicles, and a few Strykers mounted with those new Leonidas-IIIs—the high-powered microwaves. They're incredible drone killers. But they are coming by sea."

"Hmm, good to know. Then we have much to prepare," replied Lindqvist. He turned to his staff, speaking rapid Swedish. Orders were given, acknowledged, executed. The machinery of defense accelerated as preparations got underway.

Later, walking back to his temporary quarters, Mercer found Bertil sitting on a bench, studying the stars.

"Clear night," the Home Guard veteran observed. "Good for satellites. Yours and theirs."

"You think they're watching us now, here on Gotland?" asked Mercer.

"Always." Bertil's weathered face was thoughtful as he went on to explain. "Captain, my great-grandfather fought the Russians in 1939, in the Winter War in Finland, not here. He was one of the men who volunteered. When the Russians invaded, no one from Europe or America came to their aid—only their fellow Nordic neighbors. He said the worst part of the war was waiting. Not knowing if the Russians would come or where they might come from. Just…waiting."

"Yes, that must have been hard, not knowing," Mercer offered, his voice low. "It's different now, Bertil. NATO, technology—"

"Eh, yes and no," interrupted Bertil. He stood, joints creaking as he stretched his back. "Sure, technology changes, but men don't. Someone in Moscow looks at this island, sees opportunity. Someone in Washington sees a threat, or a way to hurt Russia and now China. And we Gotlanders, us Swedes...? All we see is home...and we wonder if we will still have one when the dust settles."

Bertil then turned to Mercer, patting him on the shoulder like a father would a son, his voice warm and proud. "I'm starting to like you, Captain. Your boys seem competent, and that's a good thing. If trouble comes, we'll need that." He paused, then added. "But enough talk of war and what might happen. Let us talk about this chess rematch you owe me."

Mercer smiled, "Sure, we can play another match tonight if you'd like. But first I need to take a moment and call my wife." He excused himself and began walking away from the building, reaching into his pocket to retrieve his phone.
****

Alex Mercer pressed the phone to his ear, smiling instinctively as Maddie's voice rang through, bright and excited.

"Alex! Oh my God, babe! You won't believe it!" she burst out, a tremble of joyful tears threading through her words.

He chuckled, warmth filling him instantly at the sound of her voice. "Slow down, Madz. What's happened?"

"The new book, Alex—it's hit number seven overall on Amazon. Number seven! It's been in the top hundred for three straight days now!"

"That's incredible!" Pride swelled in Alex's chest, almost overwhelming. "I told you, didn't I? Always knew you had it in you."

"Because you never stopped believing in me," she replied, her voice softer now, earnest and deeply grateful. "You know I couldn't have done this without you. Everything you've sacrificed...the late nights, the marketing lessons, the nanny—"

"It was worth every moment," he assured gently, picturing her face, eyes sparkling with triumph and tears. "How are my girls and my little dude?"

"They miss you terribly. Haley and Holly keep asking when Daddy's coming home, and Alex Jr. points at your picture and babbles something suspiciously close to 'Dada.'"

Alex's throat tightened, emotion thickening his voice. "I miss them so much. I miss you."

"We miss you too," she whispered, voice breaking softly. She gathered herself quickly, laughing lightly through fresh tears. "But listen to this—I checked what it says I've sold, and you won't believe it, Alex. I've sold an entire year's worth of your captain's pay in just four days. Four days—can you believe it?"

He nearly choked, astonishment flooding him. Never in a million years had he thought her hobby would turn into such a goldmine. "Madz, are you serious right now?"

"Dead serious," she laughed, triumphant and a bit mischievous. "And when all of this is over, I'm going to retire you from the Army, soldier boy."

Alex laughed softly, shaking his head, still amazed. "Oh, I don't think we're quite there yet. Let's wait and see how the rest of this series turns out, OK?"

"Ha-ha, you're jealous. You watch, buddy," she said firmly, the smile evident in her voice. "Ah, I hear junior crying. I gotta go take care of this, but you stay safe out there and hurry your butt home. I'll need to put you back to work marketing my next book."

He swallowed hard, the thought bittersweet yet enticingly real. "Will do. I'll stay safe. I'll be home to you and the kids before you know it."

"You'd better," she said softly, heartfelt urgency underscoring her words. "We need you home."

"I love you, Madz."

"Love you more, Blackjack Six," she teased gently. "Stay safe."

As Alex ended the call, he took a deep breath, carrying her words like armor against the uncertain days ahead.

This had better stay an exercise... he ruminated to himself as he headed back to the barracks and the game of chess Bertil was bound to be waiting to play.

****

Captain Alex Mercer took a moment to stretch as the vehicles came to a halt. Today marked the eighth day since his advance party had arrived on Gotland. They were nearing the end of their familiarization tour, finalizing potential positions for equipment from the 1st Battalion, 59th Air Defense Artillery Regiment that was now steadily arriving. Major Zachary Holt, the battalion's S3, had joined them the previous night, eager to scout precise locations for the launchers, radar stations, and supporting infrastructure.

The final area Mercer still needed to see lay along Gotland's rugged eastern shore, where limestone cliffs plunged sharply into the Baltic, creating a natural barrier that had witnessed Viking longships, Hanseatic merchants, and invasion fleets alike throughout history. The strategic importance of this coastline was unmistakable, even in peacetime.

Captain Elin Boström, commander of the Gotland Regiment's IRIS-T battery, had taken point for today's visit. Mercer had found Captain Boström impressive from the moment they'd first met eight days prior, struck by how seamlessly she and Bertil combined sharp tactical knowledge with a deep appreciation of the island's storied history, interspersed with casual wit and easy humor.

Today, Boström and Bertil had guided Mercer, Holt, and the rest of their small team to an overlook near Smöjen, several kilometers south of Kyllaj harbor. From this vantage point, the Baltic stretched out before them, glittering in the sunlight, with the hazy outline of Latvia faintly visible along the horizon.

Captain Boström gestured toward discreetly camouflaged equipment positioned nearby. "Right there is one of our IRIS-T radar installations," she explained confidently. "It covers this entire sector, giving us excellent visibility toward the sea and early warning against threats coming from the direction of Latvia or mainland Russia. From here, we track every vessel and aircraft crossing into Swedish waters."

"Impressive setup, Captain," Sergeant First Class Holloway remarked, clearly intrigued. "What's the radar's operational range?"

Boström smiled warmly, appreciating Holloway's genuine interest. "The Giraffe 1X radar we're operating here can reliably detect air targets up to around seventy-five kilometers out," she explained. "When it comes to smaller targets like FPVs, UAVs, and drones, its effective detection range narrows to between twenty and forty kilometers, with coverage extending up to about ten thousand meters—or around thirty-three thousand feet, for you Yanks," she added with a playful wink.

Major Holt stepped forward, studying the position intently. "Captain, your IRIS-T battery and radar capability dovetail perfectly with what we're setting up at Grönt Centrum. Once our Patriot battery is in place near Romakloster and the railway, your radar feed can directly augment our detection capabilities at lower altitudes. The Patriots will handle the higher and longer-range threats—ballistic and cruise missiles, fighter jets—while your IRIS-T provides intermediate coverage. Together, that's a robust layered defense."

"Exactly," Boström confirmed enthusiastically. "Integrating your Patriot battery with our IRIS-T network is key to comprehensive airspace management. And with your Leonidas-III high-powered microwave systems in place, we'll also neutralize drone swarms without firing a shot. I understand you plan to mount those on JLTVs and Strykers?"

"Precisely," Holt nodded. "Bravo Company, 2-503rd Infantry, will operate eight Leonidas-III systems spread strategically around our critical assets—Patriot radars and launchers, HIMARS batteries, and our key command-and-control nodes. The HPM systems will be fully integrated through NATO's Integrated Air and Missile Defence network, giving us an immediate, non-kinetic option against drone swarms and small UCAV threats."

Mercer glanced out across the Baltic once more, the cool sea breeze tugging at his jacket collar. This spot near Smöjen, with its hidden radars and commanding views, underscored exactly why Gotland had long been a linchpin of Baltic defense strategies. The systems they were now positioning represented a decisive evolution in capability—a blend of high-tech equipment and skilled professionals committed to ensuring the island remained a formidable deterrent.

"All right," Mercer said decisively, turning to Major Holt and Captain Boström. "This location is definitely a go. Let's lock it in."
****

Later That Day
Fårösund, Gotland

Captain Alex Mercer and the small convoy departed the overlook near Smöjen, leaving behind the panoramic views and the concealed radar positions. They navigated narrow roads flanked by dense pine and juniper forests, heading north toward Fårösund, where the ferry connected Gotland to Fårö Island.

Arriving at the ferry terminal, Mercer noticed the expansive Baltic stretching out before them, dotted with islands and framed by stark, windswept shores. Captain Elin Boström guided them to a strategic viewpoint near the terminal, pointing toward the horizon.

"Here, and across on Faro, near Southern Sand, there are some campsites along the beach, and some roads that lead inland, connecting the beach to the rest of the island," she explained, indicating a stretch of shoreline and how an enemy might come ashore. "If I was invading, I would come ashore here as it's a prime location for amphibious landings and quick access to roads leading out of the beach area."

Bertil unfolded a map of Faro and began to explain. "Captain Mercer, when you look at Faro, you have Southern Sand resort area in the south, and Norsta Aurer beach to the north. But only Southern Sand has immediate access to a road. It has fewer obstacles, mostly gravelly beaches—making this place ideal terrain if the opposition brings specialized landing craft."

Mercer studied the landscape, already visualizing defensive positions. First Sergeant Tanner had his camera out again, methodically documenting angles and approaches. "I take it you guys have pre-registered artillery targets?" he asked, his voice clinical.

"Yes, of course, every hundred meters. In fact, we have pre-registered coordinates for every possible beach landing location onto Gotland and Faro. This makes it easy for artillery and air units to know where to bomb depending on what kind of information we are receiving," Boström responded, pride evident in her confident tone. "This comes from decades of preparation. Each rock, every significant tree, everything has coordinates and firing solutions should the Russians and their friends try something."

Just then, a chilly gust blew off the Baltic. Mercer could swear it felt like a tension in the air had just blown over them. It reminded him of a feeling, like something bad was about to happen. It was a premonition he'd felt during his time with the Rangers, when his company would provide security or overwatch for a Delta or SEAL before it went bad.

Mercer pushed the feeling aside, then turned directly to Boström. "What's your professional assessment, Captain? If Gotland was assaulted by Russian VDV or Marines, how long could you hold out without reinforcements?"

She considered the question carefully, then turned to face the sea. "That depends of course on how large the force is that invades, but if I had to guess, with the size of our force and your own, seventy-two hours against a determined invader. Perhaps ninety-six if we trade space to buy time." Boström then turned to face Mercer directly. "But that's not the primary strategy, correct? You Americans aren't planning for a delaying action, are you?"

Mercer met her gaze firmly. "No, ma'am. We're here to win."

"Good. Then let's hope your Patriots and Leonidas-III systems are as effective as your confidence suggests," she replied, offering a thin smile.

Major Holt, who had remained quiet through most of the tour, spoke up. "With your IRIS-T batteries integrated, Captain Boström, and our Patriots in position around Romakloster and the Grönt Centrum, I feel pretty confident about our systems creating a solid, overlapping coverage of Gotland that'll extend several hundred kilometers in every direction. Should the Russians or Chinese decide to get froggy with waves of FPV drones or something like that, our Leonidas-III HPM units and Strykers will handle any drone swarms and loitering munitions. I think this gives us some good flexibility and depth in protecting critical targets against conventional and hybrid threats."

Mercer nodded approvingly. "Agreed. Especially in light of what they discovered from that Chinese cargo vessel your Navy intercepted off the coast. But that also brings me back to something I was thinking about during our last stop, Boström," he said as he looked at Bertil's map again. He pointed to Karlsvärd Fortress, at the entrance of Slite harbor. "I know this is a historical military fort, and the last time it was used was in 2011, but I can't get past how geographically well positioned this location is for protecting Slite.

"You pointed out how you have one of your Giraffe radars located near Slite, and we'll likely place one of those Leonidas systems there with a HIMARS truck. But what if we placed a platoon of soldiers on Karlsvärd, armed with Javelin ATGMs and MANPADs? We could turn that little island into a decent fortified position, especially if we pair the platoon with a mortar section and heavy weapons squad," Mercer explained.

Colonel Lindqvist seemed to agree. "It's not a bad idea, Captain. It does come down to manpower. We just don't have enough soldiers to man all the positions we should. I'd like to broach this topic with your battalion commander and my own leadership. I don't particularly like the idea of having your battalion scattered across three different locations like this. It leaves you too thin in too many areas and not strong in any one particular spot. But that is a political question that is above my pay grade. For now, let's finish the site survey and prep for the arrival of the rest of your equipment and people."

The ride back toward Roma was subdued, each occupant absorbed by their thoughts. Upon arrival at the tactical operations center, they were met with an unexpected sight: a cluster of civilian cars bearing official Swedish government plates.

"Great, speaking of politics," Colonel Lindqvist muttered with thinly veiled annoyance. "It would appear we have our Stockholm observers visiting today."

Mercer chuckled at the familiar feeling. *I guess the military perspective of politicians is universal, even here in Sweden…*

As Mercer and Colonel Lindqvist exited the vehicle, one of the bureaucrats made his way toward them. He extended a hand toward Colonel Lindqvist. "Colonel, good to see you again."

Lindqvist smiled pleasantly, shaking his hand. "Likewise, Deputy Minister. If you'll allow me, this is Captain Alex Mercer. He's the company commander for Bravo Company, Second Battalion, 503rd Airborne Infantry," the colonel introduced.

"It's a pleasure to meet you, Captain. I'm Deputy Defense Minister Eriksson," the slender man said. He adjusted his rimless glasses. "Don't mind us. We are just checking in, here to assess how the integration of your forces into the defense of Sweden is going."

"Things are going well, Deputy Minister. The majority of the American forces begin to arrive in the coming days," interjected Lindqvist diplomatically.

"Oh, that's good to hear. Hopefully, some of the residents will understand their presence is just temporary. You would be surprised how some residents are already expressing concerns about their pending arrival," Eriksson cautiously warned.

"It's nothing personal against you or your men, Captain," he said to Mercer. "It's just that American forces tend to draw attention— sometimes unwanted attention, some argue."

Mercer got the hint and interjected firmly but respectfully, "We understand, sir. We're mindful of that, and that is why we are looking to maintain a minimal footprint. No unnecessary presence in civilian areas. Out of sight, out of mind."

"Hmm, that's good to hear. Public perception remains sensitive," Eriksson pressed, looking directly at Mercer. "I appreciate the 'out of sight, out of mind' mentality, but perhaps some community engagement might reassure some skeptical locals? You know, show the human side of NATO operations if you will."

Tanner coughed quietly, suppressing amusement at the thought of paratroopers conducting soft community outreach.

"Perhaps once the units and their equipment have fully arrived, we can consider how to do something like this," Lindqvist replied, ending the discussion.

As the delegation departed, Bertil appeared silently beside Mercer, observing the civilian cars leave. "Politicians…they want safety without soldiers, security without weapons. An impossible balance."

"Same everywhere, I guess," Mercer laughed. "Don't worry, Bertil. They'll appreciate us quickly enough if things turn ugly."

"If," Bertil echoed solemnly. "A small word with large consequences."

Mercer gathered his team later that evening inside Roma's tactical operations center. Maps and laptops filled the tables, powered by strong Swedish coffee. First Sergeant Tanner briefed on the main body's imminent arrival, detailing housing arrangements and logistics. Major Holt outlined Patriot battery positions near Gråtmon, with secondary sites identified to the north and east.

Before adjourning, Mercer revisited Eriksson's point about community relations. Ideas circulated: language training cards, sports matches with locals, structured activity to minimize friction. Yet Mercer knew the best reassurance came from effective defense.

As his team dispersed for the night, Mercer paused, staring across Gotland's landscape now fading into twilight. Stepping outside, he felt the Baltic breeze again, crisp and invigorating. Soon, NATO's pledge to Gotland would be tangible, embodied by soldiers ready to hold the line. Only time would reveal if their preparations would be tested, but until then, readiness was their watchword.

****

March 19, 2033
Klara Hedevig's Apartment
Innerstad, Visby
Gotland, Sweden

The kettle clicked off just as the front door opened. Klara Hedevig didn't move from the window. She watched the mist crawl across the rooftops of southern Visby, soft tendrils of dampness rolling inland from the sea.

"You left the lock undone again," came her boyfriend's voice, boots thudding as he entered. "One of these days, I'll walk in and scare you half to death."

Klara turned just enough to offer a faint smile. "Maybe that's what I was hoping for."

Lars snorted. "Well, if you want a scare, I've got news for you." He shrugged off his field jacket, tossed it over the back of the chair, and ran a hand through damp, wind-mussed hair. "You remember how we were told it would just be one company of American paratroopers?"

"Bravo Company, right? The ones at the Grönt Centrum in Roma?"

He dropped into the kitchen chair, rubbing his face. "Yeah. That's changed. Everything's changed. The Chinese Foreign Minister opened his mouth yesterday—made it official that the PLA and Russian Navy have their little love nest up in Kaliningrad. And guess what? The PLA restored that old Soviet air base outside Gvardeysk."

Klara stiffened slightly. She kept her back to him, pouring two mugs of tea with practiced calm. "I thought that base was derelict."

"So did Stockholm. So did NATO. But turns out the Chinese have been quietly rebuilding it for years. And now, we find out there's a full PLA amphibious task force exercising with Russian Marines. So now, NATO wants to move all their American paratroopers, consolidated here on Gotland."

He accepted the tea with a tired nod. "Whole regiment's coming. Not just Bravo. Alpha Company is taking over Vidhave Eco Lodge and some surrounding property. Patriot missile crews and C2 elements are moving in with them."

Klara sat slowly across from him. "That's...a lot more people."

"Yeah, no kidding," he replied, clearly irritated. "Charlie and Delta Companies are going to be billeted near the P18 compound and the Tofta Range." He shook his head. "That area's going to look like Fort Bragg East by next week. We were never set up to house a full regiment. I've got HVAC techs flying in from Malmö and Stockholm, commercial tenting companies on twenty-four-hour call. We're bringing in those massive, long tents with integrated flooring and climate control—you know, the ones they use for disaster relief? We're converting half the logistics park in Slite to house gear and overflow billets."

"Sounds like a nightmare," Klara said, voice low, distracted.

He laughed bitterly. "You have no idea. We're about four trailers of portable toilets away from losing our minds."

"This is going to impact the lodging I had set up for the Baltic Wings Festival near the airport, isn't it?" she asked.

"Yeah, it probably is," Lars answered. "And I can't guarantee it won't affect any of your other bookings with the huge amount of influx coming in."

"Damn. This is going to be really inconvenient for both of us, then," Klara replied.

Lars put his head into his hands. "It's going to be a *very* long week...at least I have you to make it better."

"Aw, I'm so sorry all of this is coming down on you all at once," Klara responded soothingly. She stood up and gave him a hug from behind before massaging Lars's shoulders.

Although she did her best to play the role of empathetic and dutiful girlfriend, she had moved behind him partly so she wouldn't have to work as hard to control her face. Her thoughts were spiraling. Eight of her operatives had confirmed lodging near the airport. Vidhave was only fifteen minutes west by car. If Alpha Company was taking over the area, that entire plan was compromised. Worse, the Patriot unit and their support teams would make any movement toward the airfield a much riskier proposition.

Lars slowly relaxed his shoulders under the influence of her strong hands. He sighed. "Thank you for this. You always know how to calm me down."

"Of course," Klara replied cheerfully. "I'm here for you."

After another moment or so, she slipped back down into her seat and took another sip of her tea. "So when does Alpha Company arrive, my love?"

"They're already off the boat. Staging now in Visby Harbor."

Her stomach tightened.

"Well, how can I help make this whole situation better for you?" she asked.

"I can think of one thing," Lars said with a wink. "But it will have to wait. I still have to coordinate power grid assessments with Region Gotland and find a local contractor who can deliver six hundred meals three times a day until the field kitchens are operational. Honestly, I just came here for breakfast and to vent. I have to be out the door again in fifteen."

She reached over and placed her hand on his. "Lars, I am so sorry. We'll get through this…together. Let me fix you breakfast," she replied.

In no time flat she had some toasted rye crispbread and jam on a plate for him, which he accepted with gratitude. As soon as he ate it, he rose from the table, kissed her on the head, and left.

Once the door closed, Klara allowed herself to curse quietly under her breath. "This is going to mess up all of my hard work!" she said to herself. Now instead of the original one hundred and fifty or so US paratroopers her operatives had planned on encountering, they'd be up against about six hundred of them. Not to mention, these huge areas being taken over would absolutely impact her housing plans before and during the festival.

She needed to get to the office as soon as possible. Her morning observation walk would have to wait.

As soon as she stepped into her work area, Klara went straight for her laptop. She logged in, turned on her VPN, and didn't even bother checking the birding websites yet. This amount of information would be very difficult to transmit through one of the boards. Instead, she went right for her Tuta email account, where she wrote a draft email that she would never send. She had just finished typing when she noticed another draft email besides the one she had been writing.

The message was simple: "Team modified. Eight Russian attendees of the Baltic Wings Festival have changed their travel plans, and Chinese attendees will be taking their place."

For the second time that morning, Klara swore. Russians could blend in. But Chinese? In Roma? In Vidhave?

She stood abruptly and crossed to her laptop. Everything was unraveling. And the Americans weren't even fully unpacked yet.

She exhaled, forcing herself to slow her breathing and concentrate.

Time to pivot, she thought. *Time to adapt. Before the window closes entirely.*

Chapter Twenty-One:
Welcome to the Edge

March 21, 2033 – 0730 Hours
North Ramp
Andersen Air Force Base, Guam

Tropical rain hammered the tarmac in sheets. The squall had rolled in fast, turning the morning sky the color of old steel. Wind gusts shoved the C-17's tail as hydraulics lowered its cargo ramp with a mechanical groan.

Jodi Mack stood just inside the hangar bay, tablet tucked under her tactical jacket as rain hammered the flight deck. Water pooled around her boots, trailing wet prints across concrete still warm from the previous day's sun. Outside, forty-eight Taiwanese sailors and marines stood in formation under the deluge. Their digital blue uniforms clung to them like a second skin, soaked and dripping—but not a single one shifted or grumbled.

Good, she thought. *They'll need that kind of discipline.*

"Skinny Poo's probably watching this through a spy satellite," Mick muttered, checking his watch. "Counting heads. Measuring shadows."

She glanced at Mick, still smirking at the nickname "Skinny Poo." It had been born in 2013, when a photo of Xi Jinping and Obama walking alongside each other caught the attention of a savvy internet troll in Taiwan. He'd replaced the two with a caricature of Winnie-the-Pooh and Tigger. Xi was Pooh, obviously, and as the meme went viral, Beijing lost its mind.

They banned the meme, scrubbing search results and declaring Pooh an "enemy of the state"—but it was too late. Taiwanese netizens had already weaponized it into a national pastime. Subtle mockery was disguised as cartoon humor. These jabs, that censors couldn't always catch and Beijing couldn't laugh off, lived on.

When Xi died, his handpicked successor had inherited more than just the presidency. He'd inherited the meme. He was lankier than Xi, colder in demeanor, but no less authoritarian. When an internet troll called him Skinny Poo, the name stuck, like a middle finger dressed in honey.

"I think that's the last of them," Mack commented, watching as the final ROC operator descended the ramp. According to her roster, he should be Commander Tang Muyang, a submarine warfare specialist with ten years in Taiwan's navy. Observing him, Mack noted how his eyes swept the hangar, cataloging exits, defensive positions, potential threats. It was the kind of automatic threat assessment that came from years of living next door to a hostile giant.

"That's our lead student," Mick noted. "Downloaded his file last night. Smart cookie. MIT exchange program, systems engineering."

"Perfect." Mack tapped her tablet, pulling up the training schedule. "He'll need every neuron firing to handle what we're teaching."

The formation marched into the hangar, boots splashing through puddles. Up close, Mack could see the tension in their faces. Young men and women who'd grown up watching PLA destroyers probe their waters, counting missile batteries pointed at their homes. Last week's vote in Beijing had stripped away any remaining illusions. The PRC's declaration that Taiwan would be included in the new customs inspection routine under the guise of their new drug enforcement act was a blockade in all but name. It was still yet to be determined if the US and the rest of the international community would adhere to the inspection terms or test Beijing's appetite for direct conflict.

"Welcome to Guam," Mack called out, her voice carrying over the rain drumming on metal. "My name is Jodi Mack, but you can call me Mack. I'm one of the TSG trainers from a company called Anduril Industries. Prior to Anduril, I was a lieutenant in the US Navy, specializing in unmanned underwater vehicles. This is my TSG counterpart, retired Chief Warrant Officer Three Michael Matsin. He spent twenty-six years in the US Navy and is a encyclopedia of all things related to unmanned naval warfare."

"Just Mick, or Chief," he added. "Save the formalities for people who care."

A few tight smiles cracked through the formation's discipline.

"You're here because your government bought the best unmanned systems money can't normally buy," Mack continued. "Seeker-class XLUUVs that can hunt subs autonomously for thirty days. Hammer Shark sprint torpedoes that'll make a *Song*-class submarine look like it's standing still. Zealot surface vessels that turn your coastline into a no-go zone."

She paused, studying their faces. "But hardware's just expensive junk without operators who know how to use it. That's where we come in."

"Ma'am"—Commander Tang raised a hand—"the systems you mentioned—they're American designs. Will we have full operational authority?"

"Good question." Mack appreciated the directness. "Short answer, yes. Long answer, you'll have Lattice AI integration giving you tactical control while strategic oversight remains within your command structure. Think of it as Netflix for naval warfare—you pick what to watch, but the algorithm suggests what might kill you."

Nervous laughter rippled through the ranks.

"Look, some decisions aren't ours to make and have been forced upon us," Mick interjected. "This latest decision by the PRC to include Taiwan in their drug enforcement act inspection regime is a case in point. But we're not here to debate policy or what happens next. We're here to train you on some equipment that gives your leaders some options and the PLA some pause." His humor evaporated as he addressed the elephant in the room head-on. "We all know this customs inspection regime starting April fifteenth is a threat to the very survival of your country. Our job isn't to decide what happens next. That's a political question we elect leaders to decide. What Mack and I are here to do is make sure that if they try to enforce this blockade, they'll be fishing ChiCom destroyers out of the Taiwan Strait."

Thunder rolled across the airfield. The lights flickered, emergency power kicking in smoothly.

"Questions?" Mack asked.

A young petty officer, barely twenty-one by the look of him, raised his hand tentatively. "The vote last week… they really mean it this time?"

The hangar fell silent except for rain and distant thunder.

"They've meant it every time," Mack said quietly. "Difference is, this time they think they can win. Our job—your job—is to make that calculation so costly they'll choke on it."

She gestured to the equipment containers being offloaded from the C-17, each one stenciled with cryptic designations: XLUUV-SEEK-7, CAN-USV-12, MINE-CAP-3.

"Ten days," she announced. "That's what you get to master systems that take our operators months to learn. We'll run you eighteen hours a day. Sleep will be a luxury. Mistakes will be painful. But when you leave here, you'll be able to turn the waters around Taiwan into a graveyard for anyone stupid enough to test you."

"Including West Taiwan's finest rust buckets," Mick added with a wolfish grin.

This time the laughter was genuine. Even Tang cracked a smile at the joking reference to mainland China as "West Taiwan" instead of the People's Republic of China.

"Ground rules," Mack continued. "Everything you see here is classified beyond classified. The Chinese have assets throughout the Pacific trying to steal what you're about to learn. Trust no one outside this group. Use only secured comms. And if someone approaches you offering money for information…"

"Report it immediately," Tang finished. "We've had the briefings."

"Good." Mack stepped aside as ground crews began moving the first container into the hangar. "Grab your gear and follow Chief Reyes to billeting. PT formation at 1400. First classroom session at 1500. Tonight, you learn to think like the machines you'll command."

The formation broke, operators collecting seabags and equipment cases. Mack noticed how they moved—alert, professional, but with an undercurrent of urgency. They understood the stakes.

"Think they're ready for this?" Mick asked quietly.

Mack watched Tang directing his people, organizing them into work details without being asked. "They better be. Clock's ticking, and Skinny Poo's not known for patience."

"Speaking of which…" Mick pulled out his phone, showing her a news alert. "PLA Navy announced another 'training evolution' near Matsu. Three destroyers, carrier group standing by in reserve."

"Pressure tactics." Mack shrugged, but her jaw tightened. "Let them posture. In ten days, these kids will have the tools to make that carrier group think twice about entering the strait."

The squall began to ease, sunlight breaking through in patches. Steam rose from the tarmac as tropical heat reasserted itself. Mack looked at her tablet one more time, reviewing the compressed training schedule. Ten days to teach submarine hunters how to command robot wolves. Ten days to help David sharpen his rock-slinging skills.

No pressure, she thought, then called out to the ROC contingent. "One more thing. Anyone here seen *The Empire Strikes Back?*"

Confused nods and raised hands.

"Good. Because, as Yoda said, 'Do or do not, there is no try.' Except here, 'do not' means your country drowns in landing craft. So let's make sure that doesn't happen."

She turned to Mick. "Think I should ease up on the movie quotes?"

"Nah." He scratched his beard. "If you can't find wisdom in eighties action flicks, what's the point of defending democracy?"

Tang appeared at her elbow, having settled his people. "Excuse me, Mack, one question. These XLUUVs—they're truly autonomous? No tether to a base?"

"Yes. Thirty days of underwater hunting, all on their own. Here, let me show you something." She pulled up a schematic on her tablet. "These bad boys have onboard AIs that can process and identify acoustic signatures, classify threats, and even predict submarine behavior patterns over time. You designate the zones they operate in, and you control and program the rules of engagement they use. After that, they're killer whales with torpedoes for teeth."

"Amazing. And what if the PLA tries to jam our communications?"

"Ah, well, that's the beauty of autonomy." Mick leaned in. "Can't jam what doesn't need to phone home. These things will keep hunting even if every satellite burns and every radio tower falls."

Tang studied the schematic, fingers tracing torpedo loadouts and sensor arrays. "We've theorized such systems. To see them real…"

"Yes, it's impressive. We've moved well past theory, Commander," interrupted Mack as she closed the tablet. "It's time we welcome you to the future of naval warfare. Population: you."

Tang smiled at her brashness.

"Come on," Mack said, leading them deeper into the complex. "Time to turn you into ghost whisperers. Except your ghosts will be carrying Mark 48 torpedoes."

Outside, the squall had passed completely now, leaving behind that electric clarity that came after tropical storms. As Mack looked behind the hangar, she knew somewhere out there, beyond the horizon, Chinese satellites were certainly watching, counting, analyzing.

Let them watch, she thought. *By the time they understand what we've taught here, it'll be too late.*

Behind her, forty-eight voices began calling cadence as Chief Reyes led them to their quarters. The sound echoed off hangar walls, mixing with jet engines and distant thunder.

The countdown to April fifteenth had started. Time to contact was steadily approaching.

****

March 22, 2033 – 0600 Hours
TSG Operations Control Center
Apra Harbor

"Simulated contacts bearing one-six-zero. Depth forty meters. Speed five knots and climbing."

Mick stood behind a pair of ROC sailors hunched over their console. The green trace of the Seeker-class XLUUV ghosted across the bathymetric map, showing the depth and shape of the underwater terrain. Sonar pings highlighted a target track just beyond the shelf drop. The ops trailer smelled of coffee, electronics, and nervous sweat.

"What's your call, Petty Officer Liang Zihao?" Mick kept his voice neutral.

The young sailor's fingers hovered over the Engagement Authorize key. On screen, the Seeker's AI had already classified the contact: PLAN Type 039C submarine, confidence eighty-seven percent. The autonomous hunter circled like a shark, maintaining perfect acoustic shadow while calculating firing solutions.

"It's... it's requesting permission to engage," Liang said, voice tight.

"That's because we're in training mode." Mick tapped the screen. "Fully autonomous, this thing would've already put two Mark 48s in the water. You've got eight seconds to authorize or abort."

Liang glanced at his partner, then stabbed the Authorize key. "Weapons free."

The display erupted in data streams. Two torpedoes separated from the Seeker, their tracks diverging to bracket the target. The submarine contact immediately accelerated, diving for the thermocline. Too late. The first torpedo detonated beneath its keel, the second finishing what physics started.

"Kill confirmed," the AI announced in its eerily calm voice. "Returning to patrol pattern."

"Outstanding." Mick clapped Liang on the shoulder. "Except for one thing. Check your IFF overlay."

Liang's face went pale as he pulled up the identification layer. The "enemy" submarine now showed friendly markers—a Japanese *Soryu*-class on scheduled transit.

"Well, that complicates things," he muttered in Mandarin.

"Yeah, just a bit. You sank an allied sub." Mick leaned against the console. "Look, the PLA knows our allies' signatures too. They'll spoof, they'll deceive, they'll try to make you kill friendlies. That's why we have human oversight."

Commander Tang watched from the supervisor's station, taking notes on a secured tablet. "How often do they attempt acoustic spoofing?"

"During my time in the Navy, every time we sailed through the South China Sea," Mick replied bluntly. "Your Seeker's AI is good, Commander—scary good—but it's not perfect. It learns from every engagement, sure, but the enemy learns too."

He pulled up another scenario. "OK, we're going to reset and try this again. This time we're running the Matsu Gap. Petty Officer Wang, you're up."

The display refreshed. Three Seekers appeared in formation, patrolling the narrow waters between Matsu Island and the Chinese mainland. Mick had programmed this one himself—a nightmare scenario of overlapping sonar coverage, civilian traffic, and hostile submarines trying to force the strait.

"Mission parameters," he announced. "Prevent any submerged transit while avoiding civilian casualties. You've got six hours of battery on each Seeker before they need to surface and recharge. Oh, and the PLA just declared another 'live-fire exercise' in your patrol box."

Wang's team huddled over their stations. Within minutes, they'd repositioned the Seekers into a picket line, using Lattice AI to coordinate overlapping sonar coverage. Smart, but predictable.

"Incoming surface contact," one operator called out. "Container ship, bearing zero-nine-five."

"Let it pass," Wang ordered.

Mick suppressed a smile. The ship passed directly over Seeker-2's position. The XLUUV's AI immediately detected the acoustic anomaly—something heavy had just detached from the container ship's hull.

"Contact! Subsurface separation from merchant vessel!"

"It's a parasitic mini-sub," Commander Tang identified quickly. "We've been monitoring the PLA's experiments with them."

"Ah-ha. Good catch," complimented Mick as he watched Wang's team continue to react. "But heads up, you've got bigger problems."

The display began to light up with new contacts. What looked like a group of routine fishing vessels heading to sea had just dumped dozens of active sonar buoys, creating a wall of acoustic noise. Behind the screen, two Type 093 nuclear attack subs sprinted for the gap.

"They're herding us," Wang realized. "Trying to force our Seekers out of position."

"So, what do you do?" pressed Mick.

Wang's fingers flew across his console. "Seeker-1, ignore the noise. Maintain station. Seeker-3, shallow dive, get below the thermocline. Seeker-2..." He paused, calculating. "Sprint north, then cut engines. Drift onto their flank."

The display updated in real time. The Chinese subs, confident in their acoustic cover, maintained their sprint. They never detected Seeker-2 drifting silently into their baffles.

"Fire when ready," Wang ordered.

Four torpedoes lanced out. The lead Type 093 managed an emergency blow, broaching like a wounded whale before the weapons found it. The second tried to dive but ran straight into Seeker-3's firing solution.

"Splash two," the AI reported.

But the mini-sub had slipped through during the chaos.

"You stopped the main force but missed the infiltrator," Mick noted. "In real combat, that could be carrying special forces, mines, or worse. Tang, what's your assessment?"

The commander stood, addressing his sailors. "We're thinking like surface warriors, not submariners. The Seekers give us reach, but we need to think in three dimensions, multiple layers."

"Exactly." Mick pulled up a new display showing the full undersea battle space. "Each Seeker can deploy sixteen micro-mines from its payload bay. Create choke points. Channel the enemy where you want them."

Outside, dawn painted Apra Harbor gold. Through the trailer's reinforced windows, they could see the actual Seeker units in their cradles, technicians running final checks. Each one cost twenty-eight million dollars—less than a tenth of a manned submarine but with similar capability in confined waters.

"Let's talk real-world employment," Mick continued. "Your coastline has three major approach routes for amphibious assault. The Penghu Channel, the north approach past Keelung, and the southern route through the Luzon Strait. How many Seekers would you need for effective coverage?"

The room erupted in discussion. Some argued for concentration of force, others for dispersed operations. Tang let them debate before speaking.

"Twelve per approach, minimum. But that assumes perfect coordination."

"Which brings us to Lattice." Mick activated the holographic display, showing a three-dimensional network of interconnected nodes. "This isn't just a command and control tool. It's a hive mind for your robot fleet. Each platform shares data, learns from others' experiences, adapts tactics in real time."

He highlighted vulnerability points. "But it's also your greatest weakness. The PLA's been developing quantum computing specifically to crack AI networks. They hack their way into Lattice, they own your fleet."

"Ouch. Countermeasures?" Tang asked.

"Compartmentalization. Firewalls between tactical and strategic layers. And this." Mick held up a physical key. "Manual override, hardwired into each platform. It's a Stone Age solution to a Space Age problem."

Petty Officer Liang raised his hand. "Sir, the battery limitation. Six hours seems…"

"Inadequate? Yeah, it is." Mick shrugged. "That's why you rotate. Always have a third of your force charging, a third in transit, a third on station. Or…"

He pulled up another slide showing modified Taiwanese fishing vessels.

"Tender ships. Disguised as trawlers but carrying charging stations. The Seekers surface at night, quick charge, and they're back in the fight."

"The PLA will target them," Tang observed.

"Of course they will. Which is why you defend them with these bad boys." The display showed Zealot USVs, bristling with missiles and autocannons. "Surface escort for your subsurface hunters. Combined arms, autonomous style."

The morning wore on. Scenario after scenario, each more complex than the last. The ROC operators began thinking less like traditional sailors and more like orchestra conductors, managing a symphony of autonomous systems.

During a break, Mick found himself outside with Tang, both men watching the actual Seekers being lowered into the harbor for afternoon live trials.

"Your thoughts, Commander?"

Tang was quiet for a moment. "It changes everything. For decades, we've planned for heroic last stands. Brave men dying to slow the invasion. This…" He gestured at the robots. "This gives us a chance to win."

"Only if you use them right." Mick lit a cigarette, ignoring base regulations. "The PLA's not stupid. They're developing countermeasures as we speak. Drone swarms to overwhelm your Seekers, EMP weapons to fry their circuits, cyberattacks on Lattice."

"Then we adapt faster." Tang's jaw set. "We have to."

"Exactly. That's the spirit." Mick flicked ash into the harbor. "Tomorrow we run the nightmare scenario. Full invasion fleet, contested electromagnetic environment, degraded communications. Think your people are ready?"

"They'll have to be." Tang watched his sailors through the trailer window, bent over their consoles with fierce concentration. "That vote in Beijing last week... it was meant to end us."

"Then let's make sure they choke on the attempt." Mick crushed out his cigarette. "Yoda was wrong about one thing. There is 'try.' And trying to invade Taiwan after we're done here will be the PRC's last mistake."

They headed back inside. The next scenario was loading—a hundred PLAN vessels approaching with their barge bridges and civilian vehicle ferries loaded with battalions of armor and infantry fighting vehicles, hundreds of PLA aircraft, communications jammed, satellites offline.

Time to teach these kids how to fight blind and mute.

Chapter Twenty-Two:
Steel Horizon

March 22, 2033
1030 Hours Local Time
Bemowo Piskie Training Area, Northeast Poland

"Assassin Two-Two, this is Assassin Two-Seven. I've got eyes on ridge. We've got FPV drones above and in the tree line," Torres's voice crackled over the internal comms. He'd barely called out his warning when, a second later, the Leonidas-equipped Ripsaw on the flank fired a directed pulse into the sky. Torres watched through his commander's independent thermal viewer in satisfaction as the pair of commercial-grade quadcopters dropped like flies into the Polish mud. The threat had been eliminated before it could ruin their day.

Unlike conventional weapons, the electromagnetic pulse made no sound when it fired. There was no crack of the sound barrier breaking, no swooshing sound of a rocket motor or missile accelerating—just a faint electrical hum, then silence where rotors had once buzzed.

"Assassin Two-Seven, Romeo One-Alpha, targets eliminated, targets eliminated," Warrant Officer Marrick announced over the battalion net. "Shifting autonomous patrol route to Grid November-Kilo-Four-Seven."

A sharp crack split the air. Then another. The M5's 30mm autocannon tore into a drone-controlled target vehicle disguised as a Russian BMP-3. The unmanned target erupted in a shower of sparks and shredded composite material before igniting, adding to the realism.

"Holy—" Private First Class Munoz jumped in surprise from the sudden eruption of machine-gun fire and cannons going off outside as the exercise got underway. "Whoa! Those are live rounds that Polish watchtower is firing over top of us!"

"Damn right they are," Torres growled from his commander's station. "They're firing well above us to simulate what it will sound like when it's the real deal, Private. We train as we fight. No do-overs when Ivan comes knocking. Now stay focused. Head in the game, guys."

Their tank moved with the rest of the platoon as they advanced further into the training range. The whole scene was surreal, far more realistic than the range they'd trained on at Bliss. As they approached a wooded area, the hairs on the back of Torres's neck tingled. He keyed his mic. "Gunner, traverse right. Watch that wood line."

"Copy that," Sergeant Burke replied. The turret whined as their 120mm smoothbore cannon tracked to the right of the scarred training area. More tracers arced overhead—red streams of 7.62mm mixed with the stuttering bark of the louder .50-cal, firing somewhere to their left.

A pyrotechnic artillery simulator exploded nearby, adding yet another layer of realism to their training. Some crazy Polish engineers had rigged canisters filled with loose rocks and dirt to be thrown into the air to rain down on their vehicles as they drove by. It greatly increased the pucker factor of their training.

"Assassin Two-Seven, this is Assassin Two-Six." Lieutenant Novak's voice cut through, trying to project calm over the chaos. "Polish element reports movement along grid Papa-Romeo-Two-Eight-Eight-Seven-Six. Probable OPFOR armor."

Another explosion erupted, closer this time. Smoke canisters popped along the ridgeline, obscuring thermal sights with thick gray clouds.

"Roger, Assassin Two-Six. Assassin Two-Two moving to overwatch."

"Driver, ford that creek, then find us a berm near the tree line," Torres commanded. "We need defilade to cover First Platoon's advance."

Specialist Boone responded instantly. The seventy-ton M1E3 lurched forward, turbine screaming. They plunged into the shallow creek, water spraying in the air as they did. The tracks churned through the muddy bottom, finding purchase on the rocky streambed without missing a beat.

As they exited the far bank, another salvo of artillery simulators detonated behind them, close enough to pepper the turret with dirt clods. Boone spotted what Torres wanted—a natural earthen berm created by years of erosion, just high enough to hide their hull and drove toward it.

"Perfect, Boone. Ease her in."

The Abrams settled into its hull-down position with mechanical precision, Boone feathering the throttle until only the turret and the business end of the M256 smoothbore protruded above the scraped berm. The turbine's whine dropped to a whisper—its fifteen hundred shaft horsepower idling like a caged predator.

Torres pressed his face against the CITV's padded eyepiece. The commander's independent thermal viewer painted the battlefield in stark contrasts—white hot against black cold. Through the drifting smoke from their earlier engagements, the next-generation FLIR cut through the visual clutter like a scalpel through flesh.

He spotted movement in the trees; something was darting between the birch trees and pines. Heat plumes from diesel engines soon appeared, betraying the OPFOR vehicles crawling through their scripted dance. They were the T-90M surrogates—tracked drone targets with bolt-on visual enhancers, making them look like Russian tanks. They executed their pre-programmed routes with robotic precision. Beyond them, the fixed targets lurked in scraped fighting positions, their IR-suppression blankets turning the forty-ton steel monsters into hidden ghosts, at least to the untrained eye.

"Contact front, tank. T-72 at our eleven o'clock!" Burke called out with the practiced precision of a man who'd found what he was hunting. His hands danced across the gunner's control handles—not frantic, but precise. "Whoa, scratch that. It's a pair of T-90s, not T-72s. Six hundred meters moving from our eleven o'clock position to our three o'clock...hang on. I'm still searching the treeline."

Burke continued his search with the thermal sights as he swept right, the magnification jumping from three-power to ten with a flick of his thumb. "Torres—I got three more tanks, right side of those pines to our four o'clock. They're in hull-down position, T-72 profile. Six hundred and twenty meters."

"Got it! Load sabot. Gunner—target left T-90," Torres commanded, his words following the precise cadence drilled into every tanker at Fort Moore. No wasted syllables. No confusion. In combat, confusion killed.

The ballistic computer system absorbed the data like a digital deity of destruction. Wind speed, air density, barrel drop from the previous rounds fired—all processed in nanoseconds.

But Munoz was already moving. His right knee snapped the knee switch, and the ammunition ready rack door retracted with a hydraulic hiss. The sabot round sat waiting—forty-five pounds of tank-killing precision. He grabbed it, pivoting his body as he rammed it home. He slammed the breech shut.

"Sabot up!" His palm struck Burke's shoulder, letting him know the gun was ready to fire.

Burke never stopped tracking the T-90 as it continued to move. The stabilization kept the reticle dead center on its turret ring.

"Fire!" Torres shouted.

"On the way!"

BOOM!

The Abrams bucked. Sixty-eight tons of steel compressed against the torsion bars as the main gun roared to life. Downrange, the sabot petals separated in a brief metallic flower before the penetrator—a depleted uranium dart—punched through the target.

Orange smoke erupted from the pyrotechnics, confirming their kill. Four seconds had elapsed from contact to kill. In combat, four seconds was forever. Here, it was good enough.

"Target identified!" Burke was already traversing right. "Engaging second T-90!"

The dance continued—acquire, engage. Each evolution was smoother than the last. Torres watched his crew work with grim satisfaction.

No wasted motion. No hesitation.

Outside their tank, more artillery simulators exploded, continuing to add to the surreal scene around them. Torres spun his commander's independent thermal viewer through a full 360-degree sweep, checking their flanks and rear while Burke maintained his sight picture on the tree line. Through the CITV, he caught glimpses of the battle unfolding—Polish K2s maneuvering through smoke, their 120mm guns thundering. An M5 Ripsaw darted between burning target hulks, its autocannon chattering.

"Target, eleven o'clock, static T-72!" Burke called out, already tracking.

"Fire and adjust!" Torres confirmed, continuing his scan. There wasn't anything behind them yet, but that could change fast.

"Up!" Munoz had another sabot ready.

"On the way!"

The gun fired again. The brass base from the combustible casing spat out of the breach, clanking against the floor as Munoz readied the gun to fire.

Torres had nearly completed his sweep when he caught movement in his peripheral vision—black specks against gray sky.

"Drone swarm, three o'clock high!" he called over the company net.

The sky filled with angry hornets—thirty-plus FPV drones converging from multiple vectors. Some carried training munitions, others just cameras, but in combat each would pack enough explosive to mission-kill a tank.

"All Warrior elements, air threat inbound!" Novak called. "Leonidas systems to auto-engage!"

The M5-CD variants swiveled their high-power microwave emitters skyward. There was no visible beam, just drones tumbling from the sky like poisoned birds.

Ten down, thought Torres. *Fifteen. Twenty...not enough.*

The drone operators or the AI controlling them was reacting to the HPM and scattering, making it harder for the Leonidas system to fry their circuitry.

"We got leakers! They're getting through!" Munoz's voice cracked, tangible fear in it now. This might be training, but those drones looked too real as they dove at their position.

The surviving drones evaded erratically, moving with inhuman speed as they bore down on them. In real combat, this was exploding death on a stick flying at a hundred-plus miles per hour. Torres watched in horror as one of the little nightmares zipped around several trees before aiming for a Polish tank to their left. Drones had gotten through. Vehicles were lost.

The Polish K2 to their left popped a red smoke grenade as simulated flames—hit by a drone carrying a training marker. The crew bailed out, playing dead as per the exercise rules as they watched the others continue on.

Torres pushed the loss aside and put his head back in the game as he ordered his tank back on the move. "Assassin Six, Assassin Two-Seven, displacing to next firing position!" Torres radioed.

Seconds later, Novak called. "All Assassin Two elements, retrograde to Phase Line Blue!"

As they backed off the tree line under a hail of simulated fire—explosions, tracers, and smoke—it looked like the combat footage they had trained on from Ukraine. By the time they reached the rally point, half the company of tanks was dead. The M5s were toast.

"ENDEX, ENDEX," Iron Six's voice boomed across the net. "Exercise complete. Return to Assembly Area Alpha for debrief."

The battlefield fell silent except for the whine of the tank's turbine engines. Torres climbed from his tank, legs shaky from adrenaline. All around him, tank crews emerged looking shell-shocked. The combination of live ammunition, overhead tracers, and constant explosions had achieved its purpose. This felt real; it felt terrifying.

"Wow. Holy crap, that was insane," Burke muttered, pulling off his CVC helmet. Sweat plastered his hair to his skull.

"That was...educational," Torres corrected. He watched the Ripsaws return to their staging point, moving in perfect formation despite the chaos. Those machines had performed well, but the drone swarms had still broken through.

It was time to learn from this controlled disaster and figure out what went wrong, what went right, and what they could do better.
****

1245 Hours Local Time
Assembly Area Alpha
Bemowo Piskie Training Area

The after-action review took place in the same converted hangar, but the atmosphere was different. Crews sat straighter, paying closer attention. There was nothing like live rounds and explosions to focus the mind.

"You are dead," Lieutenant Colonel Cunningham announced without preamble, addressing the assembled companies. "If this were real combat—we just lost forty percent of the battalion. Why?"

This time, no one rushed to answer. The live-fire exercise had stripped away comfortable assumptions.

"Because you still think this is a game," Cunningham continued. "When artillery falls, when tracers fly, when drones swarm— you hesitate. You think. You die."

He clicked through footage from the exercise. Tanks bunched up under fire. Crews slowed to react to the drone threat. Perfect kill zones had been created by predictable movement.

"The Ripsaws performed well," Major Lathrop added. "They identified threats, engaged targets, maintained precision under fire. But look here—" He highlighted a moment where an M5 sat motionless while its controlling crew dealt with their own crisis. "When humans panic, machines become expensive targets."

Warrant Officer Marrick stood. "Sir, the data shows the autonomous systems achieved—"

"That's great. But machines don't bleed," Cunningham cut him off. "Your machines killed targets, Chief. But they couldn't adapt when the enemy changed its tactics. They failed to recognize the trap until too late."

Torres found himself nodding. The Ripsaws had performed their programmed tasks perfectly. But war wasn't a program.

"Sergeant Torres," Cunningham pointed at him. "Your crew. What did you learn?"

Torres stood slowly. "That we need to train harder, sir. The noise, the chaos—it got to us. My loader froze up when things got loud. My driver overcorrected under fire. We survived on instinct, not skill."

"Honest assessment. Continue."

"The integration with the Ripsaws is still clunky. When our tank is fighting for survival, we can't manage the unmanned systems effectively. It's like trying to play piano while drowning."

There were a few chuckles from the crowd. Gallows humor ruled among tankers.

"So what do you propose?" asked Lieutenant Colonel Cunningham.

"Repetition under stress, sir. Run this exercise daily if we have to. Live rounds, explosions, maximum chaos. Do it until managing Ripsaws under fire becomes muscle memory, not conscious thought."

"And the fear?" Lathrop's eyes narrowed. "When real missiles fly, when your soldiers begin to die?"

Torres thought of the stories he'd heard the veterans of Iraq, Afghanistan, and Syria—of their tanks getting nailed by Iranian-provided explosively-formed penetrators during the heights of the Iraq War. The discovery that EFPs penetrated the armor of main battle tanks had been shocking.

"Sir, fear keeps you sharp. It's a good motivator. But I've always believed it's training that keeps you alive. I'd say we need more of the latter to manage the fear," Torres explained.

Cunningham nodded slowly. "That's an astute answer, Sergeant. I agree. Tomorrow, we run this again. And again after that until the battalion stops thinking and starts fighting. This has to be second nature, people. Action, reaction."

Major Lathrop pulled up a slide for everyone to chew on. It showed the casualty projections for what a real conflict in the Suwałki Gap might look like. The numbers were sobering.

Cunningham resumed speaking. "In two weeks, we begin Steel Forge—a combined arms exercise with the entire division as well as our Dutch, Polish, and German NATO partners. The exercise will include attack helicopters, fighters, drones, artillery, and rocket artillery. Why? Because we train as we fight, and we fight as we train. We do this so when the balloon goes up—nothing changes. It's muscle memory. Act, react—without hesitation."

Cunningham paused, letting that sink in.

"I know some of you think this is extreme—that I'm pushing our battalion too hard, risking too much in training." His voice hardened. "You all remember how the Ukraine War played out—suicide drones and World War I–style trench warfare? That's what happens when you lose the ability to maneuver, when a force gets drawn into an urban fight inside of villages and cities. It bogs you down; it traps you into a war of attrition instead of a war of maneuver. We are tankers. Maneuver warfare is in our DNA. It's how we fight. The wars of tomorrow will be fought with everything we practiced today—drones, AI, electronic warfare, and violence of machines at the speed of AI."

Torres found himself nodding along. It was cold, but it was the truth. He smiled when he saw Captain Morrison, his company commander, step forward. "Sir, Alpha Company is ready for the challenge. We'll train until it's second nature."

"Good. Because if China moves on Taiwan, if Russia moves here"—Cunningham gestured toward the east—"there will be no learning curve. You will fight with what you know, or you will die learning."

The briefing continued, but Torres found his mind drifting to his crew. Munoz especially—the kid had talent, but Torres was concerned he might freeze under pressure. They'd need focused drills, stress inoculation.

Maybe I'll partner him with Burke more, he thought. *Let the steady calm of our gunner rub off on him.*

After dismissal, Torres gathered his platoon. "Listen up. What happened today was a wake-up call. We got our bells rung because we weren't ready for this kind of chaos." He looked at each of his soldiers. "That changes now. Starting tomorrow, we train under maximum stress. If you can't handle the training, you're going to struggle when it's real."

"Sergeant"—Munoz raised a hand tentatively—"the explosions, the tracers—it felt real out there."

"Good. That's the point." Torres softened slightly. "Look, I know today was rough. But every mistake we make here is one we won't make when lives are on the line. Real combat is worse—no reset button, no second chances. We train hard so we can fight easy."

He turned to Warrant Officer Marrick, who'd joined their huddle. "Sir, we need to work on the Ripsaw integration. That drone swarm hit us hard."

"Agreed. I'll have my guys work on drone detection and interception. That won't happen again."

"Perfect." Torres addressed the group again. "One more thing. What I said in there about not having do-overs? I meant it. We're in the business of making the other guy die for his country. That's an ugly truth, but it's *our* truth. The better we get at our job, the more of us come home. Questions?"

None came. They understood the stakes.

"All right. Recovery operations in thirty minutes. Make sure your track is squared away—we roll again at 0700 tomorrow."

As the soldiers dispersed, Lieutenant Novak approached. "Wise words, Sergeant. Think they'll stick?"

"They'd better." Torres watched Munoz helping Burke check their tank's optics, already moving with more purpose.

"Because the major's right—if this kicks off for real, we won't get a learning curve," said Novak.

"I know. The guys know too," Torres replied softly. "Tomorrow's another day. We'll do better."

They'd keep training until the fear became fuel, until chaos became clarity. Because somewhere east of them, they knew Russian and

Chinese forces were running their own exercises. And they weren't planning to lose either.

Chapter Twenty-Three:
Thunder Feather

March 27, 2033 – 0900 Hours
Deepwater Training Range
30 Nautical Miles West of Guam

The command center's air conditioning fought a losing battle against forty bodies crammed into a space meant for twenty. Jodi Mack stood at the primary display, watching Hammer Shark torpedo feeds stream across the holographic projection. The converted destroyer tender *Emory S. Land* rolled gently in two-foot swells, her combat information center now serving as the nerve center for today's exercise.

"Speed check. Sixty knots confirmed. Terminal phase lock-on in five seconds."

The Hammer Shark's nose dipped in a final surge, water cavitation bleeding from its flanks as it sprinted toward a decommissioned tank landing ship playing the role of a PLAN Type 075 amphib. The one-way weapon had traveled forty nautical miles to reach this point, guided by nothing but its onboard AI and preprogrammed mission parameters.

"Three... two... one... impact."

The display flared white. When the feed cleared, the target ship listed heavily to port, a forty-foot hole torn just below her waterline. The Hammer Shark had detonated its five-hundred-pound warhead with surgical precision, right at the vulnerable joint between hull and machinery spaces.

"Target neutralized," Chief Petty Officer Huang announced, trying to keep the excitement from his voice. "Time from launch to impact: thirty-seven minutes."

"Not bad." Mack circled the impact point on her tablet, transmitting the analysis to all stations. "But check your depth sensors. What do you see?"

Huang frowned, pulling up the data. His face fell. "It... it ran shallow the last thousand meters. Breach probability was eighteen percent."

"Eighteen percent chance the PLA spots your torpedo wake and has time to deploy countermeasures." Mack let that sink in. "In the strait,

216

with that murky water and all the commercial traffic? Maybe you get away with it. But maybe you just wasted a cool eight million dollars and gave away your launch position."

Commander Tang moved between the stations, observing his sailors' work. "The AI should have maintained optimal depth."

"Should have, but didn't." Mack pulled up the Hammer Shark's decision tree, a cascading waterfall of calculations made in milliseconds. "See here? It prioritized speed over stealth in the terminal phase. Why?"

The room studied the data. Finally, a young ensign named Zhao raised her hand. "Tidal current. It detected a following current and tried to maximize velocity."

"Exactly. The AI made a tactical decision based on incomplete data." Mack highlighted the relevant code. "In programming, we call this an edge case. The Hammer Shark trained on thousands of simulations, but never this exact combination of current, depth, and target profile."

She turned to face the room. "This is why we're here. Not to teach you which buttons to push, but to understand how these things think. Because in five weeks, when Skinny Poo sends his invasion fleet, you won't have time for debug cycles."

Mick's voice crackled over the intercom from the weather deck observation post. "Mack, we've got dolphins playing in the target area. Might want to delay the next shot."

"Copy that." She switched displays. "All right, people. While nature takes its course, let's talk about the Hammer Shark's real magic— cooperative hunting."

The hologram shifted to show a simulated PLAN carrier group: one Type 003 carrier, two Type 055 destroyers, three Type 054A frigates, and a supply ship. Classic Chinese naval formation, bristling with defensive systems.

"Single Hammer Shark versus this?" Mack asked. "You're throwing rocks at a fortress. But watch what happens with a coordinated attack."

She initiated the simulation. Eight Hammer Shark units launched from different vectors—some from submarines, others from disguised merchant vessels, two even fired from a stealth corvette from fifty miles away. The torpedoes immediately began talking to each other through quantum-encrypted burst transmissions.

"Wow. They're sharing data," Tang observed. "Building a collective picture."

"Uh huh. More than that." Mack zoomed in on the lead torpedo. "They're negotiating amongst themselves. Watch."

The Hammer Shark swarm steadily began its approach toward the carrier group. The PLAN's defensive systems activated the moment they detected the first torpedo—decoys, jammers, active sonar, even counter-torpedo torpedoes. The Hammer Sharks scattered, some chasing false targets, others going silent.

Then something beautiful happened.

The surviving Hammer Shark units regrouped, their AI collectively recognizing the deception. They redistributed targets based on damage probability, approach angles, and remaining fuel. Two torpedoes even went dark, loitering in place while their brothers drew defensive fire.

"Holy hell," someone whispered.

The attack unfolded like a deadly ballet. Torpedoes feinted high, drawing defensive fire, while others slipped through the noise below. The carrier's escorts found themselves turning to engage threats from every quadrant, their overlapping defense zones suddenly full of gaps.

When the simulation ended, the carrier listed dead in the water, both destroyers were sinking, and a frigate burned from stem to stern.

"Six Hammer Sharks expended," Mack tallied. "Total cost: forty-eight million. Damage inflicted? One carrier group mission-killed. That's a thirteen-billion-dollar trade in your favor."

"True, but they'll adapt," Tang said quietly. "The PLA will develop countermeasures."

"Of course. I'm sure they already are." Mack pulled up some intelligence photos that US Naval Intelligence had cleared for her to share. They showed Chinese naval bases with new acoustic arrays, towed decoys designed specifically for high-speed torpedoes, even experimental directed-microwave weapons for underwater use. "Which is why we don't rely on any single system."

Mick's voice returned over the speakers. "Dolphins have cleared the test range. We are cleared to resume the exercise."

"Outstanding. Petty Officer Wang, your team's up." Mack reset the range display. "This time, you're programming a Hammer Shark for harbor infiltration. Target is a destroyer tied up at pier. Defenses include anti-torpedo nets, patrol boats, and active sonar. Show me how you thread that needle."

Wang's team huddled over their tablets, fingers flying across the interface. The Hammer Shark's programming screen looked like abstract art—decision trees branching into probability clouds, behavioral parameters expressed in mathematical notation.

"Sir," Wang said after ten minutes, "we're ready."

"Launch when ready."

The Hammer Shark slipped into the water with barely a splash, its pump-jet propulsion nearly silent. On the display, it immediately dove deep, hugging the bottom contours.

"Conservative approach," Mack noted. "Trading speed for stealth."

The torpedo crept forward at eight knots, less than a quarter of its maximum speed. Every few minutes it would stop entirely, passive sensors drinking in the acoustic environment. When a patrol boat passed overhead, the Hammer Shark actually buried itself in the bottom sediment, playing dead until the threat passed.

"Jesus," Mick's voice came over comms. "That's not a torpedo, that's a sea snake."

Three hours later—compressed to twenty minutes in simulation time—the Hammer Shark reached the harbor mouth. Antitorpedo nets blocked the obvious approaches, but Wang's programming had anticipated this. The weapon located a gap where tidal flow had shifted the net anchors, just wide enough for its sleek body.

"Threading the needle," Ensign Zhao breathed.

Inside the harbor, new challenges arose. Commercial traffic, police boats, active sonar pinging from shore installations. The Hammer Shark wove between obstacles like a living thing, its AI making thousands of microadjustments.

Then it found the destroyer.

"Target acquired," Wang announced. "Initiating terminal run."

The Hammer Shark had two options: impact the hull directly or swim beneath and detonate under the keel. Wang's programming chose option three—neither.

The torpedo surfaced just long enough for its optical sensor to verify target identity, then dove again. It swam beneath the destroyer, past it, then turned back toward the pier. When it detonated, the explosion destroyed not just the ship but a significant section of the dock infrastructure.

"Mission kill plus infrastructure denial," Mack said approvingly. "The destroyer's not just sunk—it's destroyed the pier. Well done."

But Wang wasn't celebrating. He stared at the aftermath display, calculating casualties from the dock explosion. "Collateral damage. Those were civilian dock workers in the simulation."

"Yes, they were." Mack's voice softened. "This is the reality of autonomous weapons. Your programming, your ethics, your choices— they all matter. The Hammer Shark will do exactly what you tell it, so you better be damn sure what you're telling it is right."

The room fell quiet. Outside, the real ocean sparkled under the tropical sun, peaceful and deceptive.

"Let's talk rules of engagement," Mack continued. "The Hammer Shark can discriminate between military and civilian targets, but only if properly programmed. It can abort attacks if conditions change, but only if you build in those safeguards. Every line of code you write is a moral decision."

Tang stepped forward. "In a shooting war, those distinctions become difficult."

"I agree. They do." Mack nodded. "Which is why we train. Which is why you're here. Because when Skinny Poo sends his fleet, you'll need to stop them without becoming the monsters they paint you as."

She pulled up footage from the Russia-Ukraine conflict— autonomous sea drones striking bridges, ports, naval vessels. "This is your future. Precise, lethal, but bounded by law and conscience. The Hammer Shark gives you reach. Lattice gives you coordination. But judgment? That stays human."

Mick entered the command center, shaking water from his cover. "Hate to interrupt the philosophy seminar, but weather's building. We've got maybe two more runs before we need to secure."

"Copy that." Mack turned back to her students. "Final exercise of the day. Commander Tang, I want you to program a Hammer Shark for the ultimate test—discrimination drill. Mixed military-civilian harbor, degraded visibility, jamming environment. Show me you can still put warheads on foreheads without killing innocents."

Tang moved to the programming station, his team forming around him. As they worked, Mack pulled Mick aside.

"They're getting it," she said quietly. "The technical stuff, the tactics. But I wonder if we're preparing them for the real cost."

Mick gazed through the porthole at the target ship, still burning from the morning's exercise. "Nobody's ever ready for that. But when the alternative is watching your country disappear?" He shrugged. "You do what you gotta do."

"Yeah." Mack watched Tang's team work, young faces intent on their screens. "Let's just hope we're teaching them to win, not just die more efficiently."

"Amen to that." Mick checked his watch. "Speaking of which, you heard the latest? PLA's moving another carrier group toward the exercise area."

"The *Fujian*?"

"And escorts. Big metal middle finger to anyone watching."

Mack felt the weight of the timeline pressing down. Less than three weeks until April fifteenth—three weeks to turn these sailors into robot wranglers capable of stopping an armada.

"Then we better make every minute count," she said.

On the display, Tang's Hammer Shark entered the water, beginning its discrimination run. Time to see if human judgment could be encoded into silicon and steel. Time to see if David's sling was smart enough to find Goliath's eye.

Chapter Twenty-Four:
The Environment Waits for No One

March 28, 2033
Gotland, Sweden

It was 0945 hours as the black Mercedes electric-powered vans hummed quietly up the gravel road, their low whine almost drowned out by the constant wind gusts rolling off the Baltic. Klara Hedevig stood at the edge of the Näsudden wind array, jacket pulled tight, smile pulled tighter.

The turbine blades above them spun in lazy circles, casting slow-moving shadows over the tour group. Two investors in green energy from Singapore were bright and smiling; Klara was happy that they wouldn't need an interpreter as they also spoke English. An NGO from Japan had sent three of its representatives to investigate Sweden's advancements in sustainable energy. A Spanish investment firm had also sent three of its people with an interpreter. Rounding out the delegation were eight Chinese "energy executives," all dressed in tailored overcoats.

"I hope you'll find this a compelling example of Sweden's offshore wind capabilities," Klara said. "These were retrofitted in 2030 to accommodate a new Siemens blade stabilization system. They're still running at ninety-eight percent efficiency."

The Chinese interpreter relayed her words in Mandarin, and the Spanish interpreter did her magic. The rest of the group understood her tour in English. One of the Chinese officials nodded. Another pointed southwest—toward the coast road. A small convoy of JLTVs rumbled in the distance, just visible through the mist.

Cao Ju, the interpreter for the Chinese group, didn't wait for Klara to comment. He spoke quietly to the group in Mandarin, then turned to Klara. "They ask if this is part of the recent deployment."

Klara hesitated, then gave a calculated nod. "Yes. US Army vehicles. Likely from the 173rd Airborne. They've increased their footprint here following recent developments in Kaliningrad and along the Suwałki Gap."

One of the officials—the shortest of the group, with sharp eyes and an arctic-blue scarf—asked a clipped question in Mandarin, which

Cao translated without embellishment. "How many soldiers have arrived? And where are they being housed?"

Klara turned her body slightly to shield the conversation from the wind, or from prying lenses, should any be watching. "I'm not totally sure. I've been told a regiment of paratroopers is likely around six hundred. As to where they are staying, I've heard some are staying in Roma, near the Grönt Centrum. I believe some are staying near the airport, while the rest are staying with the Gotland Regiment at Tofta."

Cao's left eyebrow rose, but he said nothing to her as he relayed the information.

The man in the scarf looked satisfied. He pulled out a small notebook, scribbled something, then turned his gaze back to the turbines.

"And this system here," Klara continued, raising her voice slightly, "feeds into the southern grid loop that powers Klintehamn and portions of Burgsvik. Grid balancing is managed from a control center in Hemse."

Cao repeated the energy cover story with professional ease. Klara noted how none of the officials so much as looked toward the turbines. Their eyes were scanning the tree line—counting trucks and estimating patterns.

A man from the Spanish group raised his hand politely and asked in English, "What's the primary materials source for the turbine blade retrofits? Are you relying on domestic composites or importing from Germany or Denmark?"

Klara welcomed the break in tension. "Great question. The newer stabilizers are sourced through a joint Nordic supply network, mostly Swedish and Danish composites. The blade tips are still imported from a German subsidiary, but that may shift to local manufacture next year."

One of the Singaporean investors chimed in, her tone bright. "And what's the projected maintenance cycle at your efficiency rate?"

"Fourteen to sixteen months per full diagnostic rotation," Klara replied. "We operate three drone teams for visual inspection and blade diagnostics. The offshore variants have a slightly longer cycle thanks to lower particulate exposure."

Several heads nodded, satisfied. The tension faded slightly—at least among the non-Chinese participants.

Klara took a step forward and lowered her voice, speaking directly to Cao. "You'll see supply convoys running east–west across this road through the end of the week. They're repositioning HIMARS launchers and counter-UAV systems to the central corridor. There may also be Patriot radar assets mobile near Slite and Roma."

Cao didn't need to translate that. Every man in the group understood English better than they pretended.

Klara forced a pleasant tone. "Shall we move to the vans? The next site has active biogas processors and may smell... less than inviting."

The group nodded as one. The man with the scarf lingered a moment longer, eyes squinting toward the coast road.

Klara didn't breathe until he turned to follow.

****

Grönt Centrum, Gotland

The Roma biogas plant stank of wet fermenting compost, but Klara preferred the odor to the silence of the van ride. She pushed through her rehearsed speech with mechanical precision.

"...and this anaerobic digestion system is fed by agricultural waste from farms across central Gotland. It produces both heat and electricity, with minimal transmission loss to the surrounding district."

Across the road, visible through a tree line were armored Humvees, stacks of cargo containers, and a row of folding tents braced against the spring wind. All signs of Bravo Company's presence.

"Are those... military assets?" one of the Chinese officials asked—in English.

Klara paused just a beat longer than she should have. Her eyes flicked toward Cao.

"Temporary," she said carefully. "Part of a Swedish-led training initiative. Best not to linger your attention on them too long. There are cameras. Sensors."

Cao began translating, but she stepped closer and lowered her voice.

"Tell them, politely, that they are being watched, just like I am. If they start pointing, they'll be having a much shorter visit to the island."

Cao's mouth tightened. He relayed the message. The response from the man in the scarf came swiftly—a terse phrase in Mandarin and a hard glance toward Klara.

Cao hesitated. "He says... you are too forward. That such disrespect is noted."

Klara straightened her blazer. "Then he's free to file a complaint with my director. After we're safely off the island."

For a few tense seconds, no one moved. Then the scarfed man gave a curt nod, and the rest of the group shifted their attention back to the tour.

A Spanish delegate leaned closer to his interpreter and asked something in hushed tones. After a brief exchange, the interpreter looked to Klara. "He's asking how the plant manages methane capture and if excess gas is sold back to the national grid."

"Good question," Klara said, seizing the chance to reset the tone. "Yes, we capture and scrub the methane for purity, then it's piped into the local grid under a regional agreement. Roughly twelve percent is sold back to mainland suppliers during peak capacity."

One of the Singaporeans added, "Do you foresee hydrogen conversion scaling up here in the next three years?"

"It's being discussed," Klara replied smoothly. "The infrastructure's viable with modest retrofits. But it depends on funding commitments from both Stockholm and Brussels."

Klara continued, her voice crisp. "As I was saying, this plant handles over two thousand tons of biological input annually. Our newest digesters were installed in late 2031 and have improved conversion rates by nearly twelve percent."

Behind her words, the rhythmic thud of heavy boots sounded from the tree line. A small patrol, four soldiers in full gear, rifles at low ready, passed along the perimeter, eyes scanning in all directions.

Cao glanced over, then returned his gaze to Klara. "You were right," he said under his breath. "We're being watched."

Klara didn't break stride. "Good. Maybe they'll think I'm actually here for the digesters."
****

Tofta Solar Pilot Site

They'd reached their final stop for this tour. What was supposed to be a dormant limestone pit repurposed for solar research was now less than a kilometer from Charlie Company's new motor pool and RBS-70 SHORAD platforms.

As Klara delivered a rehearsed briefing on photovoltaic soil integration and regional output modeling, she noticed several of the visitors drifting too close to the western ridge. The Spanish and Japanese delegates remained near the marked display area, nodding along politely, while the Singaporeans took photos of the demo plots and panels. But it was the Chinese delegation who were again testing the boundaries.

She moved swiftly. "Please remain near the installation markers," she said with forced cheer. "That ridge is unstable and marked for erosion monitoring."

Cao quickly translated.

Still, one of the Chinese officials, a tall man with gray temples and leather gloves, continued up the incline.

From the ridge, he would see at least a half dozen Leopard tanks parked under camo netting, visible through breaks in the sparse trees.

Klara reached him just before the crest. "Sir, for your safety, I must insist—this is an off-limits zone."

The man turned slowly, his expression unreadable. Then he nodded once and stepped back, rejoining the others below.

A Singaporean investor tilted her head toward Klara. "Are these solar arrays active already or just in testing?"

"Still in pilot phase," Klara replied smoothly. "We've logged six months of seasonal data and are preparing a transition report to submit to Region Gotland's energy board. If funded, full deployment will follow within two years."

One of the Japanese delegates asked, "Have you had issues with ground stability from the old quarry base?"

Klara nodded. "Some. Drainage improvements were done last autumn, and we've layered erosion controls over the eastern edge. The rest of the ridge, as you've seen, is not meant for foot traffic."

Cao approached quietly. "They are getting impatient," he murmured. "They want details you have not provided."

"They'll get what they get," Klara muttered. "Unless they want to risk the entire operation."

She gave a tight smile as she returned to the group.

"To the untrained eye," she said, pitching her voice for the onlookers possibly monitoring their conversation, "this may seem like an ordinary solar soil integration platform—but it's one of the most efficient in Scandinavia. It's been field-tested to survive Gotland's harshest winters."

Cao translated dutifully. The officials nodded, but their eyes lingered westward.

Klara's hands remained still, but her mind raced. Back home, the red go bag in her closet was ready. Inside was a forged Estonian passport, euro cash, SIM chips, and a ferry ticket to Riga hidden in a birding field guide.

If this tour went sideways—if just one patrol got curious—her window to vanish would slam shut.

She exhaled, then gestured toward the vans. "We'll finish at the café just ahead. Excellent saffron bread and no patrols."

They followed without protest. No one spoke. The only sound was the sea wind—and the faint clatter of tank tracks shifting positions in the forest.

****

A Few Hours Later
Visby, Gotland

The bell above the café door chimed softly as Klara stepped inside. The warmth and the scent of strong coffee, cardamom buns, and clean wood floors enveloped her like a blanket. She pulled down her scarf, glad to be out of the wind.

Annika stood behind the counter, pouring espresso into a demitasse with the precision of a surgeon. Her sharp eyes flicked up. "Look who finally returns to civilization. I was beginning to think you'd defected to Stockholm."

Klara offered a tired smile. "Only for a few hours. Green energy waits for no one."

Annika raised a brow. "Green energy, or government guests? Someone saw your convoy down by Tofta. You looked very... official."

Klara winced internally. Of course someone had noticed. "Part of the Baltic Resilience & Renewables Initiative," she said casually, sliding onto a stool. "There are some NGOs and investors from Japan,

Singapore, Spain, and China. Mostly technical experts from their clean energy board. They wanted a tour of our infrastructure—wind, solar, and biogas—to see the latest tech our Swedish industry has come up with. I think it's going to lead to some new business for a few of our local companies."

"Ah, that's great. That explains the large convoy of guests. Your tour looked like a foreign minister's motorcade," Annika pressed.

"Ha-ha, yeah. I suppose it does," Klara replied smoothly. "I think with all the uncertainty around the world these days, countries are looking for ways to insulate their sources of power in ways that don't leave them dependent on the whims of a dictator deciding he wants to take over his neighbor."

Annika made a noncommittal sound and handed another customer a flat white. "Yeah, I suppose you are right. Are you still planning that bird-watching thing?"

"The Baltic Wings Festival?" Klara nodded. "Absolutely. There will be a lot of attention from ecotourists, especially now that NATO's decided to treat Gotland like a forward base."

Annika narrowed her eyes but said nothing.

Klara leaned in, voice soft. "It's not what it looks like, I promise. They're bureaucrats. Stiff, boring, and constantly jetlagged. I spent half the day explaining anaerobic digesters and the other half making sure they didn't trip over SHORAD cables."

That earned a short laugh from Annika. "Well, if anyone can wrangle that crowd, it's you."

"Exactly," Klara said. "It's all harmless. Besides, I'd rather be arguing solar grid stability than listening to more NATO artillery echoing across the coast."

Annika gave her a skeptical once-over, then poured Klara her usual tea and joined her at the bar. "If you say so. Just don't bring any drama to my café."

"Wouldn't dream of it," Klara replied sweetly, though she could still feel Cao's last glare burning behind her eyes.

She sipped her St. Hans Blend slowly, portraying a practiced calm on the outside. But inside, she was already rewriting the contingency plan for her escape.

Just in case.

****

Klara Hedevig's Apartment

The light in Klara's kitchen was low, and the blinds were drawn tight. She moved with silent efficiency, opening a sideboard that held folded linen and placemats—at least on the surface. Behind the stacked tablecloths, a thin false backing slid away, revealing a narrow compartment no larger than a shoebox.

Inside was the red go bag: matte fabric, unbranded, soft-sided. It contained a rolled bundle of euro notes—none larger than twenties—a slim RFID-shielded wallet with two different national ID cards, a burner phone, and an Estonian passport in the name of Liisa Tark.

Next to it sat a nylon pouch with a handful of USB drives, a small GPS tracker, and a clean SIM pack. She checked everything, fingers moving fast but methodically.

Then she closed it, slid the panel back into place, and refolded the linens with care.

In the bathroom, she flushed a single index card she'd used to sketch a new extraction route—from Visby to Nynäshamn via the early freight ferry, then across to Riga by bus.

She would begin staying more nights at Lars's place—claiming it helped her sleep better with him gone so often. That way, if anyone came snooping here, they wouldn't find her home. And Lars wouldn't have an excuse to stop by unannounced. It also meant less chance of him stumbling on her other contingencies, like the key to the storage unit on the north end of town—rented under a different name—that was currently secured inside her makeup bag. Inside that unit, she'd started storing nonperishable food, a field medical kit, a few changes of clothes, and a collapsible bicycle.

Tonight, she'd head to the co-op market and use self-checkout to withdraw small amounts of cash using her debit card—never more than a few hundred kronor at a time. She would spread these withdrawals out over multiple stores, over multiple nights.

She opened her laptop next. The VPN connected through a shell in Latvia, then routed into Prague. On her screen, she launched a secure text pad and updated her off-site checklist:

1.   Rotate the phone.
2.   Update ferry schedules.

3.   Buy burner charger with power brick.

4.   Prepare second go bag.

She stared at the screen for a long moment before minimizing the window and pulling up the birding website she used as her cover.

She added a cheery post about the upcoming white-tailed eagle observation walk, then shut the laptop and leaned back in her chair.

The room was quiet, save for the soft ticking of the kitchen clock. Outside, the wind howled faintly across the eaves. Klara exhaled slowly.

It was all about timing now. She wasn't sure whether she'd see the trap before it snapped shut.

Chapter Twenty-Five:
Brotherhood Before the Storm

March 28, 2033 – 1930 Hours Local Time
Krasnawie Pub
Drawsko Pomorskie, Poland

Torres smirked at Novak. The scent of charred meat and cheap vodka drifted through the chill, growing stronger the closer they got to the noise. The pub door creaked open, spilling a wave of heat and sound. Torres stayed close behind Major Kowalski, squinting into the steamy air as Polish rock music thundered from hidden speakers overhead. His eyes adjusted to the amber glow and the crush of bodies—talking, shouting, singing all at once.

"Welcome to the *real* Poland!" Major Kowalski boomed over the noise, steering them through the crowd. "Not NATO Poland. Not fake Hollywood Poland... but *real* Poland!"

The place was everything a proper soldiers' dive should be— scarred wooden tables, faded military patches covering the walls, and a bartender who looked like he'd killed men with his bare hands. Polish and American voices mixed with the clinks of glasses and bursts of laughter.

"This is our tradition," Kowalski said as they neared a corner table. A handful of Polish soldiers spotted him, nodded, then stood and disappeared into the crowd without a word. Torres, Novak, and the Major slid into the newly vacated seats. "Before every deployment, we drink. We eat. And we become brothers. Tomorrow we could die—but tonight, we regret nothing but the hangover."

Torres caught Novak's uncertain look. The lieutenant was still learning that when in Rome, do as the Romans do.

"Relax, LT," Torres murmured. "We're building trust with allies. It's part of the mission."

Sergeant Burke, PFC Munoz, and Specialist Boone squeezed into the pub behind them, eyes wide. Even Staff Sergeant Granger and his crew had come, leaving Delaney back to watch the platoon.

"Sergeant Torres!" A familiar Polish sergeant appeared—the HET loadmaster from Gdańsk, whose gold tooth was gleaming. "You made it! Janusz Kowalczyk, but everyone calls me Kowals."

They shook hands; the Pole's grip was practically crushing.

"First round is mine," Kowals declared. "For successfully moving American steel across Polish roads without destroying single bridge!"

A cheer went up from the Polish NCOs at nearby tables. Someone slapped Torres on the back hard enough to rattle his teeth.

"What are we drinking?" Munoz asked nervously.

"Żubrówka!" Kowalski produced a bottle like a magician. "Bison grass vodka. Polish tradition since 1600s."

"Major, I should probably—" Novak started.

"Lieutenant, in Poland, refusing first drink is grave insult." Kowalski's eyes twinkled. "You wouldn't insult your allies, would you?"

Shot glasses appeared. The vodka was pale green, almost glowing.

"*Za wolnosc nasza i wasza!*" Kowalski raised his glass. "For our freedom and yours!"

"Heard that before," Burke muttered. "Usually right before things go sideways."

They drank. The vodka burned sweet and herbal. Munoz coughed. Boone's eyes watered. But they all kept it down.

"Good!" Kowals pounded the table. "Now we eat. Then we drink properly."

Platters materialized—pierogi, kielbasa, dark bread, pickles. The Polish NCOs insisted on explaining each dish, arguing over whose grandmother made better bigos.

"Try this." A Polish tank gunner, Corporal Nowicki, pushed a plate at Torres. "Tatar. Raw beef. Makes you strong like Polish cavalry."

Torres took a bite. *Not bad, actually*, he thought. *Like upscale bar food back in El Paso.*

"So, Sergeant," Nowicki continued in accented English. "Your Abrams. Seventy tons, yes? Our K2s, only fifty-five. How you not destroy every road?"

"Carefully," Torres admitted. "Your HET crews did good work."

"Polish logistics, best in NATO." Kowals refilled glasses without asking. "We move anything. Tanks, missiles, broken American dreams…"

The table laughed. Even Novak was loosening up, discussing tactics with a Polish lieutenant.

"Your robot tank," said another Pole to Burke. "It really thinks?"

"That's what they tell us." Burke accepted another shot reluctantly. "Haven't seen it do much but follow us around yet."

"Like my wife's cousin," Kowals declared. "Follows everywhere, says nothing useful, costs fortune to maintain."

More laughter filled the room. Torres felt the tension of the past few weeks beginning to ease. He understood these men and they understood him.

Different flag, same life.

"Sergeant Torres." Kowalski leaned in close, his voice dropping. "May I speak frankly?"

"Of course, Major."

"My men—they are good soldiers. But they remember history. Russians to the east have invaded many times. Each time, we fight. Each time, we lose. Then we fight again." He paused. "This time, with Americans beside us, maybe different ending."

Torres met his eyes. "I agree, Major. Let's hope it doesn't come to that. If it does, we'll be here, and we'll make 'em pay for every inch of Polish land they try to take."

"I like you, Sergeant. Plain spoken. I believe you. But belief and history…" Kowalski shrugged. "We shall see."

A commotion near the bar drew their attention. Polish soldiers were clearing a space, pushing tables aside.

"What's happening?" PFC Munoz asked, alarmed.

"Arm wrestling," Corporal Nowicki grinned. "Polish tradition. Visitors must compete."

"Oh, hell no," Boone started to protest, but Kowals was already dragging him forward.

The impromptu tournament drew the whole pub's attention. Boone, wiry and quick, lost immediately to a Polish sergeant built like a concrete bunker. Munoz lasted longer through technique but eventually succumbed.

"Americans getting soft," someone called out in accented English.

That's when Burke's Nebraska farm boy pride kicked in. "All right, that's it." He rolled up his sleeves, revealing tatted forearms and muscles like bridge cables.

His opponent was Corporal Wojtek Górski, who Torres recognized as a tank loader from one of the Polish tank companies. He had a similar build, and a similar quiet confidence.

They locked hands. The pub fell silent.

"*Na trzy*," Kowals said. "One... two... three!"

The table creaked. Both men's faces reddened with effort. Neither arm moved.

"Come on, Burke!" Munoz shouted.

"*Dawaj*, Wojtek!" the Poles countered.

Thirty seconds passed. Then a minute. Sweat beaded on both faces. Then, incrementally, Burke's arm began to bend until he couldn't hold it anymore.

The Poles erupted. Money changed hands. Górski slapped Burke on the shoulder, then both men grinned and shook hands.

"Good match," Górski said simply.

"Rematch when we get back," Burke promised.

"Sure, I'll gladly take more of your American dollars from you," Górski muttered with a grin, then quickly raised his glass. "But tonight, we are here!"

More vodka appeared. Torres tried to pace himself, but the Poles were insistent. Every toast meant something—to fallen comrades who had volunteered to fight in Ukraine or Afghanistan, to NATO, to someone's grandmother who'd killed three Nazis with a pitchfork during the Second World War.

"You have family?" Nowicki asked Torres during a lull.

"Wife. Four kids." Torres pulled out his phone, showing a photo.

"Beautiful family. I have two daughters." Nowicki shared his own photos. "They think I drive tank to work like normal job. Don't understand why Daddy sometimes gone for months."

"Mine are starting to understand," Torres admitted. "I'm not sure if that's better or worse."

"Worse," Kowals interjected. "When they understand, they worry. When they worry, you worry. Better they think we play with big toys."

Staff Sergeant Granger appeared at Torres's elbow. "Sergeant, you might want to check on your loader. He's not looking so good."

Torres glanced over and shook his head. Munoz was doing shots with three Polish privates, and appeared increasingly green.

"Munoz! Time to switch to water."

"I'm good, Sarge!" Munoz protested, then hiccupped.

"That's not a suggestion, Private."

The Poles good-naturedly switched to beer, saving Munoz's dignity as they passed him a bottle of water. Torres made a mental note to have Gatorade ready in the morning.

"Your lieutenant," Major Kowalski observed, "he reminds me of myself when young. All theory, no practice."

Torres watched Novak deep in conversation with a pair of Polish officers, hands moving as they discussed maneuver warfare.

"He'll learn. They all do eventually."

"In Belarus, perhaps." Kowalski's expression darkened. "You've seen the intelligence?"

"Some of it," Torres replied. "I'm just a Sergeant First Class—not an officer like yourself."

"It's OK. I share with you. Across the border, we face the Russian First Guard's Tank Army and Chinese 81st Group Army—easily six hundred main battle tanks and enough artillery to level Warsaw." He knocked back another shot. "They call it exercise. We call it preparation."

"Wow, that's a lot of tanks. I guess that's why we're here, Major. We can't let you Pols have all the fun if things kick off," joked Torres.

"Yes. The famous American deterrence." Kowalski smiled sadly, brushing off his joke. "You know what we call American military strategy? 'Fight to last European.'"

Torres winced. He didn't have a good answer for that. He changed the subject and started talking sports. It gave him a chance to brag about his son, a future baseball star.

As the night wore on, someone produced an accordion—because *of course* there was an accordion. Polish folk songs mixed with American cadences. Burke tried to teach them "Blood on the Risers," which the Poles loved once they understood the words.

"Gory, gory, what a helluva way to die!" they sang, mangling the pronunciation but nailing the sentiment.

Torres found himself at a table with Kowals and a few other Polish NCOs, the universal brotherhood of sergeants transcending language barriers.

"Tell me," Kowals said, vodka making his English looser. "Why you do this? Could make more money in civilian world, yes? No one shooting at you."

Torres thought about the question before responding. "I was dirt poor when I joined. The Army gave me a chance to do something with myself, and besides, I come from a long line of soldiers in my family. In fact, a Torres has served in uniform since the days of the Republic of Texas. My great grandfather served in World War II, my grandfather in Vietnam, my big brother in Iraq, and now me. After sixteen years of this, it's who I am. I can't imagine doing anything else."

"Hmm, same." Kowals nodded. "My son says I'm crazy. Says I should drive truck for Amazon. Better pay, he says. But Amazon doesn't stop Russians."

"To crazy men who stop Russians." Torres raised his glass.

"And Chinese," another sergeant added. "Don't forget Chinese."

"How could we?" Górski gestured broadly. "They own half of Africa, building bases everywhere. Soon they'll want Poland too."

"Have to go through us first," Burke interjected, swaying slightly.

"Through all of us," Nowicki agreed. "NATO Article 5. Attack on one…"

"Is attack on all," the table finished in unison.

There were more drinks, and more stories. Kowals told about his father, who'd driven tanks for the Communists but secretly helped the Solidarity movement during the 1980s. Nowicki's grandfather had fought at Monte Cassino with Anders's Army. Every Pole had a story of resistance, of fighting against impossible odds.

"This is why," Kowalski said quietly to Torres, "we must be brothers. Not just allies on paper. Brothers. When the storm comes—and it will come—we must trust absolutely."

Torres understood completely. You couldn't build that kind of trust in briefing rooms or training areas. You built it here, over vodka and war stories, creating friendships and bonds that transcended cultures and language.

"Sergeant Torres!" PFC Munoz appeared, definitely drunk now. "They're doing toasts. Said I should make one for America."

"That's... actually that's the lieutenant's job, Munoz," Torres replied.

"LT's in the bathroom. Come on, Sarge. For 'Merica!" Munoz slurred his words.

The pub suddenly quieted. Torres found himself standing, glass in hand, facing fifty Polish and American soldiers.

"I'm not good at speeches," he began. "But I do know this. Sixteen years ago, I took an oath, to defend the Constitution against all enemies. It didn't say anything about *where* those enemies might be."

He saw nods of agreement around the room.

"Now I'm five thousand miles from home. My daughter asked me the other day why. 'Why Poland? Why now?'" He paused. "I told her because a free Poland means a free Europe. A free Europe means her and siblings sleep safe in Texas. It's not complicated. It's not some grand conspiracy or somehow about American imperialism. It's about honoring your word and standing shoulder to shoulder with our allies. That's it. It's that simple."

He raised his glass higher.

"Major Kowalski quoted a saying to me earlier. 'For our freedom and yours.' He's right. And it works both ways. So here's to the Polish tankers who'll be on our right flank. To the Polish infantry who'll hold the line. To the Polish people who know the price of freedom better than most. And here's to us, the 4th Battalion, 70th Armor, the most decorated tank unit in the Army."

He switched to the bit of Polish he'd memorized on the flight over.

"Niech żyje Polska!"

The pub exploded. Poles pounded tables, shouting approval. Someone started singing the Polish anthem. Then the Americans countered with "The Star-Spangled Banner." Then both groups tried to sing both anthems simultaneously, creating a patriotic cacophony.

"LT, it's time to go," Torres told Novak, who'd returned looking pale. "We need to get out of here before someone decides we need to do another round."

Novak gave him a weak smile and nodded in agreement. They gathered their soldiers, said their goodbyes. Handshakes became embraces. Phone numbers were exchanged. Promises were made to continue meeting up after each exercise.

Outside, the March air bit sharp and clean. Stars wheeled overhead, unpolluted by city lights.

"That was…" Novak paused, searching for words. "Not what I expected, but a lot of fun."

"Real diplomacy happens at the ground level, LT." Torres steadied PFC Munoz, who was drifting to the right as they walked toward the parking lot. "The State Department signs treaties. The Army makes them work."

They piled into the duty van, Sergeant Burke taking the wheel as their lone designated driver.

"Sarge," Specialist Boone asked from the back, "you really think it's going to kick off? Like, for real?"

Torres looked back at his crew—they had young faces, flushed with alcohol and camaraderie.

"Hard to say, Boone. I think we train like it will. The rest is above our pay grade."

But as the van started, he thought about Major Kowalski's words. The storm was coming. They all felt it.

The van rumbled through empty streets back to the base. Behind them, the pub still glowed with light and life. Polish and American voices still mixed in song.

Tomorrow, they'd be back to being professional soldiers. Checking equipment, running drills, preparing for an exercise everyone pretended was routine.

But tonight, they'd been brothers. And when the storm came— if it came—those kinds of bonds might make all the difference.

Torres's phone buzzed. He had another text from Maria. "Kids asleep. House feels empty without you."

He started to type a response, then stopped. What could he say? That he'd spent the evening drinking with Polish tankers? That everyone here expected war but pretended otherwise? That he missed her like a physical ache but couldn't come home?

Instead, he typed, "I love you. I miss you. Hug them for me."

"Always do. Stay safe soldier and return to me."

He pocketed the phone and closed his eyes. Żubrówka swirled in his stomach. Tomorrow would bring headaches and PT and the endless preparation for a war they hoped wouldn't come.

But tonight had been good. Tonight had been necessary. Because Kowalski was right. When the storm came, they'd need to be more than allies. They'd need to be brothers.

Chapter Twenty-Six:
Azure Surge

March 29, 2033 – 0800 Hours
Fleet Operations Building
Naval Base, Guam

Mick settled into the observation chair as six large displays flickered to life. Each screen showed a different angle of the Zealot USV—a sleek unmanned predator bristling with weapons. The name Zealot suited it perfectly: It was relentless and uncompromising. It was the same USV the US Navy was integrating into their autonomous surface fleet, a crossbreed between a cigarette boat and a porcupine.

"Zealot-1 through 6 are on station," the range safety officer announced. "Weather is clear, Sea State Two, winds from the northeast at eight knots."

"Perfect conditions," Mick muttered to Commander Tang. "Which means nothing like what you'll face in the Strait."

"Have you heard how the deliveries of the Seekers have been going?" Tang asked in a hushed tone as the trainees continued to filter into the room.

Mick subtly turned his back to the trainees, speaking at an equally discrete volume. "I have. I was told as of last night, the final delivery of the forty-eighth Seeker was offloaded and moved into the Zuoying Naval Tunnel Complex. I was given a tour of the facility a few weeks ago. I have to admit, Commander—that place is impressive. Something about secret underground submarine bases is just cool."

Tang grinned at him. "They are great. Did they show you how it connects to the Gaoping River Military Storage Tunnels? If they didn't, remind me to give you a tour when we return to Zuoying. Should the mainlanders attack, this is where we plan to ride out the missile barrages until it's safe to leave."

"Neat. Well, looks like it's time to get this show on the road," Mick replied, gesturing for the commander to take a seat with the others as he prepared to start.

Staring at the men and women who'd decide the fate of the battle that might determine the outcome of the war, he began. "Good morning! I hope you got a good night of sleep because today is going to be a busy day," Mick said to his trainees. "For the past couple of days, we have taught you the ins and outs of how to use and fight the Seeker XLUUVs. Now it's time to shift gears and introduce you to the USV displayed on the monitors behind me. We call this beauty the Zealot. It's the US Navy's version of the Zealot fast-attack unmanned surface vessel. Now before we begin, let's review the weapons loadout for this bad boy."

Having had two cups of coffee and a Zyn pouch, Mick was feeling good as the caffeine and nicotine surged through his veins. He pulled up the specifications. "As you can see from the display, the Zealots pack a hell of a punch. Each of them carries four AGM-114L Longbow Hellfire missiles, two FIM-92M Stingers for air defense, and a M134 minigun in a CROWS turret with five thousand rounds of 7.62mm full metal jacket therapy for those pesky patrol boats. Last but not least is a two-hundred-and-fifty-pound explosive charge in the bow, should your Zealot run out of ammo or find an appropriate target to ram. With a maximum speed of up to forty-five knots and a combat range of six hundred nautical miles, this thing is a beast. It's going to be a nightmare for the ChiComs to try and defend against. But you want to know what makes it a real terror?"

Mick tapped the screen, showing the USV's sensor dome.

"This. Radar, infrared, acoustic, and electromagnetic—all feeding an AI that thinks faster than any human crew or operator." He let that sink in. "This isn't just a boat—it's a constantly learning predator, prowling the waves and defending the shores of Taiwan. This is going to be the thing of nightmares for your enemies," explained Mick with a sadistic smile.

Petty Officer First Class Tsai raised her hand. "The acoustic sensors. Can they coordinate with our Seekers?"

"Outstanding question." Mick pulled up the network architecture. "Through the use of the Lattice AI system, it creates a mesh network between all of our platforms. If your Zealot spots a submarine periscope, that data instantly updates every Seeker in range. This also works in reverse, meaning this tool allows for all of your networked unmanned autonomous vehicles to share sensor data and targets between each other."

He switched to tactical view. Taiwan's western coast materialized in bathymetric detail.

"Scenario time. PLA amphibious group approaching Penghu. Twenty ships including three Type 071 amphibs." The room's energy shifted. This wasn't theoretical. "You've got six Zealot units. David versus Goliath, Pacific edition."

Red icons populated the display. "Primary threats—Type 022 Houbeis. Fast-attack boats doing fifty knots on wave-piercing hulls. Eight YJ-83 missiles each." He zoomed on the missile specs. "NATO calls them CSS-N-8 Saccades. With a three-hundred-sixty-four-pound warhead, one hit ruins your whole day."

"What's the range of the Longbows, and how does the targeting system work?" asked Petty Officer Tsai.

"Eight klicks." Mick highlighted engagement zones. "Fire-and-forget targeting. Lock, launch, move. Sea-skimming profile makes them hard to counter. HEAT warhead punches through anything in the PLA inventory."

He spent the morning showing combat footage. They watched Ukrainian sea drones harassing Russian warships and Houthi swarms in the Red Sea. They saw success and failure, frame by frame.

"Yesterday's lessons become tomorrow's tactics." He paused the final video—a Russian corvette listing after a drone strike. "This is real, people. You adapt or you die. Simple as that."

The day blurred into tactical discussions, targeting priorities, swarm coordination. Mick pushed them hard, watching exhaustion battle determination on young faces. By 1800, they moved with more confidence—smooth, efficient, lethal.

"OK, let's call it. Outstanding work today." He killed the displays. "Tomorrow, we run through our final live fire and test some of the lessons we've taught you. We'll be firing Hellfires and Stingers, blowing stuff up. For now, I want you to get some chow, then grab some rack time. I'll see you tomorrow. Dismissed."

As they filtered out, chattering in Mandarin mixed with military English, Commander Tang lingered behind.

"I think they're ready," he said quietly.

Mick popped a fresh Zyn, contemplating Taiwan's odds. "They'd better be."

As they stepped outside, Guam's tropical evening painted the sky orange. Mick had seven weeks until his contract ended. Only seven weeks to transform these kids into warriors who could hold the line when—not if—Beijing made its move.

His phone buzzed; his wife, Sarah, was checking in from California. He'd call her later, spin stories about routine training while preparing for anything but. His mind was racing too much to talk to her right now. "Slow is smooth." He muttered his old submariner's mantra. "Smooth is lethal."

Tomorrow they'd arm the boats. Tonight, he'd pray his students never needed to unleash them.

Chapter Twenty-Seven:
Burgers & Battle Plans

April 3, 2033 – 1714 Hours Local Time
Vidhave Eco Retreat, Gotland

The evening air hung warm and still, more like mid-May than early April—one of those rare Baltic gifts when winter releases its grip early. Lieutenant Colonel Patrick Brenner stood before the massive grill, turning elk steaks and wild boar sausages with practiced precision, the aromatic smoke of juniper wood chips rising into the cloudless twilight sky.

"Daniels, bring me that platter for the root vegetables," Brenner called out, wiping sweat from his brow with his sleeve. Command Sergeant Major Eric Daniels appeared with a carved wooden serving board, grinning at the sight of his battalion commander playing Viking chef. The gesture wasn't lost on anyone—here was their leader, on what might be the eve of history, personally preparing a feast for his officers.

The Vidhave's staff had outdone themselves, transforming the eco lodge's pavilion into something from the sagas. Overhead, strings of warm lights crisscrossed between the timber beams like stars caught in a net, while strategically placed torches cast dancing shadows that evoked ancient mead halls. The long wooden tables—already part of the pavilion's rustic charm—now bore checkered cloths weighted with platters of grilled root vegetables, lingonberry sauce, and fresh rye bread. Swedish and American soldiers sat shoulder to shoulder, passing bottles of Gotlands Bryggeri and sharing stories that bridged a thousand years of warrior tradition. Colonel Lindqvist moved among them like a Norse chieftain, his weathered face bright with satisfaction at seeing his idea brought to life—two militaries becoming one force over fire and fellowship, the eternal bond of those who stand watch against the darkness.

Captain Alex Mercer stood near the rough-hewn bar the Vidhave staff had improvised, nursing a Gotlands Bryggeri as he watched the evening unfold. The unusually warm air carried the scent of juniper smoke and grilling meat across the pavilion, where Swedish and American officers had begun finding their seats at the long tables.

Colonel Anders Lindqvist approached through the amber torchlight, moving with the confident grace of a man on his own ground.

"Your battalion commander knows his way around a grill," Lindqvist observed, accepting the beer Mercer offered. His eyes tracked Brenner's movements—the practiced efficiency, the care with each cut of meat.

"Rangers lead the way, sir. Even at Viking feasts," Mercer replied, noting how Lindqvist's weathered face cracked into a genuine smile.

"We shall see if your Texas beef can stand against our island elk," the colonel said, but his tone held warmth rather than challenge.

Mercer watched his fellow officers settling in—Captain Elin Boström had cornered Major Holt near the pavilion's edge, her hands already sketching IRIS-T integration patterns in the air. Captain Joran Lindholm and CSM Daniels had found common ground over tank warfare, their animated gestures suggesting they were refighting some past battle. Even now, with platters of food appearing on the tables, the shop talk persisted—until First Sergeant Walcott materialized with fresh beers and gentle admonishments about leaving work for tomorrow.

"Gather round!" Brenner's voice carried across the pavilion as he set down his spatula. The conversations gradually died as officers drifted toward the tables, Americans and Swedes intermingling naturally now after weeks of joint preparation.

As they took their seats, Mercer found himself between Sergeant First Class Holloway and a Swedish Home Guard captain, the tables groaning under the weight of the feast—grilled elk steaks, wild boar sausages, root vegetables charred to perfection, fresh bread, and bowls of lingonberry sauce that gleamed like garnets in the torchlight.

Colonel Lindqvist rose slowly, beer in hand, waiting for the last conversations to fade. When he spoke, his voice carried the weight of centuries.

"There is an old saga," he began, his English touched with the rhythm of his native Swedish, "about a king who asked his warriors why they fought. One said for gold. Another for glory. But the wisest warrior said, 'I fight for what stands behind me, not what lies ahead.'"

The pavilion had gone completely silent, even the crackling of the torches seeming to pause.

"Look around you," Lindqvist continued, gesturing to the mixed gathering. "Americans who left families five thousand miles away. Swedes who could be home with their children tonight. Why are we here?"

He let the question hang in the warm air before continuing.

"We are the sons and daughters of Vikings, of Minutemen, of those who stood at Thermopylae and Valley Forge. Different flags, same blood—the blood of those who stand between the darkness and the light." His voice grew stronger. "We train for peace, yes. We hope for it. But when the storm comes—and it will come—we become what we must become."

Mercer felt the truth of it in his bones. Around him, faces had grown serious, the weight of history and purpose settling over them like armor.

"Behind us," Lindqvist said, his voice dropping to almost a whisper that somehow carried to every corner of the pavilion, "are our children playing in gardens. Our wives sleeping peacefully. Our parents growing old in freedom. That is why we become savage when we must. Not because we love what is in front of us, but because we love what is behind us."

He raised his beer higher.

"To the warriors of Gotland. To the Sky Soldiers of America. To the brotherhood forged in preparation for battles we pray never come." His eyes swept the gathering. "But if they do come, may our enemies learn why free men have always been the fiercest fighters— because we choose to be here. We choose to stand watch. We choose to be the shield."

"*Skål!*" the Swedish officers roared.

"Airborne!" the Americans responded.

As they drank, Mercer caught Brenner's eye across the table. His battalion commander gave an almost imperceptible nod—this was why they'd organized tonight. Not just to eat and drink, but to forge something deeper. Tomorrow they'd be back to patrol schedules and defensive positions. But tonight, under the stars and torchlight, they were becoming what they'd need to be if the worst happened.

The feast continued late into the evening, stories flowing as freely as the beer—tales of Swedish winters and Texas summers, of tank battles in Iraq and peacekeeping in Kosovo, of fathers who'd stood watch on this same island during the Cold War. History and present merging over fire and fellowship, creating something new from traditions old as warfare itself.

When they finally departed into the warm night, walking back to their scattered positions, Mercer knew something fundamental had shifted. They were no longer allies coordinating a defense. They were brothers preparing to hold the line.

****

Following Day
April 4, 2033 – 0900 Hours Local Time
P18 Headquarters, Gotland Regiment

Captain Alex Mercer sat in the darkened briefing room, watching the EUCOM J2 representative cycle through classified slides. The room held only company commanders and above. These were the American and Swedish officers who needed to understand the bigger picture beyond Gotland's shores.

"Gentlemen, what you're seeing is acceleration across all domains," the briefer, a Marine colonel, stated flatly. "Yesterday, PRC Foreign Minister Qiao announced that their Baltic naval facility is now fully operational. They're claiming it's to protect shipping from increased piracy and secure their Arctic passage interests."

The slide changed to show Kaliningrad's expanded facilities.

"Additionally, they've reactivated the old Chernyakhovsk Air Base. Officially, it's a training facility for nations purchasing Chinese military aircraft. Unofficially, it's a forward operating base ninety minutes from every Baltic capital."

Mercer noticed Colonel Lindqvist's jaw tighten at that assessment.

"Here's where it gets interesting," the briefer continued. "NSA and GCHQ intercepts indicate growing friction within EDEP leadership. Russian intelligence is expressing alarm at the scope of Chinese force deployment to the Leningrad district. SVR reports describe PLA units billeting in civilian areas due to insufficient military housing— something Moscow didn't anticipate or approve."

A new slide showed force dispositions across Eastern Europe.

"The Iranians are reportedly furious. They signed up for an exercise, not what they're calling 'Chinese adventurism.' Our assessment is that Beijing may have overplayed their hand, creating fractures in the alliance before the exercise even begins."

The briefer paused, letting that sink in before moving to the Pacific situation.

"Meanwhile, the CCP voted unanimously yesterday to implement their 'civilian customs inspection' regime for Taiwan-bound vessels. Starting today, randomly selected cargo ships will be directed to mainland ports for inspection. Noncompliance risks boarding and seizure."

The reactions came rapid-fire through diplomatic cables displayed on screen:

"Taiwan's President called it 'a blockade by another name.' Japan's raised their alert status and begun consultations with allies. The Australian PM urged calm while warning Beijing they're pushing toward conflict. Most dramatically, the Philippines revealed documents from a captured PRC intelligence operative detailing plans for seizure of the Palawan Islands as part of a broader First Island Chain Strategy."

Mercer watched Lieutenant Colonel Brenner lean forward at that last piece.

"Secretary Hallsworth reminded Beijing, quote: 'The People of China prosper through international cooperation, not isolation born of aggression.' Strong words from State."

The briefer clicked to his final slide.

"EUCOM and NATO assessment remains that EDEP is a psychological operation, saber rattling on an unprecedented scale, but still theater. We're maintaining current readiness levels while monitoring for escalation indicators. Questions?"

Silence greeted him. After he departed, Brenner stood.

"All right, maybe Brussels is right. Maybe it's all for show." His voice carried the skepticism his face showed. "But we're not betting lives on 'maybe.' New training priority effective immediately—every soldier drills medical response daily. Casualty evacuation, pressure dressings, tourniquet application. If bullets start flying, I want muscle memory saving lives."

He continued, pacing now. "Counterdrone procedures at every level. Yes, our systems have degraded their effectiveness, but assuming the enemy won't adapt is how you end up dead. Personal jammers, Leonidas systems, manual tracking, I want you to drill it all."

Colonel Lindqvist stood as Brenner finished. "The Americans prepare for the worst, and so will we. Home Guard increases surveillance of unusual activity, strangers asking questions, people where they shouldn't be, you know what to look for. Our air-defense units will integrate fully with the Patriot battery, ready to respond within seconds, not minutes."

He looked directly at Captain Bertil. "Your people know this island better than anyone. They are our eyes and ears. Tell them to trust their instincts—if something feels wrong, report it."

As the meeting broke up, Mercer walked back to his vehicle in the strengthening morning sun. The contrast struck him—peaceful Swedish countryside, farmers tending fields, children waiting for school buses, while he carried knowledge of gathering storms across half the globe.

Back at Grönt Centrum, he found his platoon leaders conducting PT, soldiers calling cadence as they ran past the old barracks. Normal military routine on an extraordinary day. He wondered how much to share, how much would help versus hurt.

First Sergeant Tanner appeared at his elbow. "How was the briefing, sir?"

Mercer watched his soldiers for a moment, young faces, eager, trained, but untested in what might be coming.

"Informative, Top. Let's you and I grab coffee. We need to adjust some training priorities."

For now, he'd give them what they needed to survive. The bigger picture about the Chinese bases in the Baltic, possible fracturing of alliances, and blockades disguised as inspections, they could wait. His job was to keep these soldiers alive and fighting when abstract threats became concrete reality.

If EUCOM was wrong, if this exercise was more than theater, they'd find out soon enough.

Chapter Twenty-Eight:
Black Tracks, Cold Steel

April 5, 2033
2130 Hours Local Time
Suwałki Corridor – East of Białystok

The tanks thundered across the field in a bounding overwatch formation, with one group of tanks covering the others while they advanced. The roar of tank engines echoed through the valley as Alpha Company assaulted a simulated defensive belt. Muzzle flashes lit up the night as they reached the first obstacle line—rows of dragon teeth anti-tank obstacles interlaced with barbed wire in front of a tank ditch deep enough they'd need specialized engineering vehicles to cross.

Surging forward from behind Torres' platoon came a trio of engineering vehicles with attached Sapper teams—combat engineers trained in breaching complex obstacles and fortified positions.

The four Abrams tanks in 2nd Platoon laid down suppressive fire as a pair of M5 Ripsaws flanked out ahead, scanning the trench line for enemy ATGM teams with thermal optics and LIDAR pings.

"Loader, AMP!" Torres barked as he spotted a target his gunner should have.

"Gunner, shift—bunker complex, eleven o'clock, six hundred!"

"Identified!" Burke's Cajun drawl cut through the noise.

"Fire!"

"On the way!"

The 120mm main gun cracked. A moment later, the target bloomed in a flash of simulated fire and smoke—another OPFOR strongpoint taken off the board.

Live rounds punched into earthen berms behind the targets. The crack of tank cannons mixed with the steady hammer of coaxial machine guns. Overhead, illumination rounds burst like miniature suns, casting stark shadows across the obstacle belt.

"Sapper element is moving up," Lieutenant Novak reported from Alpha-21. "Assassin Two-Three and Two-Four, suppress flanks. That tree line's hot."

"Gunner, coax—fixed fire, trench line, ten o'clock," Torres ordered, eyes locked on the flickering IR signature along the berm line.

"Identified," Burke replied.

The M240 coax opened up with a stuttering burst, red tracers stitching the edge of the trenchworks. Alongside, Alpha-22 and -23 joined in, hammering suppression with coax and .50-cal fire from the commander's remote operated weapon station. The engineering vehicles surged forward under the covering fire from Torres's platoon.

Moving abreast of them, a pair of M1150 Assault Breacher Vehicles advanced in staggered formation to the obstacle line. One of the ABVs fired its MCLIC, a rocket-dragged line charge that arced high before slamming down across the dragon teeth and tangled concertina wire.

"Fire in the hole!" an engineer called over the company net.

A concussive blast ripped across the obstacle belt—flame, dust, and shrapnel shearing through the concertina wire and dragon teeth. Smoke hung low as the breaching lane began to take shape. Without delay, a Joint Assault Bridge vehicle crept forward, aligned with the cleared gap. The JAB vehicle deployed its bridging array across the shallow anti-tank ditch. The span locked into place with a metallic clank.

"Assassin Two-Two, Castle Two-One," came the call over the company net. "Lane is clear. Bridge set. Passage open for armor."

"Copy, Castle. Alpha Two-Two moving," Torres replied, keying his throat mic.

To his left, an M5 Ripsaw crossed the newly created bridge and pushed out toward Phase Line Dallas, its turret sweeping side to side. Torres tracked it on his multi-function display. A thermal ping bloomed behind the far berm—a small, fast, humanoid heat signature.

"Possible missile team, eleven o'clock," Burke announced.

"Loader—switch out Sabot. Give me AMP!" Torres snapped.

"Copy," Munoz replied, already reaching. He ejected the sabot shell and locked in the Advanced Multi-Purpose round. "AMP up!"

"Gunner—send it," Torres said.

"On the way."

The 120mm barked, hurling the programmable round downrange. The round detonated mid-air, showering the target's cover with shrapnel. The thermal signature winked out.

"Good effect," declared Burke excitedly.

"Good shot! Maintain overwatch," Torres congratulated, settling back into his seat. "Driver, get us on the move and across the bridge. Assassins Two-Three, and Two-Four, follow behind us."

Specialist Boone got them across the bridge quickly and safely as the Ripsaws cautiously advanced ahead of them. Torres felt like they were steel wolves being unleashed, searching for targets to kill.

"Contact! BMP, ten o'clock! Five hundred and fifty meters!" The Ripsaw's sensors had found something. Its 30mm autocannon barked, tracers walking across a concealed position. The remote-controlled target vehicle—dressed up to look like a BMP-3—shuddered under the impacts.

Torres heard an explosion near his tank.

Close. Too close.

"What the hell was that?" Munoz asked.

"Another Sapper charge," Boone called from the driver's position. "It looks like Beast element breached the obstacle line we just cleared."

"Don't worry about Bravo Company. Stay focused on our area," Torres interjected, redirecting their focus.

Tanks all around them advanced deeper into the exercise area. The night erupt in controlled violence. The sound of artillery simulators continued unabated, the noise barely audible inside their armored cocoon. Smoke grenades popped at random locations, obscuring thermal sights. Yet through it all, their robotic Ripsaws prowled ahead, marking targets for the main force to destroy.

"We've got problems." Burke's voice was tight with concentration. "Assassin Ripsaw Two just went dark."

Torres checked his display. The blue diamond representing the M5 had turned amber—damaged or destroyed.

"Simulated RPG strike," Romeo One Alpha reported, frustration bleeding through his professional tone. "Assassin Ripsaw Two is combat ineffective. Transferring sectors to Assassin Ripsaw Three."

It was a lesson learned the hard way: unmanned didn't mean invulnerable.

"Boone, watch that crater on your left," Torres coached as they entered the breach. The kid was holding steady, but breach operations tested every driver. One wrong move meant thrown track or worse.

"I see it, Sergeant. Nice and easy."

Torres kept his head on a swivel as their tank continued through the course, watching for the inevitable counterattack. In the Russo-Ukraine War, both sides had learned to pre-register artillery on their own obstacles.

"Incoming! Incoming!" someone screamed over the company net.

The world outside their tank exploded.

The sound of artillery simulators bracketed their position. Pyrotechnic charges exploded, throwing rockets, dirt, and debris into the air to rain on them—simulating shrapnel hitting their vehicle. As Torres watched the scene unfold around them through his commander's independent thermal viewer, he saw Assassin Two-Four slide sideways on some loose soil. It threw a track as a tree branch got caught in the gear teeth, stopping their vehicle.

"Assassin Two-Four's immobilized," Staff Sergeant Delaney reported, voice steady despite the chaos. "Continuing to engage."

"Assassin Two-Three, cover them," Novak ordered. "Two-Two, with me. We're pushing through."

Torres felt pride swell as he listened to Novak take charge with an air of authority and confidence he didn't have four months ago when he'd first shown up. The lieutenant was growing into the role, making decisions under pressure. "Roger, Assassin Two-One. Assassin Two-Two's with you."

They cleared the obstacle belt into hell as more targets appeared.

"Contact front! Multiple vehicles!" Burke's hands flew over controls. "I count three T-90s, three o'clock, 450 meters. Load Sabot!"

"Copy, load Sabot!" Munoz replied, already reaching. He ejected the AMP shell and locked in the Sabot round. "Sabot up!"

"On the way."

BOOM!

The 120mm cannon belched flame as it hurled the depleted uranium lawn dart across the four hundred and fifty meters in fractions of a second. Sparks erupted against the armored hull of the T-90 main battle tank. The other tanks were hit in rapid succession as Novak joined the fray.

Downrange, the target vehicles died in a shower of sparks. But four more appeared, their exterior silhouettes giving them away as BTR-90 armored personnel carriers. Then to Torres's surprise, a trio of target vehicles that appeared to be T-90s emerged from deeper within a nearby copse of trees to their four o'clock position.

"Two-Two, they're swarming us," Novak called, his voice tense. "All Assassin elements, action front. Establish base of fire."

The other platoons of the company spread out in a hasty line formation anchored on Torres and Novak. The tanks found whatever cover the terrain offered while firing at the defenders. This was the critical moment—they had successfully breached into the enemy rear area. It meant they were exposed to more enemy kill zones, but they also had the chance to really wreck the enemies' day.

"Assassin Ripsaw Three has visual on enemy command post," Romeo One Alpha announced. "Grid Papa-Romeo-Two-Five-Seven. Requesting permission to engage with Javelin strike."

"Permission granted," Captain Morrison replied instantly. "Prosecute and take 'em out!"

Torres watched his display as the remaining M5 locked onto the target. In real combat, its Javelin launcher would send a missile arcing into the night. Here, computers calculated the hit probability and awarded the kill.

"Command post destroyed," the exercise controller announced. "OPFOR C2 degraded."

The defensive fire slackened. Without coordination, the remote-controlled vehicles reverted to basic programming—still dangerous, but predictable.

"All Assassin elements, advance!" Captain Morrison commanded. "Objective in sight!"

The company surged forward. Torres caught glimpses of other platoons maneuvering—First on the left, Third swinging wide right. Textbook company team breach and assault.

"Loader, how we doing on ammo?"

"Eight sabot, four AMPs remaining," Munoz replied promptly. The kid was finding his rhythm, combat stress focusing him now instead of freezing him up.

"Two-Two, infantry in the open, one o'clock," Novak called.

Torres saw the thermal mannequins representing dismounted infantry. In combat, these would be the enemy's last reserve, trying to stop the breakthrough.

"Burke, coax. Troops in the open—eight o'clock, two hundred meters!" Torres shouted.

The coaxial machine gun chattered, walking tracers across the target array. The exercise controllers marked them destroyed, one by one.

And then, suddenly, it was over.

"Objective secured," Morrison announced. "Cease fire, cease fire. ENDEX."

Torres slumped in his seat, adrenaline crash hitting hard. Around them, the battlefield fell silent except for idling engines and the crackle of burning simulators.

"Nice work, Boone," Torres praised. "That was textbook driving through that breach, Specialist. Well done!"

"Thanks, Sergeant." The kid sounded exhausted but proud. "Though I about filled my pants on more than one occasion. That has to be the most realistic tank course I've ever seen."

"Man, you ain't joking, Boone. If you didn't pucker a little on this course, you weren't paying attention," Burke drawled.

They pulled into the assembly area as dawn broke. Maintenance teams swarmed over vehicles, checking for exercise damage. Torres found Staff Sergeant Granger standing beside Two-Three, staring at his tank.

"You OK, Granger?" Torres asked.

"That was intense, Torres. If Assassin Ripsaw Two hadn't marked that position first..." Granger shook his head. "Those robots saved our bacon tonight."

It was true. Despite losing one M5, the unmanned vehicles had identified threats faster than human crews could have managed. The integration was working.

"Sergeant Torres!" Lieutenant Novak approached, Captain Morrison and the company executive officer in tow. "Outstanding work tonight."

"Thank you, sir. The platoon performed well."

The XO, First Lieutenant Washington, studied him with calculating eyes. "Walk with us, Sergeant First Class."

They moved away from the vehicles, finding privacy behind a maintenance shelter. Dawn painted the Polish countryside gold, but Torres felt the weight of what was coming.

"I'll cut to it," Washington said. "The CO and I have been watching you. Your platoon has the best gunnery scores, highest readiness rates, and now this—flawless execution under pressure."

"It's a team effort, sir."

"Ah don't be modest," Captain Morrison interjected. "Your leadership makes the difference. Which is why we need to talk about contingencies."

Torres felt his stomach tighten. He knew where this was going.

Washington continued, "Listen, if this balloon goes up—and between us, intel says it might—we need depth in our leadership. If something happens to me or the CO, or hell, Novak..."

"You're the glue holding this platoon together," Morrison finished. "But we might need you to hold more than that. If the company officers are taken out, are you ready and able to step up? To take command of the company if it comes to that?"

The question hung in the morning air. Torres thought of his crews—Burke and Munoz, finally clicking as a team. Granger, steady as a rock. Delaney, turning his poetry into deadly precision. The kids would become killers if they had too.

"If it comes to it, sir. I'll do whatever the mission requires."

"Good. I know you will." Captain Morrison clapped his shoulder. "I know this sounds morbid, me asking you this. But it's important for me and the other officers in the company to know which of our NCOs can set up and take charge if things really get ugly. During World War II, tank crews died pretty quickly. Hell, we saw how fast tank crews got chewed up in the Russo-Ukraine War. I just need you to think about it and be ready in case this exercise in Belarus spills over into NATO territory."

Torres nodded. "I understand, sir. I appreciate the confidence you have in my ability to lead should it come to it. I'll do what has to be done."

Morrison smiled. "I like that about you, Torres. You'd make a hell of an officer if you ever decided to put in for your commission. But enough of that. Get your guys some rest. We've got recovery operations at 1000, then Major Lathrop wants to review what went right, what went wrong, and what could go better. The battalion plans to run the exercise again tomorrow night."

"Wow, no rest for the weary."

Morrison laughed. "There never is, Sergeant. There never is."

As the officers departed, Torres stood alone, watching the sunrise. Somewhere to the east, past Belarus, Russian and Chinese forces conducted their own exercises. Training their own crews, testing their own integration of man and machine.

The M5 Ripsaws sat in a neat line, battle damage already being repaired by contractors. In a few hours, they'd be ready to fight again. No fatigue. No fear. No doubt.

But they couldn't hold ground—couldn't make the choice between legitimate target and war crime. They couldn't inspire scared kids to be more than they thought possible. That still took people...flawed, tired, magnificent people.

"Sergeant?" Munoz appeared, looking haggard. "Maintenance wants to know about that track tension issue."

"OK. I'm on my way." Torres took one last look at the sunrise, then turned back to his work. Because somewhere out there, the next war was waiting. And when it came, it would come at machine speed, with human souls paying the price.

It was time to make sure his people were ready.

****

Seven Hours Later
Barracks, Białystok Training Area

Torres sat on his bunk, tablet propped on his knees. The FaceTime connection struggled with the base's overloaded Wi-Fi, but Maria's face finally resolved on screen.

"Hey, baby," she said, and just hearing her voice made his chest tight.

"Hey. Kids asleep?"

"Finally. Carlos fought bedtime for two hours. Kept saying Daddy promised to read him a story."

Guilt twisted in his stomach. "I did. Lost track of time with the exercise."

"He'll live." Maria's smile didn't reach her eyes. "How are you?"

"Tired. Cold. Missing you."

"How's the training going? You guys ready to show the Russians what's what?"

Torres forced a laugh. "If they're dumb enough to try something, yeah. Though honestly, I think this is all just saber rattling. No way Moscow wants a real fight with NATO."

"That's good. The news makes it sound worse."

"News always does. If it bleeds, it leads. We're just here as a deterrent. Wave the flag, show some strength, everyone goes home." He kept his voice light, confident. No point worrying her with his doubts.

"Speaking of home..." Maria's expression shifted. "Miguel's in trouble at school again."

"Ugh, what now?"

"Cutting classes. Third time this month. Coach called—said if Miguel misses one more class, he's off the team for the season."

Torres sat up straighter. "Whoa, hold up, Maria. He's skipping school?"

"No, just his afternoon classes. He shows up in the morning and for practice after school. He disappears between eleven and three. It's starting to tank his grades, Ramon."

Torres sighed audibly in frustration. "OK. Put him on, Maria. I'll handle this."

"Ramon—"

"Put him on, Maria," he said with a bit more heat than he meant to.

She disappeared. He heard footsteps, muffled arguments, then Miguel's face filled the screen. Even at fourteen, Torres could see the athlete in him—broad shoulders, quick eyes.

"Hey, Dad. How's it going in Poland?"

"Don't 'hey, dad' me, Miguel. You want to explain yourself?"

Miguel's cheeks flushed as he shrugged. "School's pointless, dad."

"Oh really? Pointless? You know what's pointless? Throwing away a gift most kids would kill for."

"Oh, come on, dad. It's just a few classes—"

"No, Miguel, it's not. We're talking about your future here." Torres leaned forward. "You know what your fastball clocked at last week?"

"Eighty-seven," Miguel answered with genuine pride.

"That's right. Eighty-seven miles per hour—at fourteen, Miguel. Do you have any idea what that means?"

Miguel shrugged again, but Torres saw interest spark in his son's eyes.

"It means scouts are already asking about you. It means you could have college paid for. Hell, it means you could go pro if you keep developing. You could land a multimillion-dollar contract, Miguel. But you know what else it means?"

"What?"

"It means nothing if you can't stay eligible. No grades, no team. No team, no scouts. No scouts, no multimillion-dollar contract."

"Oh, come on, dad. It's not that bad. I'll always have baseball—"

"Oh, yeah? Where? The parking lot? Your backyard? You think the Astros are scouting kids who got kicked off their high school team for being too stupid to show up for algebra?"

Miguel's jaw tightened. "I'm not stupid."

"Then stop acting like it. You've got a gift, Miguel. A real shot at something special. How many kids in your school can throw eighty-seven?"

"None."

"How many in El Paso?"

"Maybe... two or three?"

"And how many of them are ditching class?"

Silence.

"Miguel, I'm not there to drag you out of bed or make sure you show up for class. Your mom's working doubles to pay for the transmission that decided to take a crap on us three hundred and two miles after the warranty expired. You want to help? Stop making her worry about whether you'll graduate."

"Ugh, these classes are sooo boring—"

"Life's boring. You think sitting in this tank for hours is exciting? You think your mom loves checking IVs at three a.m.? We do it because it gets us somewhere better."

Miguel's defiance cracked slightly. "The other kids say baseball's just a game."

"The other kids are jealous. They see what you can do, know they can't touch it. So they try to drag you down to their level. That what you want? To be just another kid with excuses?"

"No."

"Then what do you want?"

Miguel looked away, then back. "I want to pitch in the majors."

"Say it again."

"I want to pitch in the majors."

"Then you have to start acting like it. Major leaguers don't skip class. They don't give coaches reasons to bench them. They show up, do the work, and earn their shot." Torres softened his tone. "You've got something special, son. Please don't waste it because sitting in history class is boring."

"What if I'm not good enough, dad?"

"Then you fail trying, not because you were too lazy to show up. But, Miguel? You are good enough. I've watched you pitch since you were eight. You've got the arm. You've got the focus. You just need the discipline."

Miguel nodded slowly. "Coach says there might be scouts at the regional tournament."

"Oh, wow! That's amazing, Miguel! When is it?"

"It's in six weeks," Miguel explained, excitement returning in his voice.

Torres looked off screen for a moment before returning to face his son. "OK, Miguel. Then you've got six weeks to fix your grades and show those scouts you're worth investing in. Do you think you can you do that? Turn your grades around to show 'em you've got brains to go with that arm?"

"Yeah, I think I can do that," Miguel confirmed.

"You think, or you know?"

"I know I can."

"Good. Because if you make the majors, you're buying me season tickets."

Miguel cracked a smile—the first real one Torres had seen. "Let me guess...behind home plate?"

"Ah come on. I'm your father, not your agent. I'll take the bleachers. I just want to see my boy play, and live the baseball career I never had vicariously," Torres joked.

Maria reappeared as Miguel left. "Thank you, Ramon. I've been trying to get through to him for weeks."

"It's OK, Maria. He just needed to hear it different. How are you holding up?"

"I'm OK. Tired. The hospital's been crazy with all this flu going around. The auto shop said the transmission should be repaired in a couple of days. What luck, the damn warranty running out when it did," She paused. "Are you really not worried? About the situation there?"

"Eh, not really. The Russians talk big, but they know better. They got their asses kicked in Ukraine. I doubt they're looking for a repeat." He felt bad about lying to her, but protecting her was more important.

She smiled. "Good. I sleep better thinking you're just doing training over there."

"That's all this is. Big, expensive training," he replied.

They talked for a few more minutes—Carlos's preschool adventures, Sophia's science fair project. Normal life continuing an ocean away.

"I should go," Maria finally said. "Early shift tomorrow."

"Maria—"

"Come home safe, OK? Even if it is just training."

"I will. Love you."

"Love you too."

The connection ended. Torres stared at the blank screen, then tossed the tablet aside. Down the hall, someone laughed. Polish voices mixed with American—the two forces had started mingling more naturally.

His phone buzzed. Text from Burke: "Pub run. You in?"

Torres considered. He should sleep. Tomorrow brought more training, more preparation. But his mind was racing—Miguel's future, Munoz's struggles, the growing weight of keeping everyone ready.

"Give me five," he typed back.

******

0130 Hours Local Time

Hussar's Rest Pub, Białystok

The pub reeked of sweat and spilled beer—a universal constant in military watering holes. Torres pushed through a crowd of Polish tankers to find Burke holding court at a corner table.

"—so there we are, in Latvia, six clicks off the railhead, knee-deep in mud, and my driver locks up the steering system trying to drift an Abrams like he's in *Fast & Furious*," Burke was saying, his Louisiana drawl thickened by beer and bravado.

The Poles roared with laughter. One of them—a sergeant from the K2 company—wiped tears from his eyes as he leaned in. "During Iron Spear last year, our crew ran over our own drone on day one. Commander screamed, 'That was twenty thousand euros!' Then blamed the Americans for making it too quiet."

"But did you finish the lane?" Burke asked, raising his glass.

"Tak! Drone was gone, but gunner hit every target. Even the ones we weren't assigned!"

"Combat effective," Torres said dryly, sliding into the seat beside Burke. "That's all that matters."

Another round arrived. Laughter thickened. No politics, no doctrine—just soldiers telling stories from training rotations that had started to feel more like a prelude than preparation.

"Sarge!" PFC Sellers waved from across the table. "Settle a bet. Can the Ripsaw really engage twelve targets simultaneously?"

"Theoretically," Torres said carefully, noting the mixed company. "Never seen it tested."

"Because it's fantasy," declared a Polish corporal. "Machine cannot think like gunner. Cannot feel battlefield."

"Doesn't need to feel," Marrick's voice cut through. The warrant officer sat at the bar, nursing something clear. "It just needs to calculate faster than you can blink."

The Pole turned. "You are robot officer, yes? Tell me—your machine, it knows difference between soldier and farmer with rifle?"

"Thermal signature, movement patterns, weapon recognition—"

"I ask simple question. Does. It. Know?"

Marrick's jaw tightened. "It processes thousands of data points—"

"So no."

The table went quiet. Torres saw hands drifting toward bottles—not for drinking.

"Different tools for different jobs," Torres interjected. "Ripsaw spots targets. We decide what to shoot. System works."

"Until it doesn't," the Pole insisted. "Ukraine teaches us—war is chaos. Your pretty robots, they like order. What happens in chaos?"

"We adapt." Novak appeared, Captain Sikora beside him. "Just like you did. Just like everyone who survives does."

Sikora nodded approvingly. "Well said. Another round for my American friends! To adaptation!"

The tension broke. Conversations resumed, war stories flowing with the alcohol. Torres noticed Marrick remained at the bar, isolated in his certainty.

"Walk you back?" Torres offered an hour later, finding the warrant officer still nursing the same drink.

"I'm good."

"Wasn't a question, sir."

They left together, stepping into the sharp Polish night. Their breath steamed in the cold air.

"They don't get it," Marrick said finally. "The capability we're fielding. It'll change everything."

"Maybe. But those guys? They've been watching Russia's moves for years. They've earned their skepticism."

"Skepticism's fine. But they act like I'm trying to replace them."

Torres stopped walking. "Aren't you?"

Marrick turned, surprised. "What?"

"Be honest, sir. Five years from now, ten—you really think we'll need tank crews? Or will it all be Ripsaws, controlled from bunkers in Nevada?"

"That's not—" Marrick paused. "I don't know. Maybe. But right now, we need both."

"Right now." Torres resumed walking. "That's all any of us have. Right now, your machines need us to tell them what to kill. Second that changes, we're all obsolete."

"You'd rather we stick with pure human control? Let kids die because they're slower than algorithms?"

Torres thought of McDermott, his growing confidence. Of Munoz, fighting through his hesitation. Of his own son, chasing dreams in Texas.

"I'd rather we remember that someone has to live with the consequences," he said finally. "Your Ripsaws will kill more efficiently. But they won't carry the weight after."

They reached the barracks in silence. Inside, exhausted soldiers grabbed what sleep they could before morning brought another day of preparation.

Torres paused at his door, checking his phone. A text from Maria: "Miguel went to all his classes today. Even stayed after for tutoring. Whatever you said worked."

He smiled, pocketing the phone. Small victories.

Tomorrow they'd train again. Perfect the integration of man and machine. Prepare for a conflict everyone said wouldn't happen.

But tonight, his son was back on track. His loader was working through his fears. His crew was ready.

For now, that was enough.

Chapter Twenty-Nine:
Silent Guardians

April 8, 2033 – 0230 Hours
2nd Naval District Headquarters, Secure Operations Center
Magong Naval Base, Penghu Islands

The early-morning air hung thick with salt and humidity as Michael "Mick" Matsin exited the building housing the underground bunker, stepping into the night air. It felt good to escape the ops center buried beneath twenty feet of concrete and rebar that separated the world above from the nerve center below. As the fortified command post for the ROC Navy, it had been built to survive whatever Beijing might throw at it. It was a constant reminder of the threat under which the people of Taiwan continued to live.

As Mick pulled his Unplugged encrypted phone from the pocket of his cargo pants, he checked the time difference, noting that if it was 0230 here, that meant it was 1130 the morning before back home in Ventura County. His wife, Sarah, would be finishing her morning run along the beach, probably stopping at that coffee shop along Main Street she loved. The same place where they'd had their first date twenty-eight years ago, when he was a freshly minted fire control tech and she was finishing her nursing degree.

He pressed Call, and the phone rang twice before her voice filled his ear. "Hey, sailor."

"Hey yourself." Mick leaned against the building's concrete wall, still warm from yesterday's sun. In the sky above, the stars wheeled through gaps in the scattered clouds, the same stars she'd see in twelve hours. "How's the weather back home, Sarah?"

"Seventy-two and perfect. The beach was gorgeous this morning." She paused. "And you?"

"Hmmm, well, it's humid and tropical, kind of what you would expect of an island," he responded, omitting, of course, the air raid sirens they'd tested earlier, or how often and brazenly the PLA Air Force had been violating the Taiwanese ADIZ, or Air Defense Identification Zones, the closer they got to April 15. "It kind of reminds me of that time when we were stationed on Guam or Hawaii."

"Yeah, those were happy times... Mick..." Her voice carried that tone, the one that cut through twenty-six years of marriage and five kids' worth of deflection to get at the truth. "I'm not sure if you see any news over there, but the rhetoric from Beijing is getting worse. They're calling Taiwan a 'festering wound that must be cauterized.'"

He winced as he listened, then tried to say something. "I've heard some of it, Sarah—"

"Hey, don't 'Sarah' me. I've spent twenty-plus years as a Navy wife. I know when you're downplaying things." He could hear her setting her coffee mug down, that distinctive sharp clinking sound it made, ceramic against the quartz countertop of their kitchen. "I know the money is good, and we could use it. But twelve hundred and fifty a day doesn't do us any good if—"

"I know, you're right." He cut her off, the words coming out rougher than intended. She was concerned, that was all.

Below his feet, through twenty feet of rock, rebar, and concrete, forty-eight ROC naval personnel tracked every surface contact within two hundred miles. Kids, really. Same age as their oldest, the one serving on USS *Intrepid*. "The training's going well. They're quick learners. If anything happens, they'll be ready."

"It's not them I'm worried about."

A maintenance crew drove past in an electric cart, tools rattling. Mick waited until they passed. "Seven more weeks. Contract ends May thirty-first. Jodi's already got us booked on the first flight to Guam, then home."

"You promise?"

"Would I lie to my favorite nurse?" He teased.

"You'd try to protect her from worrying." But he heard the smile creep into her voice. "How's Jodi? Still making those terrible movie references?"

"Yup, yesterday she told the ROC Marines that operating the Zealot USVs was like 'giving Maverick a boat instead of an F-14.' They just stared at her."

Sarah's laugh filled the distance between them. "Tell her she needs newer material."

"I'll add it to the list, right after 'stop calling President Ouyang Skinny Poo in front of the Taiwanese admirals.'" He laughed.

"She doesn't!"

"She does. They love it." Mick checked his watch. Fourteen minutes into his fifteen-minute break. "Listen, I need to—"

"I know. Back to the cave." She sighed. "Mason called yesterday. The *Intrepid*'s in Yokosuka for resupply. He sounds good. Tired, but good."

Their oldest, following his father's path but in a Navy transformed by silicon and autonomy. "Tell him I'm proud of him next time he calls."

"Tell him yourself when you get home." A pause. "I love you, Michael Matsin. Come back to me."

"I always do, Sarah." The words were ritual, promise, prayer. "Love you too."

"Mick?" she asked, not wanting the call to end.

"Yeah, I'm still here?"

"Whatever's coming, whatever you're really preparing them for, just... be careful. The kids need their father. I need my husband," she said, her voice wavering.

He closed his eyes, feeling the weight of everything unsaid. The PLA naval buildup they'd tracked all week. The way the Taiwanese operators had stopped joking during drills. The grim efficiency that had replaced nervous energy.

"I'll be careful," he said. "I promise."

"Okay." She didn't sound convinced, but she let it go. Twenty-six years of marriage meant knowing which battles to fight. "Call me tomorrow?"

"Of course. Same time," he responded automatically.

"Good. I'll be here."

The connection ended, leaving him alone with the night sounds of distant waves against the harbor walls. Mick looked at his watch. *Time's up.* Fifteen minutes of normal life of being a husband instead of an advisor, of pretending the world wasn't balanced on a knife's edge.

He straightened his 511 shirt—old habits died hard—and headed back to the blast door. His key card chirped, the heavy mechanisms disengaging. The door swung inward, revealing the stark fluorescent world below.

He walked down the reinforced concrete stairs, past the emergency equipment lockers and radiation detection systems until he approached another checkpoint, presenting his credentials to an ROC

Marine, who scanned them with the thousand-yard stare of someone who'd been awake too long. He waved him in, and Mick entered the sprawling ops center.

Two dozen workstations monitoring everything from underwater sensors to satellite feeds. The main display showed the Taiwan Strait in real time, every contact tagged and tracked. Merchant traffic flowed in predictable lanes, but everyone watched for anomalies. For the patterns that would signal Beijing's patience had finally run out.

"Coffee, sir?" Master Chief Petty Officer Liang appeared at Mick's elbow, offering a steaming mug. The stocky Taiwanese sailor had the weathered look of someone who'd spent decades on these islands, watching the mainland's growing shadow.

"Thanks, Master Chief." Mick accepted the ceramic cup, noting the faded 146th Fleet insignia. "Local blend?"

"Penghu specialty. We grow it near the old Dutch fortifications." Liang's English carried only a trace accent. "Fifteen years I've been drinking this mud. Helps with the night shifts."

Mick sipped the coffee, admiring the kick of caffeine he felt almost immediately. The stuff was strong enough to wake the dead, with an undertone of something floral. He moved toward the autonomous systems console where Jodi Mack hunched over the displays, tracking their underwater sentries.

"Welcome back to the Bat Cave," she said without looking up. "Your Seekers are being good little robot sharks tonight. One of our Hammer Shark one-way UUVs is maintaining a perfect acoustic shadow on that *Song*-class sub we've been trailing."

"That's good. It means everything is working the way it's supposed to," Mick replied.

He turned to look at the rest of the operations center stretched before them. Three tiers of workstations descending toward a massive digital display. The main screen showed real-time shipping traffic, each vessel tagged with registration data. Two dozen contacts moved through the strait's shipping lanes, their paths traced in phosphorescent lines.

"Busy night tonight," Mick observed.

"Always is." Master Chief Liang Zihao gestured at the display. "That container ship, the *Ever Progress*? Makes this run twice weekly. The fishing fleet from Xiamen? They push our territorial waters every dawn. We know them all by name."

A side door opened. Admiral Han Junjie entered, followed by his staff. The operations center snapped to attention.

"As you were," Han commanded in Mandarin, then switched to English. "Mr. Matsin. Ready to turn our archipelago into a fortress?"

"That's the plan, Admiral."

Han approached the tactical display. Despite his sixty years, the admiral moved with a swimmer's grace. "Master Chief, bring up the defensive overlay."

The screen transformed. Penghu's ninety islands appeared in topographic detail, military installations glowing amber. Missile batteries dotted the landscape—Hsiung Feng III sites marked in blue triangles, Sky Bow III positions in blue squares.

"Gentlemen, be seated." Han waited as officers filled the briefing area. Mick recognized some faces from previous training sessions. Commander Tang Muyang from mine warfare. Lieutenant Colonel Wu from the 503rd Armored Brigade. Fresh-faced Ensign Huang clutching a tablet like a life preserver.

"For those of you joining us today, sorry about the early hour. Some things are best done under the cover of darkness, when the fewest people are able to see what we are doing," Han began. "I would like to introduce you to Mr. Matsin—he is from the company TSG and responsible for training our people on how to properly use and employ the equipment they have brought. His team is also helping us establish a training and maintenance program that will ensure this becomes an enduring program," explained Admiral Han, a smile spreading as he continued. "This equipment his company is providing is going to change how we look at naval warfare. In fact, these expensive gifts can swim and think for themselves."

A few nervous chuckles rippled through the room. They were David, standing before the proverbial Goliath.

Han's expression hardened. "Make no mistake, people. Penghu stands between the mainland and Taiwan. We are the cork in the bottle. For seventy years, we've prepared for the day they might come. Now, with our American friends' help, we add new teeth to our defenses should they try."

He nodded to Commander Tang. "Commander, brief them on our underwater situation."

Tang stood, laser pointer in hand. "Yes, sir. What you are looking at is the Penghu Channel. It runs seventy meters deep at its center. The Penghu Waterway"—his laser traced the southern passage—"reaches a depth of one hundred twenty meters. Deep enough for submarines running silent to pass through."

The display zoomed, showing underwater topography. "These trenches between our islands are like highways for enemy subs. Our diesel boats patrol when they can, but..." He shrugged. "Two submarines cannot be everywhere."

"Exactly. That's where we come in," Mick said, joining the conversation as he stood. "Jodi, why don't you talk about the Seeker?"

Jodi Mack nodded from her workstation, a new image appearing on the monitor. "Good morning, gentlemen. Let me introduce to you Seeker—your new underwater sentry."

The display shifted, revealing a sleek, torpedo-shaped vehicle rotating in 3D. "This is the US Navy Seeker-class XLUUV. It's thirty-nine feet or twelve meters in length and three meters in diameter. Basically, it's a robotic mini submarine designed to hunt other submarines with either a trio of Copperhead-500s or six Copperhead-100 AI-torpedoes."

Ensign Huang raised a tentative hand. "You said it's robotic. Does that mean it's autonomous, and if so, how autonomous is it, ma'am?"

"Good question, Ensign." Jodi highlighted the vehicle's sensor dome. "Each Seeker carries an AI brain trained on thousands of submarine acoustic signatures. It can differentiate between whale song and a Type 093's reactor cooling pumps at fifty kilometers, sometimes further."

"Wow, that's incredible. And what kinds of rules of engagement are we able to set on this thing?" Lieutenant Colonel Wu interjected.

Mick fielded this one for Jodi. "Whatever you like. We recommend using layered authorities. In patrol mode, they observe and report. In threat mode, it requires human authorization to engage. In terminal defense mode, if hostile forces are actively attacking inside the geofence you've created, they'll hunt independently based on the rules and parameters you set."

Admiral Han leaned forward. "And these Hammer Shark mines—why don't you explain that a bit more?"

"Sure, so the Hammer Shark mines are what we like to call next-generation smart mines," Jodi explained. "In the past, mines were laid in the likely path a warship would travel. These are different. Instead of hoping for an enemy ship to cross its path, it'll seek it out if it enters its detection field. When they're deployed, they're essentially in a dormant status until activated by acoustic or magnetic signatures matching the threat library of the onboard brain. Once a match is made, the mine will wake up, verify the target, and attack it from below."

Master Chief Liang whistled softly. "Incredible. The waters themselves become our ally."

"Exactly." Mick pulled up deployment maps. "Tonight, we position twelve Seekers in the deep channels. The Hammer Shark fields go here"—he marked approaches to major harbors—"integrated with your existing coastal defenses."

"And how do they coordinate?" Commander Tang asked.

"Through the Lattice AI system," Jodi answered. "Think of it as a conductor orchestrating your defensive symphony. Your Hsiung Feng batteries, our autonomous systems, your preregistered artillery, it's all linked together to work in support of each other."

Admiral Han stood, hands clasped behind his back. "Mr. Matsin, I've defended these islands since I was Ensign Huang's age. I've seen the mainland's forces grow from coastal patrol boats to carrier battle groups. Tell me honestly, will these machines make a difference?"

Mick met his gaze. "Admiral, in the Russo-Ukraine War, ten men with drones stopped entire armored columns. Tonight, we're giving you three hundred underwater drones that never sleep, never miss, and never retreat. Yes, sir. They'll make a difference."

Silence settled over the room. On the main display, commercial traffic continued its eternal dance, unaware that beneath those waves, the nature of warfare was about to change.

"Master Chief," Han commanded. "Alert the fishing cooperative. We'll need six boats ready by 0400."

"Already done, sir. Captain Koh selected crews with naval reserve experience."

"Good." Han turned to his officers. "Gentlemen, for seventy years we've promised to hold these islands. Tonight, we begin keeping that promise. Commander Tang, your team deploys first. Questions?"

Ensign Huang raised his hand again. "Sir, what if the mainland detects our deployment?"

Master Chief Liang answered before Han could speak. "Ensign, they've been watching us for decades. They see what we want them to see." He gestured at the commercial traffic. "You think we chose tonight randomly? That container ship will block their satellite pass at 0420. The fishing fleet creates perfect sonar clutter. We've done this dance before."

"Just never with robotic dancers," Commander Tang added.

Han checked his watch. "Two hours until deployment. Mr. Matsin, anything else?"

"One thing, Admiral." Mick set down his coffee. "My team's been training your sailors for six weeks. They're ready, Sir. Trust them."

"Trust." Han savored the word. "Easier to trust men than machines."

"Fair enough. Then trust the men who control the machines."

****

Lucky Dragon
Magong Harbor

The civilian section of Magong Harbor reeked of diesel and fish. Mick stood on the *Lucky Dragon*'s deck, watching ROC sailors load equipment under cover of routine maintenance. The modified trawler's hold concealed racks designed for XLUUV deployment.

"Nervous?" Jodi's voice crackled through his earpiece.

"Always am before an op."

"This isn't combat, Mick. Just very expensive fishing."

He smiled. "Tell that to my gut."

Captain Koh emerged from the wheelhouse. The seventy-year-old skipper with skin like weathered teak was former ROC Navy, having commanded a destroyer before retiring to take over his family's fishing business.

"We're ready, Mr. Matsin." Koh's English was accented but precise. "My grandson's boat will follow as backup. Boy did five years in the submarine service."

"That's great. I appreciate the help, Captain."

Koh spat over the rail. "Mainland bastards have been stealing our fishing grounds for years. About time we put some teeth in these waters."

Commander Tang approached, his team wheeling the first XLUUV on a concealed trailer. The autonomous submarine was wrapped in tarps, looking like any other piece of maritime equipment.

"First package ready," Tang reported. "Ensign Huang will monitor from here. Chief Liang's team has the deployment cradle prepared."

Mick checked his tablet, confirming Lattice connectivity. Each XLUUV showed green on the network, their AI cores initialized but dormant.

"Remember," he told Tang, "these aren't torpedoes. They're hunters. Once we activate them, they'll patrol for thirty days before needing recovery. They'll learn every sound in these waters."

"Including our own submarines?" he asked.

"Yes. Already programmed with your acoustic signatures. They'll ignore friendlies unless fired upon," Mick explained.

Tang nodded slowly. "During the Third Taiwan Strait Crisis, I was a junior lieutenant. We listened to their submarines circle our islands, helpless to stop them. Now..."

"Now you hunt back," Mick replied.

The deployment team worked with practiced efficiency. Within minutes, the first XLUUV was secured in the trawler's modified hold. Eleven more would follow on five other boats.

Master Chief Liang appeared, smartphone in hand. "Satellite pass in forty minutes. Weather's holding, light fog rolling in from the southwest. Perfect conditions."

"I'd call that divine providence," Captain Koh muttered. "My grandfather said the sea goddess Mazu protects these islands. Maybe she sends fog when we need it."

"I'll take help from any source," Mick replied.

Ensign Huang approached hesitantly. "Mr. Matsin? I've been studying the AI protocols. What happens if communications are jammed?"

"Good question, Huang." Mick pulled up a schematic on his tablet. "Like Jodi and I showed you guys during the training, each unit has three layers of decision-making. Primary is networked through Lattice. Secondary uses the local mesh networking between the units. And tertiary, should the other two systems become jammed or unavailable, is fully autonomous based on the preprogrammed parameters you provide it."

"So even if we're cut off..."

"They keep hunting. That's both the beauty and terror of autonomous systems, Ensign," Mick answered. "Once awakened, they don't need us anymore."

The young officer paled slightly. Commander Tang clapped him on the shoulder. "That's why we maintain strict deployment protocols, Ensign. These are tools, not masters. We're still the ones who give the orders."

"It's still incredible. Tools that think," Huang murmured.

"Hey, focus on the mission," Tang ordered. "We can philosophy later."

By 0400, the small fleet was ready. Six fishing boats, crews of mixed civilians and naval personnel, each carrying death in their holds. Mick stood beside Captain Koh as the *Lucky Dragon*'s engine rumbled to life.

"Heading?" Koh asked.

"North first. Deploy along the Penghu Channel's eastern edge." Mick showed him the route on a waterproof chart. "Twelve positions, spaced for overlapping coverage."

"I know these waters. Fished them forty years before you were born." Koh's hands were steady on the wheel. "That deep trench near Xiyu? Perfect ambush point. Current pushes south. Anything transiting there has to fight it or go around."

"Exactly. That's why we're putting two units there."

The flotilla departed separately, maintaining normal fishing patterns. The *Lucky Dragon* led, her navigation lights reflecting off black water. Behind them, Magong's lights faded into predawn darkness.

"Contact," Chief Liang reported from the radar station below. "Mainland surveillance vessel, thirty kilometers northwest. Maintaining standard patrol pattern."

"Let them watch," Koh said. "We're just fishermen heading for the morning catch."

Mick activated his tactical display. The six boats appeared as blue dots, their paths converging on predetermined coordinates. Each deployment point had been selected for maximum coverage of submarine transit routes.

At 0420, they reached the first position. The container ship *Ever Progress* passed two kilometers north, its bulk blocking the latest Chinese surveillance satellite.

"Now," Mick commanded.

The deployment team worked in darkness, guided by red-lens flashlights. The XLUUV slid down specialized rails, entering the water with barely a splash. On Mick's display, its icon shifted from white to blue as systems activated.

"Unit One deployed," Ensign Huang reported from his monitoring station. "All systems nominal. AI initializing."

"Set patrol parameters," Mick instructed. "Patrol depth forty meters, pattern Alpha-Three. Threat library loaded?"

"Confirmed. Seven hundred twelve acoustic signatures in memory," Ensign Huang confirmed.

With the first unit deployed, they moved methodically and with purpose to the next position. By 0500, six units were in the water, their icons forming a defensive line across the channel. The *Lucky Dragon* rendezvoused with the other boats in a fishing ground twelve kilometers northeast of Magong.

"Perfect," Captain Koh announced, cutting the engines. "Now we fish."

The crews deployed nets and lines, maintaining their cover. Below, the XLUUVs began their patrol, artificial minds learning the rhythm of these waters.

"Lattice shows all units operational," Jodi reported via secure comm. "Acoustic returns normal. They're hunting."

Commander Tang joined Mick at the rail, watching the dawn brighten the eastern sky. "My grandfather fought the Japanese here in 1895. My father faced the Communists in 1958. Each generation, same islands, different weapons."

"Different kind of war now," Mick said.

"Is it?" Tang pulled out a cigarette, hands cupping the lighter flame. "The year has changed, but the stakes remain the same. They want these islands. We want to keep them, and these machines will help us do that."

Mick thought about that. "Agreed, but I wouldn't oversimplify the complex nature of autonomous warfare."

"Of course not. But the purpose remains human." Tang exhaled smoke into the salt breeze. "We defend our home. Your machines just help us do it better."

Just then a pod of dolphins broke the surface nearby, their sleek forms arcing through the waves. Below them, twelve artificial predators began learning their hunting grounds, patient as death itself.

"Contact update," Chief Liang called. "Mainland vessel changing course. Coming to investigate."

"Let them come," Captain Koh said. "We're legal. Fishing permits all in order. They want to count our catch? Fine. They won't find what swims beneath."

Mick watched the surveillance vessel's approach on radar. The game of cat and mouse that had played out in these waters for decades continued. Only now, the mice had grown metal teeth.

"All units deployed," he reported to Jodi. "The guardians are in place."

"Roger that. Admiral Han sends his compliments. Phase one complete."

Mick allowed himself a moment of satisfaction. In six hours, they'd transformed Penghu's underwater approaches into a lethal maze. Any submarine attempting to transit would face a gauntlet of tireless hunters.

Ensign Huang appeared from below, tablet glowing. "Sir? Unit Seven just reported acoustic contact. Biological—it's a whale pod transiting south. It's incredible. The AI correctly identified and ignored them."

"That's good. See, this is why we spent weeks training the recognition software." Mick studied the data briefly. "I like it. This is exactly what we want. The system's learning. Every contact is making it smarter, more effective. That means it's becoming more lethal."

"I agree with the general premise and idea. But this is also what worries me," the ensign carefully admitted.

"I am glad this worries you, ensign," Commander Tang interjected. "It means you're thinking independently, beyond what you have been taught. That's a good thing but remember—no matter how smart the AI becomes, we're still the ones holding the leash. Never forget that."

The mainland surveillance vessel from earlier had closed to five hundred meters. Then, as quickly as it had appeared, it abruptly turned away, apparently satisfied with the fishing fleet's legitimacy. As the sun rose over the Taiwan Strait, painting the water gold and crimson, the fishing boats hauled their nets in, filled with the morning catch.

Lurking below the waves, the real catch had already been made. They'd successfully deployed the twelve Seeker XLUUVs to begin their silent prowl of the depths surrounding the Penghu archipelago. Within a few more days, they'd have successfully transformed the islands into a trap. The next time the PLA Navy wanted to test the waters, they would find them filled with mechanical sharks, hungry and patient.

"I think we're done for now, Captain. Take us home," Mick ordered.

"Aye." Koh revved up the engines. "We did a good morning's work. I feel my grandfather would be proud. He fought a different war, but it's the same spirit."

As the *Lucky Dragon* turned toward Magong, Mick sent a final message to Jodi: "It's done. Silent guardians deployed. The sea wall is complete."

Her response came immediately: "Good copy. Phase two begins tonight. The coastal wolves are ready to prowl."

Mick smiled as he read her message. He secured his equipment and went below. In twelve hours, Elena Bell, the new TSG contractor, would take the next watch, hiding their *Zealot*-class surface drones along Taiwan's western shores. Layer by layer, they were building an autonomous defense that would turn the Taiwan Strait into an unmanned hellscape—a phrase the former IndoPACOM Commander Admiral Sam Paparo had predicted nine years earlier.

But first, breakfast. Even waging digital warfare required human fuel.

The *Lucky Dragon* chugged toward home, her crew whistling traditional fishing songs, nets heavy with tuna and mackerel. Just another morning in the Penghu Islands, where fishermen had become warriors and the sea itself had grown silicon teeth.

Chapter Thirty:
Coastal Wolves

April 12, 2033
Budai Township Fishing Port
Chiayi County, Taiwan
23 Kilometers South of Dongshi, Western Coast

Elena Bell checked her dive watch—0500 hours. High tide was in ninety minutes. Through the warehouse's salt-crusted windows, she counted seventeen fishing boats preparing for the morning catch, their diesel engines warming in the predawn drizzle.

Perfect cover, she thought.

The old salt processing warehouse smelled of rust and brine. Once, Budai had supplied salt to half of Taiwan. Now the abandoned buildings served a different purpose. Elena ran her hand along a Zealot USV's sleek hull, marveling at the engineering. Eight months ago, she'd been piloting these USVs for the Navy. Now, she was hiding robotic boats in Taiwanese fishing villages and getting paid handsomely by TSG for her efforts.

"Coffee?" Ensign Lin appeared at her elbow, offering a thermos. The kid couldn't be older than twenty-two, but his eyes held the intensity of someone who understood the stakes.

"Thanks." Elena accepted the cup, noting the Tsoying Naval Base insignia on his jacket. "You're up early."

"Couldn't sleep. Too excited." Lin's English was flawless, probably perfected at one of Taiwan's military academies. "First real deployment of autonomous systems. We're making history."

"History's overrated," Elena muttered, sipping the bitter brew. "I prefer boring deployments where everyone goes home."

A door banged open. Master Sergeant Sun materialized from the rain, his marine recon team ghosting behind him. The sergeant's expression suggested he'd rather be anywhere else than babysitting American contractors.

"Perimeter's secure," Sun reported in accented English. "But we have a problem."

Elena's hand instinctively moved toward her concealed sidearm. "Define problem, Sergeant."

"Old Tau from the morning market says strangers were asking about 'new equipment' at the harbor. There were two men, mid-twenties with mainland accents. They left before dawn."

"Hmm, could be nothing," Ensign Lin offered hopefully.

"Yeah, or it could be a ChiCom SOF unit conducting surveillance of the area," Elena countered. She activated her encrypted comm. "Morning, Mick. You got a minute?"

Mick's voice crackled through her earpiece from Penghu. "It's early, and I haven't had my coffee yet, but go ahead, Shark Two."

She smiled, stifling a laugh before turning serious. "Our Marine overwatch may have detected a possible compromise. He received a local report of a pair of military-aged males with mainland accents showing interest in our activities."

A pause followed. "Your call, Elena. You're on scene," Mick advised.

She weighed the options. Abort, and they'd lose weeks of preparation. Continue, and they might walk into a trap. Through the window, oyster farmers were already heading out, their flat-bottomed boats loaded with cultivation gear.

"Mission's too important and we're short on time. We'll proceed," she decided. "But we adapt. I'll update you if anything changes. Shark Two out." Elena disconnected the call, then turned to Ensign Lin. "Can your mesh network handle distributed activation?"

The ensign's fingers flew over his tablet. "Yes, ma'am. Each USV can activate independently based on proximity triggers. No central command signal needed."

"Good. We scatter the units more than planned. Make them find all of them."

Master Sergeant Sun grunted approvingly. "Finally. Someone who thinks like a marine."

The warehouse doors rolled open. Chief Petty Officer Chang of the Coast Guard entered, water streaming from his rain gear. Twenty years of service showed in his hardened face and careful movements.

"Weather's getting worse," Chang announced. "Northeast monsoon's picking up. Seas building to two meters."

"Perfect," Elena said. "Rough seas mean fewer observers."

Chang's expression soured. "Also means more danger for my fishermen. These aren't Navy crews, Ms. Bell. They're civilians with families."

"Who volunteered to help defend their homes," Captain Koh interjected, entering behind Chang. The fishing cooperative leader moved with a destroyer captain's bearing despite his seventy years. "My boats, my choice, Chief Chang."

Elena watched the tension between the two men. Chang was sworn to protect civilian maritime traffic. Koh, on the other hand, had an understanding that sometimes civilians had to become warriors.

"Gentlemen," she interrupted. "We have six hours to position forty USVs along twenty kilometers of coastline. Let's focus."

She pulled up the deployment map on a waterproof display. Budai's coastline appeared in detail—oyster platforms extending two kilometers offshore, abandoned salt pans creating a maze of channels, and fishing ports dotting the shore.

"Original plan was four units per platform, ten platforms total." She adjusted the display. "New plan: two units per platform, twenty platforms. Harder to find, harder to destroy all at once."

"More trips," Captain Koh observed. "More exposure."

"But better survivability," Sun added. "I like it. Defense in depth."

Ensign Lin studied his tablet. "I can modify the mesh network protocols. Each pair of USVs will create a local node. Destroy one, the other adapts."

"Do it." Elena turned to the deployment teams. "Check your equipment. We launch in thirty minutes."

The warehouse erupted in controlled chaos. ROC sailors wheeled USVs toward concealed trailers. Each unit was wrapped in fishing nets and tarps, disguised as aquaculture equipment. The Zealot's angular hull disappeared beneath convincing camouflage.

Elena inspected each unit personally. The USVs were engineering marvels—four meters long, semisubmersible, carrying four naval Hellfire missiles and a two-hundred-and-fifty-pound warhead for terminal attack. But it was their AI that made them truly lethal. Each could identify, track, and engage targets autonomously or in coordinated swarms.

"Ma'am?" A young sailor approached nervously. "Unit Seventeen shows a fault in its IFF transponder."

Elena checked the diagnostic display. The Identification Friend or Foe system showed intermittent failures. "Pull it. We don't deploy anything that might target friendlies."

"But that leaves us with thirty-nine units…"

"Better thirty-nine reliable wolves than forty with one rabid." She marked the unit for repair. "War's about trust, sailor. We trust these machines to kill the right targets."

Chief Chang reappeared, smartphone in hand. "Coast Guard radar reports Y-9 surveillance aircraft, fifty nautical miles west. Routine patrol pattern so far."

"So far," Sun echoed darkly.

Elena considered their options. The Y-9's sensors could detect unusual activity, but the rain and sea state would degrade their effectiveness. Still…

"We adjust timing," she decided. "Launch in three waves, mixed with regular fishing traffic. Ensign Lin, can you slave some USVs to fishing boat navigation?"

"Already done." The ensign showed her his screen. "They'll mirror fishing vessel movements until activated. Anyone watching will see normal traffic patterns."

"Outstanding." Elena felt a flutter of pride. These kids were good. "Captain Koh, which boats are ready?"

The old captain consulted a handwritten list. "Six boats first wave. All with veteran crews. My nephew commands the lead vessel— five years in the Navy, knows these waters like his own palm."

"Perfect. Master Sergeant, I need your marines dispersed among the boats. If we have mainland assets watching…"

"Already planned," Sun interrupted. "Two-man teams per vessel. Civilian clothes, concealed weapons. Anyone tries to board, they'll meet resistance."

Elena nodded. The plan was coming together despite the complications. Outside, rain intensified, drumming against the warehouse roof. Through the murk, she could see oyster platforms stretching into the gray dawn—perfect hiding spots for mechanical predators.

"Movement," one of Sun's marines reported. "Vehicle approaching from the north. Not local plates."

Everyone tensed. Elena moved to a window, peering through the rain. A white van approached slowly, headlights probing the darkness.

"Weapons ready," Sun ordered quietly. His marines faded into shadows.

The van stopped fifty meters away. A door opened. An elderly woman emerged, followed by two younger men carrying boxes.

Chief Chang laughed. "Breakfast delivery. Mrs. Chen's famous rice porridge. She comes every morning."

Elena exhaled slowly. "Christ. This place has my nerves wound tight."

"Good," Captain Koh said. "Nervous keeps you alive. Complacent gets you killed."

Mrs. Chen's crew distributed steaming containers. Elena accepted a bowl gratefully, the hot porridge warming her core. Around her, sailors and marines ate quickly, fueling for the work ahead.

"Five minutes," Elena announced. "First wave launches."

The warehouse doors opened. Rain slashed horizontally, driven by the monsoon winds. Six trucks emerged, each pulling covered trailers. To any observer, they looked like standard aquaculture transport.

Elena climbed into the lead truck with Ensign Lin and two ROC sailors. Captain Koh's nephew, a compact man named Zhao, took the wheel.

"The oyster platforms are two kilometers out," Zhao explained as they drove. "We'll use the service channels. Local boats only—mainlanders wouldn't know the routes."

They descended toward the harbor, windshield wipers fighting the downpour. Budai's fishing fleet bobbed at moorings, crews preparing despite the weather. Elena counted over forty vessels—perfect concealment for their operation.

The truck stopped at pier seventeen. Elena jumped out, rain immediately soaking through her jacket. The deployment team worked fast, transferring USVs to a waiting oyster boat. Each unit splashed into the vessel's holding tank, hidden beneath legitimate aquaculture equipment.

"Go," Elena commanded.

The boat departed, diesel engine churning gray water. Through the rain, she could barely track its progress. Five more boats followed, each carrying their deadly cargo toward predetermined platforms.

"Shark Two, this is Overwatch," came Sun's voice in her earpiece. "Drone contact. Small quadcopter, approaching from the east."

Elena's pulse quickened. "Commercial or military?"

"Unknown. But it's heading directly for the harbor."

She made a quick decision. "Continue deployment. Act natural. Lin, can you jam it?"

"Not without revealing our capabilities," the ensign replied.

"Then we ignore it. Everyone maintains cover."

The drone buzzed overhead, cameras swiveling. Elena forced herself to appear calm, just another worker loading boats in the rain. The quadcopter circled twice, then headed north.

"It's gone," Sun reported. "But expect company. That was reconnaissance."

"All the more reason to hurry," Elena replied.

The first wave reached the oyster platforms. Through binoculars, she watched crews deploying USVs into concealed cages beneath the farming structures. From the surface, nothing appeared unusual—just aquaculture workers maintaining their equipment.

"First wave complete," Captain Koh reported. "Twelve units in position."

"Second wave launches in twenty minutes," Elena commanded. "Different routes, different platforms."

She used the interval to check systems. Each deployed USV showed green on Lin's network display. The mesh was forming, creating an invisible web of sensors and weapons along Budai's coast.

"Ma'am?" Chief Chang appeared at her elbow. "That Y-9 changed course. Now heading southeast. Toward us."

Elena calculated distances and times. The surveillance aircraft would be overhead in forty minutes. They needed to finish before then.

"Accelerate timeline," she ordered. "Waves two and three launch together."

"That's a lot of boats moving at once," Chang warned.

"Better than getting caught mid-deployment."

The remaining trucks rolled out. Elena watched twenty boats depart in seemingly random directions, their courses actually precisely calculated to reach different platform clusters. Rain provided cover, but also made the work dangerous. Two-meter swells tossed the small vessels.

"Unit Twenty-Three deployed," a voice reported. "Platform Fourteen secure."

"Unit Twenty-Four in position. Mesh network confirmed."

The reports continued. Elena tracked progress on her tablet, watching the defensive line take shape. Each USV pair created a node in the network, linked to coastal radar stations and missile batteries. When activated, they would transform from hiding to hunting in seconds.

"Contact!" Sun's voice was sharp with urgency. "Fast boat approaching from the north. Not local configuration."

Elena grabbed binoculars. Through the rain, she spotted a sleek patrol craft moving at high speed. Military lines, no visible weapons, but clearly not civilian.

"Coast Guard?" she asked Chang.

The chief shook his head. "Wrong hull design. That's mainland Maritime Militia. Unofficial navy."

"How long until our boats return?"

"Fifteen minutes minimum."

That's too long, Elena thought. The militia boat would reach the platforms before then. Elena weighed the options, and none were good.

"Ensign Lin, activate Units Nineteen and Twenty. Minimal signature, surveillance mode only."

"Ma'am, if they detect active sensors…"

"Better than them finding boats full of military hardware. Do it."

Lin's fingers danced over the controls. Two kilometers offshore, a pair of USVs awakened, sensors probing the approaching vessel.

"Target identified," Lin reported. "Type 022 hull, modified for intelligence gathering. Electronic warfare suite active."

"They're hunting for signals," Elena realized. "Looking for our network."

The militia boat slowed near platform seven. Through binoculars, Elena watched crew members photographing the oyster farming structures. They were methodical, professional.

"They know," Sun stated flatly. "Someone told them where to look."

Elena's mind raced. If the mainland knew about Budai, the entire coastal defense network was compromised. Unless...

"Lin, can you make our USVs mimic commercial navigation radar?"

The ensign's eyes widened with understanding. "Make them look like fishing boats? Yes! Give me thirty seconds."

His fingers flew over the keyboard. On the display, USV signatures shifted, now appearing as standard fishing vessel returns.

"Brilliant," Chang murmured. "They'll see what they expect to see."

The militia boat continued its patrol, scanning each platform. They found nothing unusual—oyster cages, maintenance equipment, and what appeared to be small fishing boats sheltering from the storm.

"Y-9 now twenty kilometers out," a lookout reported.

"Come on," Elena whispered, watching their boats race back toward the harbor.

One by one, the deployment vessels returned. Crews quickly unloaded equipment, maintaining the pretense of normal operations. The militia boat completed its sweep and turned north, apparently satisfied.

"Last boat docking," Captain Koh announced.

Elena checked her watch. The Y-9 would be overhead in minutes. "Everyone inside. Normal harbor operations only."

They retreated to the warehouse as the surveillance aircraft's drone filled the air. Elena watched through windows as the Y-9 circled Budai, sensors probing. Rain and electronic countermeasures would limit their effectiveness, but not eliminate it.

"All units showing operational," Lin reported quietly. "Thirty-nine Zealot USVs successfully deployed. Mesh network stable."

Elena allowed herself a moment of satisfaction. Despite the complications—suspected compromise, surveillance pressure, weather challenges—they'd succeeded. Budai's coast now bristled with hidden teeth.

"Shark One, this is Shark Two," she reported to Mick. "Coastal wolves are in position. The pack is ready to hunt."

"Outstanding work," Mick replied. "Any complications?"

"Mainland knows something's up. Militia boat sniffed around, but found nothing actionable. Recommend advancing activation timeline."

"Agreed. Jodi's working on that issue. Get your team back to base."

Elena gathered her people. Master Sergeant Sun approached, his earlier suspicion replaced by grudging respect.

"Not bad for a contractor," he admitted. "You think like an insurgent. I approve."

"High praise from a marine," Elena replied.

Chief Chang shook her hand. "You kept my fishermen safe while accomplishing the mission. That's all I asked."

Captain Koh smiled through his exhaustion. "My grandfather smuggled weapons against the Japanese. My father ran supplies during the White Terror. Now I hide robot boats. Each generation finds its way to resist."

Ensign Lin finished backing up his data. "Ma'am? The mesh network is learning. Every boat that passes, every radar return—it's building a baseline of normal activity. In a week, it'll be able to identify anomalies instantly."

"That's the idea," Elena said. "Smart weapons for smart warfare."

They loaded into vehicles for the return journey. As they left Budai, Elena took one last look at the coast. Peaceful fishing village, oyster platforms bobbing in the waves, morning catch being sorted at the docks.

But beneath the surface, thirty-nine mechanical wolves now prowled. When the time came, they would rise from hiding, missiles ready, AI minds calculating attack vectors. The Taiwan Strait had grown silicon fangs.

"You did good today," Mick's voice came through her earpiece. "Get some rest. Tomorrow, we integrate with the main network."

"Copy that." Elena closed her eyes, exhaustion hitting hard. "The coastal wolves are ready. God help anyone who tries to land on these beaches."

As their convoy headed inland, the Y-9 completed its surveillance run and turned west. Its cameras and sensors had captured thousands of images—fishing boats, aquaculture platforms, normal coastal activity.

They'd seen everything. They'd seen nothing.

In the digital age, the best camouflage was normalcy. And death now swam hidden among the oyster cages of Budai, patient as the tide itself.

Chapter Thirty-One:
The Forest Places Things

April 13, 2033 – 1645 Hours Local Time
Tree Line East of County Road 143, Near Botbaldevägen Junction
Rastplats Hallute Backe, Gotland

Captain Bertil Sonevang pressed himself deeper into the pine needles, ignoring the damp seeping through his ghillie suit. Thirty-two years of teaching history had taught him patience. Three decades in the Home Guard had taught him when patience might get you killed.

Through his thermal monocular, two figures moved along the forest trail like tourists who'd memorized their role too well. North Face jackets, expensive ones. Zeiss binoculars hanging just right, and camera bags that cost more than most Gotlanders made in a month. It all looked perfect.

Too perfect, too Gucci in his mind.

"Nyqvist," Bertil whispered into his throat mic. "Status?"

"Eyes on POI," Sergeant Albin Nyqvist responded from forty meters north of the persons of interest. "They're stopping again. Same pattern as yesterday."

Bertil tracked the pair through his optic. The taller one, Asian features, maybe Korean or Northern Chinese, knelt beside a limestone outcropping. His companion, stockier with Slavic cheekbones, maintained watch while consulting what looked like a birding guidebook.

Except birders don't GPS-mark defensive positions, Bertil thought grimly.

This was the second day his team had shadowed some people affiliated with the "Baltic Wings Conservation Group." Two days of watching them photographing approaches to the Patriot battery positioned three kilometers northeast. Two days of them sketching "geological formations" and landmarks to rapidly identify specific locations.

After the news they had heard about Kaliningrad, the sudden appearance of Chinese and Russian Marines conducting joint amphibious drills had everyone's teeth on edge. Stockholm and NATO higher-ups had ordered increased surveillance of all foreign groups on

Gotland. What the increased scrutiny found made Bertil's old soldier instincts scream—danger.

"Wait, hold up." Nyqvist's voice tightened. "The tall one's got something."

Peering through his thermal, Bertil watched the Asian man produce an object of some sort from his pack. It looked cylindrical, matte gray in color, about the size of a large thermos. He couldn't spot any commercial markings, not that it mattered.

"I'm recording it," Corporal Emma Lindgren confirmed from her position. The digital camera captured a high-definition video of the scene, relaying it to the 2-503rd Battalion's S2 shop and the P18 command post in real time.

The taller man knelt closer to the ground, placing the device into a shallow depression beside the outcropping's base. The stockier man standing nearby produced a small tool that looked like a modified pH meter as he knelt down and pressed it into the ground nearby. The man's movements were quick, smooth and professional. It was clear he'd done this before, many times.

The stockier man retrieved a stick of chalk from the pocket of his jacket and made a small mark on the limestone, three dots and a line. Bertil wasn't sure what it meant, but he recognized reconnaissance markings when he saw them. It reminded him of something his grandfather had shared with him about his experience fighting the Soviets in the Winter War in neighboring Finland.

"Maybe it's an acoustic sensor," Bertil murmured softly. "Or something worse."

The pair stood, brushing dirt from their knees. The Asian man turned his wrist, checked his watch, a military tell if Bertil had ever seen one. Civilians checked phones. Soldiers checked watches.

The pair began to move, continuing down the trail toward the coastal overlooks. Just two more nature lovers enjoying Gotland's beauty. Except nature lovers didn't emplace surveillance devices along trails leading to Patriot launchers and HIMAR vehicles.

Bertil reached for his radio, keying a different frequency. "Blackjack Six, Blackjack Six, this is Hemvärn Lead. Priority traffic. How copy?"

Captain Mercer's voice came back almost immediately. "Good copy, Hemvärn. Send it."

"Blackjack, we have confirmation of two POIs, possible foreign nationals. Break. Emplacing unknown device on the road in the vicinity of grid seven-tree-niner-four-two-eight. Request immediate consultation."

"Hemvärn, wait one," responded Mercer.

Bertil could picture the American captain in the TOC at the Grönt Centrum, probably pulling up the grid on his tactical display. Since the start of the Kaliningrad exercise, he'd been glad to see the Americans had stopped pretending this was a routine deployment. Pretense had a way of getting people killed.

"Hemvärn Lead, Blackjack Six. That grid puts you danger close to Route Apple." Mercer used the coded designation for the Patriot battery's primary logistics corridor. "Can you maintain observation?"

"Affirmative. But, Six, there's a problem. They're using reconnaissance markers along the route. If I had to guess? They're Spetsnaz or trained by them."

The encrypted channel stayed quiet for three heartbeats before it crackled to life.

"Copy all. I'll round up a team. We're eight mikes out. Do not, I repeat, do not attempt to recover that device until we arrive. How many devices have you spotted so far?"

"Just the one so far. It could be acoustic or possibly a ground sensor. I'd wager they're building a surveillance net."

"Yeah, or a targeting grid," Mercer replied grimly. "Hold your position. We're moving."
****

1713 Hours

Mercer arrived like his Ranger training had taught him—fast, quiet, and ready for war. The ISV materialized from the forest road, engine barely audible. The eight paratroopers dismounted with practiced efficiency, weapons at the low ready, heads on a swivel.

As the paratroopers approached, Bertil emerged from his hide, shedding the ghillie hood. "Captain Mercer. The POIs moved northwest, toward the Bungenäs overlook," Bertil greeted him, pointing in the direction of the trail they had gone down.

"Damn, Bertil. You almost gave me a heart attack." Mercer shook his head as his soldiers lowered their rifles. "OK, show me this device you mentioned."

Bertil nodded, motioning with his head for them to follow him. They moved carefully through the forest, Bertil's Home Guard team falling in with the Americans as they fanned out. No friction, no confusion. Two weeks of joint patrols had built trust in each other's abilities.

When they reached thirty meters from the limestone outcropping, Staff Sergeant Anna Chen raised her hand sharply. "Hold here, sir," she called out, her voice carrying quiet authority. "Let me scan the area before we advance. If there's a proximity sensor, I'd rather not trigger it blind."

"Good call, Staff Sergeant," Bertil acknowledged with approval.

Chen gave him a brief nod, already reaching into her patrol pack for the detection wand. She extended the device's antenna with practiced efficiency, waiting for it to initialize before turning toward where Bertil had indicated the chalk marker. The scanner hummed softly as she swept it in precise overlapping arcs, her eyes never leaving the display.

"That's... unexpected," Chen murmured after a moment, brow furrowing at the readout. "If they'd placed any kind of sensor—seismic, acoustic, thermal—I should be detecting electromagnetic emissions. But I'm getting nothing. No RF signature, no magnetic anomalies. The area's reading completely clean."

"Interesting," Mercer said, exchanging a glance with Bertil.

The Swedish lieutenant shifted his weight, clearly troubled. "I don't doubt your equipment, Sergeant, but my team watched them place something. We have video confirmation."

"I believe you, Lieutenant," Chen replied, already flipping open the scanner's side panel. "Could be tourists, could be something else. Let me recalibrate this before we make assumptions." Her fingers adjusted the frequency range with the confidence of someone who'd done this countless times. "Some newer devices can remain completely passive until triggered, producing no emissions until activation. They're designed specifically to defeat standard detection protocols."

She closed the panel and resumed scanning, this time using a different sweep pattern.

"See, Holloway?" Mercer said with mock seriousness. "This is why Battalion sent us Chen. That high-tech gear is more complicated than our simple knuckle dragger brains can grasp. It requires at least a thirty-five on the ASVAB just to operate it."

"Ha-ha, try eighty, sir," Chen shot back without looking up from her work.

"Ah, cut the chatter, both of you," Sergeant First Class Holloway interjected, though his tone held amusement. "Just be grateful we've got Chief Long and Staff Sergeant Chen running our EW section now. Remember that disaster we used to have, Anders?"

Mercer couldn't suppress his laugh this time. First Lieutenant Jerry Anders had been part of their unit for seven months, claiming expertise in drone warfare and electronic countermeasures. Within weeks of his arrival at the company, it became painfully clear he couldn't tell a frequency scanner from a metal detector, let alone interpret what it was detecting. When he was replaced with a warrant officer and NCO who lived and breathed electronic warfare, it transformed their capabilities overnight. Knowledgeable soldiers paired with the proper tools were a force multiplier a commander dreamed of.

Mercer eyed Chen as she waved her wand in precise patterns he didn't understand, much like he suspected a wizarding student from Hogwarts would in one of those Harry Potter books he'd read growing up. Glancing over to Bertil, who made his way next to him, he saw a growing look of annoyance at how long this was taking.

"Chen, you got an ETA on how much longer this is going to take before it's safe to make a visual inspection of this thing?" asked Mercer, to the relief of his Swedish counterpart.

Chen kept a neutral face as she shrugged. "Could be minutes, could be hours. If it's GPS-linked, might not activate until—"

"Eliasson, what are you doing?" interrupted Bertil as he called out to one of his soldiers.

Mercer and Chen turned in the direction of the mystery device. One of Bertil's soldiers, Private Henrik Eliasson, had started moving toward it.

"I'm moving around this outcropping to see if I can get a visual on the device," replied the young soldier, continuing to cautiously move forward. "Ah, there, I can almost see it now—"

Chen's scanner suddenly shrieked a warning. The display lit up with flashing yellow lights.

"Oh God! It's got a proximity activation sensor!" Chen shouted loud enough for the soldiers around her to hear. "Everyone back, *now!*"

Eliasson froze as she shouted. He turned to look at them, a look of confusion etched on his face. "What do I—"

Before he could speak, the sound of a soft click echoed off the limestone outcropping when a black cylinder the size of a coffee can launched a meter into the air. For a split second, it hung there—then it detonated.

BOOM!

The clap of the explosion shattered the calm of the forest. The blast, not meant to shatter trees or carve a crater, exploded hundreds of tiny steel fragments in all directions. A hypersonic scythe designed to maim rather than kill.

Eliasson, standing closest to the device, had borne the brunt of the blast. The explosion had tossed his body like a rag doll, hurling him backward through the air before crashing in a heap. His body hit the ground ten meters away, immediately screaming a raw, primal sound that cut through the ringing in everyone's ears.

"Medic!" someone shouted. Then a second voice shouted a call for help, urgently pleading and screaming in pain.

Through the smoke and dirt, Mercer rolled onto his side, picking himself off the ground. Surveying the situation around him. He saw soldiers, his and Bertil's, scattered, some still standing, their weapons trained outward, others picking themselves off the ground like him.

Turning his eyes toward the screaming, he saw Private Eliasson, torn branches and leaves around him, his face contorted in agony. His training kicked in and he moved with purpose as he approached the gravely wounded soldier, assessing his wounds and determining what to do next.

Eliasson's body was a torn and bloody mess. His left leg was gone below the knee, nothing but shredded meat and exposed bone, blood oozing with each beat of his heart. His right leg, while still attached, was torn open from hip to ankle, spurting arterial blood. His torso seemed OK, the body armor having absorbed the worst of the shrapnel, but both his arms were peppered with fragments. Deep gashes had found the gaps in his armor.

Corporal Gustav Holm, who'd been moving to pull Eliasson back, was on the ground clutching his right thigh. Dark blood seeped between his fingers. "Holy crap, I'm hit! Oh God, I'm hit!" he shouted through gritted teeth.

"Hang on, I'm coming!" Mercer heard Specialist Rodriguez shout as he ran toward Holm, ignoring a piece of shrapnel sticking out of his left arm.

"Move! Move! Move!" Sergeant First Class Williams was shouting as he sprinted forward with his aid bag. "Tourniquets now! Control that bleeding!" he ordered one of the soldiers nearest him.

The training kicked in as the paratroopers and Home Guard soldiers converged on their wounded. Williams went straight to Eliasson, ripping the individual first aid kit from the man's battle belt.

"Hold him down!" Williams commanded as Eliasson thrashed. Two soldiers pinned the screaming man's shoulders down while Williams worked the IFAK. He quickly applied the tourniquet on the left leg first, positioning it high and tight above the knee. As he twisted it tight, the blood seeping out stopped, but his screaming intensified.

"Keep holding him! The first tourniquet's on. I need to apply another!" Williams shouted. "Eliasson, I've got to apply another one to stop the bleeding," Williams told him as he tightened the tourniquet.

"Here's another." Chen tossed Williams her IFAK, then grabbed her radio. "Blackjack Base, this is Blackjack Six-Echo. We've been attacked. I need an emergency medevac to our position. Stand by for grid. Break. Grid seven-tree-niner-four-two-eight. I have at least three wounded. One is urgent critical. Traumatic amputation and severe extremity trauma. How copy?"

There was a short pause after she ended her call before the radio chirped to life. "Blackjack Six-Echo. Good copy on last transmission. Medevac spinning up from Visby. ETA twelve mikes."

"Twelve minutes!" cursed Williams. "Tell 'em to hurry, Chen. He may not have twelve minutes!"

Mercer watched as Williams now had both tourniquets on Eliasson, but it was clear he was going into shock. His screams had faded to whimpers, his eyes losing their focus. "I need more pressure dressings. Find me some more!"

While Williams worked on Eliasson, Bertil knelt beside Holm, helping to apply direct pressure to the wound on his thigh. The corporal's face was clammy and ghost white. "Hey, Gustav, stay with me. Look at me, look at my eyes."

"It burns," Holm gasped. "It burns…"

"That's good, man. It means you're alive." Bertil kept pressure on the wound while another soldier positioned a pressure dressing over the wound. "Just hang in there, Gustav. You're going to be fine."

Rodriguez had sat himself against the trunk of a tree. He'd cut away at his uniform, exposing his arm, revealing a six-inch gash. It had cut deeply, but it wasn't life-threatening. One of the other soldiers was already wrapping it, his combat lifesaver bag sitting next to him.

"Who's got morphine!" Williams called out. "We need one over here!"

One of the medics produced two auto injectors from his bag. He tossed one to Williams, then applied the other to Holm. Within seconds, the wounded men's faces began to relax as the pain meds took hold.

"Hey, we got choppers inbound. We need a landing zone now!" Mercer barked. They had almost forgotten to find a clearing for the helo, having been so busy trying to stabilize their urgent critical that they'd almost forgotten. "Over there—find us a thirty-meter radius. Move!"

The soldiers scattered, some expanding the security perimeter while others worked to clear branches and debris in a nearby clearing. In the distance, they started to hear the distinctive thumping of rotor blades. The sound of the helicopter closing in on them.

Chen appeared at Mercer's shoulder, her scanner still in hand. "Sir, that device… it's still transmitting. Low-power beacon. And there's something else." She showed him the display. "It's emitting a GPS signal. Military-grade, encrypted."

"Whoa, what are you saying?"

"Sir, I'm saying whatever that device was it's still active and transmitting," she explained.

"Good grief." Mercer cursed and looked at the blood-soaked ground where Eliasson had fallen. "That thing is likely transmitting our coordinates to whoever is on the other end. We need to move out of this area until we can get EOD to neutralize this thing and figure out who it belongs to."

Seconds later, a helicopter thundered overhead, a Swedish HKP 16 with medical crew aboard. It settled into the hastily cleared LZ, rotor wash whipping branches and dust into a frenzy.

"Come on! Let's go! Let's go!" the flight medic was shouting as he jumped out with a stretcher team.

They loaded Eliasson onto the stretcher first. The kid, barely twenty, had slipped unconscious. The medics worked with practiced efficiency, getting IV lines started as they moved.

Holm went next, still conscious but fading. Then Rodriguez, who tried to wave off help until Mercer ordered him onto the bird.

As the helicopter lifted off, Bertil stood beside Mercer, both men watching it disappear into the darkening sky.

"That was my fault, Captain," Bertil said quietly. "I should have maintained better control of my men."

"No, Bertil." Mercer's voice was hard. "This isn't on you. It's on them. The bastards who planted it." He turned to face Chen. "Is your bag of tricks able to tell how many more of these things are out there?"

She shook her head. "No, sir, it can't. But if they're placing them along every major route…" She didn't need to finish. He knew the implications.

"Damn. We need to alert all units. Nobody approaches suspicious markers without notifying your team and EOD." Mercer pulled out his radio, then paused. "And, Bertil? Your man Eliasson, I think he's going to make it. He may have lost the leg, but he'll live."

Bertil nodded slowly, but his eyes remained fixed on the bloodstained forest floor. In the distance, they could still hear the helicopter beating its way toward Visby Hospital.

As the sound of the helicopter continued to fade, the forest settled back into uneasy quiet. They roped off the area, marking it for EOD, and then loaded up into the vehicles and headed back to the Grönt Centrum to debrief on what had just happened.

****

Following Day
April 14, 2033 – 0830 Hours Local Time
Grönt Centrum, Gotland

The conference room smelled of strong coffee and a sleepless night. Lieutenant Colonel Patrick Brenner sat across from Colonel Anders Lindqvist, both men looking like they'd aged years in the past twenty-four hours. Captain Mercer stood near the wall map, favoring his left side where debris from yesterday's blast had left bruises despite his body armor. Bertil sat carefully in a chair, his arm in a sling. He'd returned from the hospital against doctor's orders.

"Three locations checked since dawn," Major Stenqvist, Lindqvist's S2, reported. "All negative. Whatever network they were building, yesterday's incident seems to have spooked them into going to ground."

"Or they finished whatever their mission was," Captain Bradley, Brenner's S2, added grimly. "Seven groups over two weeks. Even if each only placed a dozen devices…"

"That's over eighty potential sensors or mines," Brenner finished. "Ah, this could get ugly."

Lindqvist rubbed his temples. "Stockholm's sending their best EOD-Forensics team. Should arrive by 1400. The National Police Commissioner held a press conference this morning. They're promising to bring the perpetrators to justice."

"Justice." Bertil's voice carried bitter amusement. "This isn't a crime. It's war preparation."

"True, but the public doesn't know that yet," Lindqvist replied. "And perhaps it's better they don't. We're already seeing panic buying in Visby's stores. If people knew the true scope…"

"Yeah, they'd begin to flee the island," Bertil finished.

Mercer pulled up imagery on his tablet. "Sir, we checked the two locations Bertil identified. First was nothing, just some geology students taking samples. But they were nervous, kept asking why American soldiers were questioning them."

"The whole island's on edge," Brenner observed. "Can't blame them after yesterday. How's Private Eliasson?"

"Stable," Bertil answered quietly. "They saved the right leg, but he'll never walk normally again. Twenty years old." His good hand clenched. "Twenty years old and maimed by cowards who hide bombs in our soil."

The room fell silent. Through the window, they could see increased security patrols, Swedish soldiers and American paratroopers working in mixed teams, everyone tense, everyone watching the area around them.

"It's not just us," Bradley said, pulling up regional intelligence reports. "The Baltics are going crazy. Estonia's mobilizing their reserves. Latvia's requested additional NATO assets. Everyone's spooked by those Kaliningrad exercises."

"As they should be," Stenqvist added. "Joint amphibious operations two weeks before the scheduled EDEP exercise? Either they're incompetent at scheduling, or—"

"Or they're accelerating their timeline for something we don't know yet," Brenner finished. "It's like they're moving pieces into position early."

Lindqvist's phone buzzed. He glanced at it, frowning. "Speaking of escalation..." He turned on the wall-mounted television. "You need to see this."

The screen showed a press conference in Manila. General Emilio Sarmiento, the Philippines' National Security Advisor, stood at a podium, his weathered face set in hard lines.

"—will not stand by while the PLA attempts to starve out the peaceful people of Taiwan. We will continue to deliver humanitarian aid, including food and medicine, to our democratic neighbors, without interference."

"Oh crap, just what we need," Bradley muttered. "He's calling the PRC out."

Sarmiento continued: "The PLA has no authority to deter, deny, or delay those shipments in international waters. If a single Filipino vessel is harassed or boarded, it will be met with swift consequences. I trust Beijing understands what that means."

The news feed switched to a response from Beijing. Major General Ren Xiaojun, the PLA's attack dog and spokesperson, stood before a bank of microphones. Even through the television, his contempt was palpable.

"General Sarmiento speaks with the arrogance of a bygone era. Taiwan is a domestic matter of the People's Republic of China. Your so-called 'deliveries' are provocations, thinly veiled attempts to challenge our sovereignty."

"Wow, would you listen to this bastard?" Mercer said under his breath. "Who does he think he is?"

Ren continued: "If Manila wishes to test the resolve of the People's Liberation Army Navy, it will have its answer soon enough. The inspections begin tomorrow. I suggest you advise your captains accordingly... before someone miscalculates."

Brenner muted the television. "Tomorrow. April fifteenth. Tax day in America, and the same day as their 'customs enforcement' is supposed to start."

"It's all connected. Has to be," Bertil said slowly. "The devices here, the exercises in Kaliningrad, now this confrontation in the Pacific. They're synchronizing events."

"Yeah, multiple pressure points," Bradley agreed, pulling up a global map. "You got the Taiwan Strait, the South China Sea, the Bering Sea, and the Baltic Sea. Pick your poison. We've got four geographically different locations, all under threat at the same time. They're trying to force us to choose where to respond, where to place the limited forces we have."

"Well, in my mind, they've already chosen where to attack," Lindqvist added grimly.

A knock at the door interrupted the conversation. A Swedish communications specialist entered the room, looking shaken. "Colonel, priority message from Stockholm. The forensics team was able to analyze that partial fingerprint we sent them last night from the device."

"Oh, they did? That's excellent. What did they find?"

"A match—a Red Notice, actually. Wanted, detain on sight," the specialist informed them.

"Really? What does a Red Notice mean again?" asked Brenner, turning to Lindqvist.

"An Interpol Red Notice is similar to your American FBI Most Wanted list or your terrorist watch list. It's an international law enforcement bulletin," explained Colonel Lindqvist. "It means our suspect is wanted internationally for serious crimes."

"Huh, impressive work by your forensics team," Brenner commented. "What more can you tell us about him?"

The comms specialist nodded, then explained, "The man's real name is Hung Minghao, age thirty-seven. He entered the EU through Amsterdam three years ago using sophisticated forged documents— biometric passport, fabricated employment history, everything. The identity held up through multiple security screenings." The specialist paused. "He's been operating as a cultural attaché at the PRC embassy in Stockholm for the past eighteen months."

"How sophisticated are we talking?" Bradley asked.

"State-level," the specialist replied. "Our intelligence assessment suggests MSS 6th Bureau—their elite foreign operations division. He's not just a spy, he's an assassin. The Red Notice links him to the murder of a Taiwanese intelligence officer in Prague two years ago."

"Jesus," Brenner breathed. "An MSS assassin operating here for eighteen months."

Lieutenant Erik Norling, the communications specialist, shifted the folder in his hands. "There's more, sir. Swedish Intelligence was just informed this morning that British MI6 has been hunting this man for over a year."

"The Brits?" Lindqvist leaned forward. "Why weren't we told?"

"They only connected the dots yesterday when we sent the fingerprints through Interpol channels," Norling explained. "Zhang Wei first appeared on their radar in Gibraltar. Local police confronted him photographing an American submarine entering the naval base. When they tried to question him, he assaulted both officers—killed one with his bare hands, left the other in a coma."

The room went cold.

"The only reason they knew it was him," Norling continued, "was a Royal Navy CCTV camera that caught the entire assault. Crystal-clear footage of his face, his methods. Professional, efficient, brutal. He disappeared before backup arrived."

"And now he's here," Bertil said quietly. "On my island."

"The British want him badly," Norling added. "The officer he killed had three children. But Swedish intelligence has convinced them—with American backing—that the strategic value of surveillance outweighs immediate arrest."

Brenner turned to Bradley. "State's involved?"

"Has to be," Bradley replied. "If we can map his network now, during this critical period with the PRC, it's worth more than one arrest."

Lindqvist nodded slowly. "So we watch. We wait. We see who else crawls out of the shadows."

"A cold-blooded killer walking free on Gotland," Mercer said. "That sits well with everyone?"

"No," Brenner replied firmly. "But if grabbing him means a dozen other operatives go dark, potentially right before they activate? We can't afford that trade."

"The British aren't happy," Norling admitted. "But they're cooperating. For now."

"OK, then for now we wait, we observe, and we see who else he might lead us to." With that, Lindqvist stood to signal the meeting was over.

Chapter Thirty-Two:
Network Rising

April 14, 2033 – 1000 Hours
Hengshan Military Command Center – Joint Operations Center,
Sublevel 3
Taipei, Taiwan

The holographic display came to life, painting Taiwan's maritime domain in three dimensions. Jodi Mack watched four hundred seventeen blue icons materialize across the projection—each representing an autonomous weapon now lurking in the strait's dark waters. The assembled brass fell silent.

"Gentlemen," Jodi began, her voice carrying across the Joint Operations Center, "welcome to the future of naval warfare. I am proud to report that as of today, we have completed the final delivery and deployment of all manned and unmanned underwater vehicles, naval surface vessels, counterdrone systems, loitering munitions, short-, medium-, and long-range cruise missiles, and last but not least, short- and long-range surface-to-air missile defense systems. If you are ready, I can provide our final update and answer any lingering questions you might have before we hand the system over to you and your forces."

The Joint Operation Center sat three stories beneath the Ministry of National Defense at the base of the Yangmingshan Mountain range in the Shilin District of Taipei. The JOC hummed with barely contained energy as the leaders of Taiwan's military met for what might be the final time with all of them present in the same room. At the end of the meeting, the leadership of the country would begin to disperse to different command posts, on the off chance that one or more of them became the subject of a PLA attack.

Present in the room and leading the discussion for the military was Admiral Han Ji-cheng, the Commander of the Navy, and the man who had led Taiwan's efforts to integrate unmanned and autonomous vehicles into naval strategy. His counterpart, Lieutenant General Wu Jian-tai, the Commandant of the Marine Corps, had also been instrumental in preparing the Marines to counter the anticipated landings for which they knew the PLA Army and Marines had been training vigorously for years. President Ma Ching-te, along with the Air Force

Commander, General Tseng Zhaoming, and the Commander of the Army, General Guan Li-jen, sat quietly as they listened to the brief. Not in the room (for security reasons) were the Minister of Defense, the NSB Director, and the Director of Intelligence, who would listen to the meeting from a separate, secured location.

Admiral Han Ji-cheng, Chief of Naval Staff, leaned forward in his command chair. The silver-haired sixty-two-year-old admiral had watched the growth of the PLA Navy from a coastal patrol force to a true blue-water navy across his career. His expression remained carefully neutral as he listened to the TSG representative give them a final update before declaring their program ready.

"Ms. Mack." Han's English was precise, academic. "You're asking us to entrust our nation's defense to machines that think for themselves. Forgive my skepticism."

"Skepticism's healthy, Admiral." Jodi manipulated the holographic controls. The display zoomed, focusing on the Penghu archipelago. "These aren't just machines. They're force multipliers. Let me demonstrate."

She highlighted a cluster of icons near Magong Naval Base on Penghu's main island. "Mr. Matsin's team deployed twelve Seeker-class XLUUVs five days ago. Since then, they've logged over eight hundred hours of autonomous patrol time. Colonel Hsu, what has your information warfare section observed?"

Colonel Hsu adjusted his Marine-issued glasses, consulting his tablet briefly before replying. "Three PLA submarines transited the Penghu channel. We identified them as Type 093 attack submarines, running silent. Our diesel boats never would have detected them."

"But the Seeker did." Jodi pulled up acoustic traces. "Here, here, and here. Each submarine tracked continuously for twelve hours. The AI identified them by their pump signatures, reactor cooling patterns, even crew movement rhythms. The machines never tired, never lost contact."

Vice Admiral Lo Hua, Han's deputy, studied the data intently. "Incredible. What about rules of engagement? What stops these units from attacking?"

"Excellent question." Jodi expanded the display, showing decision trees. "Four-layer authorization protocol. Layer one: passive monitoring only. Layer two: active tracking with human notification.

Layer three: weapons free with human authorization. Layer four: autonomous engagement if Taiwan is under active attack."

"And who controls these layers?" Lo pressed.

"You do. Specifically, this room does." Jodi gestured to the command stations. "The entire system operates under your authority, not ours. Think of it as the world's most sophisticated watch officer—one that never sleeps."

Lieutenant General Wu Jian-tai of the Marine Corps stood, his bulk imposing even among the seated officers. "I see a lot of graphs and neat videos, Ms. Mack. And while many of my officers speak highly of the equipment TSG has provided, I have ten thousand marines preparing to counter beach landings and protect critical infrastructure. It's clear how your robot fish helps the Navy, but what about my marines?"

Jodi smiled. This was the question she'd been waiting for. "General, may I show you Tainan scenario seven?"

Without waiting for permission, she activated a tactical simulation. The hologram shifted, showing Taiwan's western coastline in detail. Red icons appeared—showing a massive simulated amphibious force.

"Here we see one hundred twenty landing ships approaching the shore as they disembark their force," she narrated. "We now have six hundred amphibious assault vehicles nearing the beach. A traditional defense would require your marines to meet them at the waterline. The casualties in this scenario would be…"

"Catastrophic," Wu finished grimly. "We've run these scenarios before."

"Exactly. Now watch this." Jodi activated the autonomous defense network. Blue icons swarmed from hidden positions. "Thirty-nine Zealot USVs launch from Budai alone. Each carries four Hellfire missiles. That's over one hundred fifty precision strikes before they close for kamikaze attacks."

The simulation played out in accelerated time. USVs weaved between landing craft, missiles launching in coordinated volleys. Ships exploded, burned, and sank. The neatly organized invasion formation dissolved into pure chaos and destruction.

"Meanwhile," Jodi continued, "Sea Guardian smart mines activate beneath the first wave." More red icons vanished. "Next, the Seeker XLUUVs hunt the escort submarines protecting the amphibious assault ships." The video simulation showed numerous underwater battles erupting across the display.

General Hsu watched his marines' beach positions remain untouched as the invasion fleet died at sea. "How many reach the shore?"

"In this simulation? Seventeen percent. Your marines are mopping up survivors, not struggling to survive against wave after wave of landing craft."

"God in heaven, it's a slaughter," someone whispered.

Major Lin from Submarine Squadron 256 raised his hand like an eager student. "The Seekers—they can coordinate with our diesel boats?"

"Yes, but not just coordinate," Jodi replied. "They enhance them. Your submarines are quiet but limited by crew endurance and battery life. Seekers can scout ahead, maintain contact while your boats position for attack. You become wolfpack leaders, not lone hunters."

She pulled up real-time footage from a Seeker patrol. The underwater view showed murky darkness pierced by sonar returns. A massive shape materialized—a commercial freighter's hull passing overhead.

"This is live?" Admiral Han Ji-cheng asked.

"Ten minutes ago. Unit Seven, patrolling the Penghu deep channel." Jodi enhanced the image. "Watch the AI work."

Data cascaded across the screen: acoustic analysis, hull configuration, prop cavitation patterns. Within seconds, the AI identified the vessel: "Motor Vessel *Changsha*, Chinese registry, container ship, normal transit pattern, threat level minimal."

"It learns, General," Colonel Hsu observed. "Every contact improves its database."

"Exactly," Jodi confirmed. "In five days, our units have cataloged over three thousand vessel signatures. They know what belongs and what doesn't."

An alarm chimed, signaling a real-time alert. Jodi's fingers flew over controls.

"What is it?" Han demanded.

"It's another cyber probe against our firewall. Let me check its origin... ah, of course, ATP1—Shanghai," explained Jodi. Lines of code scrolled across a side screen. "It's Unit 61398, 2nd Bureau, from the PLA

Strategic Support Force. It's the same hacker teams constantly probing the US Pentagon back home."

Colonel Hsu's team scrambled to respond, but Jodi remained calm. "Watch as the AI handles it with Colonel Hsu's team," she directed.

The Lattice system visualized the attack—red tendrils probing for vulnerabilities. Blue defensive protocols activated, adapting in real-time. Within seconds, the probe was isolated, analyzed, and rejected.

"Each time they attempt to hack our systems, the attack pattern's been cataloged," Jodi explained. "Next time, Lattice will recognize it in nanoseconds. Like antibodies learning diseases."

Vice Admiral Lo studied the defense. "Impressive. But what about physical attacks? Jamming, EMP?"

"Distributed architecture," Jodi replied. "Destroy our satellite links, the mesh network continues. Jam radio frequencies, fiber optics take over. EMP a command node, decision-making distributes to surviving units. We've built redundancy into redundancy."

She activated another display. "Let's run drill alpha-seven. Simulated saturation attack on Taiwan."

The hologram exploded with threats. Two hundred ballistic missiles arced from mainland launch sites. Cruise missiles hugged wave tops. Aircraft swarmed from multiple vectors.

"Traditional defense would require human controllers to prioritize, assign, and engage," Jodi narrated. "Reaction time: minutes. Reaction time using the Lattice AI..."

The AI had already begun responding before she finished speaking. Tien Kung III batteries swiveled, tracking priorities. Naval units adjusted positions. Autonomous systems prepared to engage low-altitude threats, while Patriot batteries engaged cruise and ballistic missile threats.

"Seven milliseconds," she finished. "Human-like decision-making at machine processing rates."

The simulation played out. Interceptors launched in perfect sequence. USVs engaged sea-skimming missiles. Electronic warfare systems activated, spoofing and jamming. The massive attack whittled down to manageable numbers.

"Eighty-seven percent interception rate," Jodi reported. "Compared to sixty-two percent with traditional command and control."

Admiral Han stood slowly, approaching the hologram. His fingers passed through a glowing icon representing a Seeker patrol. "In my career, I've seen warfare evolve from guns to missiles to networks. Now you bring us thinking weapons."

"Is that acceptance, Admiral?"

Han turned to face her. "My great-grandfather fought the Japanese with bamboo spears. My father faced Communist gunboats with American destroyers. Each generation gets the weapons it needs." He paused. "Before I sign off on final delivery of this, show me more."

Jodi suppressed a smile. The hard part was over; he'd accepted the system. "Sure. Let's discuss integration with your existing systems."

She pulled up Taiwan's defense architecture. The Po Sheng C4ISR network appeared as a neural web connecting bases, radars, and command centers.

"Lattice AI doesn't replace the Po Sheng system you have," she explained. "It enhances it. Think of Po Sheng as your nervous system, Lattice as reflexes. Conscious thought when you have time, instant reaction when you don't."

"And the Americans?" General Hsu asked pointedly. "Does this tie us to their systems?"

A delicate question. Jodi chose her words carefully. "Lattice AI can operate independently or integrate with allied networks. If US Seventh Fleet intervenes, we can share targeting data instantly. If not, you retain full autonomous capability."

"Convenient flexibility," Lo observed.

"Realistic flexibility," Jodi countered. "We've learned from Ukraine. Allies help, but self-reliance wins."

Another alert. This time, Jodi's expression sharpened. "Admiral, we have acoustic detection. Three contacts, bearing two-seven-zero, range forty kilometers from Penghu."

The room tensed. Han stepped to the command position. "Classification?"

Data flowed across screens. The AI analyzed patterns, compared signatures. "PLA Navy Type 093 attack submarines. Hull numbers five-zero-seven, five-one-one, unknown third. Depth two hundred meters, speed eight knots, heading one-eight-zero."

"They're probing our defenses. Getting in position for tomorrow," Lo stated.

"Interesting development. What are our options?" Han asked Jodi.

"Currently, twelve Seekers are within intercept range. Your submarines *Hai Lung* and *Hai Hu* are sixty kilometers northeast, too far for immediate response. We can maintain passive tracking or..."

"Or?" asked Admiral Han.

Jodi stared at the admiral, debating if she should say what was on her mind. "Or we could demonstrate a capability they don't believe you have. I could have the Seekers ping them. Ring their bell, and let 'em know we see them—and they're alive because we *let them be*."

Han considered. Around him, staff officers waited. The weight of decision hung in the air.

"Let's hold off. I don't want to tip our hand just yet. I want this to be a surprise should it come to that."

As the final presentation came to an end, Marcus Harrington, who had been listening from the TSG headquarters in Virginia, chimed in.

"Admiral Han," Harrington began without preamble. "I trust you are happy with the system and capabilities of our products?"

"Mr. Harrington," replied Han. "Your weapons are as advertised, and you delivered on time."

"Excellent. Good to hear, Admiral Han. Jodi, are you ready for phase authorization to pass control of the systems to the Armed Forces of the Republic of China?"

She glanced at Han, who nodded. "Yes, sir. They are ready to take final control of the system."

Harrington's expression sobered. "OK. Admiral Han, when we give you full activation, that means the AI can engage independently if you authorize it. If Taiwan comes under attack, it will respond according to its programming. There are no take-backs, no abort codes once you set it. The genie stays out of the bottle."

"We understand, Mr. Harrington," Han answered. "Tomorrow, Beijing begins their 'customs inspections.' We'll need every advantage if they decide to take this kinetic."

"Very well." Harrington entered his authorization code. "May God help us all. Lattice AI, offensive protocols authorized. Authentication codes have been transmitted to your secure email."

The holographic display shifted. Blue defensive icons turned amber—armed and ready. Status boards showed weapons systems transitioning from safe to standby.

"It's done," Jodi announced. "Four hundred seventeen autonomous weapons now stand ready. Admiral, you command the most lethal naval defense network in the Pacific."

Han studied the display, watching his mechanical fleet patrol. "We're not just defending anymore," he said quietly. "We're hunting."

As if in response to his words, another alert sounded. This time, they were being notified of a priority intelligence report from Chao Ming-hsien, the head of their intelligence agency.

Chao's face appeared on one of the monitors. "Admiral, we are receiving a flash message from the American INDOPACOM liaison in Hawaii. They are reporting an increase in ships from the PLA Eastern Theater Fleet, preparing to depart the Ningbo Naval Base. They estimate a force of around thirty-six surface combatants, and an unknown number of submarines are preparing to head south, toward us."

"Thank you for that, Director Chao. Colonel Hsu, how long until they reach the strait?" Han asked.

"Forty-eight hours at standard cruise," Hsu replied. "Twenty-four if they push hard to join the existing ships already on station."

"Then we have one day to prepare." Han turned to Jodi. "Can your machines handle a full fleet?"

She met his gaze steadily. "Admiral, during the Russo-Ukraine war, a single well-trained, well-equipped drone unit would routinely blunt entire battalion and brigade-sized attacks. In contrast, you have four hundred and seventeen SMEs working alongside your sailors and marines with the most advanced AI-controlled naval platforms ever built. Yes, I think we can handle them."

"We'd better, for all of our sakes," replied Admiral Han before adding. "Ms. Mack, I'd like you to remain here as my liaison. I want to make sure I can call upon your TSG expertise, should this go kinetic."

"When, not if?"

Han's smile held no humor. "April fifteenth is tomorrow. Beijing set this deadline. They'll keep it." He addressed his staff. "Alert all commands. Set condition two throughout the fleet. Inform the President—the autonomous guard is active."

As officers scrambled to implement orders, Jodi found herself alone with the holographic display. Four hundred seventeen icons pulsed with patient menace. Each represented an angel of death, held in check by silicon synapses and the human wisdom of when to unleash them.

Elena's voice crackled through her earpiece. "Aquarium, this is Shark Two. Coastal wolves report unusual activity. Multiple fast boats departing Xiamen harbor."

Jodi brought up the video feeds from a trio of maritime sentry towers on Kinmen Island, giving her a view of the harbors around Xiamen used by the PLA Navy. Sure enough, they showed multiple *Houbei*-class missile boats and a pair of corvettes putting to sea. "That's a good copy, Shark Two. Aquarium is tracking the situation. Maintain position."

Mick joined the channel from Penghu Station. "Aquarium, Shark One is detecting an increase in submarine activity around Dongsha Atoll and the approaches to the Penghu Islands. Seekers-5 and 7 have identified five *Yuan*-class conventional submarines, two heading toward Dongsha, the other three toward Penghu," Mick reported.

He paused a second before he continued. "Aquarium, Seekers-4 and 6 also detected four *Yuan*-class submarines and two *Shang III*-class nuclear-powered attack subs en route to the Luzon Strait. Be advised, these are likely trying to break out into the Pacific or get around to Taiwan's east coast. How copy?"

"Good copy, Shark One," Jodi murmured. "I guess tomorrow we'll find out if they plan to enforce this new inspection by force."

Jodi watched as the tactical picture unfolded around Taiwan. She thought of Sun Tzu's ancient wisdom: "All warfare is deception." In terms of deception, she felt they had delivered masterfully in this regard. They'd hidden their unmanned autonomous killer ships, disguised among fishing boats and oyster farms. They'd mined the paths approaching the shores of Taiwan with thousands of smart mines anchored to the ocean floor, all connected via an undersea mesh net that would allow the AI to coordinate their surface and subsurface attacks faster than any human could.

When Jodi expanded the tactical picture from Taiwan to the strategic view of the Pacific, however, it didn't make sense. The deployments of PLA Navy ships from the East and South Sea Fleets were commensurate with the actions leading up to tomorrow. What puzzled her was everything else. In theory, the PLA Navy should have been deploying all its vessels to support this new customs regime, especially in the East and South China Seas, where it was likely to encounter resistance. Instead, this past week, they'd watched as large swaths of the North Sea Fleet sortied out of the Yellow Sea, past South Korea and into the Sea of Japan.

A few days later, this force of PLA warships had linked up with the Russian Pacific Fleet at the Vladivostok Naval Base, supposedly part of the Pacific EDEP exercise scheduled to start in May. Then, to everyone's surprise, a dozen PLA Navy conventional and nuclear-powered submarines had made an unannounced port call at the Russian Kamchatka Submarine Base in Rybachiy. Jodi knew the TSG contract was specific to Taiwan. Still, she couldn't shake the feeling that Taiwan wasn't the main event. Something else was up...something big. She just didn't know what it was yet.

Chapter Thirty-Three:
Amber Watch

April 14, 2033
2130 Hours Local Time
Forward Staging Area – Near Augustów, Northern Suwałki Corridor

The thermal feed ghosted across the display, revealing faint flickers of heat behind a hedgerow—too angular, too deliberate. Torres leaned over Marrick's shoulder, eyes narrowed beneath his helmet. "That's not deer."

The tanks sat cold beneath camouflage netting, their engines silent, hulls sunk into hardened berms carved into the Polish countryside. No headlights. No idling turbines. No chatter. The M5 Ripsaws stood motionless in sentry mode—running on battery power, their turrets slowly scanning sectors like wolves in the grass.

"Probably wild boar," Marrick murmured, adjusting the drone's thermal settings. "But I'll tag it for monitoring."

Torres straightened, his joints protesting after hours of stillness. Around them, Alpha Company held the line—fourteen M1E3 Abrams and their robotic wingmen scattered across three kilometers of forest and farmland: silent, watching…waiting.

This wasn't training anymore.

"I'm walking the line," Torres said quietly. "Keep me posted on any changes."

Marrick nodded, eyes never leaving his screens. The warrant officer had grown thin these past weeks, living on energy drinks and determination. The burden of managing both manned and unmanned assets was telling.

Torres stepped out of the command vehicle into the Polish night. The air hung warm and still, unseasonably mild for April. Low fog drifted between pine breaks, muffling sound and blurring the tree line.

Perfect weather for infiltration, he thought.

He moved without night vision, letting his eyes adjust naturally. After twenty minutes, the darkness revealed its secrets—the bulk of camouflaged tanks, the geometric shadows of fighting positions, the faint glow of red-filtered lights where crews maintained their vigil.

At Alpha-22, he found Burke on watch, thermal sight slowly traversing their sector.

"All quiet?" he asked.

"Quiet as a crypt, Sarge." Burke didn't look away from his sight. "Munoz is catching some shut-eye. Kid was wound tighter than a spring."

"He's not the only one." Torres climbed onto the hull, settling beside the loader's hatch. "You good?"

"Been better. Coffee's cold, can't smoke on watch, I'm out of Zyn, and my back's killing me." Burke finally glanced over. "But yeah, other than that, I'm good. You?"

Torres chuckled, but didn't answer immediately. A few kilometers to their front, the forest ended at abandoned farmland. Beyond that, somewhere in the darkness, lay Belarus. And beyond that…a lot of people with guns and armored vehicles.

"My sister called yesterday," he said finally. "Said our parents are scared. News is talking about Taiwan, about Russian and Chinese ships massing in the Sea of Japan. She asked if I'm in danger."

"What'd you tell her?"

Burke shrugged. "I lied. Said we're safe, that I'm where I want to be."

Torres eyed him. "And if it all goes sideways…both theaters at once?" He thought of the classified briefs, the movement of Russian forces, the Chinese "training exercises" that looked more like invasion prep.

"I don't know, Sergeant. I guess we'll see what happens," Burke finally replied.

They sat in companionable silence, watching the darkness. Somewhere to the south, a Ripsaw's thermal camera detected movement and flagged it—another boar, according to the algorithm. But every alert tightened nerves already stretched thin.

Torres' radio crackled softly. "All Assassin elements, this is Assassin Six. Be advised—Polish infantry platoon will be moving through approximately one klick to your front in the next twenty mikes. They're conducting their own border patrol. Do not engage, they are friendlies. Acknowledge."

"Assassin Six, Two-Seven copies all," Torres acknowledged.

Twenty minutes later, Burke whispered, "There they are. Movement, bearing zero-seven-zero. About nine hundred meters."

Torres tracked them through his thermal sight: a full platoon of Polish infantry moving in a tactical column as they advanced through wooded terrain. Their movement was purposeful but unhurried—a routine patrol, not a combat operation.

"Our allies are out earning their pay," Burke observed quietly.

"Yeah, just like us." Torres watched the Polish soldiers continue their patrol, disappearing and reappearing between the trees. Soon, they were just heat signatures again, then nothing. The forest returned to its empty vigil.

"You know what I'm thinking about?" Burke said after a long pause. "My kids' summer vacation. Wife wants to take them to Disney. I told her I'd think about it."

"Disney in July? You're braver than I thought." Torres allowed himself a smile. "Mine want to go camping in Colorado. Real camping, not this tactical bivouac nonsense."

"Think we'll make it back for summer?"

Torres considered the question. They'd been here six weeks already. The rhetoric from Moscow and Beijing came in waves—sometimes threatening, sometimes conciliatory. Meanwhile, soldiers on both sides sat in the woods, watching each other across invisible lines.

"Yeah, I think so. This feels like… posturing. Both sides are showing teeth, but nobody really wants to bite." He adjusted his thermal sight, scanning the empty forest. "Few more weeks of this, some diplomatic breakthrough—everyone goes home with stories about that time we almost started World War Three."

"Stories and without a combat patch," Burke added.

"Yeah, I can live with that." Torres thought about his kids, about mountain trails and campfires without tactical significance. "Besides, armies are expensive. Keeping us all out here, burning diesel, wearing out equipment—someone's going to run the numbers and decide talking is cheaper than posturing."

"From your mouth to God's ear, Sarge."

They settled back into silence, watching the darkness. Somewhere out there, Polish infantry continued their patrol. Farther east, Russian and Chinese forces probably sat in their own positions, having

314

similar conversations. Everyone waiting, watching...hoping cooler heads would prevail.

Torres allowed himself to imagine it—flying home, hugging his kids, complaining about the heat at Disney World or the mosquitoes in Colorado. Normal problems. Peaceful problems.

"Three more hours until shift change," he said finally.

"I can make it three more weeks if it means we all go home," Burke replied.

"Roger that." Torres continued his scan, but his mind was already halfway to summer vacation. Sometimes hope was all you had on a dark night in Poland, waiting for a war nobody really wanted.

Chapter Thirty-Four:
What Do You Know?

April 14, 2033
Baltic Resilience & Renewables Initiative Office
Visby, Gotland

Besides the Tuta email account that Klara usually checked for messages from her handler, Viktor Mikhailov, there were certain times of day that she knew to check another account in the drafts folder. Many times, there was nothing there, but the message she had just opened was about to change everything for her.

"Crap," she said aloud as soon as she realized the drafted message was from the Russian asset who'd been with the person who'd placed the explosive device on Gotland.

"I didn't know this Chinese guy was bringing the GPS jammer and that other device with him," he explained. "We weren't supposed to implant the device until two days before the actual event. I was just putting down indelible chalk marks where we needed to place our equipment. When we had walked several miles away, I heard it go off and knew we had a big problem."

Klara was absolutely freaking out at this point. She couldn't even begin to think what to do.

"The Chinese guy is trying to pretend like nothing happened," her asset continued. "He returned to his housing that I think you set up for him on Gotland."

She cursed, fighting the urge to slam her fist into the wall.

"Your brothers are proceeding as normal, but if we are detected and there's no way to escape, we plan to execute our operation, even though it's early."

Klara put her head in her hands. Years of planning and preparation had gone into the events of the upcoming weeks. She had been disciplined and careful. And now, if she didn't play this just right, it could all be thrown away because of one impatient Chinese operative.

I have to find out what Lars knows, she realized. *I need to see how bad this is.*

****

Later That Day
Lars Gustafsson's Apartment
Visby, Gotland

Klara flirted with her boyfriend while he made dinner, walking behind him and giving him a hug, and then playfully whispering in his ear.

Lars smiled, turned to her and gave her a kiss. "Not yet, my love. My meal is going to be a masterpiece, and I'm almost done."

"Oh, all right, spoilsport," she teased. Klara plopped down in the living room to wait and turned on the news. They were talking about what was happening on Penghu in Asia.

Lars overheard the reporter. "You know, this is kind of a big deal," he said. "No one knows what's happening next. "There could be a shooting war between China and Taiwan."

"That sounds very serious," Klara remarked.

"It is…" His voice trailed off. "All right, enough of the news. Dinner is ready."

He placed bowls of fish stew with root vegetables on the table, along with a pan of boiled new potatoes. Although she was definitely playing a role, Klara was grateful that her boyfriend was such an excellent cook.

"It smells amazing, thank you," she said, kissing him on the cheek as she sat down.

They hadn't been eating long when Lars got a text message, and all the color drained from his face.

"What's wrong?" Klara asked.

Am I blown? she wondered.

"Something terrible happened, an explosion of some kind," Lars explained. "Three of my Home Guard friends were flown to the Visby Hospital. One of them just got out of a pretty major surgery. It's not clear if he's going to make it."

She had never seen Lars quite this upset—he was practically shaking. "I'm going to visit," he declared, standing.

Klara gently placed a hand on his shoulder. "Let me come with you," she offered.

He fought back tears and smiled weakly. "That would be nice, actually."

"Just let me put the rest of this away, and we'll head out," said Klara.

At least this way, I can find out what happened, and how much the soldiers know, she thought.

****

April 14, 2033
Visby Hospital
Gotland, Sweden

The fluorescent lights in the hospital hallway buzzed faintly overhead, their sterile glow casting long shadows down polished floors. Klara followed Lars past the reception desk and toward the observation wing where the Home Guard soldiers had been admitted.

The place smelled like antiseptic and recycled air. Lars walked quickly, fists clenched, his face pale and tight. Room 212 was just ahead.

Inside, two soldiers were already awake and propped up in their beds, IV drips attached to their arms. Both looked up as Lars entered—then visibly relaxed.

"Lasse!" one of them called, voice hoarse but eager. "Hell, man, you should've seen it."

Lars smiled tightly and crossed the room. "You scared the crap out of us, Niklas. You look like a bomb hit you."

Niklas gave a weak laugh. "Close enough."

The other soldier, who Klara recalled was named Jonsson, was watching her with vague recognition. "Hey. Klara, right? From the energy thing? Weren't you at Lars's birthday party?" he asked.

"I was," she said, keeping her tone warm but neutral. "I'm so sorry you're both here. We heard it was bad."

Niklas gestured toward the third bed, its curtain drawn and lined with medical monitors that hummed softly. "It was worse for Kalle. They don't know if he's going to pull through. Internal bleeding, shrapnel… he was closest to whatever blew."

Lars swallowed hard. "What the hell happened?"

Jonsson shook his head. "We saw some strange markings in a restricted woodland plot—chalk lines, I think. We got closer and saw someone burying a disc of some kind near a service road. We went to check it out, but the person was way deep in the woods before we could

318

get to them. Kalle was inspecting the edge of the device when it blew. I swear, there wasn't even a trip wire."

"It wasn't some buried artillery shell?" Lars asked.

"No way," Niklas answered. "It wasn't old. Looked like a fresh plant job. Modern casing."

Jonsson nodded. "We were just doing recon, man. Nothing aggressive. No digging. It still went off."

Klara fought to keep her expression composed. She folded her hands in front of her coat to hide her trembling fingers.

"What do the police say?" Lars asked.

"They're treating it like sabotage, maybe terrorism," said Niklas. "They've cordoned the area and called in the bomb squad from Stockholm."

Jonsson added, "But nobody knows who placed it. No cameras. Just started to look at it, and then boom."

Klara exhaled slowly, letting herself lean against the window frame. Her heart was still racing, but the weight of the dread in her chest subsided.

They don't know, she realized. *Not yet.*

One of the machines behind the curtain gave a dull beep. A nurse entered, checked the vitals of the unconscious man, and adjusted the IV line. She gave them all a tight smile and slipped out without speaking.

Lars stood there in silence for a moment. Then he reached over and gripped Jonsson's shoulder. "I'm glad you two are OK."

"Still hurts like hell," Niklas grunted, adjusting his bandages.

"You're lucky," Klara said gently. "It could've been much worse."

They both nodded. Then, mercifully, the room fell into quiet conversation—Lars asking after families, Niklas joking about the food, and Jonsson grumbling about hospital gowns.

Klara listened, chimed in when needed, and mentally marked every detail they didn't know.

For now, she was safe.

****

April 15, 2033
Lars Gustafsson's Apartment

Visby, Gotland

Klara's boyfriend came home a little early that evening.

"How are your friends at the hospital?" she asked.

"Better," Lars replied, giving her a hug. "Kalle is stable now. They said it looks like he will pull through."

"That is so good to hear," Klara replied. Her voice conveyed relief and compassion for his friend, but she also wondered if the third soldier knew something his friends did not.

"I haven't started dinner yet, but I bought salmon," Klara explained.

"That's right, it's your turn tonight," Lars replied.

"I know I'm not as good a cook as you, honestly, but I feel that it's only fair for me to share the load," Klara explained.

"No need to downplay your food," Lars answered. "I love your meals."

She smiled and set to work cooking some baked salmon with dill and lemon, which she accompanied with a side of quinoa, steamed broccoli, and cold cucumber salad. Lars turned on the news while she cooked.

When the news turned to events in Asia, Klara saw it as an opening. "Lars, do you think this stuff happening in Taiwan with China places Gotland in danger?" she asked. "You know, because of the Chinese presence in Kaliningrad and this big EDEP exercise?"

Her boyfriend replied, "I don't know, but everyone is jumpy."

As she started placing dinner on the table, Lars's face lit up. "Oh, I almost forgot to tell you," he said. "We caught a lucky break on who might have placed the explosive device."

"Really?" Klara asked. Based on his tone, she was sure it wasn't linked to her, but her heart beat faster all the same.

"It appears they managed to obtain some footage of the guy the Home Guard thought they saw placing the device. It turns out the person had an Interpol Red Notice on him for the murder of a police officer in Gibraltar."

"No way!" Klara replied, answering in a way to make him feel like she was showing interest in him, but all the while, her mind was racing.

"Yeah," Lars continued. "Then he got caught snooping on a submarine arriving at the naval base some eighteen months ago."

"Wow," Klara answered.

"The guy was apparently working as a cultural attaché at the Chinese embassy in Stockholm," Lars continued, "but in reality, he's more likely a spy, possibly looking to do some sabotage stuff on Gotland ahead of the EDEP exercise. No one is really sure. It's unclear if he's still on Gotland or if he escaped off the island on one of the late-evening ferries."

"Oh, man. Do I need to be worried?" she asked.

"Honestly…I don't know," Lars replied. "There's a lot of scary stuff going on in the world right now. It's best to keep your wits about you, for sure."

Klara went in for a hug, allowing Lars to comfort her, and also giving her a moment to contemplate where this left her.

Is this going to compromise my mission? she wondered. The wheels turned in her mind.

After dinner, she told Lars, "With everything going on, I think I need to go home and notify members of the Baltic Resilience & Renewables Initiative of the recent events on Gotland. I probably should also run some damage control, so people won't back out of my Baltic Wings Festival."

Lars was concerned, but he understood and offered to walk her to her apartment.

Once she arrived, she opened her laptop and began to create an encrypted document. Klara began making a list of "suspicious things" that she had noticed about the Chinese investors and NGO members that were a part of her recent tour of Gotland. In the document, she noted how she'd worked with groups like this in the past, so she hadn't initially thought anything of it, but with all that had happened, now it seemed like some of the things they'd done might be a part of something bigger. She noted how they were trying to get too close to military lines when touring the Tofta Solar Pilot Site, and how they were asking too many questions about the military presence on Gotland.

This will work, she thought to herself.

Klara didn't give this log of events to her boyfriend yet, but she decided to keep it in her back pocket as a "get out of jail free" card just in case she got questioned. If asked why she'd waited, she could claim that she didn't want to seem racist, so she was waiting to gather more information, but ultimately she became scared of what might happen if she unwittingly aided in this heinous act.

I'm not going to compromise years of work on a Russian op for a few incompetent, impatient Chinese agents, she thought.

After mulling over her details and editing her document into a polished gem, Klara went to sleep. She rested peacefully in the knowledge that if she had to turn in a few Chinese operatives and burn them, she would do so, saving years of work with the Russians.

Chapter Thirty-Five:
The Fog of War

April 15, 2033 – 0745 Hours
Type 055 Destroyer *Zunyi*
120nm Southwest of Penghu

"Contact bearing two-four-five, twenty-three kilometers. MV *Kalayaan Spirit*, Philippine registry." Lieutenant Commander Zhu Mingzhe's voice carried crisp professionalism, despite the obvious tension of the moment. They were finally doing it—bringing the renegade province of Taiwan home to its native people.

"Captain, escorts have been spotted. Radar signatures confirm one ROC *Kang Ding*-class frigate and two *Tuo Chiang* corvettes," reported Lieutenant Commander Zhu.

Captain Shen Tao acknowledged with practiced calm, his fingers tracing the outline of the sealed envelope beneath his uniform. Inside were Admiral Deng's orders and the personal guarantees his crew and officers wouldn't be hung out to dry should things not work out the way the politicians intended. In a calm yet firm voice, he asked, "Distance to inspection zone boundary?"

"Eight kilometers, Captain. They'll cross it in approximately twelve minutes at current speed," confirmed Lieutenant Commander Zhu.

The South China Sea stretched impossibly blue through *Zunyi*'s bridge windows, the morning sun painting the water in shades of deceptive tranquility. It was perfect visibility—ideal for engagements, terrible for hiding. Every action would be witnessed, recorded, and judged.

Shen turned to Lieutenant Commander Zhu. "I'm headed to CIC. You have the bridge."

Zhu acknowledged as Shen made his way to the combat information center. As he passed through the hallways into the guts of the ship, he saw his sailors moving about, attending to their duties like nothing was happening. They were calm, prepared and ready for whatever was about to happen.

"Captain entering CIC," announced one of the enlisted sailors as Shen entered the darkened room. He saw a large digital map of the area displayed on one giant monitor. Another showed the air space around them, while a third tracked potential undersea threats.

Seeing his XO, Commander Gong Jun, Shen ordered, "Give me a status report on the squadron disposition."

Commander Gong acknowledged, directing his attention to the monitor that showed the tactical display of their current disposition. His ship, the *Zunyi*, a Type 055 destroyer, was leading a formation of two Type 052D guided missile destroyers and four Type 054A guided missile frigates with enhanced ASW capabilities. To further enhance his squadron's interdiction capability were four Type 056A corvettes: fast, nimble ships with the ability to transition to subhunters, should his squadron encounter any undersea threats.

As impressive a display of Chinese naval power as this was, the presence of the twelve converted fishing trawlers with the People's Maritime Militia spread across kilometers of ocean gave his squadron the ability to spread a vast net across the shipping lanes approaching the Taiwan Strait. No ship would escape inspection unless authorized by his superiors.

"As you can see, we have the shipping lanes approaching the Penghu archipelago covered with Maritime Militia trawlers labeled Lotus One through Twelve," Commander Gong explained. "About an hour ago, the trawler labeled Lotus Seven spotted a Filipino freighter on a course that would take it to Magong Harbor, Penghu. They have been moving to interdict the vessel since they spotted it."

"Interesting," Shen commented. "Barely eight hours into the new rules, and we already have our first ship attempting to disregard them." He looked at the names of the ships in his squadron, then asked, "The *Tongling* appears to be closest to that Filipino ship, along with Lotus Seven. Direct the *Tongling* to move closer to get in position to board it if they refuse to comply once we contact the ship's captain."

Gong reached for the radio receiver and began issuing orders. They had barely made it past breakfast before they had their first cargo vessel looking to violate the inspection order.

Barely ten minutes had gone by when the closest of the militia trawlers contacted them. "Dragon Lead, this is Lotus Seven," the voice of the militia commander crackled with excitement.

"Lotus Seven, this is Dragon Actual. Go ahead," Shen responded directly. He recognized the need and value of having the maritime militia involved in this operation, but that didn't mean he liked using them. His experiences with them thus far had done little to ameliorate the lack of professionalism in how they conducted themselves in their interactions with the Navy. They were subordinate to him, not the other way around.

The radio crackled. The trawler's captain was noticeably excited as he realized he was talking directly to the squadron commander. "Ah, Dragon Actual, sir. The Filipino vessel has continued to ignore our hails. As we grew closer, the vessel picked up speed. I am requesting permission to initiate close approach and attempt to slow it down."

Shen hesitated. He motioned for Commander Gong to activate the ship's Type 347G EO tracker and get them a visual of the freighter in question. Seconds later, the optical tracker had locked onto the MV *Kalayaan Spirit*, nine nautical miles off the starboard bow. The image sharpened—despite the haze. The trawler Lotus Seven was a kilometer off the port side of the vessel.

Shen held the radio receiver against his chest as his mind reviewed the rules of engagement for the tenth time that day. The ROE were clear. He was to use the militia vessels to create confusion, force noncompliance, and then use that noncompliance to board the vessel and seize control of it.

"Captain, we have a problem," Gong interjected before Shen could give the order for Lotus Seven to proceed. "Sir, those *Tuo Chiang* corvettes we spotted an hour ago are accelerating toward the *Kalayaan Spirit*. They may try to place themselves between Lotus Seven and the cargo vessel. This is going to place them dangerously close to the *Tongling*."

Lifting the radio receiver to his lips, Shen said, "Lotus Seven, we have two *Tuo Chiang* corvettes moving to intercept you. I want you to maintain current position. Observe and report only."

"Affirmative, Dragon Actual. Observe and report, out."

This was exactly what concerned Shen about the operation. If the ROC Navy decided to intervene... things could escalate quickly. The *Tuo Chiang* corvettes were fast and stealthy multimission corvettes. They could reach speeds of up to forty-five knots, and bristled with eight Hsiung Feng III medium-range supersonic anti-ship missiles with five-hundred-pound warheads and a range of four hundred kilometers if they were the extended-range variant. Further complicating things, the *Tuo Chiang*s also carried twelve of the ROC's vaunted Sky Sword II surface-to-air missiles. Shen had been told these were very close to the US Navy's SM-2 missile. Altogether, these stealthy corvettes were a threat to his squadron he couldn't ignore.

"Commander Gong, sound battle stations and pass the word to the rest of the squadron to be prepared to engage the *Tuo Chiang* corvettes," Shen ordered. "I'm going to try and to speak with the captain of this vessel to see if we can defuse the situation before it turns kinetic on us."

Shen then directed his comms officer to get him a channel on the international frequency he knew the civilian freight would be monitoring. Keying the radio, Shen announced, "MV *Kalayaan Spirit*, this is Chinese Navy warship *Zunyi*. You are entering the sovereign waters of the People's Republic of China and have been selected for customs inspection under the Drug Enforcement Act of China 2033. You are hereby ordered to reduce speed and prepare to be boarded."

His call was met with static for several long minutes. Then a voice in accented English responded: "Chinese warship *Zunyi*, this is *Kalayaan Spirit*. We are in international waters on lawful transit to Magong Harbor, Penghu. Your inspection authority is not recognized by international law. We are continuing on to our destination."

Shen was disappointed in the response, but he had expected nothing less. The only countries acknowledging this new law were the countries already aligned with China and EDEP. The Western-aligned countries friendly with the US and NATO decried the law as a thinly veiled attempt at embargoing Taiwan. Shen noted his communications officer was already recording the interaction and documenting it for the inevitable inquiry and after-action report.

He was about to respond when Zhu, his operations officer, interjected. "Sir, you might want to see this. We are detecting new aerial contacts entering our battlespace. It looks like our air picture is about to get crowded." Zhu brought up a digital overlay of the tactical airspace around them. He was right—the sky was filling fast.

As if the stealth corvettes shadowing their formation weren't enough to deal with, a mix of friendly and potentially hostile aircraft were now converging toward weapons range.

Vectoring in from the mainland were six J-10 fighters, their IFF beacons transmitting clearly. But what drew Shen's attention were the ghostly placeholders trailing behind them—it appeared they had the company of some stealth fighters flying dark, their radar cross-sections nearly invisible to the *Zunyi's* AESA arrays.

Anticipating Shen's question, Zhu explained, "Sir, those placeholders are for the four J-20s. The only reason we even know they are there is because they are transmitting short-burst encrypted telemetry on the SkyLink combat channel. Before you ask, it's passive pickup only—no emissions. They're flying in coordinated formation behind the J-10s as cover."

Shen studied the flight path and spacing. Those J-20 pilots were smart—maintaining offset altitude and trailing distance, masked by the J-10s' radar signature. But their digital handshakes confirmed their identity: friendlies, so his air-defense systems didn't mistakenly label them hostile.

"Thank you, Zhu, for that explanation. Go ahead and assign them a discreet tracking label so we don't have a blue-on-blue incident," Shen ordered, then added, "And, Zhu—keep their identifiers suppressed on our shared displays. No need to advertise to anyone else that we've got stealth on station right now."

"Yes, Captain," Zhu confirmed as he relayed the orders to the sailors manning the AESA systems.

He leaned forward slightly, eyes fixed on the expanding battlespace. It was getting crowded—fast.

Sir, we're detecting multiple tracks inbound from Magong and Chiayi Air Base," Zhu said, a sharper edge in his voice now.

Shen stepped beside him, eyes narrowing at the tactical overlay. From the east, an ROC P-3C Orion maritime patrol aircraft was approaching low and slow, along the edge of their engagement window. Shen wasn't overly concerned with the Orion itself. What did concern him were its escorts. The P-3 was being escorted by four of the ROC's newer F-16 Vipers, flying in a loose formation to either side of the Orion with their AESA radar actively scanning for targets.

"Whoa, those aren't reconnaissance drones," Gong muttered beside him. "Those Vipers could be carrying a pair of Harpoons or, if we're really unlucky, a pair of HF-2s."

Shen didn't respond immediately; his mind was racing with calculations. For the moment, the Vipers were staying just outside his engagement envelope, a hundred kilometers from his ship. It was a thin line, and those Vipers could rapidly close that distance. But the Harpoon-ER and the Taiwanese Hsiung Feng III both possessed a range greater than a hundred and fifty kilometers. They didn't need to close in on his squadron to pose a threat to his ships.

Suddenly, appearing behind them, new radar tracks from the direction of Chiayi airbase blinked into view. It was another group of four more Vipers joining the party, spreading out in a wide arc.

"Captain! We're showing new contacts from Magong airbase. They just launched more aircraft," Zhu announced loudly, his voice sounding somewhere between excited and scared. "It looks like their indigenous fighters, those Ching-Kuo IDFs. They're probably air defense interceptors."

Shen clenched his jaw. The ROC's air presence was solidifying into a multi-axis threat. This posturing was turning into something, an escalation that was rapidly moving beyond his ability to control.

"This isn't good, sir," Gong said quietly. "This is quickly turning into a powder keg waiting to blow."

Before Shen could respond, a shrill alarm blared throughout the CIC. One by one, GPS signals marking their position and the ships around them began to flicker. The positional data they regularly received from the BeiDou-3 satellites overhead began to waver, then spiked. One second, it was showing them miles practically inside the Penghu Islands, then it was placing them adrift in the South Pacific.

"Captain, we're being jammed!" the electronic warfare officer shouted in a panic. "I'm showing GPS degradation across all bands. Sat comms with headquarters just dropped—I can't get a signal lock."

"Calm down, Lieutenant!" Shen barked angrily. "We've trained for this. Revert to backup systems and get me a status report on what's happening around us and with the rest of the squadron."

The lieutenant seemed to regain himself when the screens inside the CIC flickered several times before shutting down. Commander Gong typed feverishly at his terminal when the monitors returned. "Captain, I think our systems are in the process of being hacked. I'm initiating a hard reboot of our systems now," Gong relayed to him as the monitors turned off again.

The CIC erupted in a flurry of reports and cross voices as static flooded the comm channels that were still working. Seconds later, the monitors returned, and icons on the digital display appeared. Then they began disappearing or freezing once again.

Zhu looked up from his station. "Sir, we've lost contact with the squadron," he exclaimed. "We've lost the aircraft feed. We're being jammed across multiple broadband emitters. It's saturating every channel. I can't localize the source!"

"Sir, underwater contacts!" The sonar operator's voice cracked. "Multiple... dozens... behavior pattern unknown!"

Shen rushed to the sonar station. The display showed contacts moving in perfect synchronization—too fast for conventional submarines, too organized to be torpedoes. Then it came to him...they could be unmanned underwater drones racing toward the ships of his squadron. The track closest to one of his ships was the frigate *Qinzhou*.

"That track right there"—Shen pointed to it—"what's the range to the *Qinzhou*?"

"It's, um, it looks like it's passing directly beneath—"

The sound of the blast reverberated through the CIC. The shockwave of the blast buffeted the *Zunyi*, despite the two-kilometer distance between them and the *Qinzhou*. In that moment, Shen knew that no matter what happened next, he'd just lost whatever control of the situation he'd thought he had. His squadron was under attack, and he had no idea how it had happened or who had fired the first shots.

Chapter Thirty-Six:
First Blood

April 15, 2033 – 0745 Hours
Hengshan Military Command Center – JOC
Taipei, Taiwan

The emergency klaxon shattered the predawn quiet of the Joint Operations Center, its piercing wail cutting through the low hum of electronics and hushed conversations. Major General Yen Jiachun's coffee mug froze halfway to his lips as the main display wall erupted in cascading alerts.

"We're receiving an emergency transmission on VHF channel sixteen!" Captain Hsu Lichung's fingers flew across his console. "It's a Filipino merchant vessel—three-five nautical miles west of Magong Harbor."

The speakers crackled to life with heavily accented English. "Mayday, Mayday, Mayday! This is Motor Vessel *Kalayaan Spirit*, Philippine registry. We are requesting immediate assistance. We have Chinese warships attempting to board us. My God, they're firing warning shots at us! We need help! We are in Taiwan territorial waters! We are requesting immediate assistance. Can anyone hear us?"

General Yen set his mug down with deliberate calm, though his pulse quickened. They had known this was a possibility. Still, they had somehow hoped it wouldn't come to this. Now that it had, they had to deal with it.

"This is unacceptable!" Yen exclaimed. "In our own territorial waters at that. Get me a visual of the situation, if it's available. Let's get it on main screen," Yen ordered, whipping the JOC into action. "All stations—Navy and Air Force, give me a tactical picture of what we're looking at, now!"

The Joint Operations Center, manned by officers and senior NCOs from the Army, Navy, Air Force, Marines, and now TSG, moved with practiced efficiency. Monitors populated quickly with real-time data from Manta One, their Zephyr S pseudosatellite, maintaining its silent watch from its perch at seventy thousand feet over southern Taiwan. The infrared feed painted the Taiwan Strait in ghostly whites and grays, each heat signature tagged and tracked by the AI-assisted targeting system. It identified eleven PLA Navy vessels, denoting them as angry red diamonds, arranged in a loose crescent around a single blue square—the *Kalayaan Spirit*.

More data concerning the situation continued to flow into the JOC from a P-3 Orion, which had just completed its third pass of the area since coming on station two hours ago. Seconds later, a live video appeared on a monitor; the feed had been piped in from one of their Teng Yun UAVs, circling above Magong Naval Base.

"Get a confirmation of that PLA surface composition. I want to know what we're dealing with," Yen directed, focusing his operators' attention.

The naval liaison officer, Commander Qiu Shaozheng, stared intently at his monitor before speaking. "I've got it. We're looking at one Type 055 destroyer, designated *Zunyi*. Two Type 052D guided-missile destroyers. Four Type 054A frigates." He paused, double-checking his screen. "Four Type 056A corvettes. Plus...damn, twelve maritime militia trawlers on top of it...and they're moving in closer, possibly going to attempt to board them."

"Unbelievable. They really think they can just violate our territorial waters like this." Yen's voice carried the shock of the moment and the weight of the reality that this was really happening. A total of twenty-three foreign military vessels had entered their territorial waters in pursuit of a single merchant ship.

"What's the air picture looking like?"

Major Ke Jianhao, the Air Defense Coordinator, spoke up from his station. "We are tracking six J-10s inbound from the northwest, bearing three-two-zero. Currently ninety miles out, on intercept vector for our P-3 and our fighters on combat air patrol over Penghu," he calmly replied before his brow furrowed. "Um, we're also getting intermittent returns from the Patriot's phased array tracking radar at Penghu Airport. It's probably a stealth contact—maybe J-20s, but they're ghosts for right now. We can't get a confirmation yet."

The J-20s were China's fifth-generation stealth fighter, a counter to the American F-22 Raptor and the F-35 Lightning IIs. Until they engaged another fighter, dropping their stealth profiles to fire their missiles, they were phantoms.

Another burst transmission on the emergency frequency aired over the radio. "Chinese Navy vessel. This is *Kalayaan Spirit*. We are a civilian bulk food carrier in Taiwan waters. We will not submit to your boarding request or—"

A new voice cut in, speaking accented but clear English. "Motor Vessel *Kalayaan Spirit*, this is People's Liberation Army Navy vessel *Zunyi*. Under provisions of the Drug Enforcement Act of China 2033, you will stop your vessel immediately and prepare to be boarded for customs inspection. Any attempt to ignore these instructions or proceed to your destination will be considered a hostile act and treated accordingly."

Jodi Mack looked up from her station, clearly shocked by the brazenness of the command. In the days leading to this event, Admiral Han had personally requested to have a TSG liaison embedded in the JOC. Her expertise in the autonomous systems with which TSG had augmented the Navy and Marines had made her the go-to advisor.

Jodi seemed to shake off the surprise of the situation. Her fingers danced across her workstation as she correlated data feeds from the numerous sensors surrounding Penghu. "General, we have vessels in the area," she called out. "They are already responding."

She cast her screen to one of the monitors on the wall. "Sir, Shark One at Magong confirms we have the frigate *Chen De* and the corvettes *Wan Chiang* and *Fu Chiang* on patrol nearby. They're redirecting now to converge on the merchant's position."

"Time to intercept?"

Commander Qiu checked his plot. "Eight minutes for *Wan Chiang*; she's closest. *Chen De* is twelve minutes out. The *Fu Chiang* is bringing up the rear at fifteen."

The math wasn't on their side. The PLA boarding teams could be on that merchant in five minutes and at least one of the fishing trawlers was already practically on top of them.

"Sir!" Master Sergeant Lin Meiqing half-stood at her console. "We're detecting an electromagnetic spike from the PLA formation. They are going active with their fire-control radars."

The *Kalayaan Spirit*'s captain came back on the radio, fear bleeding through the static. "To anyone who can hear this, we are a civilian vessel in Taiwan waters! Chinese Navy ships are attempting to board us. This is an act of piracy! We are requesting help immediately!"

General Yen's jaw tightened. Listening to the calls for help and not being able to do anything about it was killing him inside. He wanted to scream but knew it wouldn't change anything. Every second this situation went unchecked meant lives at risk.

"To hell with it," he muttered to himself. The legal justification was clear.

"Get me Shark One," Yen ordered.

"Sir, Shark One is online," Captain Hsu confirmed seconds later.

"Shark One, Fortress Actual. How copy?"

"Fortress Actual. Good copy. Go for traffic," came the cool, professional response from Mick. While Jodi remained in Taipei, Michael Matsin had stayed on Penghu to assist Commander Tang and his sailors in manning the various autonomous vessels deployed around the Penghu Islands.

"Shark One, what's the status on your unmanned systems? Do you have something in play near the civilian ship in distress?" General Yen asked.

Mick's gravelly voice came through clearly. "Affirmative, Fortress. We have six Seeker XLUUVs deployed and loitering on station. We have another twelve Zealot USVs holding at launch point Huay-Two. Just say the word, and we'll engage."

The autonomous systems were their hidden edge against the PLA Navy. Months of secret training with TSG were about to pay off. But once revealed…their surprise would be gone.

"General." Mack's voice carried urgency. "Sir, we have confirmed submerged contacts entering the battlespace. Two Type 039C diesel-electrics, based on acoustic signatures. They're positioning to cut off our surface units from Penghu."

General Yen was about to respond when his air liaison officer called out a new threat.

"New air contacts!" Major Ke called out. "Dragon-Eye is reporting those J-10s accelerating and being vectored toward Penghu. Time to merge with our combat air patrol—six minutes."

"What alert fighters do we have on deck?" Yen asked.

"We're launching four Vipers from Penghu Airport. Another six IDF fighters are launching from Tainan." Ke's hands flew over his console as he continued to call out the status of the fighters on strip alert. "But, General, those ghost returns of possible J-20s—we're starting to get some better returns on them. Nothing we can lock up, yet, but there's definitely something stealthy out there."

"Sir, should I alert Admiral Han and General Tseng?" interrupted Captain Hsu.

"Yes. Immediately. I want full command staff to the JOC now!" General Yen ordered as he watched the converging forces on the display. "And set Readiness Condition Two across all commands and facilities."

The radio crackled again. Commander Qiu looked up sharply. "Sir, our frigate the *Chen De*—they're reporting the sight of PLA helicopters launching from the PLA frigates. It looks like a pair of Z-9s in assault configuration."

"Weapons status on all forces?" asked General Yen.

"Currently weapons hold, per standing orders," Commander Qiu replied.

Yen felt the weight of this moment. Being the first to fire meant bearing responsibility for starting the war. But in their own waters, with a civilian vessel under threat...

"Maintain weapons hold," he ordered. "But all units, prepare for defensive action. The moment they—"

"Vampire, Vampire, Vampire!" Commander Qiu's voice cut him off. "We have missile launch from PLA corvette *Tongling*! It's a C-803 heading for *Wan Chiang*!"

The JOC erupted. On the main display, a red line streaked from one of the Type 056As toward the approaching ROC corvette.

"*Wan Chiang* attempting evasive maneuvers," Qiu reported. "Deploying countermeasures—"

The red line merged with the blue triangle representing *Wan Chiang*.

"Direct hit!" Qiu's voice cracked. "*Wan Chiang* is hit amidships. She's reporting heavy damage, fires onboard."

Yen's decision crystallized in an instant. "All units, weapons free! Repeat, weapons free! Engage all PLA forces in our territorial waters!"

The tactical display exploded into chaos. Blue lines—Hsiung Feng III missiles—erupted from *Chen De* and *Fu Chiang*, racing toward the PLA formation. The Type 052D destroyers responded with their own volleys, HHQ-9 interceptors rising to meet the incoming threats.

"Shark One, execute Piranha Protocol," Yen commanded. "All autonomous systems, prosecute submerged contacts."

"Copy, Fortress. Seekers going active. Zealots launching now."

On the display, six new blue dots appeared beneath the surface as the XLUUVs abandoned their silent runs and went to attack speed. Twelve more streaked from Penghu's hidden coves—the Zealot USVs racing toward the PLA surface formation at sixty knots.

"Sir, GPS interference increasing," Captain Liao Renjie reported from the EW station. "BeiDou constellation is attempting to override civilian signals."

"Execute jamming protocols. Deny them satellite navigation."

"Dragon-Eye is defensive!" Major Ke shouted. "J-10s attempting missile lock. Our CAP is engaging."

The main door burst open. Admiral Han Ji-cheng strode in, still buttoning his uniform jacket, with General Tseng Zhaoming right behind him. Their eyes took in the tactical display—a maelstrom of missiles, countermeasures, and maneuvering forces.

"Who fired first?" Han demanded.

"PLA corvette *Tongling* launched on *Wan Chiang*," Yen reported. "Direct hit. We are now weapons free in defense of our waters."

On the screen, one of the red diamonds suddenly flashed and disappeared.

"Splash one!" Commander Qiu announced. "*Qinzhou* is hit. Multiple Hsiung Feng impacts. She's breaking up."

But the PLA response was swift and overwhelming. More missiles filled the air, and the ghost contacts Major Ke had worried about suddenly materialized.

"J-20s dropping stealth!" Ke warned. "Four bandits, they're on our CAP flights!"

The calm before the storm was over. In the space of ninety seconds, the Taiwan Strait had become a killing field.
****

April 15, 2033 – 0724 Hours
2nd Naval District HQ, Secure Operations Center
Magong Naval Base, Penghu Islands

The tactical display erupted in crimson as the first C-803 antiship missile streaked across the screen. Mick Matsin gripped the edge of the console, watching the inevitable unfold in real time.

"Impact in five seconds," Commander Tang announced, his voice steady despite the sweat beading on his forehead. The secure operations center beneath Magong Naval Base hummed with controlled chaos—operators called out targets, electronic warfare officers jammed frequencies, and the constant ping of sonar returns from their deployed assets rounded out the cacophony.

The red line merged with *Tajiang*'s icon.

"Direct hit," Tang confirmed. "She's taking water. Damage control teams responding."

Vice Admiral Lo Hua stood rigid behind them, eyes locked on the master display. "Return fire. All units, weapons free."

Mick's fingers danced across his control interface, managing six Seeker-class XLUUVs prowling beneath the churning waters. Each autonomous submarine carried three Copperhead-500 AI torpedoes, their neural networks trained on PLA acoustic signatures. "Shark One confirms Piranha Protocol active. My girls are hunting."

"Dragon-Eye is taking fire!" The air defense coordinator's voice crackled through the speakers. "Multiple Fox Threes inbound!"

On the display, six J-10s bore down on the lumbering P-3 Orion. Four F-16s broke formation, afterburners blazing as they moved to intercept.

"Vipers engaging," someone called out. "Fox Two, Fox Two!"

The aerial ballet played out in digital clarity. Sidewinders and PL-12s crisscrossed the sky. Two J-10s exploded immediately, then a third. An F-16 took a missile to the port wing, spiraling down in flames. The remaining Vipers pressed their attack with savage precision.

"Splash four, five, six!" The air coordinator's excitement died in his throat. "New contacts—fast movers from the northwest. Stealthy signatures resolving—"

"J-20s," Admiral Lo said grimly. "Four of them."

Mick watched the stealth fighters materialize on the scope like phantoms becoming solid. They'd waited, let the F-16s expend their missiles on the J-10s. Now they'd struck.

"Dragon-Eye is hit! She's going down!"

Three more F-16s vanished from the display in rapid succession, overwhelmed by the J-20s' beyond-visual-range missiles. But Penghu's defenders weren't finished.

"Patriot battery has lock," Tang reported. "Birds away!"

Two PAC-3 interceptors roared skyward. The J-20s, caught transitioning from stealth to attack profiles, tried to evade. Two weren't fast enough—orange blossoms marked their deaths at thirty thousand feet.

"*Chen De* is launching Harpoons," Tang called out, tracking the ROC frigate's desperate counterattack. Eight anti-ship missiles leaped from their canisters, racing toward the PLA formation.

The response was immediate and overwhelming. The Type 055 *Zunyi* and her escorts filled the air with HHQ-9 interceptors. Most of the Harpoons died in flight, but two punched through, slamming into a Type 054A frigate.

"*Qinzhou* is burning," someone reported. "But *Chen De*—"

The *Kang Ding*-class frigate never had a chance. Four YJ-83s converged on her position. Her CIWS sprayed tungsten desperately, claiming one missile. The other three found their mark.

"*Chen De* is gone." Tang's voice carried no emotion. Just fact.

The last *Tuo Chiang* corvette, *Fu Chiang*, fought like a cornered wolf. Her crew launched every Hsiung Feng III in her magazines before the Type 054As bracketed her with concentrated fire. She rolled over and sank in less than ninety seconds.

"Sir!" An intelligence officer pointed at his screen. "Massive launch detection from the PLA destroyer group!"

Mick's blood chilled. He knew what was coming. "Cruise missiles. They're going for the base."

The display lit up with new tracks—twenty-four CJ-10 land-attack cruise missiles in the first wave, their turbofan engines pushing them at six hundred miles per hour toward Magong.

"All defensive systems online," Admiral Lo commanded. "Weapons free on all incoming vampires."

Patriots roared off their rails. The new Roadrunner-M interceptors—Anduril's latest counter-cruise missile system—streaked skyward at Mach 5. The sky above Penghu became a killing field of intersecting vapor trails.

"Fifteen vampires destroyed," the air defense coordinator reported. "Nine leakers inbound!"

"Second wave launching," someone else shouted. "Another twenty-four cruise missiles!"

The command center shook as the first CJ-10s found their targets. Lights flickered. Dust cascaded from the ceiling. The deep boom of explosions penetrated even their hardened bunker.

"Roadrunner magazine is empty," Tang reported. "Patriots engaging second wave."

More intercepts. More leakers. The bunker shook harder this time; a monitor crashed from its mount. The lights died for three seconds before emergency power kicked in.

"Surface radar is gone," an operator called through the smoke. "We've lost Pier Seven and the fuel depot!"

Another explosion came, this time closer. The floor bucked beneath their feet. Admiral Lo steadied himself against a console, blood trickling from a gash on his forehead where debris had struck.

"Enough," he growled. "Commander Tang, Warrant Matsin—unleash the sharks."

Mick had been waiting for those words. His fingers flew across the interface, transmitting new targeting priorities to his three assigned Seekers. "Shark One prosecuting surface targets. Seekers-1 through 3 going active."

On his screen, the XLUUVs abandoned their silent stalking. Pump jets engaged, pushing them to forty knots as they closed on their targets. The AI-assisted fire control systems had already computed optimal attack angles.

"Seeker-1 has firing solution on Type 052D, hull number one-seven-three," Mick announced. "Launching Copperheads."

Three torpedoes separated from the XLUUV, their own AI brains taking over as they sprinted toward the destroyer. The PLA ship detected them immediately, launching decoys and maneuvering hard. But the Copperheads had trained for this, their neural networks processing acoustic returns faster than any human operator.

"Impact in thirty seconds," Mick reported, already shifting Seeker-2 toward a pair of Type 056 corvettes. "Seeker-3, target that damaged 054A."

Beside him, Commander Tang worked his own trio of Seekers with equal precision. "Submerged contacts identified. Two Type 039B diesel-electrics and—" He paused, double-checking the acoustic signature. "One Type 093A nuclear boat. Bold of them."

"Not for long," Admiral Lo said through gritted teeth.

The first explosions erupted beneath the PLA formation. The Type 052D *Nanjing* took two Copperheads amidships, her hull cracking like an egg. She listed immediately, secondary explosions rippling through her magazines.

"Scratch one destroyer," Mick announced. "Seeker-2 engaging corvettes."

But the PLA had awakened to the threat. ASW helicopters dropped sonobuoys in frantic patterns. The Type 056A corvettes, designed for antisubmarine warfare, began active pinging with their hull-mounted sonars.

"They've got Seeker-2," Mick reported as his display showed the XLUUV caught in overlapping sonar beams. "She's running, but—"

A Yu-8 rocket-assisted torpedo found its mark. Seeker-2 died in a flash of pressure and flame.

"Seeker-2, snapshot on that corvette, bearing two-seven-zero," Mick commanded. The last of his XLUUVs fired desperately before diving deep. One Copperhead found its target—the *Tongling*, already damaged from earlier fighting, broke in half and sank.

Tang's submarines were having better luck with the submerged targets. The Type 039Bs, optimized for coastal ambush rather than open water maneuvering, couldn't match the Seekers' speed or AI-driven tactics.

"First Type 039 is breaking up," Tang reported clinically. "Seeker-5 has the nuclear boat. Launching all torpedoes."

The Type 093A fought hard, launching countermeasures and diving for the thermocline. But three Copperheads with networked targeting were too much. The nuclear submarine imploded at four hundred meters, taking ninety-six souls with her.

"Zealots engaging surface targets," another operator announced.

Mick switched his display to track the twelve USVs racing at sixty knots toward the PLA maritime militia. The unmanned boats split into wolf packs, their Hellfire missiles reaching out toward the converted trawlers. But the PLA had learned from Ukraine's maritime drone attacks. Type 056 corvettes moved to screen the militia vessels, their 30mm cannons and HQ-10 missiles creating walls of steel.

"Zealots-3 through 7 are gone—8 and 9 are pressing the attack," someone reported.

Two trawlers exploded as Hellfires found their mark. Another took a suicide charge from Zealot-Twelve, the two-hundred-and-fifty-pound warhead turning the vessel into flaming wreckage. But it wasn't enough. Nine of twelve USVs died in the attempt.

The command center shook again as another cruise missile found something topside. Emergency lighting flickered. Smoke thickened despite the ventilation system's efforts.

"Damage report," Admiral Lo demanded, wiping blood from his eyes.

"We've lost the main radar array, two Patriot launchers, and the northern pier complex," his aide reported. "Casualties are… significant."

Mick looked at his display. Three Seekers were still operating, out of six. Three Zealots limped home. Against that, they'd sunk one destroyer, three corvettes, two diesel submarines, and a nuclear boat, plus several militia vessels.

He locked eyes with Commander Tang. Both understood the grim calculus. They'd bloodied the PLA's nose, proven their autonomous systems could kill. But the base was burning, the ROC surface fleet was decimated, and this was only the beginning.

"Sir," the communications officer called out, voice cracking. "Flash traffic from Fortress. The mainland has launched ballistic missiles. Impact time…eight minutes."

Admiral Lo closed his eyes for just a moment. When he opened them, they burned with resolve.

"Sound general quarters. All remaining assets to maximum readiness." He looked at Mick and Tang. "Gentlemen, we've just started World War Three. Let's make sure we're still here to finish it."
****

April 15, 2033 - 0824 Hours
Hengshan Military Command Center – Joint Operations Center
Taipei, Taiwan

The tactical display painted a grim picture as damage reports flooded in from across northern Taiwan. Jodi Mack's fingers flew across her console, correlating data from surviving assets. Red damage indicators spread like blood across the digital map—Penghu burning, the northern naval bases under bombardment, aircraft falling from the sky in uneven exchanges.

"Magong Control, this is Fortress. Report your status." Major General Yen's voice carried forced calm as he attempted contact for the fourth time.

Static answered. Then a burst of interference took hold of the line before a haggard voice broke through. "Fortress, this is… this is Commander Tang, Magong Control. Admiral Lo is KIA. We've lost primary C3 capability. Multiple cruise missile impacts. Base is operational but degraded. Shark One—Matsin—is wounded but functional."

Jodi's stomach clenched. Mick had survived, but barely. The entire TSG control element at Magong had taken a beating.

"Aquarium." Yen appeared at her shoulder. "Can you take control of the Shark assets?"

She was already pulling up the authentication protocols. "Give me thirty seconds to establish uplink." Her fingers danced across the interface, rerouting command authority through backup satellite channels. One by one, the surviving Seeker XLUUVs checked in. "I've got eight operational units from the original eighteen. Six are damaged but mobile. Four, no response—presumed destroyed."

Admiral Han Ji-cheng moved behind her, studying the underwater battlespace. "Lieutenant Mack, you now have full undersea warfare authority. Whatever those things can do—do it."

"Aye-aye, sir." The old Navy acknowledgment came automatically. She'd been out for three years, but muscle memory died hard.

"Air picture update!" Major Ke Jianhao's voice cut through the controlled chaos. "Six IDFs from Tainan intercepting PLA fighters over Penghu. Four F-16s joining from Chiayi."

The aerial engagement unfolded with brutal asymmetry. The newly arrived J-20s, invisible until they chose to engage, struck like phantoms.

"Multiple missile launches detected," Ke reported, voice hollow. "IDFs are defensive—no lock on the J-20s. They can't see them to shoot back."

One by one, the indigenous fighters vanished from the display—fourth-generation aircraft helpless against fifth-generation stealth. The F-16s fared no better, their radars finding only empty sky until the moment PL-15 missiles appeared on their threat receivers.

"All aircraft down." Ke's words fell like hammer blows. "No kills on the J-20s. They're already extending, probably Winchester on missiles."

"Northern sector reporting!" Commander Qiu Shaozheng called out from his navy liaison station. "Multiple surface engagements. *Chi Yang* is gone—magazine detonation. *Kee Lung* took three YJ-83s, breaking up. Missile boats *Hai Ou*, *Hai Ying*, and *Hai Peng* all confirmed sunk."

The numbers were staggering. In less than ninety minutes, the ROC Navy had lost a third of its surface combatants.

"Vampire, vampire!" Captain Hsu Lichung's warning snapped everyone's attention to the main display. "Thirty-six cruise missiles inbound—northern vector. Targets appear to be Keelung Naval Base and Weihai Camp."

"All AMD assets, weapons free," Major General Yen ordered. The Air Force commander had been quietly coordinating the air defense battle, but even his composure was cracking.

Patriots and Roadrunner-M interceptors rose to meet the threat. The engagement played out in compressed time—explosions blooming across the sky as the defensive systems found their marks.

"Thirty intercepted," Hsu reported. "Six leakers. Impact in twenty seconds."

They could only watch as the remaining CJ-10s found their targets. Two slammed into Weihai Camp, the army facility disappearing in twin fireballs. Four more hit Keelung—the naval logistics hub and 131st Fleet Command building taking direct hits.

"Ma'am, I'm tracking massive acoustic activity," Chief Petty Officer Zeng Minghui said from his station. "PLA submarine surge. They're pushing everything they have through the strait."

Jodi's hands moved with practiced efficiency, tasking her Seekers. Eight operational units against what looked like an entire submarine fleet. But the XLUUVs had one advantage—they were already in position, silent and waiting.

"Executing Wolfpack Seven," she announced. "All Seekers going active. Time to earn our pay."

The autonomous submarines revealed themselves simultaneously, their AI-driven targeting systems processing multiple contacts. *Song*-class diesel boats, built for coastal ambush, found themselves the hunted rather than the hunters. The older boats, some dating back to the 1990s, had no answer for the Copperhead-500s' advanced guidance.

"Seeker-7 confirms two Song kills," Jodi reported, watching the acoustic returns. "Seeker-9 has three more. These boats are sitting ducks."

The *Yuan*-class submarines, more modern with air-independent propulsion, tried to fight back. But the Seekers had been designed specifically to counter diesel-electric boats—their AI trained on thousands of hours of acoustic signatures.

"Six *Yuan*s down," Jodi reported, her voice steady—professional satisfaction tempered by the sobering scale of destruction. "Seekers-13 and 14 have expended all Copperheads. I'm routing them to an alternate rearm and refit site near the northern coast—possibly Port Shen'ao or, if needed, they'll swing south around Taiwan to a secure harbor on the East Coast," she added. Her autonomous undersea hunters had just sunk more enemy tonnage in a single engagement than any force had achieved since the Second World War.

As several of Jodi's Seeker-class XLUUVs slipped away, their torpedoes expended, she shifted control to another Seeker that had been loitering near Pengjia Islet. Few outside the upper echelons of naval intelligence understood the strategic importance of this tiny outpost, located just sixty-three kilometers northeast of Keelung City. The remote ROC Navy installation formed a critical node in the US–Japan–Taiwan undersea surveillance network, commonly referred to as a regional SOSUS grid. Arrays of seabed-mounted hydrophones and passive acoustic sensors monitored PLA submarine movements as they transited the Miyako Strait—a vital gateway into the Western Pacific and the contested waters surrounding the Ryukyu Islands, including Okinawa.

As Seeker-11 synced with her workstation, Jodi leaned forward, eyes narrowing on the display. The autonomous unit had been shadowing a pair of Type 054A *Jiangkai II*-class frigates for several hours. Sensor readouts confirmed the ships had recently fired multiple salvos from their H/PJ26 76mm deck guns—likely targeting the ROC Marine garrison defending Pengjia Islet's maritime and aerial surveillance towers.

Her brow furrowed as she scanned the acoustic and thermal traces. The Seeker's hydrophones had detected the rhythmic blade signatures of rotary-wing activity—probably Harbin Z-9s or Ka-28 Helix ASW helicopters—launched from the frigates' flight decks. Jodi suspected an assault force may have been inserted to seize the island's critical sensor infrastructure.

She pushed the thought aside. That fight would be someone else's problem—hers was beneath the waves. Her mission was clean, cold, and lethal.

She queued the firing solution. With three Copperhead-500 AI-guided torpedoes loaded, she reserved one for contingencies and released the other two. The Type 054As were decent antisurface platforms with respectable air defense capabilities, but their antisubmarine warfare suites were notoriously underpowered—an exploitable weakness. Moments after launch, the torpedoes arced into intercept vectors, their onboard targeting AI adjusting course to exploit known vulnerabilities: the zones closest to the VLS magazine compartments.

The first detonation sent a geyser of flame and steel punching skyward. The second torpedo hit just aft of the bridge. Both frigates erupted within seconds, the blast patterns consistent with internal magazine detonations. Two more enemy warships reduced to burning wreckage.

Jodi exhaled slowly. She found herself wishing absurdly that the Seeker had a camera feed she could save—something to mark the moment. Not for glory. For proof. For memory.

"Hot damn! Nice shooting, Jodi!" called out Chief Petty Officer Zeng Minghui from the adjacent console, his voice rising above the rumble of status updates.

"Don't thank me yet, Chief," she replied, her cheeks warming with a mixture of pride and dread. "Seeker-12 just flagged a new contact—Type 052D destroyer. It's practically begging to become an artificial reef."

A dry chuckle rose from Commander Qiu Shaozheng, seated a few consoles down. "If we weren't living through the end of the world, ma'am, I'd say that's the funniest damn thing I've heard all week." His jaw unclenched slightly, the tight lines of tension softening at her remark.

She placed Seeker-11 back in autonomous loiter mode and jumped to Seeker-12 and resumed the next hunt. As the battle beneath the waters of Taiwan churned from robotic death, Jodi began to feel a surge of hope with each passing victory. The autonomous systems she'd mastered during her time in the Navy were proving their worth around Taiwan. *You know, maybe we can—*

"General Yen!" Captain Hsu's voice interrupted her thoughts, his voice raw and shaky. "Manta Two is reporting launch detections from the mainland—they're ballistic missiles. Oh God. There's lots of them."

The main wall display shifted to show the stratospheric ISR feed aimed in the direction of mainland China. Launch plumes bloomed from multiple known launch locations across China's eastern provinces like deadly flowers arcing into the sky.

"Someone confirm those launch sites and what kind of missiles those are," General Yen ordered forcefully, though the color from his face had already drained, along with Jodi's hopes.

"Stand by. Confirmation coming in now—Base 96166 near Guangzhou. We have twelve DF-16 missile tracks," responded Hsu, his voice growing more strained with each report. "Base 96111 at Puning. Sixteen launches confirmed, DF-17 hypersonics." Hsu paused for a second as more data continued to come in. "Here comes another volley, this one coming from Base 96421 at Yong'an. Looks like twenty DF-21Ds. We have launches coming from Base 96417 at Huidong—appears to be a total of eight DF-26s."

Admiral Han stepped forward, his face granite. "Total count. What are we looking at?"

Captain Hsu didn't look up from his screen. "Still compiling, sir. It's heavy—but not saturation-level."

"It's confirmed. Two hundred thirty inbound tracks," Hsu said, voice flat. "Mixed load—ballistic and cruise. DF-16s, -17s, -21s, -26s, plus CJ-10s. Time to impact: eleven minutes for the hypersonics, fourteen for the rest."

The JOC fell silent. Fingers hovered over keyboards. Radios hissed.

"No signs of mobile launchers redeploying," Hsu continued. "No bomber launches. No MRLs on the move. Could be a single-phase strike."

Han's eyes shifted to the main monitor. "Any tracks on Okinawa? Guam? Are the Americans or Japanese being hit?"

"Negative, Admiral," Hsu said quickly. "No second-theater expansion. No launches toward US or JSDF assets."

A ripple of restrained relief moved through the room.

"Targets?" Han asked, eyes still locked on the growing constellation of missile arcs.

"They're coming in now," said Major Ke Jianhao, scanning the filtered trajectory data. His voice sharpened with each word.

"Zuoying Naval Base. Adjacent Tsoying Shipyard. Leshan Long-Range Radar. Dongsha Island Garrison. Anping Naval Base, Tainan. The Army Command HQ, Taoyuan. Army Special Forces Command—Longcheng Barracks complex."

He hesitated—one more line of data was populating.

"And the Longtan Combined Maintenance Depot. That's under Third Regional Support Command. Also in Taoyuan."

Everyone in the room exhaled, like they'd been punched in the gut.

"Damn it," Han muttered, jaw clenched. "They're gutting our second strike."

As the seconds stretched for what felt like minutes, the missile tracks continued to advance toward them. Each of the glowing red tracks was hundreds or even thousands of pounds of explosive power racing toward them.

"OK, we have trained and prepared for this moment," General Yen began. "We all knew this day might come, and now it has. This is no longer a drill. This is real. I want all missile batteries active, Patriots and Sky Bow IIIs, even the new Roadrunners-Ms. All ballistic and cruise missile defenses are weapons free to engage targets at will, maximum rate of fire. Do what we can to protect the targets in Taipei—Ministry of National Defense Headquarters, and the Hengshan Military Command Center. Kaohsiung and the Zuoying Naval Base, and the Army Command HQ, Taoyuan, are the priority targets we should focus our efforts on defending," General Yen ordered.

Yen received a nod of approval from Admiral Han as he took charge of the missile defense situation, reminding everyone they had a job to do.

As the situation continued to unfold, Jodi found herself standing, staring at the hundreds of missile tracks bearing down on them. It suddenly became real. More than a dozen of those tracks were heading for the building above her—if those Patriots missed, she could die in the coming minutes. For the first time in a long while, she began to pray.

"First intercepts in ninety seconds," someone announced.

Jodi met General Yen's eyes. The old soldier managed a tight nod—acknowledgment of her contribution, and what they'd achieved today despite what might happen next. She'd bloodied the PLA Navy today, sending more tonnage to the bottom of the ocean than anyone since World War II. But now, in this moment as missiles closed in on them, none of that mattered.

"Impact in thirty seconds!" shouted someone.

"Oh God—brace for impact!"

****

From the Authors

Miranda and I hope you enjoyed *The Gotland Deception* and the beginning of our newest thriller series. If you're ready to continue the story, you can pick up *The Suwałki Crisis*, Book Two in the series. It is currently available for preorder on Amazon.

I want to share something personal—something that may sound strange to some. I felt a calling to write this series. A pull. A quiet, persistent voice inside telling me this story needed to be told.

That inner voice—some might call it instinct, others faith—has saved my life more than once. It guided me through harrowing moments during my time in Iraq, and again during tense situations while working across Europe. I've learned to trust it.

So why this story? Why now?

Because I believe we're living at a turning point. Our nation, our world is standing at the edge of the greatest industrial and technological revolution since the dawn of electricity: the rise of Artificial General Intelligence. While our political and corporate leaders debate how to wield it, our adversaries are already preparing to weaponize it.

And that's why I felt compelled to write this story.

If you truly value something—your family, your freedom, your homeland—you should be willing to protect it, to fight for it. Ask any parent what they'd do to protect their children, and you'll understand what I mean. It's no different at the national level.

Yes, every country—whether in Europe, Asia, or here in America—has its flaws. But those flaws don't define us. What does define us is how we rise to defend what matters most.

Captain Alex Mercer's story is one of honor and sacrifice. He's a man who began his service as an enlisted soldier before earning his commission. He represents the warrior-scholar—someone who leads from the front and never forgets where he came from.

Sergeant First Class Ramon Torres reflects my own upbringing—a man who didn't come from much but used military service as a way to provide for his family, improve himself, and continue a legacy of service to his country.

As this series unfolds, you'll meet other characters like Alex and Ramon—men and women who understand the cost of freedom, who know that service matters, and that allies matter. And that, sometimes, war must be fought—not out of hatred, but out of love for what we refuse to lose.

As a veteran of the Iraq War, I understand war in ways I wish I didn't. I've lost more friends to suicide than to bullets. I carry the physical and emotional scars of that war, as does Miranda—and even our children. But despite everything we've endured, I would answer the call again in a heartbeat if my country needed me. Not because I believe it's perfect. But because I believe it's worth it.

As we step into an uncertain future, I want to ask something of you—something hard. Show patience. Show kindness when you can. Show resolve when you must.

We can't control the world around us, but we can control how we respond to it. If I choose to respond with grace, and you do the same, that ripple effect—small at first—can change lives.

As a wise man once said: "Be the change you want to see in the world."

If you are ready for the next chapter in this World on Fire series, you can purchase your pre-order copy on Amazon. It's our goal to release our books ahead of schedule, but every now and then you have to allow for a little "kid" factor with a young family. The *Suwalki Crisis* is set to release on December 23, 2025, right before Christmas. If we finish it early, we'll release it early. If you pre-order your copy now, it'll appear on your Kindle the moment it's released.

Thank you again for all your support over the years. It's meant a lot to Miranda and me, and our three kids. In the meantime, we are down to the final book in our Rise of the Republic series, *Into the Schism*, that will end this incredible series. To our pleasant surprise, this series and the Monroe Doctrine series have both achieved Amazon KDP All-Star status for quite some time, ranking among the Top 100 most-read series in the science fiction and thriller genres for thirty-four consecutive months. If you haven't tried this series yet, you're missing out on one of the most-read series of the 2020s.

We also launched the start a new sci-fi spinoff series within the Rise of the Republic universe called Battles of the Republic—starting with *The Intus Invasion*. You can purchase your copy here. In this series, we will follow the career progression of several characters we began introducing in books ten, eleven, and twelve of the main Rise of the Republic series. Battles of the Republic will allow us to explore the untold campaigns and the stories of the men and women who fought them.

As always, we appreciate each and every one of you that take the time to read our books. We definitely couldn't do this without you. If you've enjoyed *The Gotland Deception*, we would love it if you could take a moment and write a review on Amazon and Goodreads for us. Early reviews make a huge difference in the success or failure of a new book or series, and it's how new readers discover our books. As full-time writers, we do live on the sales of our books. For us to continue writing full-time and bringing you the stories you love, we will need your continued support. We hope we have earned it through the years and countless books and stories we've given you.

All our best,

James Rosone and Miranda Watson

Abbreviation Key

1MC	1 Main Circuit (Shipboard Public Address)
A3	Deputy Chief of Staff of Operations for the Air Force
AAR	After-Action Review
ABV	Assault Breacher Vehicle
ACV	Amphibious Combat Vehicle
ADA	Air Defense Artillery
ADIZ	Air Defense Identification Zones
AEGIS	Advanced Electronic Guided Interceptor System
AESA	Active Electronically Scanned Array
AIP	Air-Independent Propulsion
AIS	Automatic Identification System
AMP	Advanced Multi-Purpose
AMRAAM	Advanced Medium-Range Air-to-Air Missile
APC	Armored Personnel Carrier
APOBS	Anti-Personnel Obstacle Breaching Systems
AR-HUD	Augmented Reality Heads Up Display
ASVAB	Armed Services Vocational Aptitude Battery
ASW	Anti-submarine Warfare
AT	Anti-Tank
ATGM	Anti-tank Guided Missile
AUV	Autonomous Underwater Vehicle
AWOL	Absent Without Leave
AWACS	Airborne Warning and Control System
BMC-R	Battle Management Control Room
BMP	Russian infantry fighting vehicles
BRICS	Brazil, Russia, India, China, and South Africa
BTR	Russian armored personnel carrier
CAP	Combat Air Patrol
CCP	Chinese Communist Party
CCTV	Closed-Circuit Television
CHIMERA	Common High-Assurance Internet Protocol Encryptor Interoperable Manager for Efficient Remote Administration

CIA	Central Intelligence Agency
CIC	Combat Information Center
CITV	Commander's Independent Thermal Viewer
CIWS	Close in Weapons System
CMC	Central Military Commission
COSCO	China Ocean Shipping (Group)
CRI	Refers to the MIM-104C PAC-2 CRI interceptor (a modernized version of the original PAC-2 Patriot missile)
CSM	Command Sergeant Major
DEAC	Drug Enforcement Act of China
DEFCON	Defense Readiness Condition
DHS	Department of Homeland Security
DIA	Defense Intelligence Agency
E3	Newer generation of Abrams tank
EA	Engagement Area
EDEP	Eurasian Defense Economic Pact
EMCON	Emission Control
EMP	Electromagnetic Pulse
ENDEX	End of Exercise
EOD	Explosive Ordnance Disposal
ETA	Estimated Time of Arrival
EUCOM	European Command
EW	Electronic Warfare
FBI	Federal Bureau of Investigations
FLIR	Forward-Looking Infrared
FPV	First-Person View (type of drone)
GCHQ	Government Communications Headquarters (UK intelligence)
GDP	Gross Domestic Product
GEAB	Gotland Energy AB
GEM-T	Guidance-Enhanced Missile, Tactical
GPS	Global Positioning System
GRU	Russian Intelligence
HEAT	High-Explosive Anti-tank
HEMTT	Heavy Expanded Mobility Tactical Truck
HET	Heavy Equipment Transport
HIMARS	High Mobility Artillery Rocket System

HPM	High-Power Microwave
HSwMS	His/Her Swedish Majesty's Ship
HUD	Heads Up Display
HVAC	Heating, Ventilation, and Air Conditioning
ICS	Interim Contractor Support
IDF	Chinese fighter aircraft
IFAK	Individual First Aid Kit
IFF	Identification Friend or Foe
IR	Infrared
IRIS-T	Infrared Imaging System Tail/Thrust Vector-Controlled
ISR	Intelligence, Surveillance, and Reconnaissance
ITAR	International Traffic in Arms Regulations
JAB	Joint Assault Bridge
JLTV	Joint Light Tactical Vehicle
JOS	Joint Operations Center
JSDF	Japan Self-Defense Forces
JSOC	Joint Special Operations Command
KIA	Killed in Action
LIDAR	Light Detection and Ranging
LNG	Liquid Natural Gas
LT	Lieutenant
LUMES	Master's Degree Program in Environmental Studies and Sustainability Science
LZ	Landing Zone
MANPADS	Man-Portable Air Defense System
MARCOM	Allied Maritime Command
MCLIC	Mine Clearing Line Charge
METOC	Meteorology and Oceanography
MMO	Massively Multiplayer Online (video games)
MP	Military Police
MRE	Meals Ready-to-Eat
MRL	Multiple Rocket Launcher
MSE	Missile Segment Enhancement
MSS	Ministry of State Security (Chinese version of secret police, FBI, and CIA combined)

MTU	Motoren- und Turbinen-Union, a well-known German manufacturer of high-performance diesel engines and propulsion systems.
MV	Motor Vehicle
NATO	North Atlantic Treaty Organization
NCO	Non-Commissioned Officer
NGO	Non-governmental Organization
NOFORN	No Foreign Dissemination (classification level)
NSA	National Security Advisor OR National Security Agency
NSB	Naval Submarine Base
OCP	Operational Camouflage Pattern
OPFOR	Opposing Forces
OPSEC	Operations Security
PC	Personnel Carrier
PDW	Personal Defense Weapon
PFC	Private First Class
PLA	People's Liberation Army (Chinese Army)
PLAN	People's Liberation Army Navy (Chinese Navy)
PMC	Private Military Contractor
POI	Program of Instruction
PRC	People's Republic of China
PT	Physical Training
REFORGER	Return of Forces to Germany
RFID	Radio Frequency Identificatio
RHIB	Rigid-Hulled Inflatable Boat
ROC	Republic of China (Taiwan)
ROE	Rules of Engagement
RO/RO	Roll-on, Roll-off
S2	Intelligence Officer
SACEUR	Supreme Allied Commander Europe
SCIF	Sensitive Compartmented Information Facility
SEAL	Sea, Air, and Land (Navy special forces)
SECNAV	Secretary of the Navy
SFC	Sergeant First Class

SHAPE	Supreme Headquarters Allied Powers Europe
SHORAD	Short-Range Air Defense
SIGINT	Signals Intelligence
SME	Subject Matter Expert
SOCEUR	Special Operations Command Europe
SOSUS	Sound Surveillance System
SUV	Sports Utility Vehicle
SVR	Russian Foreign Intelligence
SVTC	Secure Video Teleconferencing
TAO	Tactical Action Officer
TC	Tank Commander
TF	Task Force
TOC	Tactical Operations Center
UCSD	University of California, San Diego
UN	United Nations
USN	United States Navy
USNS	United States Naval Ship
USS	United States Ship
USV	Unmanned Surface Vehicle
UUV	Unmanned Underwater Vehicle
VDV	Soviet Airborne Forces
VHF	Very High Frequency
VLS	Vertical Launching System
VPN	Virtual Private Network
XLUUV	Extra Large Unmanned Undersea Vehicle
XO	Executive Officer

THE END